Forgiveness

L. Thomas Cook

Deer Hawk Publications

FORGIVENESS is published by:

Deer Hawk Publications, an imprint of Deer Hawk
Enterprises
www.deerhawkpublications.com

Special thanks to Paulette Thomas for giving permission to
use her photo for the cover

Cover design: Ray Polizzi

Library of Congress Control Number:

Printed in the United States of America

Chapter 1

"911, what's your emergency?"

Damn good question.

It was one that Mya Westcott couldn't answer: at least, not at the moment.

She had to admit she wasn't sure what happened. All she knew with certainty was that her body lay below her on the cream bathroom tile while blood drained from it like a leaky hose. She was naked, face up, her right arm extended above her head, her left arm resting by her side; her eyes shut tight and her mouth frozen in an open-mouthed scream.

The problem, it seemed, was Mya Westcott was no longer *in* her body.

She floated near the ceiling and she didn't even know how to fly.

It was like a dream: a horrible, out-of-body dream that had begun with a sharp pain, her heartbeat pounding so fast there was no way her system could withstand it, and, finally, her heartbeat slowed and faded. Background sounds muffled like underwater acoustics. She rose from her flesh, fought the sensation, flapping her arms wildly. However, with no weight to ground her, she drifted upward. The room spun and then stopped. Suddenly, everything came into focus. Words began to amplify as if someone had turned up the volume. Oddly aware, she recognized her daughter's hysterical sob.

"My mother is…Oh God…my mother!"

She looked down to see Rachael kneeling on the floor, the phone clutched tightly in one hand while she reached for and simultaneously recoiled from the body. Once more, she heard the stoic voice of a woman on the other end of the phone.

"Try to calm down," the emergency operator said.

Calm down?

Blood pooled around Mya's earthly body. The glass shower door was sprayed with red. Splatters of blood dripped down the wall. More blood trickled from the corner of Mya's mouth. She hovered about six feet above her body and saw herself turning gray.

Wake up! Wake up!

Mya stretched out her arm to grasp her body, believing it was her last chance, but it was as if the flesh and bone vessel locked her out. She helplessly watched as her body turned gray.

If this is death, my death, then panicking is the appropriate thing to do.

"Is your mother breathing?" the operator asked.

Rachael struggled to respond. In her hand, she held a knife, the blade dripping blood. "I don't know. She's not moving. There's blood everywhere. Help her, please!" Her sorrow-filled pleas turned into begging. "Send someone. An ambulance. Someone help her."

"Help is on the way. Tell me your name. Do you feel a pulse?"

"My...my name is Rachael. Rachael Westcott and...I can't...I don't know if she has a pulse." She put the phone down on the floor, hesitated, then placed two fingers on Mya's wrist. Holding the phone once more, she said, "I don't feel a pulse. Please, send help now!"

"Did you see what happened to her?"

"She's been stabbed!"

Blood thickened on the bathroom floor. Mya floated to Rachael. She reached for her twenty-two-year-old daughter, but felt nothing. She looked at her fingers. They were translucent. She looked in the mirror directly behind Rachael and couldn't see herself at all.

What in the hell is happening?

Rachael's pleading cries continued as she knelt by her mother. Her tears dropped into the pooling blood that flowed from the shower toward the sink cabinet. She let Mya's bloody, limp wrist fall with a thud. When Mya's hand hit the floor, blood splattered onto Rachael's sleeve and face. A strand of Rachael's blond hair stuck to her damp cheek. When she tried to brush it away, blood from Mya streaked in its place.

"Don't cry, Rachael," Mya said, but her words, like her touch, were useless. She hovered above her naked body again, unable to figure out how in the world her forty-five-year-old body ended up down there while she drifted toward the ceiling.

Am I dead?

She yelled Rachael's name, but the young woman was deaf to it.

A tear slipped down her cheek.

Can ghosts cry?

"My sweet girl." Mya tried again to touch Rachael's shoulder, but instead of something solid, her hand disappeared into Rachael's back.

Rachael shivered. She reached for the spot Mya tried to touch. For a second, Mya hoped, but when Rachael shivered again and left a bloody imprint on the shoulder of the blouse, Mya knew it was no good. She had her answer. This was death–*her* death. But how? And more importantly…why?

"Baby," Mya crouched next to Rachael, "I'm so sorry you had to find me like this."

The momentary silence was broken by rapid footsteps up the stairs. Mya turned to see two police officers. "Rachael, Rachael, please, Honey, cover me up. Don't let anyone see me like this."

Rachael reached for a towel to cover her mother.

"That's my girl."

"Stop!" the police officer with a black, bushy mustache ordered. "Step away from the body." Both officers were pointing guns at Rachael. "Drop the knife."

Knife? There was a knife in Rachael's hand. When had Rachael picked that up? Mya recognized the etching on the knife handle. It belonged with Mya's gourmet set.

"I said, 'drop the knife'," the officer repeated. "Put your hands up. Now!"

Rachael looked at her hand. Her mouth opened wide. She shook the knife from her grasp as if it were a snake. The steel blade clattered to the tile floor. "I don't know how…"

"Put your hands up," the officer ordered, his gun intent on Rachael.

"Don't you dare aim a gun at my daughter!" Mya stepped between Rachael and the officers.

The police rushed through her. She was nothing more than air, and, as they passed through, an electrical charge spun Mya around. When she managed to stop, she realized one of the officers had taken Rachael by the arm while the other leaned over her body.

"Leave her alone!" Mya tried to push the officer away, but her hands went through him. She reached for his arm. Once again, she couldn't grip anything solid. She followed the officer leading Rachael into the bedroom still demanding he stop, and fighting the idea there was nothing she could do to help.

The other policeman, younger than the first, leaned over Mya's body, then came in the room and announced, "She's dead."

Rachael collapsed to the floor, her head in her hands, and cried, "No. It's not possible. I never meant…I didn't mean to…." Her words dissolved into low-pitched sobs.

Mya reached for Rachael, trying to hug her, but her embrace did not hold the young woman.

4

She spoke close to her ear, "Don't cry, Baby. I'm here," but her words couldn't reach to the living.

Mya couldn't console her daughter.

They didn't see her.

They didn't hear her.

She stood helplessly by Rachael who curled into a fetal position on the tan carpet—now stained with blood from Rachael's hands, jeans, and shoes.

"Oh, Baby," Mya said, "I wish I could hold you. I'm so sorry for the argument we had this morning. I'm so sorry for..."

Suddenly, everything around her vanished, and in the distance, a brilliant light blinded her. She squinted and shielded her eyes. The light was piercing.

It pulled her toward it. She reached for something, anything to hold onto, but there was only space.

A spectrum of colors whirled around her like some kind of kaleidoscopic, vengeful tornado.

A cacophony of voices spoke in jumbled sounds.

A flash of faces. Some she knew. Some she didn't.

A rush like a wave lifted her up and tossed her around again.

Like a plane caught in a crazed spiral, she couldn't determine what was up or down, where earth met sky, or if she flew sideways. And then, everything stopped.

In a black void, she floated with only her spiritual senses—a strange, new reality—to alert her. She felt as unencumbered as a wisp of light: a ball of energy; not held back in any way. She looked down at what was once her and glowed. In that moment, she knew. Somehow, in a supernatural way that was all at once clear and surreal, she understood that she existed somewhere and nowhere. Mya's physical body had transformed into a ball of white light with a trailing tail.

The phenomena of mind seemed to be based on the action of forces rather than the matter itself. That was the only way Mya could explain what was happening to her, and her awareness of a cloaked dark shadow that moved slightly through the murky blackness.

It was like having a bad dream and facing someone or something without knowing what it was. The image came closer. The bottom half drifted along a foggy stream. Its head was bent and draped in a black hooded cloak. When it lifted its head, it had no face. There was only a hole with a foreboding blackness that emanated from where the face should have been.

Mya darted back in fear. The black hole she saw began to glow. Fire appeared where the eyes should have been. Within the core of her soul, she sensed it and those senses allowed her to hear. It spoke in a deep, seething voice though it didn't seem to have lips, "I've waited for you."

Mya heard her own quivering response though she seemed to have no mouth either, "Who are you?"

The nightmare that loomed before her whistled a macabre tune, an old song she hadn't heard or thought about in a long time.

A whoosh of air overcame her and, once more, whisked Mya away.

She changed again, this time into a wispy form of her earthly body, and tumbled heels over head, then soared upward, light as a feather.

Strangely, her fear vanished. The darkness and any confusion she had gave way to awareness and clarity she'd never known. Surrounded by the purest white she'd ever seen, she stood with her bodily form covered in a soft, creamy pale butter yellow robe; oddly her favorite color of roses.

A strong, male voice reverberated from everywhere and warmed her. "Welcome, Mya Marie Adams Westcott."

"Who is that? Where am I?" Even though she somehow knew, she still questioned it. "Am I...is this...Heaven?"

"We call it the Lobby." A woman materialized, solid and regal, as she stepped gracefully toward her. The ground, seemingly made of clouds, swirled as she moved. Her ivory gown with gold trim embraced every curve of her body. She had an ageless face with almond eyes, the color of which changed as she came closer. When she finally faced Mya, her eyes were the color of emeralds.

"I'm Tricia." She held out her hand. Mya reached for it and a spark, like an electric shock, zapped her. She pulled back. "Don't be afraid." Mya touched her hand again. It felt like soft silk.

Tricia smiled. "We're outside of what you call Heaven. The name changes according to belief. This is where souls arrive. The Lobby is where you'll be processed."

"Processed?" For the first time, Mya noticed others. She couldn't begin to count all the men and women wearing robes matching hers, who leisurely strolled or relaxed on benches quietly talking. Children, dressed in shorter robes and bare footed, giggled and chased after one another. No one seemed hurried or bothered by the end of life. While she watched, her glance drifted toward something in the distance through a hazy fog. Ten feet tall with rounded peaks, made of gold and ornamental, it glimmered from the light behind it more radiant than any imaginable.

"What do you see?" Tricia said.

"A gate. It's beautiful." Mya smiled. "Is that Heaven?"

"Everyone sees something different," Tricia said. "Your vision awaits after processing."

"What does that mean?"

Tricia pointed to a long row of people who took one small step forward after another. It looked like a line at the box office for a hit movie.

Two people at the front of the line wore long, flowing, aqua gowns. They each were looking down at gold binders in their hands. Both of their expressions were bland and, when one nodded, the next person from the line would step to them.

One of the binder people read a name. "David Ronald Sander, are you prepared to be processed?"

David Sander stood upright, shoulders back, and head high. The shaking hands at his side betrayed the illusion of confidence.

"We have reviewed the choices you made in life. Here is a list of penance and punishment." A scroll made from parchment paper was handed to David. "Upon completion to the satisfaction of this council, you may move on. Next."

They called another name. "Delores June Guttenburg, step forward."

A timid, trembling woman shuffled forward. With her head bowed and her hands clasped together, she tried to take another step but struggled to lift her feet as if some invisible weight was too much to carry.

"During your life, you made choices that cannot swiftly be dealt with on this level. We are removing you to a holding area below and just above the lowest level. Upon successful completion of penance, you may return for processing."

The woman broke down in tears. "Please give me another chance."

"You received mercy. Now, you must answer for the fate you created."

Two other spirits in deep purple gowns escorted her away and disappeared into a thick fog.

"Where are they taking her?" Mya asked. Overcome by emotions, she wanted to cry for this woman she'd never met.

"To a holding area." Tricia smiled comfortingly at Mya. "You're very compassionate. You easily feel for others. In many ways, that's a blessing." She squeezed Mya's shoulder. "Please, don't be frightened. You'll receive instructions that will answer your questions. The procedure is very organized. For some, it goes very smoothly." She took Mya's hand. Her touch was warm and gentle. "Afterward, you can rest."

"Rest." Tricia's hypnotic tone lulled Mya until a cry resonated from a far-off place, breaking her trance. Snapped awake, Mya recognized the mournful voice as Rachael's and, desperate once more, longed to return to the living world. "No." She yanked her hand free from Tricia's. "I can't rest. I have to help my daughter."

Tricia lowered her head. "I'm afraid that isn't possible."

"It has to be. I can't go until I know what happened. Until I know Rachael is all right." Mya took a small step back. "Please, I have to go home. She needs me."

"Mya, I can't allow you to return. What's done is done. There is no home besides the one waiting for you."

"You don't understand." Mya searched for a way out, a hidden exit, anything. If she got in, there had to be a way out, but her surroundings began to change. The blue dissolved, until nothing existed except a crisp, dense whiteness all around her. Her awareness and the need to find answers returned. "Something happened to me."

Tricia's emerald eyes took on a darker hue. "You were murdered."

Mya shook her head. The word and how simply Tricia spoke it, shocked her.

She fought to accept it: touching her face and staring down at her hands until she turned away. "No. That can't be right." She remembered her stiffening body turning pallid on the bathroom floor...all the blood as it congealed...her daughter kneeling next to her...

"No." Mya shook her head. Mya wrapped her arms around herself and shivered. "That isn't possible. It can't be."

Tricia lowered Mya's arms and looked deep into her eyes as if to give her strength.

"But you know it to be true."

Tricia was right. Mya knew. *But...murder?*

"How?" She didn't have any enemies. Her life, how she lived, where she lived, wasn't exactly the standard for murder. She'd seen the news, read books; she wasn't the type to be killed in cold blood.

"And what type is that?" Tricia asked with a raised brow.

Mya's jaw dropped, but for a moment, no words came out. She creased her brows and said, "How did...? Can you...?"

Tricia nodded. "Yes, I hear your thoughts. In the living world, murder can happen to anyone. It's an awful part of life that's sad, but true. It can happen to anyone."

"Not like this. This can't be the way I...that I'm supposed to...to..."

"Die."

"Don't say that."

"It's better if you accept it." Tricia's irreverent tone made it harder for Mya to argue, but Rachael's tragic cries echoed from another place.

It took all Mya's strength not to push Tricia away and run...but where was there to run? "My daughter hasn't needed me in a long time," Mya said. "I can't just leave her."

"I know how difficult this can be. Especially when it's sudden and unexpected," Tricia said. "Take solace that the violence and trauma are over." Gently, she squeezed

Mya's hand. "It's your time to move on. Everyone has a destiny."

"This isn't my destiny. It's a mistake."

"We don't make mistakes."

"Everyone makes mistakes. You aren't..." Mya covered her mouth. She believed in only one being who didn't make mistakes. This might be the place and what if Tricia was... Mya's eyes widened. "Are you...?"

"Him?" Tricia pointed up where multicolored clouds created a fluffy ceiling. It looked like rainbow cotton candy. "No. However, the one you think of did make this part of the journey meticulous and organized. This is your destiny. Unless..."

"Unless what?"

"Unless you choose otherwise."

"I can choose?" Mya's lips curved into a relieved smile. "Great. Then I choose to go back."

"That's not what I meant." Tricia shrugged her left shoulder. "Your choices are limited, and I'm afraid neither will solve the problem."

Mya didn't hide the hopefulness in her voice. "Please, Tricia, tell me and let me decide."

Tricia guided Mya to a bench and sat. She patted the spot next to her for Mya to sit. Once Mya did, she took her hand. "Any soul that arrives here is faced with choices just as they are in life. Some face simple choices, and others, much harder. The one constant factor is that there is no returning to the living form."

"Couldn't we just call this a near death experience and you zap me back in my body?"

Tricia pulled her lips inward and shook her head. "It's too late for that."

"Why? I only died a few minutes ago."

"It's been longer than that," Tricia said. "Your human shell is no longer available."

"Not available?" Mya frowned and bit her bottom lip. "Never mind. I don't want to know. So, what are these choices?"

"I've read your file and what I can tell you is that, in your case, after clearance, you may go through the gate as you saw it and spend eternity as you envision it, perhaps with those you love, in a peaceful place. Or, if you choose, you may remain in limbo, on a spirit plane."

"A ghost?"

"No, this is different. A ghost, as you call it, is an earthbound spirit. It haunts. We don't recommend that. It's unholy and isn't an option. What you may choose is to be a soul in the spirit plane, one that remains between two worlds...dimensions," Tricia said. "You retain your memories, and can see the living. I caution you, though, it's a choice that lasts for eternity and not generally pleasant."

"Why? Is room service that bad?"

Tricia smiled. "I admire your humor, Mya, especially under stress. Actually, the spirit plane appears differently to each soul. It's designed in the image the soul relates to: a courtroom for a lawyer; an operating room for a doctor. A firefighter waiting for the alarm to ring. The setting can change as often as the soul wants, but they can never leave that plane. They wander in limbo unable to interact or make a difference. For many, it's nothing more than a continuous loop."

"What about an earthbound spirit?"

"They remain in the living world. Usually, something holds them there. It might be fear of moving on or an attachment to something, any number of things. Whatever the reason, they're lost and restless. Hundreds of years in mortal time move on, they don't. Slowly, after time, they dissipate. It isn't life after death. It's usually very painful for them. They face nothing but sorrow seeing a world they can't touch, being in a place they don't truly exist. After a time, they become vengeful. They harm the living even when they don't intend to just through negative energy."

"That's it? That's my choice?"

"Or," Tricia hesitated, "you could go to the other side of the Lobby."

"The other side?"

Tricia glanced over her shoulder. Whatever she saw, Mya didn't. "That's a section we refer to as the Waiting Area."

"Waiting Area? Like in a doctor's office?"

Tricia's laugh sounded as soft as the strum of a harp. "Not exactly a doctor's office. Although, eventually, names are called. It's a place where you can think. One level is set aside for reflection before processing. On other levels, souls wait for forgiveness."

"I'm not waiting for forgiveness." Mya creased her brows. *Am I?* Since being here, the life she knew had begun to slip away one minute at a time. She had to remind herself who she was. Maybe the air, light and breezy, caused it, or the brightness, like a beautiful day at the beach, or the indescribable, overwhelming feeling of rapture. Whatever it was, as much as she loved life, it was nothing compared to this.

Mya said, "I've spent my life wondering about what comes next. I hoped it would be every good thing I imagined."

"It can be," Tricia said. Her hand, when she placed it on Mya's shoulder was warm and seemed to pulse a joy through Mya's spirit. "if you're ready."

Mya began to nod but stopped. She turned away from Tricia, trying not to give in to the bliss. "I can't. I never dreamed I'd say that, if a place like this existed, but I can't. My daughter needs me. I feel her. There must be some way."

Tricia bowed her head with a sigh. "I understand. I've given you the choices. You can stay in the Waiting

Area while you make up your mind," Tricia said. "But you haven't long. You must decide."

In the distance, Mya heard Rachael's cry. It pulled at her heart.

"If I were on the spirit plane," Mya asked, "would it be possible to reach my daughter? To tell her I love her? We've argued so much lately. I need to tell her how much she means to me. I need to let her know things I should have said. Things I thought there would be enough time to say."

"The living soul takes time for granted. There is never enough."

"So, is it possible in that plane to communicate?" Mya asked.

"It's forbidden."

"What about an earthbound spirit? A ghost? I've heard they can make contact. I've read about evidence of ghosts speaking and appearing."

"I told you, it's considered unholy. As for making contact, it's not as common as you think."

"Yes, but it is possible, isn't it?"

"And so is harm to the living. A ghost travels through a portal, and with it comes a very strong risk of other malevolent spirits attaching. Evil lurks, waiting for any opportunity. It's cunning. It manipulates easily."

Behind Tricia, a woman in a heavier robe of deep blue, listened. Mya had no idea how long she'd been there, or why her clothing and her presence were different from the others. She appeared weighed down. Her pale face and listless eyes, filled with shame and sadness, left nothing except loneliness where she stood.

"Tell her there is another way," the woman said.

"Go back to your spot, Rita." Tricia's eyes turned dark to match her harsh tone.

"Tell her," Rita said.

"What other way?" Mya looked between the two women and sensed a silent battle brewing.

"There is no other way," Tricia said. "Rita holds onto a foolish dream."

Intrigued by Rita's hand gesture that followed, Mya said, "I...I think I'll go to that waiting area you mentioned. Just for now. Just to think."

"Listen to me, Mya, Rita will fill your head with hopeless notions of things that rarely work. Besides," Tricia turned and eyed the woman with intense focus, "Rita's time is nearly expired."

"Expired? What does that mean?" Mya said.

Tricia's eyes returned to the soothing emerald color. "You've had a lot to take in. Let us save the rest for later. I can't prevent you from talking to her, but I do caution you." She stood and, in a stern tone, spoke to Rita. "Please be careful what you say and do. You've tried for a long time and it hasn't worked. Don't pull anyone else into your conflict." She glided toward a thick, foggy space where the mist parted, went through, and the exit closed.

"Come on," Rita said and led the way.

"Where are we going? What did she mean?"

"We're going to one of the holding rooms and my little spot."

"Wait." Mya stopped and took Rita's arm. "Maybe this isn't a good idea."

"You want to reach your daughter, don't you? You want to get a message to her? I can help. The only question you should be asking is how badly do you want to make contact?"

Chapter 2

The further Mya followed Rita through the Waiting Area, the more it contrasted the Lobby. Brightness, once warm and soothing, faded with every step. They went down three stairs and the air lost its sweet fragrance. Five more steps, and the surroundings changed into a dreary gray. A misty sadness washed over Mya. It felt like a heavy weight tugged on her. As she walked through the haze, the heaviness weighed her down so much she worried she would sink through the clouds swirling around her feet. She was grateful when they came to a bench where Rita suggested they sit. It was hard, and the unusual shape, uncomfortable. This wasn't a place anyone would want to sit for however long one needed to wait.

"I know it's not what you imagined." Rita let out a long, heavy breath. "But it's really not so bad. This is my spot." She glanced around with a disheartened grin that suggested to Mya she struggled to believe her own words.

"Your spot?" The space was half the size of Mya's bedroom back home but without windows to brighten it up.

"Some of us get our own spot." Rita's eyes filled with sadness and she bowed her head.

"How long have you...been here?" *Lived here? Died and stayed here?* With no clue what the politically correct terms were, Mya shrugged.

"That isn't important right now." Mya wanted to argue, but the look she continued to see on Rita's drawn face told her not to push.

Several feet beyond Rita's spot, others mulled about. No one came near them. Were there a hundred? More? It was hard to tell. They didn't stay in one place long enough to count, and it was difficult for Mya to know if she saw the same people or not. Almost everyone wore identical robes that hung to their feet like those in the Lobby, but these colors were far more drab and gloomy.

Men, fitted with dull, brown robes, stood far apart from those who wore deep purple scrubs. Women shared in the dismal attire without benefit of flowing silk or bright trim. Some, like Rita, wore dark blue fitted robes just a shade lighter than black. For the first time, Mya caught sight of a deep red patch in the center of Rita's garment, and, when Rita turned to face her, she caught a quick glimpse of a blackish wound on Rita's right temple. Rita lowered her eyes and combed strands of brown hair forward to cover it.

The people around them shuffled about, heavy with what Mya recognized as grief or regret. They labored alone with their heads bowed and rarely spoke. Even when they bumped into another person, they just moved along like sleepwalkers unaware, or, Mya suspected, perhaps very aware of situations beyond their control.

"Who are they?" Mya's heart ached for them. "Are they lost souls?"

"Conflicted souls."

"I don't understand any of this."

"Some souls are faced with doubt."

"Like me? I'm having doubts about moving on," Mya said. "This shouldn't have happened to me. I can't make any sense out of it."

"You're having trouble accepting. It gets easier."

"When I look into their faces, it doesn't seem like it does."

"Most of the ones you see here have other issues," Rita said. "Each soul is unique. Each situation in life is different. The one common aspect is the process we face when we arrive here."

"The process? I saw the line. Tricia said there's an instruction guide."

"There is," Rita said. "If you weren't scared before you read it, you will be after. Some of the souls step out of line when they read the guide. Some don't even bother to get in line. They know they're in trouble."

Mya raised her brows. "Trouble?"

"Everyone has to answer for something. The process is easier for some. They do penance and then move on. Others face something more severe."

"You mean answer for sins?" Mya glanced over at souls who cried quietly, at the ones who walked as if they had a heavy weight on their shoulders, and those who muttered to themselves. "We all have some sin."

"Some more serious than others," Rita said and looked at the floor. "The living soul forgets that. We can see with clarity what's done against us. We believe there has to be some kind of justice. When we finally face the fact that we've also committed sins against others, we suddenly don't want to answer."

"Everyone here is afraid?"

"Afraid. Ashamed. Uncertain." Rita pointed past Mya. "The group over there in brown? They're called the Seekers. They long for forgiveness and redemption from pride and greed." She waved at one woman who drifted aimlessly past. Mya smiled at her. The woman looked through them as if she couldn't see beyond her own pain.

"And the ones in purple?"

"Absolution for acts committed against others out of envy or hate."

"What if they don't receive forgiveness?"

"They have a choice to make," Rita said. "They hope time will bring forgiveness from the living, and then punishment may go easier. Most hope to find the strength to face their punishment. It's a long road ahead for them."

"Is that what the Waiting Area is?" Mya said. "Because if everyone here is waiting for forgiveness, I don't think I need that."

"Don't we all need some kind of forgiveness?" Rita's dark, chocolate brown eyes filled with tears. She closed them, and when she looked at Mya again, the tears streaked down her cheeks.

"I didn't mean to upset you."

Rita brushed away her tears and forced a weak smile. "There's so much to explain and not a lot of time. The Lobby where I met you is just the greeting area. That leads to separate levels. Levels refer to the spirit's ascension. We entered the Thinkers' level when we first came in. It's a level designated for those thinking about where they belong."

"That's where I should be. I told Tricia I wanted to come here and think." Mya stood to leave, but Rita took her arm.

"That isn't where you belong."

"But I need to decide how to help my daughter. Maybe if I talk with them—"

"The ones over there," Rita tipped her head in that direction, "can't help you. They have their own problems to consider before being called to Processing."

"Like whether to head back home." Mya could relate. She had to consider the best way to reach Rachael and wasn't convinced that being on the spirit plane was so bad. At least she could look after Rachael from there.

"There is no home, Mya." Rita placed a hand on Mya's shoulder, and the weight of it surprised her. "It's hard to explain it all, and you must be tired. New souls usually are. The journey up here is exhausting, and so is getting used to being without a body."

"Without a body? I have a body." Sure, it was see-through and a hell of a lot lighter, but Mya had arms and legs. She touched her face...that was there. Eyes in the right place. A nose. Ears. Mouth. She made a fist. The parts still worked. She inhaled and wished she hadn't. The place reeked of mold. The Lobby smelled of lavender.

19

"You should rest, but I'm afraid we're running out of time," Rita said.

"What about this spot where we're sitting? I don't understand. You brought me down some steps. Is this a different level?" Mya glanced around. The floor was as murky as the ceiling above them. "What's this place called?"

"It's a section within the Holding Area. It requires a certain type of forgiveness." Rita lowered her eyes. "A very special kind."

"I don't think I should be here. No offense, Rita, but I think I should be with the Thinkers."

"You still don't understand. It's all right. It took me a while to understand it all too. Each level has its own space. The space for the Thinkers isn't so much a place, but a level for souls to decide whether they have the courage to answer for their sins through penance or punishment, or take their chances in a dimension between here and the living world. The next level is for the Wailers. The spirit plane is not a choice. Everyone must atone for their sins. For the Wailers, it means they moan and grieve for the fate they created."

"Let me guess. The Thinkers are pretty much average people who made their fair share of mistakes and the Wailers are politicians, lawyers, and unfaithful husbands." Mya laughed.

"Listen to me," Rita took Mya's hand and led her to a corner more removed from the others, "you have to take this seriously. No soul comes here without having to answer for something." She squeezed Mya's hand and, with pleading eyes, searched her face. "Everyone here must face their true self and then let it go. It doesn't matter what your religion or your belief is, it's the same for everyone. Before any soul ascends to the final level…if they are ever able to ascend, they must move through levels and not get stuck.

The final level, the final reward, if that's how you want to think of it, is whatever you envision."

"Wailers, Thinkers, ascension, whatever. I'll handle it," Mya said and removed her hand from Rita's grasp. "Right now, I have to figure out how to reach my daughter." She stood and looked left to right with a frown, unsure of the direction to walk.

"That's why this is so urgent." Rita pointed to the right and they both strolled. "You have no idea how time works here. Your memory will fade. Haven't you felt it?"

Mya had.

The moment she arrived, her life force, or whatever they called it, began to drain. It was like her blood that spilled on the bathroom floor. It ran out of her and soon, she'd be empty.

"Now, this is very important," Rita said, her eyes intense. "Tell me the last thing you remember."

"What I remember?" She closed her eyes, but nothing came to mind.

"Concentrate."

"I'm trying." Mya closed her eyes again and took a deep breath. A vision, blurred at first, became clearer. "I...I'm on the bathroom floor. I can see myself. I don't know how long I've been there. I'm naked but not wet. I had taken a shower. My hair is a little damp but not dripping. I'm bleeding, but I can't see where the blood is coming from. It's all over the floor." She opened her eyes. "I don't want to do this anymore."

"What about your daughter?"

"My daughter?" Mya gasped. "Rachael! How could I forget?" She grabbed Rita's arms and pleaded. "Don't let her slip away. Please, help me. I can't let her slip away."

"Just relax. Take a deep breath, and focus." Rita led her to another bench and they both sat. "Take your time and visualize."

"I see a knife. My daughter is...holding it." Mya frowned. "Why was she holding a knife? She's sobbing and...police. They came and took her into my bedroom. They told her I'm dead." She gasped. "Dead. Oh, God, please tell me this is a dream." Panic rose at the same time as the urge to run. She realized there wasn't anywhere to go. Like a caged animal, she turned her head in every direction, searching for a way out. She took the first step to run until Rita grabbed hold of her arms.

"Look at me," Rita urged. She stood an inch shorter than Mya and shook her. "Look at me. You have to calm down. I wish I could say it was a dream." She tightly gripped Mya's hand. "You're still trying to deal with all of this. I know. I understand."

Mya squeaked. "Deal?" She pulled away. "I'm either about to go insane or have a heart attack."

"You're not insane, and dead souls can't have heart attacks."

"You're just a little too calm for me. If it's true and I'm dead..." She glanced around, suddenly aware of souls who stopped and stared. Irritated, she shouted, "What are you gawking at? If I'm dead, so are you."

Rita smiled over at them and waved. "Nothing to see here. New soul trying to cope, that's all." She guided Mya back to the bench and said, "Try to remember."

"Are you nuts? I don't want to remember."

"Your daughter," Rita said.

"My?" Mya creased her brows. "Oh, my God, Rachael. That's right. She...she collapsed when the police told her I was...you know."

"Dead."

"Yeah, that. Boy, you people say that word like it's nothing."

"We've had time to get used to it," Rita said.

"I don't think I'll ever get used to it."

"You have eternity to adjust," Rita said.

22

"Is that supposed to make me feel better?" Mya asked. "Never mind. The point is, Rita, Rachael is all alone, and she's still so young. I have to talk to her. I have to let her know…something. What?" Frustrated, she brushed a hand through her hair. "It's all slipping away. You have to help me. What's happened to Rachael? She must be scared out of her mind."

"Don't panic." Rita began to pace. "It's going to be okay."

"Seems I heard that before," Mya said. "When is a good time *to* panic? I don't know what happened to Rachael."

"Let's find out." Rita stopped pacing and led Mya over to something that resembled a birdbath. It looked similar to one Mya owned years ago. She got tired of cleaning it and sold it at a garage sale. "This lets us see into the living world. Not everyone likes to use it. It's too sad, but I…I check it all the time."

"What is this thing?" It was pretty, but nothing special. The sides were ceramic and smooth when Mya touched it. The bowl, made of blue, red, golden yellow, and green mosaic tile, held clear water.

"It's called the Window of Extant. It's used to keep track of the ones still in existence in the living world. I use it often. Some do when they first arrive and then they grow tired and see no reason to check on the living. As eternity passes, we forget life, as we knew it anyway. Not me." She touched the red patch on her robe. "I'm reminded every day." She wore a sad, distant look as she stirred the water with one finger.

"How long have you been here?" Mya asked again. This time, her reason was more personal…she needed to know how reliable Rita really was.

"By Earth time, five years."

"Five years? You've been in the Holding Area for five years?"

"Based on Earth time, yes. In this dimension, there is no real time. A minute could be a day. A day could be a second. Time doesn't matter when you have so much…or so little."

"Tricia said…you're going to expire?"

"Not something to worry about right now."

"Why are you in this section?" Mya glanced at the stairs that ascended to the levels they passed before. "Up, there are the Thinkers and below them, the Wailers. You still haven't named this level. What is it?"

Rita kept her gaze on the water that filled the Window of Extant. "I told you. It's just a place to wait for a special forgiveness."

"Like a miracle?"

"In a way, yes."

"What happens if you don't…find it?"

Tears sprang into Rita's eyes. "I don't want to discuss it right now. We have to focus. Here. Look into the water. Use your energy to see your daughter. Think about her. Reach in your mind to find her."

Mya strained but the water remained clear and unmoving. "I can't. Why do I feel so heavy all of a sudden?" She stepped back. "I don't like this. I feel like I'm being dragged down. It's too hard."

"You have to try."

"It's too hard. I'm scared."

"Then you don't want it enough." Rita lowered her head."

"I do. But…"

"Push away everything else and focus. You have to want this."

"All right." Mya closed her eyes. She forced her mind to picture Rachael, the smile on her face, her smoky brown eyes, the freckles on her nose, and the way she cried over Mya's dead body.

The water began to bubble.

L. Thomas Cook

"Am I doing this right?" she asked.

"Yes," Rita urged, "keep going."

The bubbles increased like a pot boiling on the stove. Slowly, an image emerged. It became clearer, more distinct, until the water settled and the vision of Rachael grew brighter.

"That's her," Mya said and laughed. "That's my daughter." She squinted, then added, "I don't know where she is. I don't recognize the place."

"Listen," Rita said.

"This has sound too?"

"Hush. Just watch and listen."

Rachael sat alone in some beige, windowless room, at a metal table with a plastic water bottle unopened in front of her and a box of tissues next to that. A pile of discarded tissues spilled over. Rachael blew her nose, crumpled the tissue, and added it to the pile.

"Ms. Westcott?" A man in a navy blue suit with a yellow and blue dotted tie, strolled in carrying a brief case. "I'm John Holmes. Your father called me."

She looked exhausted. Her usually well-kept shoulder-length hair was mussed and her eyes were swollen. She trembled in the metal chair and played with another tissue, wrapping it tightly enough around her finger to cut off the circulation. When her fingertip turned deep red, she unwrapped it, only to do the same thing again. "They wouldn't let me talk to my father. Is he all right?"

"He's worried about you." Holmes opened his briefcase and took out a legal pad.

"I've asked to talk to him a bunch of times. The police must have called him and told him about…"

"About your mother? Yes. Then he called me." Holmes sat across from Rachael and offered a dry grin. "Can I get you anything? Maybe you'd rather have a soda instead of water."

"No. I'm afraid if I eat or drink anything, I'll get sick."

"You have to keep up your strength." Holmes fussed with the knot of his tie. The gold watch on his wrist glistened under the florescent lights. The heavy band banged on the table when he placed his hands there and folded them.

"My mother," Rachael dabbed at her eyes with the tattered tissue, "they took...her body. The police never...when the paramedics came they never tried to..."

"She was pronounced dead at the scene." He stared at her like a specimen under a microscope, deciphering her every move. His freshly-shaven face revealed a spa tan. His precisely-combed brown hair didn't cover the thinning spot at the top of his head. With a hint of crow's feet around his eyes and a few gray strands around his temple, he appeared to be in his early fifties, well off, and interested. "I'd like to ask you a few questions if that's all right."

Rachael lifted and lowered her left shoulder. "I guess. I don't know what else I can say that I haven't told the police."

"The way this works, Ms. Westcott, is that I ask you some things and, of course, you may have questions for me, and then we decide if I take your case."

"Take my case?"

"Yes. You're being charged with the murder of your mother."

Mya slapped the image in the water. "That's not possible. Why would they...how in the hell could anyone think that? This is nuts."

"Are you sure?" Rita said.

"Am I sure? Of course, I'm sure!"

"You remembered her holding the knife."

"That doesn't mean...don't you dare think my daughter did this to me. She didn't. I know she didn't."

"I heard you tell Tricia you argued with her that morning."

"That doesn't mean a damn thing. Rachael and I argued. But that doesn't mean she…"

"Killed you."

"There's been a mistake. A huge mistake. I have to get down there. I have to stop this."

"How?" Rita said. "They won't be able to see you let alone hear you."

"Then I'll…I'll haunt them." Mya charged to a set of stairs with Rita right behind her.

"Slow down. Listen to me." Rita caught up and grabbed Mya by the arm. "Listen, damn it!"

"No, you listen." Mya faced Rita and pulled her arm away. "I'm not like you or them. I don't need forgiveness or to think about answering for sins. If I was here for any other reason, fine. I'd take whatever punishment I had coming and move on. But not now. My daughter is in that living world and accused of something I know damn well she didn't do. So right now, I need Tricia to tell me how the hell I get out of here and become a damn ghost."

"That's the last thing you need. Trust me."

"Why should I? You won't even tell me why you need forgiveness. Don't you think five years is a long time to wait?"

"It's just a flash up here, and I'd wait until time came to an end if that were possible. You aren't the only one with someone who needs you, someone who's all alone."

Mya lowered her voice. "I'm sorry. It's just that I haven't got time. Not if my daughter is in trouble."

"You can't become a…" Rita glanced around and softened her voice to a whisper, "ghost." She took Mya's hand and walked her back to the farthest spot again. "A ghost is the worst. It's unholy. Tricia must have told you that."

"She did. It doesn't matter. If that's the only way, I'll take my chances."

"You don't know what it means," Rita said. "Sure, a ghost might be able to appear, and now, with all the fancy equipment, they show up in photos and have their voices captured on recorders. Have you ever heard a disembodied voice? It's damn scary."

"But if I can get a message to Rachael, then being a ghost—"

"Keep your voice down." Rita looked around and above. "The clouds have ears. This is taboo to talk about, and for good reasons. It's the ultimate betrayal against our kind."

"Our kind?" Mya chuckled. "I'm sorry, but exactly what kind is that?"

"Spirits outside eternity's gate. That's a big deal. Even in the Holding Area. It offers us a chance. Believe me, some souls don't get that. Think about it, Mya. Even if you became a...you know."

"Ghost?"

"This isn't a joke. Even if you could, it's not easy. It takes years and years of practice. The soul, when it first comes here, needs rest to recharge. A ghost is pure energy. It has to learn how to harness that energy. Then there's desire. But not the kind you think. It's almost...mean-spirited, and that's what you have to watch out for. That's what evil thrives on. You have to learn how to travel the dimensions. That means assuring you're not followed or that you haven't picked up hitchhikers."

Mya flashed on the darkness she encountered on her journey here. She shuddered at the ominous image, the reptile voice, and the forbidden danger it projected all at the same time. She pushed it from her mind and tried to concentrate on Rita.

"Why do you think any proof of ghosts seem to involve hundred-year-old spirits?" Rita said. "Because of how long it takes to get good at it."

"I swear to God I wish this were some bizarre dream and I'd wake up." Mya sat on the bench and sighed.

"Well it's not, and there's more."

"Of course." Mya tossed up her hands. "Go on."

"Let's say you do get there with no problems. You manage to find the energy. Then what?"

"I let Rachael know I'm there. She's not alone."

"Doesn't sound like she is. Her father is with her."

"Her father?" Mya laughed. "He's more useless than death. I believe he loves Rachael, but there's so much she doesn't know. There's things she blames me for, and some of it I deserve, but there's more to it." She shook her head. "No, Doug Westcott is not the person she should depend on."

"Your spirit haunting her isn't the answer either. What would be the point? Either your daughter will see you and be scared out of her mind, or she'll think she's losing her mind. And let's suppose she does believe. Then what? How would she convince the others? They'll think she's crazy."

"Not if she has a photo. A voice recording."

"And do you know how many doubters would have fun with that? Even if they believed it, it still wouldn't help clear her. Have you ever heard of a ghost solving a murder and the courts allowing it? Mya, there are reasons for that. Rules. An order to life that forbids it. No one, up here or," Rita pointed down, "down there, is happy when spirits let themselves be seen, let alone recorded or photographed."

"Even so, ghosts exist, right?"

"Yes. Some are stuck in that dimension because of unfinished business."

"That's me."

"Others are stuck because a dark shadow, an evil entity traps them, holds them, and refuses to let them leave. I know angels up here who have tried to rescue them. It's nearly impossible. Evil uses trickery all the time. Spirits cry out. Angels rush in. A demon traps them. Their favorite trick? Children. They use the voices of children. Angels are compelled to help them. Humans try to help as well, but that accomplishes nothing except to feed the demon with energy and permit it to stay and grow stronger."

"That won't happen to me."

"You think you're that strong? You have no idea what demons are capable of or how many ways they have. Do you know what demons feed on? Souls. They get points or something for everyone they collect. What if, as you travel there, something attaches to you? They do that. Do you want to bring a thing like that to your daughter?"

"Of course not." As a little girl, Rachael had terrible nightmares about witches and shadows trying to eat her alive. She couldn't stand to watch horror films and on Halloween, when some kids wanted to dress up as zombies, Rachael wanted to be a princess or a rock star. "What can I do?" Mya said. "I have to help her."

"First, we have to start from the beginning and be very sure."

"I *am* sure. My daughter didn't try to kill me."

"You're right. No one tried to kill you. They *did* kill you. Before I can help, you have to be absolutely positive, and that means having an open mind. You might see things you don't want to."

"Like what?" Mya said.

"The truth. You have to be ready to gather your strength and face it. Now, get comfortable and clear your mind. Tell me everything you remember from the very beginning."

"Rita, I appreciate everything you're trying to do and I'm not worried about the truth. I just don't see how any of this will help."

"It will because I know someone. Someone who speaks *for* dead people." Rita nodded. "He's my son."

Chapter 3

"Hold on," Mya said. "You're telling me your son is—is what?" She tried to think of a way to phrase it that didn't sound ridiculous. She couldn't come up with anything except... "He sees dead people?"

"Don't be silly," Rita said and glanced around.

"You're telling *me* not to be silly?" Mya also looked around, and as she did, noticed some souls beginning to gather and stare at them.

"You have to keep your voice down." Rita eyed the gathering group, and waved nonchalantly toward them. "Hi Millie. How are you? Ed, is that you? How is everything?" She turned with serious eyes and spoke in a low voice. "No one knows except Tricia. Well, her and a few of the souls here, but it's best to keep it quiet."

"Sure it is." Mya's eyes filled with skepticism. "I guess it would be awkward if the others knew." Suddenly, Rita didn't appear as sane as before. Saying her son spoke to dead people didn't help. What did Mya know about this woman? She'd only been dead a few hours and just met her. Didn't Tricia warn her away from Rita? She advised against it, and Mya overheard her tell Rita not to involve anyone else in something that didn't work. So, was this the something?

"I'm not crazy and this could help."

Mya stood and with a nervous chuckle said, "It was nice meeting you. Good luck with all this." She slowly backed away. "Don't get up. I think I need to see Tricia. Maybe there's something else that can help me."

"There isn't. Haven't you ever put your faith in something you couldn't see or was hard to believe?"

"Sure. I put my faith in Heaven and look what that got me. I'm outside the gate." Mya didn't add that she was there with a nutcase and with her daughter suspected of her murder, she simply didn't have time for this.

"My son has a gift. He's had it since he was a child." Rita sat on the bench and looked Mya straight in the eyes. "I'm sharing this with you because I believe he can help. But, *you* have to believe, Mya. It all comes down to that."

Mya felt sorry for the woman. She carried a heavy burden of what? Sadness? Regret? "Rita, I understand you want to believe in your son and his...gift. We all believe our children are special. I went to a psychic once and trust me, it was all a con. She told me I was going to come into money and go on a trip. The only trip I went on was to the bank to get money when my car broke down. It cost me $1,200 to fix the damn thing. Actually, I did find a penny that day, but beyond that, I got zip."

"You don't understand. He really can hear the dead and he'll be able to help. You just have to want it badly enough."

"There has never been solid proof. Ask anyone. Ask Houdini. He spent years investigating and found nothing but con artists. In fact," Mya glanced around, "maybe we can find him here. He'll tell you to your face."

"Very funny," Rita said without a trace of a smile. "I'm being serious."

"Sadly, so am I." Mya caught Rita's gaze, she saw the look of despair. "All right, let's say for a minute he does have a gift, why did Tricia caution me about you? What did she mean when she told you not to get someone else involved in your conflict?"

Inhaling a deep breath, Rita slipped one side of her straight brown hair behind her ear. It exposed a four-inch hole. She quickly became self-conscious and re-combed her hair over the wound. "I've offered my help," she said, "to a few other souls but...it didn't go well. They just didn't want it badly enough or maybe they didn't really believe.

Whatever it was, it takes a certain kind of strength to reach out and even more to be heard. I think," she took Mya's hand, "no, I *know* you can do it. We have to hurry. The longer we wait, the more you'll forget."

"That's just the problem, Rita. I don't have time for something that might not work. Tricia told me about destiny. Was it my destiny to be murdered? And my daughter's destiny to be suspected of it?" Those words caused Mya to stop and think. Excited, she said, "Is there a way to check? I mean, is there somewhere up here that lists a person's destiny? I could look for my daughter's name. I could find out who decides these things and talk to them." With hope for the first time, Mya took off for the Lobby. She stopped when Rita caught up to her and blocked the way.

"There is a hall of records," Rita said, "beyond the Lobby, on the next side."

"Don't you know someone over there? Anyone who might help?"

Rita shook her head. "It isn't that simple."

Mya tossed up her hands. "Of course not. Why should it be?"

"Only certain souls of high rank have access, and even that has to be approved by," she pointed upward, "and He's not likely to approve this."

"God? Why doesn't anyone say His name? They all point up." Determined, Mya sidestepped Rita and proceeded to the Lobby. "Well, if God is who I need, then I should be able to see Him." She stopped and turned to Rita who was close behind. "How do I get to see Him?"

"You need to file a request," Rita said. "Some use the name of God. Some call Him by other names. You have to realize this place is for believers of different faiths. We just refer to Him as His Holiness or the Creator."

Mya laughed. "His Holiness seems like a fair name, but I believe in God, so that's the name I'll use."

"Fine, but He's very busy."

"So I have to fill out a request? I swear to…" Mya pointed up, "to God that I'm dreaming and I'm going to wake up soon."

"There's a long list of souls requesting counsel. A very long list."

"How long?"

"Up here, it doesn't matter. But I've heard Abe Lincoln is still waiting his turn."

"Lincoln? As in…? Are you kidding me?"

"We're all the same in His eyes."

"Jesus, this is nuts."

"His waiting list isn't as long. But even He would need permission."

Mya glanced at Rita as if she was crazy, which is exactly what she thought. "You mean I'm up here, in Heaven, and I can't see God for…a hundred years? More?"

"I told you about time. It dissolves up here into mere seconds after a while. There is no rush. No clocks. Just…space." Rita gestured around with her hand.

"So how do I find out my daughter's destiny?"

"It's locked up. You aren't meant to know."

"Not even question?"

Rita shook her head.

"How about prayer? He must hear that?"

"He does. He hears them all. And He will answer…but," Rita bit her bottom lip, "it might not be the answer you want."

"And I can't question it?" Mya combed a hand through her hair. "I thought when a person got to Heaven, everything became clear. All the reasons. All of it."

"It does. It will."

"Sure." Mya gazed at Rita. "In time, which doesn't exist up here."

"Mya, please. Let's go back to my spot. Tell me everything you remember and we can figure it out."

"Sure. Why not? My options are running out." Mya turned with Rita to head back, when she heard Tricia call her name.

"I was just coming to find you," Tricia said. She smiled at Mya and regarded Rita with little more than a nod.

"My time to think isn't up, is it?" Mya asked. "You told me I would be able to think, and I haven't decided yet."

"It's all right, Mya. I'm not here for that." Tricia took Mya's arm and brushed past Rita. "I need to speak to you about another matter." She guided Mya to a secluded corner. The solemn look on her face made Mya nervous.

"What is it? Is it about me talking to Rita?"

"No." The concern in Tricia's eyes grew. "I still wish you wouldn't, but I can't forbid it. No, this matter is more…delicate."

Mya's nervousness increased. *What now? I wasn't supposed to be in Heaven? I'm being sent to the Wailing level? I said His name out-loud and broke a rule?* She urged Tricia with her eyes and tried to remain calm. "What is it? Tell me."

"You've been invited somewhere."

Mya frowned. "Where?"

"To your funeral."

Chapter 4

Mya's eyes widened. "What did you say?" Did she hear correctly? "I've been invited to my what?"

"Funeral."

She heard correctly.

Her knees were about to give. Tricia grabbed her arm to keep her from falling.

"You don't have to go," Tricia said.

"Oh, well that's nice to know." Mya composed herself even though the light-headedness remained. If it wasn't for the fact that Tricia looked so intent, Mya would have laughed at her.

"Some souls don't wish to attend," Tricia said. "It's understandable. I'm only bringing you this option because of the prayers. Quite a few actually, and all of them with the same request that you be there. It's touching how very specific they've been. In fact, we've been inundated with many wishing for the chance to say goodbye and prayers for you to hear them."

"Nice to know." As the words settled, Mya smiled. Quite a few? It had to be her mother and father, and Aunt Rose. She was very religious, she got that from Nana—nothing could come between that woman and church on Sunday. It might also be Sarah, her best friend, the women at her book club, or Ted in accounting, he always liked her. Of course, her sister, Liz, would pray until the cows came home. Then there was Rachael, but she thought the young woman stopped praying years ago.

"The decision is yours," Tricia said.

"I can go back down? Home?

"Your home isn't there anymore, Mya."

Lost in her own thoughts, Mya barely listened. "Sure. Right. I can leave? Go back?"

"For a short time."

Mya's smile lit up her face. This would be perfect. "I can see them?"

"Yes, although they won't be able to see you. The true believers might feel your presence. And usually, at the moment of someone's death, many of the living are believers."

"Can I get a message to my daughter?"

Tricia's eyes softened. Mya could tell she sympathized, but the answer was firm. "I'm afraid not."

Mya deflated. "Why not? What's the point if I can't speak to her? Do you know that Rachael is suspected of murdering me? Do you know that?"

"I was aware." Again Tricia had that firm, calm voice—but not without feeling. She looked directly into Mya's eyes. It was getting annoying.

"Aware?" Mya's voice got louder, but she didn't care. She stared at Tricia just as intently and heard herself say, "Are you also aware she didn't do it? That she's innocent?"

"If she's innocent, then it will be proven."

"*If* she's innocent? Did you say *if*?" Mya had never known as much frustration as she faced now. So much for resting in peace.

When she was a child, her grandmother read to her from the bible. She soaked up the words and the rapture on her grandmother's face. Nana read the words like a sweet song filled with hope and joy. Much of what Nana read didn't make sense now. Mya had been a believer, led a good life, tried not to sin–too much, and what did she get in return? Murdered in the prime of her life, her daughter's life hanging in the balance, and all she got from Heaven was that justice would prevail. How was that possible? Human justice was flawed at best. Now, she began to wonder if Heaven's justice was too.

38

"My child is innocent!" Mya cried, her patience gone. "And I'd like to think Heaven would be the one place to help her!"

"There's no need to shout." Tricia's calm tone and gentle smile only irritated Mya more.

"I disagree," Mya mimicked. "I think now is the perfect time to shout. Where are all the angels, anyway? Why, besides Rita and the zombie-like souls I see shuffling around, are you the only one I've spoken too? Are you the *only* one in charge?"

"Of your process, yes." It was frustrating how patronizing Tricia was, and how little emotion she displayed. Wasn't Heaven filled with compassion as Mya's nana always told her?

"I want...no, I demand to speak to someone else," Mya said.

"I am familiar with your situation, Mya. I wish I had more to offer. For now, you must decide whether you wish to attend the funeral or not."

Mya glared at Tricia. She tried to relax. Maybe, somehow, when she was down there, she could find a way to send a message. Her contempt hidden behind a more pleasing smile, she said, "Fine. I'll go. Just tell me how."

"Your guardian will escort you."

"My what? I swear since I've been up here, my hearing has gotten worse."

"You heard me correctly. Souls may attend their funeral with their guardian."

"Why? You don't trust us?" It was a cutting remark, but what the hell, Mya's mood wasn't good, and right now, she wanted to slap the smug look off Tricia's face.

"I'm not being smug," Tricia said, "Nor am I patronizing you. That isn't my intention at all."

Embarrassed, Mya lowered her eyes. But why should she be embarrassed? "Aren't my thoughts my own? Did I give up all my rights when I died?"

"We listen to the thoughts of new souls so we can guide them. The rules about guardians apply for your protection. A soul traveling the living dimension, especially a new soul naïve to the afterlife, is susceptible to danger from other forces. We try to keep you in the light of His protection so no harm will come to you or the ones you love."

"What if I decide to stay? Does this guardian yank me back?"

Tricia could have lost patience, but Mya noticed she didn't. Maybe that was where the compassion lay. "No one will yank anyone. You would be escorted back. If you should decide to be an earthbound spirit, all the issues related to that would be explained in detail. If you decide to go back as a haunting spirit, that would be dealt with as well."

"Dealt with how?"

Tricia curled her mouth into a grin like a soft embrace. "All you need to be concerned about down there, for now, is simply to have your presence felt and offer some comfort to the living. There is no means for a message. Not the kind you think. You can whisper you love them, you can say a soft goodbye, you may even let them know you're safe. They will sense that, but the help you want to give your daughter cannot be done." Tricia cupped Mya's hands in hers. The smooth and silky feel was still there, with an added warmth that Mya could only describe as a mother's love. "You must have faith. Trust in what is meant to be."

The tender words and look in Tricia's eyes made Mya feel ashamed. Even so, the reasons she was so adamant about reaching her daughter remained just as intense.

Tricia turned and smiled toward the woman who approached them. "Mya? This is your guardian."

Mya's mouth dropped. "I…I know you. I mean, I've felt you. Anna? Your name is Anna."

The guardian grinned. She was beyond beautiful, with a light that glimmered all around her. She wore pure white with gold and silver sashes draped across her chest. A crimson braided belt hung from her waist and nearly touched the floor. Her gown kissed her feet, which were wrapped in gold sandals. In her strawberry blonde hair, she wore a crown of daisies, Mya's favorite flower. Her hair hung to her waist, and shined as bright as an evening star. Her eyes were blue, but not an ordinary blue, more like an imagined blue—wispy, calming, and gentle. A peaceful contentment emanated from her. In her presence, Mya felt safe and cherished, like she had as a child and other times in life when she wanted to give up but something inside made her keep going.

"I have been with you since you were born," Anna said. Her voice resonated like a symphony of violins and flutes. With an insight that overjoyed Mya, Anna reassured, "You know my name because you believed in me. It comes as a whisper in a dream to those with an open heart."

Mya smiled. "I don't know why I should be surprised that you understand me." It all felt so natural and yet fantastic at the same time.

"We are connected," Anna said.

"I wanted so much to believe you were there. You warned me not to ride my bike with flip-flops, didn't you? I should have listened."

Anna nodded. "A small voice in your head that tells you."

"Exactly." It was thrilling to be able to say all the things she felt yet never quite believed were real. "Nana said it was my guardian angel, but as I got older, I just thought it was my conscience or common sense."

"Your nana's light shined very bright with His love," Anna said.

Mya frowned. "Where were you when I was…when someone killed me? Why didn't you warn me? Or stop it? You could have stopped it."

Radiant and unfazed, Anna smiled with an age-old wisdom. "You already know the answer to that."

"Destiny." Mya looked down at her feet.

"I have always loved you. I have always been with you. I wept that day. Throughout your life, I shared your heartache and your fears. I will weep this day at your funeral. After that, our connection will cease to be. I will receive a new soul to watch over. A joyous time. And if you decide to move on through the gates, then I have served you well."

"I haven't decided. It isn't because you didn't do a good job, Anna. I just have to look after my daughter." Mya faced Tricia and said, "I know. My daughter has her own guardian angel, but she's my child, and I can't rest if she's in trouble."

Anna put out her hand. "Come with me, Mya. The living wait. Perhaps, in time, it will all become clear. Just remember, as you were loved on Earth, you are loved in this realm. You are not alone in your time of sorrow or indecision. You have always shown faith that what you need will come. That will never change. No matter the answers you seek or find. No matter what still remains to be. Fear is real only when we allow it. Strength is in our souls. It will find the peace it needs and you will rest."

There was something in Anna's voice. Was Anna still trying to warn her? Was it some clue or a hint meant to prepare her? There were so many questions and then…she was no longer standing with Tricia on clouds or surrounded by white. Transported without breath or motion, without blurred colors, or swirling lights, Mya arrived in a somber place.

A church.

Her church.

L. Thomas Cook

On Earth.

And, with Anna close by her side, she stood next to a coffin.

Chapter 5

The choir sang "Amazing Grace," Mya's favorite religious song from long ago. Flowers lined the altar: red roses, pink carnations, yellow and white daisies. Mya recognized the church. St. Michael's of the Angels on Winnie Street, the same church she was married in and the same church Rachael was baptized in. Over the years, Mya hadn't attended the church as she used to. It became something she did on holidays or when someone in the family married or died. Now, she was here for her death and it felt surreal at best.

A dozen or more lit candles added to the reverence. The smoke from them wafted toward the stained glass. The coffin she stood by was ivory with a bronze crucifix fastened to the top. The polished ivory finish shimmered in the warm glow of candles.

It was beautiful. All of it. The music. The casket. The flowers and the lighting. It filled Mya with contentment, a warm feeling mixed with long ago Christmases, and birthdays, the day Rachael was born. All the moments she felt loved and safe, both as a child and as a woman, washed over her.

She gazed out at the pews. A sea of black clothing and pale faces. Everyone was solemn. Some openly wept.

In the first pew sat Doug Westcott. His eight-year-old dark blue suit fit snug around his potbelly. Mya remembered the day she dragged Doug to the store to buy that suit. He groaned the whole time. Two years later, they separated after twenty-three years of marriage. That was around the time Mya stopped going to church. It really had nothing to do with the breakup of her marriage, just a sense for some time that the words of a priest no longer gave her the comfort she sought. She found more satisfaction praying on her own and in the time she spent in nature–for her that was God's true church.

And yet, there sat Doug. He wore a mustard colored tie—out of style now. She bought him that tie too. He didn't wear those things out of sentiment or because he couldn't afford new clothing. That wasn't the issue. He wasn't cheap either. His priorities were the problem. Instead of a new suit, he would much rather spend money at the track and on women. He would rather pawn, beg, borrow, and charm his way to impress women twenty years his junior than buy a suit, unless he could hock it. He was the poster boy for middle-aged men. A stereotype of what smart women should study and never approach.

Mya's biggest regret was not listening to her own intuition. She ignored the twist in her gut and the fact that her feet froze the day she walked down the aisle to marry him. She should have known he couldn't be faithful. His father hadn't been. Even while they dated, Mya had suspicions she ignored, and then she got pregnant. They married. She miscarried. Rachael's birth came a year later. Mya tried to keep the marriage going, but the distance between her and Doug grew. He had an affair. He never admitted to it, but she knew. And it probably wasn't the only one he had.

Anna placed a hand on Mya's shoulder. When Mya looked up at her, she smiled gently and in Mya's mind, she said, "That's over now. This is your goodbye."

Mya nodded. She cleared her thoughts of Doug and drifted her gaze to Rachael who stood by her father.

Rachael was crying. Her eyes swollen and her nose red, she sniffed back the tears, but more came. She looked so small in the black silk dress with her thin arms covered in a black cardigan. Mya was beside her, close enough to smell gardenia perfume Rachael always loved. She noticed that Rachael wore Mya's pearl and diamond earrings. She was glad. She wanted Rachael to have those earrings.

Rachael trembled. As if the pew in front of her was the only thing keeping her from falling, she held on tight. The young girl's sorrow was so thick it seemed to suck energy from Mya and caused her to feel weak. Anna appeared behind her and placed her hands on Mya's shoulders. Mya's energy increased as if a hundred bright lights turned on inside her. Renewed, she stood taller next to Rachael and whispered in her daughter's ear, "I'm here, and I love you."

Rachael sobbed. "I'm sorry," she whispered. "Mom, I'm so sorry."

A tear slipped down Mya's cheek. "Why did we argue so much, Rachael? I always loved you."

Rachael sniffed. "I love you, Mom."

Doug put his arm around Rachael and squeezed. "She knows that."

"I said terrible things to her," Rachael said. "I was so mad at her that morning."

"Shh," Doug said. "This isn't the time. She loved you and she knew you loved her too."

Mya inhaled Rachael's scent again. Gardenias reminded her of spring. Rachael was born on the first day of spring. Mya grinned. "I do know and I'll never forget. Don't forget me, my sweet baby."

She closed her eyes while the choir sang another song and her thoughts danced through her life. Each image floated in and out. A moment here and a brief second there. Good and bad. Voices of childhood friends, faces that brought joy, even cruel words spoken by her or others; in a flash, she relived it all. The first time she felt snow on her cheeks made her shiver as much as it had then. The lights on a Christmas tree when she was six made her just as giddy. The time she found a stray dog and wanted to keep it but the animal was happy to see its owner. All the firsts, all the in-betweens, right up to the last when her soul left the body she sometimes abused and the life she sometimes forgot to cherish.

When she opened her eyes again, she was at the cemetery beside the open grave. Mya gasped, but with Anna by her side, her fear dissolved.

Standing in a circle, people Mya knew listened to the priest recite words she'd heard before when attending funerals. Now, he spoke those very words for her.

The sun shined. She couldn't feel it on her face and for that, she was sorry. Nevertheless, she had always hoped her funeral would be on a nice day. There could be nothing sadder than a rainy, chilly day for these things.

She was glad the mourners didn't have to fight the weather. They didn't feel cold as Mya imagined her body inside the coffin did. She was grateful not to see her decaying corpse. Warmly, she grinned up at Anna, happy she was spared that sight, and the one of her autopsy. Yet, she did wonder what she wore.

"Look down at yourself," Anna said.

Mya was no longer in the pale yellow robe she wore in heaven. Instead, she was dressed in her favorite jeans and white cotton shirt. On her feet, she had sneakers stained with grass and dirt from her garden. She smiled and rubbed her hands along her sleeves. "My sister knows me," she said and looked over at Liz.

She stood behind her older sister and realized all she had to do was think of the person to be by them. In Liz's ear, she whispered, "Thank you. Take care of Rachael for me. And Mom. And Dad, and…"

She was next to Aunt Rose now. "There is a heaven," she said into the woman's ear. "But God has a waiting list to speak to Him so I can't tell Him you wish lilacs bloomed all summer. I will, though. One day, I'll see you there. I know it."

Aunt Rose smiled as if she heard the words. "Mya, I love you. We'll be together someday." The sixty-four-year-old woman dabbed her moist eyes. "And I swear we'll find out who did this to you."

The moment vanished swiftly. When Mya was conscious of it again, the mourners were moving toward their cars. "Not yet." Mya pleaded with Anna.

She thought of Rachael and that brought her to the young woman who walked beside her father toward the limo. She heard Doug say, "Rachael, we need to talk."

"Later, Daddy, please," Rachael said.

"I just want you to think about it," Doug said. "You can sign it over to me. If anything happens, and I'm sure it won't, but just in case, if you sign over the house to me, you'll be protected."

Sign over the house? That son of a bitch! That's what Doug's thinking about at a time like this?

"Don't do it," Mya said. "The only smart thing he ever did was agree to let me put your name on the deed. It wasn't that generous. The house belonged to me. I paid off the mortgage. If anything, that man owes you money. He was supposed to give me child support and most of the time, he didn't. I put you through college. He was supposed to pay half and he didn't. The house was for you, Rachael. You know that."

"I'll hold onto it for you," Doug said as he opened the car door for Rachael. "I'll only use it to borrow against or sell if we need to."

"What about the insurance?" Rachael said.

"They won't release that until the murder is solved. I do have the life insurance policy your mother named me on, but..."

Policy I named you on? No, I changed that. Wait. Did I forget one?

Doug said, "I've had some financial problems and I'll need that money." He chuckled with embarrassment the way he used to whenever Mya asked him why he was late coming home. "And there's the matter of your bail. I'm afraid we might not have much of a choice, Honey. I put up my townhouse as collateral for the bail. I know I'll get that back, you won't run—"

"Dad, I can't believe you'd say that!"

"I didn't mean it like that. But there are other expenses and we may have to use the house."

Mya leaned into Rachael and said, "Don't listen to him. He has money. He always does. He's a liar and a selfish prick. If he gets his hands on that house, there won't be a dime left for you."

"Dad," Rachael said as she stood by the car door, "when you asked me to go through mom's stuff months ago and look for that old insurance policy, I told you I felt bad. Going behind her back, even though I blame her, didn't feel right. It's obvious she forgot about that policy, or she would've changed the benefactor."

"I know. And I feel bad about it too," Doug said. "But I told you, your mother bled me dry."

"I did what?" Mya shouted in vain. "I never touched a cent. You left me in debt, you bastard! The mortgage on the house, child support, credit card debt, I worked hard to pay off all of it. We separated and you contested everything. All you did was delay the divorce with your lies that you wanted to work things out and have your family. It was all bull. You just did it so I couldn't get an accurate account of everything you owed us. And now, after all of it, you have the nerve to try this? You leave Rachael alone, Doug, or so help me…"

"I'm sorry for what Mom did," Rachael said. "But I need the house. That and the insurance policy is all I have."

"Not if you're in prison," Doug said. "I'm sorry, Honey, but let's face facts. The trial, the evidence against you. John Holmes said it isn't going to be easy."

"Evidence?" Mya said. "What evidence?"

In a flash, Mya was back in the Lobby surrounded by bright white and wearing the pale yellow gown she had on before.

"No," she said. "Anna? Anna, where are you?" She turned in circles, but Anna was gone.

"You heard enough," Tricia said, appearing in front of her.

"What evidence? My daughter did *not* kill me. Her father is trying to get the money I left for her. Something's wrong. I have to go back. I have to stop this."

"It will turn out as it is meant to be," Tricia said.

"I won't, I can't, accept that. Send me back. I wasn't finished with my goodbyes."

"Time has passed. Anna is responsible for another living soul now. You are here and need to be processed."

"No, not now. I won't." Mya ran through the Lobby. The clouds beneath her feet swirled, creating a fog. "Rita? Rita," she shouted into the mist. "I need you and your son."

Chapter 6

Mya raced down the two levels and found Rita tucked deep in the corner of her spot. The white light once again gone, dull gray filled the space so it appeared even darker than before.

Mya stopped a foot from where Rita was. Some kind of sadness encircled Rita. It wasn't something Mya could see exactly. It was more of an intense vibe that permeated the area.

Rita's eyes were closed and she had her arms wrapped around herself while she muttered something about being sorry and she had to do it but never meant to hurt anyone. She began to cry. Her tears rained down, dissolved into the vaporous cloud at her feet, and created a black hole. Mya took a hesitant step closer. She peered over the edge of the hole. It was impossible to determine how deep it went, but with each tear Rita cried, it widened and grew blacker.

"Rita?" Mya reached for her friend and then lowered her hand, not wanting to startle her. "Rita," she called again. "It's me. Mya."

Rita lifted her head. When she turned, her eyes were black circles as deep and dark as the hole. Startled, Mya backed away. Rita's eyes returned to her normal color, but the sad darkness around them remained.

"Don't be afraid," Rita said and put out her hand. "Please don't run. This is part of my penance." She lowered her head and wiped her damp cheeks. "I deserve worse than this."

"I don't understand," Mya said. The hole at Rita's feet reverted to a misty cloud and Rita's ashen face slowly changed to a pale, peachy color.

"I can't explain now. Not now," Rita said. The heaviness Mya sensed remained, and for a moment, she thought Rita might collapse.

"Are you all right?" Mya led her to a bench and sat beside her.

With a weak smile, Rita nodded. "I'm sorry I frightened you." She fussed with her hair pressing it flat to the side of her temples before she took Mya's hand in hers. "You came back. I thought maybe you'd try to stay after your funeral."

"I didn't have much choice. First I was there, and then," Mya shrugged a shoulder, "I was back here. It didn't go exactly the way I thought. But then," she laughed dully, "I guess I really didn't know what to expect." Then, she remembered. "I saw her, Rita. My daughter. I spoke to her. I think she heard me and so did Liz and Aunt Rose. At least, I think they did."

She faced Rita. Terror drove her voice as she said, "Rachael's in trouble. Her father is trying to get the house, and if I know him, he'll try to get more. There's insurance money I left her, everything in the house. He'll charm her like he always does and waste it all on gambling. Rita, he said something about the trial and evidence. What evidence could they have against her?" She flashed to the conversation she overheard at the limo. What did it mean?

"Mya, you have to stay calm."

Panicked again, Mya said, "Rita, I need your help more than ever. Tricia is pressuring me to be processed. I can't face whatever comes next until I know Rachael is all right. She's all I have. She's all that's left of me down there."

"It's going to be all right."

"How can you say that? How do we know? Time is running out. I can feel it. Going down there exhausted me. All I want to do right now is sleep, but I can't. I have to help her. The only way to do that is to find out who murdered me. But I don't know how."

"We have to start with what happened that day."

"I told you what I remember."

"You told me about the moment of your death. You have to dig deeper." Rita glanced around and lowered her voice. "You have to revisit the day of the murder. You're going to have to recall everything you can before that moment."

Mya rested her head in her hand. "I'm so tired."

"Fight it, Mya. You have to."

"Don't you think I've tried? It's all...black. Nothing."

Rita gazed around again at the other souls who shuffled aimlessly. Finally, she let out her own weary breath. "Maybe it's better this way."

"Why do you say that?" Mya looked into Rita's eyes. She couldn't help but wonder if her own held as much pain.

"Because you might not be able to face the truth. You might not be able to handle what you'll discover."

"What are you talking about?" Mya asked. "I know the truth, well, maybe not all of it, but the important part...my daughter didn't kill me."

"Sometimes we hurt the people we love without meaning to," Rita said. "You told me you and Rachael argued."

Mya got to her feet. "That doesn't mean a damn thing."

"But what if it does? To you, it might have been a little argument. Maybe for Rachael, it was more."

"How can you say that? You don't know her or me. I thought you wanted to help."

"I do."

Mya scoffed. "You have a funny way of showing it."

"The one thing I've learned since being here is a person has to face certain facts they don't want to face. Everyone says they want to know the truth, but the truth is, they really don't. Not if it's the truth they don't want to hear."

"So you think my daughter got so angry at me she...murdered me?"

"I'm not saying that. I'm just saying...what if?"

Mya shook her head. "No. There is no what if."

"Sometimes..." Rita stalled. "Sometimes we overlook things. Sometimes, we're so focused on ourselves we don't see what's right in front of us. All we think about is our own pain. A mother can love her child and still find she's guilty of...of putting her own needs ahead of her child and believing they'll understand."

Mya frowned. "What are you talking about?" Rita turned away and Mya said, "Wait a minute. Are you talking about me or...you? Rachael would never want to harm me. No matter how we argued or what we fought about, none of it would give reason for her to hate me that much."

"It's hard to know what's in their hearts or the harm words or actions can do," Rita said.

"Stop saying that. Rachael has a temper. We both do, but that doesn't mean..." Mya paused as Rachael's words at the cemetery flooded back. 'Dad, I feel bad about going behind Mom's back even though I blame her.' *Blame me? For what?* "Rachael and I have always been close. Sure, there's been a strain lately. I don't even remember what the argument was about, but I know this much, I've always put Rachael before me, and she knows it."

Did she? Is that how Rachael saw it every time I told her no?

Mya shook her head at any doubt. "I know my daughter. She's innocent."

"All right," Rita said. "If you really want to do this, we'll have to work fast. Think back to that day. Every detail could be important. Try, Mya, no matter how hard it is. You have to remember."

Mya closed her eyes and took a deep breath. She focused her energy on that morning and forced the fog covering it to lift.

*****

Mya rolled over in bed and glanced at the alarm clock that never rang. Eight a.m. She opened her eyes wider and groaned. "Damn it. I'm late."

She swung her legs over the side of the bed, yawned, and realized it was still dark. That made no sense.

Mya lifted the window blind, and when she saw the heavy, overcast clouds and the beads of rain on the window, she understood. The dreariness of it made her want to crawl back into the warm bed, pull the covers over her head, and forget the world, but she had a meeting with a client and she promised Ted Bimmerson in accounting she'd bring coffee since it was her turn.

Ted had a crush on her. Right after her separation from Doug and once a week ever since, he asked her to go out for dinner or drinks. At first, Mya was flattered to think a man would find her attractive, but then it became awkward and Ted started to make her uneasy. He seemed to know a little too much about her. He spoke about Rachael, a person he'd never met, as if he knew her. He'd ask how her soccer game or the horse show went that weekend, and when Mya questioned him about how he knew those things, he'd smile in a clumsy way and say he saw the notes written on the calendar she kept pinned behind her desk.

There were other things too: subtle things. He knew her favorite sandwich, how she preferred hot chocolate...dark with no whipped cream and a shot of cinnamon, and her favorite song; all things he claimed to learn over the years. It might be true. Mya worked for the company for fifteen years., and Ted was there the day she started.

Why she thought of that, she didn't know. It was a lousy day, rainy, and cold. The leaves had changed from bright yellows and burnt reds to bleak browns barely clinging to branches. She hated this time of year. Everything was so gray and bland. Mornings were dark, and nights were chilly and damp. The flower garden, once rich with summer colors, had faded into dead plants that needed to be tossed.

As tempting as the cozy bed was, Mya put on her slippers and shuffled down the hall. She knocked at Rachael's door, but didn't expect the girl to be there. Rachael had an early class on Mondays and was usually gone by now.

When she opened the door, she saw a lump under the blankets. "Rachael? It's past eight."

Rachael sprang up as fast as a Jack-in-the-Box. "Why didn't you wake me?" she shouted.

"I overslept too," Mya said.

"Well thanks a lot. I'm screwed now." She dropped back on the bed and covered her head with the sheet.

"Why didn't your alarm go off?"

"Why didn't yours?" Rachael hollered from under the cotton fabric. It puffed up with air like a balloon and almost made Mya laugh.

"Good question. I don't know."

"Get out," Rachael said and tossed her pillow at the door.

"Rachael, please. Do we have to start this early with one another?"

"Get out and shut the damn door." She flipped over in the bed. "I mean it."

Mya closed the door and rubbed her forehead. She felt the migraine coming and knew she'd have to eat something before she could take her medicine.

In the kitchen, she placed two slices of bread in the toaster and made coffee. Her head began to throb with the onset of a migraine. She had suffered from migraines since she was a teenager. There was a time when they got better, but as she grew older and the stress in her life increased, the headaches returned with a vengeance.

A bite of toast and several sips of coffee helped. She glanced at the clock. There was no way she'd get to work before ten at the rate she was moving.

Mya dialed the phone and a cheery voice she recognized answered. "Malone, Westcott, and Malone, this is Ms. Westcott's assistant, how may I help you?"

"Patty, it's me. I'm running late. Overslept."

"Are you all right, Ms. Westcott?"

"I'm fine, just moving a little slow this morning."

"It's the weather," Patty said. Mya could picture the perky medium blond smiling while she played with her pen between her neon purple fingernails.

"Move my ten o'clock appointment to eleven and change my eleven to tomorrow. Tell Ted I need a rain check on the coffee…and one more thing," Mya rubbed her forehead to chase away the cobwebs clinging to her brain, "Oh, yes. Put the Dell file on my desk. I'll be there by ten." She hung up.

It was good to be the boss.

It only took fifteen years to get to the top. She began at the advertising company of Malone & Malone in accounting, eventually moved to sales, and, after she worked her tail off, landed two huge contracts and one of the biggest computer companies around. That success helped make her a partner. Her salary tripled in the last five years, and after the mess Doug left her in, it was a good thing. She could finally breathe a little, and just in time: Rachael had begun college. She worried her daughter wouldn't at first. Rachael had ideas of traveling with her boyfriend and that, somehow, she'd earn money as needed.

That wasn't exactly the life Mya wanted for her. They argued nonstop about it from the time Rachael graduated high school to her twentieth birthday. In between, Mya compromised. Rachael traveled to Arizona for the winter, California for six months, and Puerto Rico for eight weeks. Mya fitted the bill and all without any financial help from Doug.

The arrangement was, Rachael would attend the local university and live at home rent-free. She would get a part-time job and Mya would pay her tuition and car insurance. Mya would try not to bug Rachael about Danny, her boyfriend, who preferred to spend the little money he earned from working part-time at a coffee shop, on his bulldog, Fetch, and on XBox games. He was the Realm of Dark Power champion according to Rachael. Luckily, they broke up two months ago.

Rachael flew into the kitchen. She snatched the last piece of toast, grabbed the cup of fresh coffee Mya just poured, and gathered her books in one fast swoop.

"I'm so freaking late," Rachael said. "thanks to you."

"Me? I don't usually wake you up. Or is that something you've added to my job description without discussing it?" Mya tried to be funny, but as the words poured out, she knew her attempt failed.

"It's called consideration, Mother."

Mya hated that tone whenever Rachael used it—which was a lot.

"I always wake up whenever I hear you thudding down the hall."

Mya huffed a laugh. "I thud?"

"Yes, Mother, you thud. You also snort. I hate it, but it wakes me up."

"Gee, I'm glad I can help." Mya laughed and wished it was because Rachael tried to be funny instead of insulting.

"I need to use your car."

Mya spun around on her heels. "What? I need my car today."

"I have a flat tire."

"How in the hell did you get another flat tire? I just paid for four new tires last month."

Rachael tossed up her hand while she slurped the coffee. "There was a pothole in the school parking lot, I guess. The tire kept getting softer and now it's flat."

"And you didn't bother to have it checked?"

"I have classes all day, projects due and a mid-term. I'm overwhelmed."

"With ceramics and poetry?"

"First you nag me to go to college, and now you're criticizing the courses I take? You didn't like Danny and you don't even ask how I am after our breakup. You probably won't like Wayne either."

"Who the hell is Wayne?"

"See. You already have that voice you get when you don't approve and you don't even know him. Well, he's a new guy I'm seeing and he's a philosophy major." Rachael looked at her mother. "I don't believe it. You just rolled your eyes at me. What's wrong now? Wayne is a deep thinker. He wants to travel to the Middle East and study with Buddhist monks. I might go with him."

"Really?" Mya swallowed the next few words that included *no freaking way* and *over my dead body*.

"On winter break he wants to go down to Mexico and observe the desert dwellers. I'll need some money. We'll be gone for three weeks."

"I'm not giving you a dime for that. Ask your father. And when you do, tell him I still want half your college tuition, and three years of child support. I'll overlook the other two years."

"It's always about money with you, isn't it? Dad has always been there for me. If it wasn't for you…"

"If it wasn't for me, what?" Mya asked, trying not to raise her voice.

"He'd still be here," Rachael shouted.

"Is that what you think?" Mya shouted back. "Is it? Or is that the bullshit he's filling your head with?" She never told Rachael about Doug's affairs or his gambling. She hadn't wanted to spoil the girl's image of her father by explaining he was never there for her and how he often lied.

"I don't care what you say or think. I'm sick of asking your permission. I'm twenty-two. I don't need it."

"But you need money. That, you'll ask for and the only answer I'm allowed to give is yes. Well, not this time. Ask your father and then scream at him."

"Dad's a good man and he loved this family. If it wasn't for you ruining everything." She gripped the doorknob of the partly-open kitchen door and screamed, "Everything. I hate you for that. I hate you! Go play with the guys at your office. Spend all your time with them for all I care. I don't need you in my life anymore."

Mya grabbed the door before she could slam it. "You hold on right now. I don't know where you're getting this stuff from but—"

"'But' nothing." Rachael stood firm with one foot out the door. "All you ever do is work at that damn office. For years. You were never here. Coming home late every night. Sometimes not coming home at all. It doesn't take a genius to figure out what's going on. And then you get separated? Yeah, real smooth, Mother. Why don't you just sew a huge red A across your chest while you're at it? And that guy, Ted? He used to show up at my soccer practice, asking me questions, and if that wasn't bad enough, now, he shows up when I'm walking across campus. He's a creep."

"Ted? I didn't know any of this."

"I bet."

"You don't know what you're talking about, Rachael. You have it all wrong."

"Sure I do. He said he wants to get to know me because I'm so important to you. That's a laugh. The only thing important to you is flirting and money." Rachael's eyes filled with bitterness. "You do realize, Mother, it's called an affair while you're married. But you've been separated for years, dangling Dad on a string, so why do you keep hiding it?"

Mya's brows lifted. "Dangling your father…Just hold on. I—I'm not dangling anyone or hiding anything. Nothing is going on with me and Ted or anyone else."

"Sure. How's the coffee club going for both of you?"

"Ted and I have been bringing in coffee since the week I started that job. There's nothing else to it."

"Really? Well, he thinks the three of us should go out for dinner and why don't I convince you? Side note, he liked that pale blue blouse you wore a month ago and you should wear it again. Yeah, he's a real charmer, Mom. He's glad that clown Thompson or Thompkins resigned so now he has you all to himself." Rachael smirked. "You picked a real winner there, Mother."

"You've got it all wrong."

"Wrong?" she screamed. "I hate you for making Dad leave and pretending to care about me at all. I hate the fact you dangle money in front of me to keep me in line just like you do to Dad." She rushed out the side of the house to the driveway. Mya's jaw hung open.

She stood in the doorway until a cold gust of wind snapped her out of the shock. Was that really how Rachael saw things? A tear ran down her cheek. All the years of hard work, endless meetings, chasing after clients, working to provide all the things Doug didn't, all misunderstood by her only child. How could this have happened? How much of it was Doug's fault?

Chapter 7

Mya wept into her hands. Rita wrapped her arms around her as she shook.

"It was awful," Mya said between sobs. "The things she said. It wasn't true. I never had an affair. I worked hard because I was trying to make up for the money Doug gambled away. And what he didn't gamble, he spent on buying women presents and going on trips. I never told Rachael any of that. Maybe I should have."

Rita hugged her. "You did the best you could."

"Rachael wasn't always like that," Mya said with a sniff and wiped her face on the sleeve of her robe. "We were so close when she was a little girl. Doug and I separated when she was fifteen. Even years before that, it hadn't been much of a marriage. At first, it was okay between Rachael and me. The first year of just her and me was fine. I did work a lot, but I thought she understood. I was trying to hold onto the house and make it possible for her to keep doing the things she loved."

"I'm sorry. For what I said before. You put Rachael first before your needs. It was stupid and thoughtless to suggest anything else."

"No. Maybe you were right. Maybe it was me wanting to hold onto things. The house. The way of life. Maybe it was what I needed and I should've seen what it was doing to her. I should have realized the more I worked, the less I gave her what she really needed. It wasn't things, it was me."

"Don't think those things," Rita said. "What you tried to do had nothing to do with putting your needs ahead of her. I was talking about selfishness. Like a mother who didn't consider what her actions might do to her child." She turned away. "I was talking about myself."

"You and your son?" Mya used her sleeve to dry her tears again. What could have been so terrible to leave Rita with such outward pain?

Rita turned back with a sad grin that lifted the corners of her teary eyes. "We don't need to talk about it right now. You have to keep remembering that day. Don't stop. No matter how hard it gets. You have to remember."

"All I remember afterwards was feeling sick to my stomach. I called work and told them I wouldn't be in at all and hold my calls. Then...I got angry. I wanted to call Doug, scream at him, and ask him why. Why did he fill Rachael's head with so many lies? He must've known how she felt. Maybe he was the one who led her to believe that stuff. And what about Ted? What was that all about? I wanted to wring his neck. How dare he go to Rachael and question her? He had no right! I thought he was weird, but to do what he did was just pathetic.

"I went to take a shower. I needed to clear my head. I don't know how long I stayed in there. The room filled with steam and I just wanted to drift away with it. My mind was racing. I think at one point I actually busted out laughing and thought I was going nuts and then I started to sob so hard my stomach caved."

"Keep going," Rita said. "Was there anything? A sound? A sense of something?"

"No," Mya said. "I put my head against the tile and felt like I was going to be sick. I don't remember anything except...steam. A lot of it. Swirling. Sort of like the clouds up here when we walk. It swirled and I felt a cold chill. I had the odd feeling someone came into the bathroom. I shut off the water. I thought that maybe Rachael had come back. That's when someone grabbed me from behind. A hand went over my mouth. I tripped backwards. My heel scraped on the lip of the shower. I saw...I saw..." Mya shut her eyes and squeezed them tight. "Something. In the mirror, for a second, a form, and I felt...a gloved hand over my mouth and then this piercing pain in my back. I fell to the floor. My eyes were covered. I felt someone stab me again and again and then…it turned black, and the next minute, I was floating above my body and looking down at…" Mya's eyed opened wide. "At Rachael. It couldn't be. She didn't do it, Rita. I know she didn't."

"How can you be sure?"

"She's my daughter."

"She was angry."

"She would never. Never." Mya took two steps away from Rita and then turned. "The hand over my mouth. It was too big to be Rachael's. And the smell. Rachael always wears gardenia perfume. That isn't what I smelled. And there's something else. Something…but I can't remember it."

"Try."

Mya could hardly stand. "I'm so tired." She felt as if she had run a hundred mile marathon.

Rita took her arm and said, "You need to rest."

"I just need a minute." Mya sat on the edge of the bench. She felt so weak, she lowered her head and closed her eyes. "What evidence do they have? Can we find out?"

Without hesitation, Rita said, "The Mirror of Extant."

Mya wished she could just lay down and sleep. She took a deep breath. The thought of Rachael alone and frightened pushed her to lift her head and look at Rita. There was little doubt in how much faith Rita had in the mirror. Mya nodded, hoping to somehow have as much faith. With Rita's help, she managed to stand.

They passed through the Holding Area to the furthest corner. When they arrived, they found the Mirror of Extant roped off.

Rita gasped and put her hand over her mouth "Tricia." She shook her head. "She's done this."

"But why?"

64

"She has her reasons. She always does."

"That's it? She has reasons? Is this jail or paradise?"

"Paradise is that way." Rita pointed up the stairs. "This is the dimension Tricia controls."

"Now what? We give up? I can't. I have to know what evidence they have against Rachael."

"There is a way," Rita said and stepped closer to Mya. "But you should know the consequences."

"I don't care. Whatever it is, I'll do it. Rita, my daughter, my only child, thinks I abandoned her. She thinks I chose work over her and had affairs. I never wanted her to hate her father, but having her hate me isn't right either." Mya paced back and forth, and the clouds whirled around her feet in a frenzy. "So help me; if I find out that Doug, that bastard, filled her head with this crap, he'll be sorry. I'll make him sorry." She stopped pacing and stood before Rita. "I mean it. I'll find a way."

Rita was silent. A look of disappointment filled her face that caused Mya to feel ashamed. "Is that what this is all about?"

Mya creased her brows. Rita misunderstood and somehow Mya had to make her realize. "No. You know that. It's about helping Rachael. She's been accused of something she didn't do."

"Then why are you talking about vengeance? If that's what you want, I can't help you." Rita sat on the bench and Mya joined her.

"That isn't what I want," Mya said. "I'm...angry. Who wouldn't be? We're speaking about my daughter. This is for her. That's what matters."

"And if you find out that Doug did tell her lies, then what?"

"I—I don't know." Mya bit her bottom lip.

"It's dangerous to be a soul filled with vengeance."

"What am I supposed to do?"

65

"Move on."

"Move on? How? How is that even possible after everything I told you?"

"Have faith that she'll find the truth."

Mya laughed. "You've been up here too long. I'm not that naïve, not anymore. All along, I thought Rachael understood and she obviously didn't. Who do I thank for that? Doug's twisted the truth."

"And Rachael didn't want to believe you. How would you make it any different if you got revenge on Doug?"

"Honestly? I'd feel better."

"And is that your purpose in all of this?"

Mya shrugged her shoulders What was the purpose? "No," she said with another dose of shame. "The purpose is to prove my daughter is innocent. It's about Rachael and not me."

Rita patted Mya's leg and smiled. "I'm glad to hear that. I hope you mean it, because there is nothing worse than a vengeful spirit." She looked away for a moment before she said, "I have something to show you."

She took Mya's hand and led her to an open area, through the Holding Area, and beyond to a place further than Mya had ventured. The surroundings changed to solid blackness and then a small glimmer of light, like a tiny ball, lit the space. Mya heard a crackle she recognized as branches and the scent of damp earth. In a flash, she was standing in the middle of a forest with dead trees and fallen limbs all around.

"What is this place?" Mya said. Dried leaves crunched under her feet.

"What do you see?" Rita said.

Mya shivered. "Woods. Dark woods and dead trees."

"Not me," Rita said. "I see an empty room and blood on the walls."

"I don't understand."

A few feet in front of them, an opening appeared. The entrance, like a vortex, swirled blackness. Mya wasn't sure whether her eyes adjusted to it or not, but the darkness began to fade a bit to expose a set of descending stairs.

Standing at the opening, Mya felt the cold. It wasn't the winter type of cold or the cold one might find in the Arctic, but a bone-chilling cold that gripped the heart and squeezed. This kind of cold could suck the last breath out of a soul and turn it to ice.

Mya held tight to Rita's hand. "What is this place?"

"Down there," Rita gestured with her head, "is a very bad dimension."

"I can see that. But what?"

Mya took a step closer. Her sudden movement surprised her. She felt compelled and took another. At the threshold, she peered in. Stairs wound down into pitch-blackness. Heat blasted upward with an intensity that reminded her of standing at the top of her grandfather's basement steps and listening as the old farmhouse furnace rattled and hissed before it kicked on. It blew hot air mixed with soot that choked her. So did this.

She heard the wails next as they pierced her ears. She covered them to block the noise, but the sound still penetrated. Mya, filled with sorrow and fear, felt the urge to take another step closer, but Rita pulled her back.

"I just want to see." Mya tried to wiggle free from Rita's hold.

"It has that power over souls," Rita said. "It will pull you closer and tempt you."

"Are there souls down there?"

Shrieks echoed from what seemed like miles away.

Mya tried to lean closer. "They need help. Can't you hear them?"

"I hear them," Rita said. "And there is no help. They made a choice long before coming here. That's the level beyond Forgiveness and Redemption. Where true lost souls and others who break sacred rules go. If we do what's forbidden," she looked back over her shoulder, "any one of us could be sent there."

"If we disobey Tricia?" Mya trembled when a growl as vicious as a wild beast shook the opening with its strength.

"It senses us," Rita said and began to pull Mya away.

Mya broke free from Rita and peeked into the entrance. "I just want to see."

As if guided, she stood at the top step. The heat on her face made her think again of her grandfather's house. Walls appeared painted in a washed out white. The door she stood next to turned to pine wood stained dark brown. She could smell the oatmeal cookies Nana baked. Her grandfather's fishing rod hung from the wall by the basement door, along with the worn out hat she loved to try on.

"Mya? Come down here," said a male voice she recognized.

"Poppy?" Mya called into the blackness.

"I need your help," Poppy said. "Don't be afraid of that old furnace. Come on."

She couldn't see her grandfather, but she knew his voice. The blast of heat wasn't so bad now.

"Poppy? Turn on the light." She stood on the top step, ready to take the next.

From within the darkness came a high-pitched whistle from a morbid tune that turned her insides colder.

It grew louder as if it was right next to her.

Mya shook, unable to move.

A roar vibrated the ground. Everything around her shook with the power of an earthquake. She began to lose her balance, teetering with her arms flailing until Rita snatched her back. They both fell to the ground. A laugh of purest evil thundered around them and then silence filled the air.

"Poppy?" Mya gazed up, and the face of her grandfather warped into Rita.

"You're all right now," Rita said. "I shouldn't have brought you here."

"What happened? What was that?"

"Evil. It tricks people."

Mya scrambled to her feet and moved away from the opening. The desire to go back to it and look again was still strong. "No. That wasn't evil. I saw my grandfather. I was in his house."

"It was a trick."

"A trick?" Mya wrestled with the image she saw and the longing she felt. "He called to me. My grandfather." The wave hit her again and she wanted to go to it. "Poppy is down there."

"He isn't," Rita said.

Mya untangled Rita's hold on her arm. "Yes, he is. He needs me."

She moved toward the opening, and Rita grabbed her again.

"He isn't down there!" Rita shouted. "Don't be fooled. Look at it. You know he's not."

Mya heard the whistle once again, followed by a bitter laugh and an eerie growl. She froze.

Shaking Mya, Rita said, "That's Hell. Look at it."

"Hell?" Mya moved back with Rita's help. Her mind clear, she saw the thick blackness as it had been all along. She smelled sulfur and dead, dry air. "I imagined it? To actually be this close? I wouldn't wish that for anybody."

"Vengeful souls can end up there," Rita said.

"Yes, I guess they could."

"Souls doing unholy things." Rita faced Mya with a hint of fear. "It could be our consequence."

Mya's breath caught. For a second, she was terrified. "I'll be careful. I won't let it turn to vengeance."

"It's not just that," Rita said. "What we're about to do might be considered unholy. Trying to reach the living. Trying to get them a message. Especially without permission. It's dangerous. If something attaches to us...if our motives aren't pure...even if they are, we're trying something that's dangerous. That place, with an empty room full of blood," she glanced over her shoulder at the entrance that still called to Mya, "could be our punishment."

Mya followed Rita's gaze. The dark opening frightened her to her core. The whistle she heard scared her even more for reasons she couldn't explain. She was somewhere that still made no sense, with a woman whose own sadness was painful to see, and playing with things she knew nothing about. Even so, Mya looked at Rita with strength that almost surprised her. "If that's my destiny, my punishment for trying to help my daughter, then I guess I'll have to face it. Tell me what I need to do, and I'll do it."

"I'll show you."

"No, I have to do it on my own. I don't want Hell," Mya eyed the suddenly-subdued entrance, "to be something you face."

"My time is nearly expired anyway."

"What does that mean? You won't be sent...there, will you?"

Rita didn't answer.

"Rita, I saw a dark really scary forest and you saw something different. Why? Why did you see an empty room with blood?"

"Everything around us is what we imagine. You saw a forest just like you saw shimmering gates. Mine is different."

"Will you be sent to Hell?"

"A level just before. A type of purgatory. It's a dimension with no end, hardly any light, where souls wander for eternity reliving the moment of their sin over and over."

"But why? Why would you be sent there?"

"If I can't receive forgiveness, one filled with understanding and unselfish love, the kind that will help lighten my soul, then I have no other place to go. It isn't possible for me to move on."

"Why do you need that type of forgiveness?"

Rita lowered her eyes. She twisted the rough fabric of her gown in her hands.

"Does this have something to do with your wound? I've seen it. Rita, did someone hurt you? Is that how you died?"

"Yes. But it isn't what you think." In a soft, quivering voice, she said, "I...killed."

Mya's breath caught. "Murder?"

"Not the way you think."

"Okay." Mya looked at Rita's tear stained face. "Then tell me. What happened? Who was murdered?"

Rita lifted her dark eyes. "Me."

Chapter 8

"I don't understand," Mya said.

"I killed…" Rita struggled with the word, "myself."

"Accidentally, right?" Mya said. "Right?" She tried to rationalize what she heard. Accidents happened. Medication got mistakenly mixed with another. Someone made a dumb move on the highway; someone not looking both ways before crossing the street. Any one of hundreds of unfortunate things people blamed on themselves could have happened. Rita was sensitive, gentle, and simple in a sweet way. It made sense she felt remorse over something that wasn't her fault.

"No." Rita kept her anguished eyes on Mya. "It was intentional."

Mya covered her mouth. "Suicide?"

"I took my own life." Rita turned from the shock on Mya's face. "I suppose you'll hate me now."

"Hate you? No. I just don't understand. Were you ill?"

"No." Rita walked slowly with shoulders slumped under an unseen weight. "There was pain. A lot of it; but not from an illness or disease. It felt like it, though. Everything inside me hurt."

"Did you see a doctor?"

Rita forced a grin. "You're trying to make sense of this. You would. You're the kind of person who would. No, Mya, it wasn't physical. It was *in* me. It hurt to get up in the morning. I hated to go out anywhere. Everything was…useless. *I* was useless."

"Sounds like depression. There's medication for that."

"I know," Rita sighed, "I tried it. Nothing helped."

"A different doctor maybe. Or different medication. Therapy."

Rita's lips curled into a sincere smile this time. "You really are trying to fix this. It's too late, Mya. Look around. There is no fixing something I did to myself."

"Depression isn't your fault. I've read articles on it. It's a very real type of illness that impacts one out of—"

"Will you stop? I know I'm not as educated as you and I appreciate you trying to find a way to make this okay, but nothing can. I tried all the doctors, the pills, all of it. In the end, it doesn't matter. I killed myself."

Mya wished she could wrap her arms around her friend and tell her it was okay, but Rita was right. Words alone wouldn't make it that way. "What made you do it? How did you find the courage?"

Rita scoffed. "Courage? There's no courage in taking your own life. My reasons?" she tossed up her hands, "Were selfish. I get that now."

"You must have felt...desperate."

Rita cleared her throat. "My reasons won't make it right."

"Tell me."

"You really want to understand, don't you? To you, it must seem so far off from what you would do or how you would handle it."

"I don't mean to judge. But, yes, I don't understand and I want to."

"How can I explain a deep ache inside that won't stop?" Rita asked. "How do I make you understand how my mind worked? I had nothing left in me. I'm not like you, Mya. You would fight, just like you are now for your daughter. Here you are outside the gate to eternity, with Tricia telling you to move on, and you knowing that would be the easiest thing to do, but you won't. You would defy them all because you believe in something...someone— even when that someone may have betrayed you."

"Rachael didn't betray me."

"See? That's faith. Well, I didn't have that. I lost my belief, all hope, and any faith in me."

"How? What could have been so bad?"

Rita shrugged. "What do you want me to tell you? Have you ever tried to face nothing every day of your life? No light. No hope. Stuck in a dark, empty hole with no bottom."

"But your son? Your family? Didn't they bring you some happiness?"

"Everything I cared about was gone or leaving. My husband left me. My son was leaving. How needed was I? I didn't have a career like you, or any real friends. I was never the social type. I never had a clue what to talk about with people. Who would be interested in me anyway? I was getting older, and I was alone."

"Sounds like you felt sorry for yourself." Mya regretted the words as soon as she said them, but it didn't alter the fact she believed what she said. "I've been there. That alone feeling sucks. I'm no one to judge. However, I can't say it's okay to do what you did."

"I know that." Tears sprang into Rita's eyes and trailed down her cheek. "I gave up. I believed I was nothing and had nothing that mattered. I forgot I had the most important thing in the world. I never stopped to think what it would do to my son. I convinced myself it was better for him. He wouldn't have to deal with a lonely old woman. He could go off, have a life, and never have to take care of me. I put my pain, my grief, ahead of him."

"Something must have caused this."

"Was I an abused wife? Did I have a miserable childhood? Is that what you're looking for? People were cruel. That's true. More than once. But the problem was with me. I couldn't handle life...or loss. When my mother passed, I felt alone in every way. Ed walked out on me. My son, Jake, he would put off his trip and his scholarship to college if I let him see how bad it was. What was the point in doing that? I was exhausted. Hiding it from him was exhausting. I'm not trying to make excuses. I'm really not. What I did falls on me."

"So why?" Mya asked.

"No easy answer. One day, I started to drink and I couldn't stop the voices in my head telling me over and over that I was a loser; telling me I was nothing and Jake would be better off without me. *I* would be better off if I gave in and let go of the pain. So, I used the only thing Ed left when he took everything else, a gun, and..." Rita brushed back her hair. The black wound was exposed. "I shot myself."

Mya took a deep breath. Her heart broke with the anguish she witnessed. Now she understood why Rita seemed full of despair. "I'm sorry." What else was there to say?

"That's why I have a red patch on my gown. It's to remind me of the blood I spilled at my own hand. This wound," she rubbed the spot on her temple, "will never heal. I've spent five years of human time with the Waiters on this level. Those souls have also committed horrible acts to themselves or others. So we spend what time we're given here praying for forgiveness."

"From God," Mya said.

"The Creator? No. He designed us to make our choices and there isn't much His Holiness won't forgive. The weight of it all belongs with mortals. I've learned that. We long for some kind of redemption. We look for forgiveness from others because of what we did in selfishness. The kind of pain we cause needs forgiveness from the ones we hurt. It isn't possible to move on without it."

"You're talking about the pain you caused yourself?"

"No," Rita said, "the kind we leave with the living. It weighs us down. We suffer with it every moment and a moment here can last for days. In my case," she flattened her hair over the wound, "once I...we expire, a moment will be an eternity lived over and over."

"You keep saying 'we'?"

"Others like me. The ones you've seen wandering."

The ones Mya thought of as "lost", who walked with their heads down and who muttered to themselves; the ones who looked through other souls with unimaginable anguish. They drifted far from the lobby and some, she noticed for the first time, seemed to drift so far away, they faded from sight. "How many have received forgiveness?"

Rita glanced at her feet. "Very few. It's rare."

"Couldn't your son give you forgiveness? Can't you reach him?"

Rita shook her head. "He won't hear me. He's learned to block his gift even more since I died. He won't listen."

"Then how do we reach him? Rita, you said he could help me."

"He can. But I'm not the one who can reach him. You have to be the one. And it has to be pure. Not for vengeance or spite. It has to be a desperate plea from someone who longs to save another."

"How can I reach him? How can I find out about the evidence they have or lead him to my killer when I don't know anything and now we can't use the mirror?"

"Follow me." Rita hurried with Mya. They headed back to the Mirror of Extant. The rope that was still in place prevented anyone from getting close to it. "I've learned a few tricks since I've been here. Mya, you have to remember what's in store for us. If Tricia finds out, and she always does, we may be sent to the lowest, most evil of places."

"I still don't want you to get into trouble."

76

Rita grinned. "My destiny is pretty much sealed. I have one last hope, and that's if you can reach my son. Maybe, somehow, he'll listen this time. But even if he doesn't, it's worth it to me to help a mother who was more than I ever was."

"That isn't true."

"We'll argue later. For now...." Rita lifted her hand and swept it to the side. A veil lowered all around them. "This will block us for now. We haven't much time."

They slipped under the rope. Rita waved her hand again and the water stirred.

"Ask your question," Rita said.

Mya focused. "What evidence do they have against Rachael?"

Rita took Mya's hand and stirred it in the water. The water began to perk and bubble.

An image came into view. Blurred at first, it cleared to a woman with shoulder-length black hair. Strands of gray poked along the roots. Her makeup, with too much blush; deep blue eye shadow; thick, black eyeliner; and ruby red lipstick, did little to hide her advancing age.

Mya pulled her hand back and the image disappeared.

"What's wrong?" Rita said. "Do you know her?"

Mya nodded. "That's Doris Ivy, my neighbor. Why would the mirror show her?"

"It has something to do with the question you asked. You need to be ready for whatever you find. I warned you about that."

Mya took a deep breath and stirred the water again. "No matter what, I won't stop this time."

The image returned. Doris put on black pumps to match her knee-length skirt. She straightened her cream silk blouse, making sure the two top buttons were undone, exposing a marquise shaped diamond on a gold chain that nestled in her cleavage.

The doorbell rang.

Doris grinned at her reflection in the hall mirror, and then changed her features to look more serious. She took a deep breath and opened the front door.

"I'm glad you could come over," she stepped back to allow the visitor inside.

Doug Westcott stepped over the threshold, and Doris shut the door.

Mya lifted her hand out of the water again.

"What in the hell is Doug doing there?" Mya said. "He couldn't stand Doris."

"You have to watch," Rita said. "If you keep stopping, the mirror won't give you the answers you seek."

"I'll watch, but this is crazy," Mya said. "I don't understand what any of this has to do with evidence."

Doug wandered further into the house, glanced around the living room, and walked to the wet bar in the corner. He poured himself a glass of bourbon as if he'd done it a hundred times. "Would you like brandy?"

"No, thank you," Doris watched Doug with a small grin. "I've been calling you for the last week. Why did it take so long for you to call back?"

Doug sipped his drink. "It's been hard, Doris. Between Rachael's arrest, the police asking me all kinds of questions, and trying to get the will read, none of this has been easy for anyone."

"It's all such a tragedy." Doris glided over to a wingback chair and sat. "I didn't mean to be thoughtless. But a man like you shouldn't be alone at a time like this."

Doug smiled wearily and put the glass of bourbon to his lips. "Why did you tell the police what you did?"

"I couldn't lie, Doug. You of all people should know that. I didn't want to say what I did, but it's the truth."

"Are you sure? Maybe you made a mistake."

"I told them exactly what I saw and heard that morning. I heard Rachael and Mya screaming at one another. It was nothing new. They argued all the time."

"Rachael blamed Mya for our separation."

"Yes, I gathered that from the screaming I overheard. I heard the things Rachael said to Mya."

"That doesn't mean...she was angry."

"I saw Rachael leave. Actually, I thought it was Mya because I saw Mya's car leave, and then twenty minutes, maybe twenty-five minutes later, the car came back. It was at least three minutes before I heard a scream. I thought they were at it again. The police and an ambulance showed up. I thought someone might have fallen. Either that, or one of them hit the other. I never guessed there was a murder."

A young man came into the room. His short, mouse brown hair, spiked with gel, looked crispy. His attempt at a goatee did nothing to flatter his thin lips and dull brown eyes. His baggy jeans, two sizes too big, hung down to show the top of his blue plaid underwear. The gray sweatshirt he wore hung on his thin frame. He silently stared at Doris and Doug.

"Hello, Burke," Doris smiled. "I didn't hear you come in."

Burke turned on his heels and left the room.

"He's very upset over this whole thing," Doris said. "You know how close he was to Rachael."

"Yes," Doug said and finished his drink. "You never liked it."

Doris guided her freshly-manicured hand over her skirt. Her one-inch nails were polished blood red and looked like claws. "Let's not get into that now. Would you like another drink?"

"No. I just wish you hadn't told the police the things you did."

"I've told you, Doug, they questioned me just like they did you."

"You didn't need to add the details."

"I just want to help. I'd think you would want the police to have as much information as possible," Doris said.

"It looks bad for Rachael."

"Am I supposed to apologize for that?" Doris studied the piece of fuzz she removed from her skirt. "I told them what I know: I heard a scream. The police and ambulance came. I rushed over to see if I could help. Rachael was covered in blood."

"She got blood on her when she leaned over to help her mother."

"Well, if that's all it was, then it'll come out at the trial."

"Along with what you also told the police."

"Would you like it better if they suspected you?" Doris said.

"Why should they?"

"Because the part I forgot to mention was I saw your car parked down the street."

"I explained that to you," Doug said.

"That's right, you did," Doris caressed her necklace like it was a pet hanging around her throat. "You said you were coming here to see me but weren't sure if Burke was home, and when you saw Rachael's car in the driveway, you thought she might notice you." She rolled the diamond between her fingers with a smug look. "You're separated, Doug. You have been for six years. If you want to see me, why shouldn't you? We shouldn't have to hide it anymore."

"It wasn't the right time to explain things to Rachael."

"We have a total of eight years together. The first two, I understand. But now? When is the right time?" Doris walked across the room to the wet bar. "You kept putting

80

off finalizing the divorce because why? Why didn't you just stop contesting the divorce and sign the damn papers?"

"I've explained. I told you I agreed to everything she wanted, but Mya kept stalling saying she wanted mediation, and coming up with ridiculous excuses. She played the courts and blamed me."

"Which is why you kept changing attorneys, and that sure as hell didn't help, did it?" Doris's lips curled in contempt. "You know something? I think I will have a brandy. Pour it for me."

"I have to go." Doug placed his empty glass on the bar.

"Not yet. I know why you're so upset with me."

"Because you don't believe me about the divorce?" Doug said. "Or because you said some damaging things about the murder? You pick."

"I told the police what I heard. That morning, Rachael screamed at Mya that she wished she was dead and she wanted to kill her."

Mya opened her jaw and eyes wide. With her finger still dripping water, she stepped back from the mirror like it was a hideous creature.

"That isn't true," she said. "Rachael never said anything like that to me. Never."

"Maybe you forgot it," Rita said.

"No. I'm pretty sure I'd remember something as cruel as that. What about Doug and that…that Doris?" Mya pointed at the bowl. "Eight years together? Together even before we separated? I should have guessed. I knew Doug was having an affair, but with that tramp? I would have never guessed that one. He prefers younger women. I bet that's why the bastard is lying to her. He's the one who contested the divorce and played the courts, changing attorneys, coming up with stupid excuses to prolong it. He did it so he wouldn't have to commit to her. Oh, he's a smart one. He left me with the debt, played around with her and probably others, and then tells everyone I stalled. That's the game he plays. He's nothing more than a cheat and a liar."

"She said she heard things," Rita said.

"She's wrong." Why would she say those lies? Mya knew Doris didn't like her and she never cared for Rachael either. Not since the time she found Rachael and Burke playing doctor in her basement. They were six years old, for God's sake. That didn't matter to Doris. She always acted as if Rachael was inferior and her precious Burke was too sweet to be mixed up with her.

"Burke, her son, was a weirdo. He was always coming over, just showing up out of nowhere. Rachael didn't want anything to do with him. She tried to be nice, but he never got the hint."

"Try to calm down," Rita said.

"Calm down? How? If that's the evidence the police have, it's all lies." Mya took Rita's hands and held tight. "We've got to get ahold of your son. I don't know what else to do. I can't leave Rachael with no one but her lying father and some jealous slut that hated me."

"We'll try." Rita waved her hand and the veil that hid them disappeared. "You need to rest. You'll have to gather all your strength if this is going to work."

"Rita Delmar," Tricia said, standing at the bottom stair to their level, "and Mya Westcott. I want to meet with both of you...now."

Chapter 9

Doris Ivy turned on a lamp in the living room, turned off the light in the kitchen, and, after she opened the basement door, switched on another light. Her heels clicked as she proceeded down the wooden stairs.

From within the tiny room, Burke heard all of his mother's movements. The room at the bottom of the cellar stairs, was barely big enough for him to stretch his long legs. Sweat ran into his eyes. The air was stale and heavy. He sniffed.

"Are you crying?" Doris asked just outside the door.

"No, Mother." Burke lied. He buried his head in his hands and stifled the urge to sob.

"You did this to yourself," Doris said. "You make me do this." She unlocked the door and stood staring down at her son's curled-up body. "I brought you a glass of milk." She put the glass on the cement floor when he didn't take it. "Drink it and stop crying. Mother is not happy with you."

"I know," Burke said. He rolled over to his other side and picked up the glass. "I'm very, very sorry, Mother."

"Of course you are. You know I'm right." Doris closed the door and locked it.

"Mother, please," Burke said. "I'll be good."

"Drink your milk."

"I don't like this milk. I want the good milk," Burke said.

"You'll get the good milk when you're good."

Doris's heels clicked as she walked to the back of the basement to start her ritual. She opened a cabinet, took out a cloth, lit a candle, lowered a veil over her face, and kneeled.

Then, muffled by the veil, she began chanting in a different language. She was calling for someone... something.

Burke covered his head, rolled up tighter into a ball, and waited for the darkness.

*****

"Follow me." Tricia glided over the carpet of clouds that swirled a fluffy mixture of indigo, dark purple, burnt crimson, and deep brown.

Rita and Mya cruised behind. Mya asked, "Why do the clouds look so different?"

"The clouds reflect Tricia's mood," Rita said, "and by the looks of them, it's not good."

In the Lobby, Tricia stopped and faced both women. Her sapphire eyes were dark and unreadable. She wasn't smiling. "Did you really think a veil around the Mirror of Extant could fool me?"

"That was my doing." Rita stepped forward. "It was my idea."

"I know that," Tricia said. "And so was taking Mya to the lowest dimension. You know the danger in that. She could have been sucked into it."

"That was my fault," Mya said. "Rita tried to warn me, but I was tricked. It won't happen again."

"It certainly won't," Tricia said.

"Is that place our consequence for challenging you? If it is, I forced Rita to help me. She had nothing—"

Tricia put up her hand. "That's enough. I know what you're both doing."

"I have to help my daughter," Mya said. "It's even worse than I imagined. People are telling lies."

"So telling lies and hiding things up here is permissible?" Tricia asked as her eyes transitioned to a dark brown. "Well, it isn't." She turned and looked directly at Rita. "Putting up veils. Really, Rita, didn't you think the clouds would warn me? And then there's the matter of you stepping under the rope I purposely put there to keep you away. You had no right."

"Rita was trying to help me," Mya said. "Is that so wrong? If there were any place designed to understand something like that, I would think it should be here. Why can't you understand I have to find some way to help Rachael before she's convicted of something she didn't do?"

"You're certain of your daughter's innocence?" Tricia asked.

Mya's eyes narrowed to slits. "Are you kidding? Of course I am! Why shouldn't I be?"

"That question tells me there is a slight chance you're not."

"That isn't so," Mya shouted.

The ground at Tricia's feet churned like storm clouds until Mya lowered her eyes and calmed down.

"Why won't you let Rita help me?" she asked.

"Rita has tried before." Tricia glared in Rita's direction. "Hasn't she told you? It was never successful. In fact, it only resulted in more suffering."

"This is different," Rita said. "Mya's motives are pure."

"Really?" Tricia eyed Mya with enough uncertainty that even Mya wondered.

What if my motives aren't *pure? They must be,* Mya decided. *This is no time to doubt myself.*

"Mya, you can't deny you're angry with your husband," Tricia said. "You question your motives and try not to doubt, but didn't you speak of making him pay? And this other woman, Doris Ivy, you feel contempt for her."

"It's true," Mya said. "I do feel those things. Who could blame me? I'm only human. *Was* human."

"Yes," Tricia said with a slight tone of superiority. "Human. Those bothersome emotions. You feel betrayed. Deceived. It all leads to nothing good."

"You're right. I do feel all that. None of it matters. Rachael is what is important to me. Her and her innocence."

"And what if you're wrong?" Tricia said. "What then? If you allow hatred and bitterness to consume you, it means eternity, *your* eternity, is at stake. Vengeance is a sin no matter the cause." Tricia placed her hand on Mya's shoulder. "I suggest you stop this now. Go through processing and move on. Let what must be…be."

"I can't," Mya said. "I just can't."

Tricia lowered her hand. "So be it. The choice is not mine."

"Don't punish Rita."

"Rita's time has come to expire."

"Don't do this," Mya said with tears building in her eyes. "I'm begging you."

"However, she has received an extension. It isn't my doing."

Mya and Rita shared puzzled looks with one another.

"What does that mean?" Mya asked.

"It means if you insist on this alternative, then it shall be. You will be granted time." Tricia waved her hand, and a glass jar filled with a cranberry-colored cloud floated in mid-air. "You have until the cloud in this glass dissolves." She took the jar and held it up into the light. "This is all the time you are permitted."

"How much time is that?" Mya asked.

"Probably not enough, but no amount would be for this foolishness." Tricia held onto the glass container and said, "You will see it thin and slowly dissolve. When the content is down to the last, the jar will be empty. Your fate. Both of your fates," she paused with a stern look at each of them, "will be determined."

"Thank you," Mya said. "We won't fail."

"None of this was my decision," Tricia said. "I was overruled. However...your fate is in my hands. What you are about to attempt goes against what we stand for. We leave destiny in the hands of those far wiser. To reach out to the living the way you imagine can only lead to confusion, and risks souls. There are already so many questions. Questions that cannot possibly be answered. Questions never meant to be answered in the living dimension. It only serves to fuel conflict between both worlds.

"There are many souls here, Mya, who left the living world through violent acts, and they face turmoil constantly. We try to counsel them here and guide them towards peace. We console them as they search for answers here."

"It isn't my answers I'm looking for," Mya said. "The risk I'm taking is for someone else."

"So I've been told. Nevertheless, vengeance can disguise itself. Evil is a trickster that can attach itself to that. If you open the portals of two dimensions, there is a very real threat that can sneak through. Because of that, I need to banish you both."

"Banish us?" Mya gripped Rita's hand. "But you said..."

"I said I am told to allow this, Mya, but not here. Not in this dimension. You will be sent to another realm where things are not always as they seem. You will have to face your fears. If you can conquer those fears and remain true to your desire to help your daughter, then have at it. However, I caution you. If the cloud dissolves before you complete your task, you will return to face whatever penance is decided.

"If you surrender to your fears, if they weaken you and take possession, or if you act in willful vengeance and it corrupts you, you will both face the lowest level for eternity. There is one more thing. Rita," Tricia paused, looking deep into Rita's eyes, "if you should reach your son, you may not ask for forgiveness. That can only come unconditionally. There is to be no mention of you. Those are the terms. Is this still what you want?"

Mya and Rita eyed each other. They both nodded.

"I will pray for you both," Tricia said.

"How will we..." Before Mya could finish her question, she was no longer facing Tricia.

Instead of light, darkness surrounded her, and the cold made her shake.

She recognized the place.

It had given her nightmares for years.

Chapter 10

Rita opened her eyes and recognized her worst fear.

She stood in the middle of an empty, windowless room. Dark red blood trailed down the four walls around her. She fell to her knees and covered her face.

When she found the courage to lower her hands and forced herself to look again, she was at the foot of a grave.

Her grave.

Somehow, she knew it was her grave, although it wasn't marked.

The grave was open. She didn't want to look, told herself not to, but she peered over the edge anyway. The ground gave. Her foot slipped, and before she knew it, she was face to face with her corpse.

Her decayed body rested with her arms crossed on her chest. In horror, Rita stared nose-to-nose at her own skull. Very little flesh remained, and what was there, appeared leathery. The jaw had dropped. No teeth remained. Bony cheekbones protruded and her eye sockets were sunken. Murky gray pupils stared back at her. She screamed. Her efforts to climb off the body didn't work. Something held her there. She screamed again.

In a hollow and whiny croak, the dead face spoke.

"You did this...to us," it said.

Terrified, Rita tried again to push off the body. Again something held her in place. When the lower jaw of the skull broke off, Rita's gut-wrenching scream turned into a sob. She tried to close her eyes, afraid to look, and even more petrified to move.

From above, something called out to her. She stopped crying long enough to hear and know that what she heard shouldn't have a voice anymore, but it did.

She lowered her hands. Back on solid ground and once more next to her grave, she saw a white mist rise slowly from another grave. Ashen and smoky, black orifices for eyes emerged while it took the shape of her departed mother. In a deep, dry rasp, it moaned and reached out a skeletal hand.

"Help me," the dead woman wailed. "Rita, why didn't you help me?"

Rita tumbled backward. She landed on hard dirt. Her eyes were open wide in disbelief and terror. "No, it can't be." She hid her face again. When she peeked, the apparition, solid and vivid, was still there.

Rita cried, "Mama? I'm sorry. I'm so sorry."

The spirit of her mother grew larger and floated over Rita's head. If Rita wanted, she could've reached up and touched the woman. She didn't. The spirit stared with morbid disgust and then, without warning, lunged at her, her face an inch away from Rita. "Why didn't you help me?"

"I should have answered the phone," Rita shrieked. "Ed left me and I just couldn't face anyone. I didn't know how sick you were. I swear." The spirit circled her.

"You never came." The figure groaned. "I called for you. I laid on that cold floor dying, waiting, and calling for you." The speed of her attacks increased. In a blurred streak, she dove in close, flew away, and came back again. Each time, she poked a finger in Rita's face, screaming the accusation. When she stopped, she pointed down and demanded. "Look."

"No!" Rita shouted.

"Look," the apparition demanded.

Rita followed the command to the grave at her feet. Dirt covered what was once exposed. The dirt aged and weeds poked through. She felt a moment of relief for not having to face her own skeleton this time. The feeling was short lived. A hand broke through the earth and a corpse, dead five years and rotting, wiggled to free itself. It screeched and clawed out of the dirt. Fingernails chipped and worm-eaten hands caked with dirt, it climbed from the ground and glared at her.

Rita trembled and squeezed her eyes shut, but nothing could block the horrible sound…a loud pop that shattered the air.

It echoed with a deafening boom. Rita didn't need to look. She knew what it was.

Still on her knees, she held the gun this time. With no control over her body, she raised her arm and placed it against her right temple.

Rita whimpered, unable to prevent the movement. "No. Please don't."

She pressed the trigger and the gun fired.

The bullet caused a penetrating wound as it devastated her frontal lobe and passed through brain tissue. Within seconds, she bled to death.

Rita's spirit floated above this image and she sobbed. But before she drifted further, something pushed her back into her body, forced her to her knees with the gun in her hand, and lifted her arm, putting the gun against her temple again. She trembled and fought not to fire the weapon, but she had no control. Once more, her finger pulled the trigger and the shot fired.

She heard a scream. Her scream.

She rose again to see her lifeless body and the damage the gun had caused, then was swept back into her body, forced to perform the act again.

*****

Mya didn't recall falling to the ground. She awoke, confused for a moment, curled in a ball, lying on an uneven, damp concrete floor in a place that smelled of mold and chilled her to the core. Her eyes adjusted to what little light there was and she looked around. From above, dead potted plants hung from the rafters while cobwebs adorned the braided ropes that kept them suspended. Lined up next to those, an old picnic basket and smaller wicker baskets were all tied to the wood beams with more braided rope. A single light bulb hung down from the ceiling, the silver pull chain also wrapped in cobwebs.

The scent of mildew and another odd odor warned her of a familiar evil; all of it some part of a faded dream she didn't want to remember.

She started at the clang and rattle behind her. The furnace. She realized where she was: her grandfather's farmhouse. A hiss, a louder rattle, the furnace ignited with the exact sound that frightened her every time she heard it as a child. She wrapped her arms around herself as she heard another pop and hiss from the burning coals.

A hot red glow flamed behind the grate, lighting up her face. The light cast shadows on the moist, stone walls behind her. One of those shadows appeared too large to belong to her.

He came out from the corner. How he got there, she never knew. He came toward her with a wicked grin, arms outstretched, reaching for her.

Mya backed away. She fell on the bottom step. He came closer. She tried to scream. Nothing came out of her mouth.

She managed to turn and run up the stairs, out the door, and across the field. In a flash, Mya was in the woods behind her grandfather's house. She recognized the place she often came as a child.

As a child of just ten or eleven years old, she used to stroll through the dense forest gazing upward beyond the tall pines to the blue sky that disappeared the further into the woods she went.

After she climbed over some stumps and made it past the trees, she'd see the railroad tracks. There, her favorite thing was to place a coin on the rails and step back while the train zoomed by and flattened it. Every time the train raced by, she clapped, and sometimes, the conductor would blast his horn.

When the train safely passed, she'd find the coin, blow on it to cool the heat, and examine how well it turned out. Content, she'd run back to share her work with her grandfather, Poppy. Her Poppy. A gentle man she adored who always chuckled with a twinkle in his eyes and admired her masterpiece.

He'd rub his chin and examine the flattened coin as if he was the distinguished judge in a 'coin flattening' contest. Slowly, he'd nod, holding Mya's anticipation for praise to the last second. "This is a good one," he'd say. "One of your best. Let's put it in the jar with the others."

It was a special time for her, an innocent time until one day...the day *he* found her.

It was autumn. A crisp smell in the air. The height of the leaf peeping season just ended. Yellows turned brown. Reds turned darker. Each step of dried leaves crunched under her small, preteen feet. Mya watched the storm clouds disappear behind the tall pines. Once the sky became visible again, she arrived at the clearing. That day, the light was dull, with gray clouds hiding the sun.

She was by the train tracks now. In her hand, she held a shiny nickel and carefully placed it on the tracks. One more check for accuracy, she readied the coin for the train. She heard the afternoon express coming. In her plaid pedal pushers and red sweater Nana had knitted for her, she kicked a damp leaf off her pink sneakers. She placed her hand on the tracks and felt the vibration of the train thundering toward her. Eager, she held her breath.

A noise in the brush behind her made her turn. A man, tall, thin, with black whiskers on his chin, and long, scruffy hair poking out from under the hood hiding part of his face, stepped out. He lowered his hood just as the sun burst out from behind a cloud. He smiled in a way Mya, as a child, never saw someone do before. It was creepy the way his lips spread into a grin and his dark eyes stared through her.

Mya backed away. He stepped closer. She almost fell onto the tracks. He kept grinning at her like her just like her four-year-old cousin, Andy, did when he saw her with a fresh-baked cookie and she knew he was going to grab it.

"It's all right, Child," the man said and took another step.

Mya's gut told her it wasn't all right at all. He took a small step and then another. Each time, he licked his lips and trailed his eyes up her body.

"I'm new to these parts," he said. "I'm hungry and lost. Can you help an old man?"

He wasn't that old. Not as old as Mya's grandfather. Maybe he was as old as her uncle Bert. He was dirty, and with every step closer, Mya could smell him. It reminded her of Papa's dog after it had run through the swamp, came back to the house wet, and covered in mud.

"I won't hurt you, Child," he said with a grin still plastered to his face that made the hair on the back of her neck stand on end. His voice and the way he kept looking at her, told her he was lying.

She turned and ran. At the edge of the woods, she stumbled over a log and he was right there at her feet. She kicked. He grabbed her leg. She screamed. He covered her mouth. Mya kicked again. Her sneaker came off. She scrambled to her feet and ran.

The train raced by. She heard it behind her as it rattled the rails. The whoosh of it blew the few remaining leaves on the trees. She turned and he grabbed her again. Mya fell back into his arms. He covered her mouth again and started to pull on her pants. He pressed his hand between her legs, as he mumbled something, but all she heard was, "Not...hurt...stop." She smelled his breath. It made her stomach churn.

He laughed while his hand worked to pull down the brand new pedal-pushers she got for her birthday three weeks before. Wet lips touched her neck. Mya spun around and pushed him with all she had.

She stumbled, falling forward and caught herself by her hands. Her pants were around her knees, so she stepped out of them as she ran. He snatched her arm. She kept trying to run, moving her feet, but he held her and kept her from gaining any distance. She tried to wiggle free. He tugged her back to his chest. She lost her balance and fell to one knee. She fumbled around and located a stick as she scrambled to her feet. With the stick, she whipped him across the face and neck. He grabbed the stick from her with one hand and his other hand went to the welt that emerged across his cheek. It gave her the chance she needed to break free.

She ran as fast as she could. Strands of her hair were caught and pulled by branches. She didn't stop. She screamed as she ran through the woods, and when she saw Poppy rush toward her, she fell on the ground crying.

Her grandfather scooped her up in his arms and brought her into the house. Her hair was filled with leaves and sticks. Her cheeks were scratched. More leaves and dirt covered her sweater. Her hands were raw with small stones embedded in the skin. Her knee was cut and bleeding.

Poppy took his rifle and stormed back to the woods. She heard two shots and shook in her grandmother's arms. Through the window she saw that Poppy's two gun blasts never hit the man who then ran off.

Later, she went into the basement and that same man slipped out from the dark corner and came at her. She ran for her grandfather's barn, heard a blast, never looked back, and hid in the loft until her grandmother coaxed her out. From that day on, Mya refused to go back into the woods. For the rest of her life, she had nightmares about the man with black eyes.

Cowered behind a maple tree where years before she'd carved her initials, Mya shook as a full-grown woman; no less frightened than she was as a child all those years ago. She reached her hand to her hair and brought back sticks and dry leaves. She had no idea how they got there. Her arms were scratched and her knee bled just as it had over thirty years ago. She glanced back over her shoulder, heard the train roar, and saw the man with black eyes step toward her.

His smile and eyes were filled with lust like before. He smelled like something rotten and evil. All around her, the woods were thicker than she remembered. There was no sky above her, only tall trees blocking any light. He took a step and then another, his filthy hands reaching for her.

Mya heard Anna's words in her head. *'Fear is only real when we allow it. Strength is in our soul.'*

Mya stood. "You're not real." Her voice shook, betraying her.

He kept coming.

She lifted her chin and fisted her hands at her sides. Voice stronger, she shouted, "You're not real!"

He reached for her, licked his lips, and smiled more.

"I know in my soul you're not real."

She closed her eyes and, when she opened them, he was gone.

Mya let out a breath. Still shaking, she looked down at herself and the cuts and blood were gone. She steadied herself until she heard a scream.

"Rita." Mya took off running.

Through the thick brush, she fought the vines that hung low. When she came out of the woods, she found Rita in an open field, slouched over on her knees, sobbing hysterically.

Mya reached for her. Rita pushed away, her eyes squeezed shut, she held her head and continued to plead with some invisible force to stop.

96

"Rita," Mya shouted and shook her, "it's me. Open your eyes. Look at me."

Rita cried. Her hand posed as if holding a gun to her temple, she sobbed. "No more. No more."

"It's not real!" Mya screamed.

Whatever terrorized Rita, Mya couldn't see, but it was obvious Rita did.

Rita pointed to the ground. "My grave. Mine. I did this."

Mya glanced down. There was nothing there. "Look at me," she said. "It's not real." She shook Rita harder, telling her to open her eyes.

Rita gazed at her friend, and, while Mya shook her, she dropped her hand.

"Mya?"

"Yes. You have to listen to me, Rita. It's not real. Whatever you think you see, it's not happening."

Dazed, Rita turned her head in all directions. "My...my mother was here and..." The field was empty. "I shot myself." She covered her face and cried again. "She was here." She pointed a shaky finger. "There. Right there. Dead. Next to me. Dead because of me. I could have helped her." Rita lowered her hands. "The gun." She looked in confusion at her empty palm. "I shot myself. It kept happening. It wouldn't stop."

"It's this place." Mya helped Rita stand. "Somehow, it's making us relive our fears."

"Purgatory," Rita said. "It must be some kind of purgatory."

"Well, whatever it is, we just have to focus on what we need to do before it's too late." She took Rita by the arm and guided her. "Come on."

They held each other's hands tightly and labored across the field and into the woods. Rita hesitated when the sky disappeared through the trees. Mya reassured her. "It's okay."

Rita pulled back. Mya held firm to Rita's arm and nodded. "We can do this."

When they came out of the woods, they saw an old gray house with a whitewashed front porch faded from the sun. Silent, they climbed the four warped steps and stood at the front door. Mya opened the loose outer screen and pushed against the aged wood door. With a whiny creak, it opened.

"Where are we?" Rita asked, afraid to step, she froze.

"My grandfather's house," Mya said. Memories flooded and a tiny grin crept across her face. This was Poppy's house: the home where she always felt loved and safe, except for that one horrible time she tried for years to forget. Her grin faded.

"I don't understand. How did you make it appear?"

Mya had no answer. She honestly didn't know how they arrived here. She simply thought of the place and it appeared. It used to be the safest place for her as a child...until it wasn't anymore. But she wouldn't let herself think about that.

Inside was dark and dusty. Mya hit the light switch. Nothing happened. She sighed at the bizarre fact that she could make a house appear but not make the damned lights turn on. On a side table, there was an old lantern and there was a box of matches in the drawer where Nana always kept them. She struck the match and lit the light.

They were in a kitchen. Pine cabinet doors hung loose from their hinges. Cobwebs dangled from the water-damaged ceiling.

On a table, there was an hourglass, and in it, a swirling purple cloud. The cloud wasn't quite to the top. Mya knew it meant their time was dissolving.

"We have to hurry," she said, studying the hourglass. "That's all the time Tricia gave us. We have to reach your son."

"I don't know if we can," Rita said. "What happened out there and now this place; I'm scared, Mya. I've never been so scared."

"We just have to concentrate. We can't let our fears stop us." Mya pointed at the hourglass. "If that cloud dissolves, it'll be too late for us, and the next place Tricia sends us will probably be worse than this."

Chapter 11

Jake Delmar balanced four grocery bags and his mail. He had a bag filled with three Boston Cream donuts clenched between his teeth, and, as he fumbled for the key in his pocket, he unlocked the door to his studio apartment without dropping anything.

"Yes, I am that good," he mumbled and bit down harder on the donut bag. After he tossed his keys on the table, he scooted toward the kitchen counter like a clown doing a juggling act. The carton of eggs, set on top of one bag, threatened to fall. He struggled to rebalance the load using his left knee as a safety net. "Hold on. Hold on," he said and reached the counter just in time to lower the bag.

He drooled with the donut bag still between his teeth, took out a half-eaten Boston Cream, and shoved the remainder into his mouth. Snatching a new bottle of Scotch from a brown bag (this is what he really wanted) he twisted off the cap and gulped a mouthful. Crumpling up the bag, he tossed it in the garbage can that overflowed with other crushed bags and empty Scotch bottles.

Pouring more of the golden liquid into a plastic cup, he sipped while he opened the mail. The first was an envelope addressed to him from his doctor. He tore it open and scoffed at the dark red ink stamped across the bill. "Overdue. Well, sorry, Doc, not this month either." The next envelope was his electric bill. "No need to open this. I'll know what they want when the lights go out." He filed it on the kitchen chair along with stacks of other late notices.

"What else do we have?" He swallowed more Scotch along with the bitter taste in his mouth. "A house for sale in a neighborhood I can never afford. How nice." He ripped that in half. "Oh, sweet. The bench saw I want is on sale at Home Depot. Twenty percent off. Nope. Still not in my price range." He flung it to the floor along with the rest of the ads for things he wanted but couldn't afford, things he wanted but didn't need, and things he needed, but were out of reach because he had other delinquent bills. He pushed all of it aside and opened the newspaper to the section of jobs he circled. It wasn't easy to hang onto jobs with the damn headaches he suffered.

He was a contractor, a good one too. That's what his boss told him when Jake explained he had to quit. Jake loved his job but couldn't tolerate those damn whispering voices only he heard. The whispers only got worse over the years. He used to block them with little trouble, but not lately, not in the last five years.

Every time his boss sent him on a job to renovate an old house, the voices crept in. Then the visions started too. Working on new buildings didn't even help anymore. They just kept coming: sorrowful pleas and mournful cries calling his name, begging him to hear, until he screamed at them to shut up and leave him alone. They tried to take over. He felt it. They wanted to use his body and force him to bend to their will. He wouldn't let them.

This was supposed to be his gift–hearing the dead, being able to read what happened and, sometimes, catching glimpses of what might happen. "A gift" is what his mother and great-grandmother told him it was: a gift he inherited, a gift he didn't want. He knew what it was like…when a lost soul took over. They brought darkness with them, and he swore to himself when he was fourteen, he would never let them in again, especially since he suffered from the time he was eleven with the dark shadows and the whistling.

The whistle tormented him.

It fooled him at first with its innocence.

Shortly after his eleventh birthday, a high-pitched, playful tune filled the air. He'd stop whatever he was doing and listen. At first, it made him smile. The tune was light and rhythmic. He'd search the house for it, thinking his mother left on the radio. He'd hear it outside and wonder if a neighbor had a record playing. He began to hum it and then mindlessly whistle it himself while he read his comics or worked on a puzzle. But then, it began to play during his sleep, waking him, taunting him. Once it gained his full attention at all hours of the day or night, the tune changed. It became less playful, more old-fashioned, haunting. It left him chilled. As soon as it began, it didn't stop, not even when he covered his ears. It no longer played in the distance. It came closer. He'd stop and listen until he felt a breath on his neck, became dizzy, and got sick to his stomach. The whistle volume increased until it filled the room.

Something overtook him. Some kind of heavy weight with an odd darkness consumed him. He no longer controlled his body. It was as if his being—what made him Jake—slipped into a black pit.

When he became conscious of himself again, he awoke along the side of a pond two miles from his house. He was crouched over drowning a cat. Both of his arms were scratched and bleeding. The cat was fighting for its life and, as it began to give up, Jake realized what was happening. He dropped the cat on the ground. It sprang back to life, hissed at him, and took off running.

The whistle sounded again in his ear. Whatever was there was right next to him. He ran from it, hands pressed over his ears. He got back to his house, ran into the closest building, the garage, and squatted in the corner, trembling. He was so afraid he didn't even dare to breathe.

He heard a high-pitched creak, a thud, and a hammer flew off his father's workbench. Then, the shadow appeared. It was solid black, ten, maybe twelve feet tall. It stretched up along the wall and then over took the ceiling. Jake rushed out of the garage. The side door slammed shut behind him, and after that, he didn't want anything more to do with his supposed gift.

His great-grandmother helped him. She had the gift too. She taught him to block it and call upon it for his purposes only and not anything else's. Then, he turned fourteen and the control was gone. He fought hard to gain it back and decided never to acknowledge it again.

For a time, it worked. During the last few years, however, something changed–something he refused to acknowledge and it made it more difficult.

Jake went over to the drawer and touched the .35 revolver he kept there. There were too many times when he held it in his hand and thought of his mother. He slammed the drawer shut. He would not be like his mother. He prayed he'd never be like her.

He turned on the TV instead and tried to relax. Lately, the headline news was the same…a young girl suspected of her mother's murder out on bail awaiting her trial. If the media had their say, she'd already be convicted and sentenced.

Jake changed the channel and caught the score of his favorite football team. He cursed. So far, this wasn't their season and neither was last year. They should play Ryan, the second string quarterback. He had soul. Jake could tell. He was psychic that way. The thought made him laugh while he drained the last drop of Scotch from his cup.

*****

"Come on, Rita," Mya said, "we don't have much time. Tell me how to contact your son." She held tight to Rita's trembling body. Rita looked tired and drained. If everything Mya learned during their time in the Waiting Area was true, Rita would need strength to carry on.

"I'm not sure we should do this," Rita said and lowered her eyes.

"What are you talking about? We have to."

"Maybe we shouldn't. Please, don't look at me like that."

"You mean confused? Pissed off? Of course I'm going to look at you like that," Mya said. "You're the one who started all of this."

"I guess I didn't think it through. I'm sorry."

"Think it through? Look, I get that you're afraid."

"I'm more than afraid. I'm petrified. I can't stop shaking. You didn't see it, Mya. My mother. Me. Our dead bodies. The gun." Rita shivered. "It was horrible."

"It wasn't real."

"It felt real to me and that was enough."

"Rita, we have to do this. We can't back out now."

"It isn't just me. I don't want to disappoint you, it's just that, my son. I couldn't protect him when I was alive. I've hurt him since I died. I don't want to hurt him anymore."

"We won't. I won't," Mya said.

"There's no way to know."

"What about all your talk on faith, hope, believing? We can't quit now. You heard Tricia. If we don't succeed, the consequences will be…well, by the look on her face and the things she said, not good. And Rita, it's more than that. What about my daughter? I have to help her. I have to."

Rita trembled. "Something is wrong. Don't you feel it?"

They stood at the kitchen table. The light from the lantern glowed and created flickering shapes on the walls. Five feet behind them, the door to the basement creaked open a few inches at a time. Mya heard the whistle, the footsteps coming up the stairs, and she rushed to the door. Slamming it, she pushed a chair under the doorknob, turned, and saw Rita slip to the floor, pointing toward the back door.

Outside, a gray mist dissolved, and in its place floated a shriveled, rotting form of a woman. The eyes, large black holes, stared through the window and then she began to pound on the door wailing, "Rita, why didn't you help me?"

Rita sobbed on the floor, cowering and begging for it to stop. Mya pulled down the blind and grabbed onto Rita.

"It's not real," she shouted over the banging on the door and the shrill of Rita's cry. She shook Rita harder until she managed to get to her to listen. "It's here to frighten us. That thing and the sounds from the basement. We can't let them. We have to focus. We have to be stronger than they are."

Rita looked past Mya, as the banging grew louder. "I'm sorry, Mom. Forgive me."

Mya took hold of Rita's face and screamed, "Tell her to go away. Tell her it's over. You have to fight your fear, Rita." Her voice began to crack. "Please. I need your help. Rachael needs you. We don't have time. Be strong. Tell her to go away. Tell her you're not afraid."

Rita latched onto Mya's hand. She squeezed it hard and, in a voice that grew more determined, she shouted toward the door, "Go away. I'm not afraid. Not anymore. I'm sorry for what happened, but I couldn't have saved your life. You're dead. It's time for you to go."

The pounding stopped.

The doorknob to the basement rattled. The high-pitched whistle of an old, haunting tune grew louder. Mya yanked the door open and screeched, "Go away! You don't belong here anymore. Now leave!"

The whistling faded and stopped. Both women held one another.

"They might come back. We have to focus," Mya said. "The cloud in the hourglass is getting smaller. How do we reach your son?"

Rita stared in a daze at the back kitchen door. Mya helped her to the kitchen table and they both sat. She closed her eyes, silently praying. She thought of her grandparents, the love she felt for them as a child, and in her mind, heard Nana read from the Bible.

After Mya opened her eyes, she looked at the table. There should have been thick dust on it, but there wasn't. The whole room looked just like Mya remembered it right down to the scent of her grandmother's oatmeal cookies.

Rita saw it all as well. "We're here because of you," she said. "You thought of this place and brought us here. That's how we reach Jake. You have to imagine him and bring us there."

"How? I don't know him."

"You'll close your eyes and picture him while I tell you about him. But first," Rita took Mya's hand, "you have to swear to me that your heart, your thoughts are pure—with no anger."

"No anger?" Mya frowned. How would that even be possible? There were so many emotions to weigh through, but at the top was definitely anger. "I can't promise that. Of course I'm angry. They arrested my daughter for *my* murder. Someone murdered me. I know it wasn't Rachael, but someone did it."

"Then we can't do this. You said you wanted to help her."

"I do. The only way I know is to find out who did this to me."

"If you have any malice at all, this isn't going to work," Rita said. "It never did in the past."

"In the past? What are you talking about?"

"I hoped this time would be different. I've tried with others to reach my son so he could help, but they held too much anger or regret. Their thoughts weren't pure and something dark always interfered. Being here with all this

L. Thomas Cook

around us, I'm more afraid. I won't risk Jake. I can't bring darkness to him."

"Maybe the something dark was you," Mya said. She saw the hurt on Rita's face and stood. "I'm sorry, but you didn't really want to help those other souls, did you? You wanted them to reach your son because he wouldn't answer you."

"You're right," Rita softly said. "My son won't answer me. He's angry about what I did. I didn't think about him. I didn't think about what taking my own life would do to him. That doesn't mean I didn't want to help the others or you. I do. You have to believe me."

"You can't ask him to forgive you. You know what Tricia said."

Rita lowered her head. "I know and I won't. It's too much to ask. I know that now. But," she looked up at Mya, "he has a gift and I know he can help you. He just…doesn't want this gift."

"Great." Mya scoffed. "Anything else you forgot to mention? Our time is running out."

"A gift like Jake's isn't easy. My grandmother had the gift. She could see things; hear things, before they happened. It almost drove her insane. My mother didn't have the gift and neither did I, but when Jake was three, we knew he had it. He would talk to things no one else could see. The older he got, the stronger the voices and the visions."

"Visions? I thought he couldn't see dead people?"

"You didn't want to believe he could hear them, so I left out the other part."

"No more leaving anything out, okay? Give it to me straight so we can figure this out. What exactly am I dealing with?"

"A gift that scared a little boy. He could see people who died and not all of them were good. My grandmother tried to help him deal with it. She showed him how to

107

control it. She died before she could show Jake anything more."

"How is any of that a gift?" Mya said.

"Because he could help people. My grandmother did. She would give people messages and help them with their suffering. Just knowing their loved one was at peace and happy, helped them. Jake's gift was special. He helped find a little girl lost in the woods. He knew when one boy at school had stolen money from another child. He brought a message to a grieving mother. When a man went missing, he brought the police to the man's body." Rita traced her finger along the rough grooves of the table. "Problems started when those things got in the newspaper and before long, kids began to make fun of him and some were even afraid of him. The worst was when he was fourteen. He started to act strangely and say things not like him at all. He ran off one night. We found him in a cemetery at the grave of a murdered man. The spirit of the man told Jake who killed him. The police suspected this person, but had no proof. The spirit told Jake where some evidence was and the man was arrested."

"That's good," Mya said.

"Except the spirit of something dark began to show. I think it was the murderer. And I think he possessed Jake. Jake never got over it. He was just a boy, but that dark spirit showed Jake everything horrible he did to kill that man and five others before that. Afterwards, Jake began to see more and more things: dark shadows that moved so fast he couldn't make out what they were. I found him one day hiding in his closet, crying. He couldn't remember some of the things he'd done. After that, he didn't want to use his gift ever again."

"So what makes you believe Jake would use his gift now?"

"Because," Rita said, "I believe your motives are good. That's why it's so important you feel that way. It was hard on Jake when his father left me and even harder after I...took my life. But you have to believe me, I was in so much pain losing Ed and then my mother. Jake deserved to have a life. He didn't need to be tied to a mother too tired and sick to get out of bed. If I had stopped to think what it would do to him, I would never have...but that doesn't matter now. What matters are your reasons for wanting to reach out to him. If you can show him you have no selfish reason, no darkness that follows, he would let down his guard and listen. His gift is still there, but buried. He needs to not be afraid of it."

"Okay." Mya took a deep breath. "I just have to clear my mind. The murderer who did this to me will answer for it through processing anyway, right? The important thing is that my daughter isn't punished for something she didn't do. How do I reach him?"

Chapter 12

"Why haven't you returned my calls?" Doris Ivy held the cell phone to her ear while she glided red lipstick across her mouth.

"I told you," Doug Westcott said, "this isn't the right time."

"Really?" Doris smirked. "It was never the wrong time before."

"My daughter is on trial for murder."

"What does that have to do with returning my calls?"

"Don't you think you could be a little more sensitive?"

"Me? What about you? I'm the one who's been waiting for years and listening to all your excuses about why the damn divorce never happened. I still don't know why we had to keep our relationship a secret. It never made sense to me."

"It would all be a bit awkward, don't you think?"

"And now that Mya is dead?"

"How would that look? You're a witness for the prosecution for Christ's sake. How would it look if everyone knew we were involved? Why are you doing this, Doris?"

"Doing what?" Doris held an eyeliner pencil in her hand. She tapped it harder and harder on top of the vanity where she sat. The glare she intended for Doug she gave the mirror instead.

"You're honestly upset I'm telling the truth about what I heard and saw? It's time you realize it, Doug, your precious daughter is a spoiled brat. I've tried to make you see it before any of this mess started. She always acted like she was a princess and the world owed her."

"Stop it. She just lost her mother for God's sake."

"And you want her to believe you're on her side so she signs the house over to you. You don't want to tarnish the image she has of you by letting her know how friendly you are with the neighbor. What if the media found out? They might start painting an ugly picture of who's telling the truth and who stands to gain the most."

"I've never heard you like this before."

Doris snickered. "Well, this is what happens when someone gets bored of your games. I could tell the police I also saw your car parked on the corner that morning and I know you weren't here to see me."

"Stop it, Doris. I mean it."

Doris grinned into the phone. "Is that supposed to scare me? Think of the scandal. If the star witness should disappear, the press would run away with it. What would the headlines be? Distraught father suspected of removing threat to daughter? Or...maybe he removed the threat to himself?" She grinned more when he said nothing. "Are you thinking it over, Doug?"

"I think you're being ridiculous."

"Am I? Or do I know more than you'd like me to? Now here's what I want: I want a little special time, just you and me. I'll meet you in one hour at our place. Now, don't grind your teeth the way you do when you don't get what you want. I just want us to have some time together, and for once, I'm deciding when." She hung up with a smile that quickly disappeared when she glanced in the mirror and caught sight of her son slipping away from the entrance to her bedroom.

She jabbed the tip of eyeliner into the top of the vanity. The point of the pencil snapped. "Burke? What have I told you about listening in to my phone calls?"

She picked up a wooden brush, and stormed into Burke's room. He sat on the edge of the bed as if expecting her. Before she said anything, he removed his shirt, turned his back to her, and gripped the bedposts. With every whack of the brush she gave him, he winced.

*****

"Sit here," Rita said. "Concentrate on what I tell you and picture Jake in your mind."

Mya let out a long breath, closed her eyes, and settled into the chair. She cleared her mind of every distraction and listened to Rita's soothing voice.

"Jake is twenty-six," Rita said. "He's five feet ten inches tall. A little on the skinny side. When I watched him through the Mirror of Extant, I noticed. I'm worried he isn't eating enough. His hair is dark brown, straight to the middle of his neck. He needs a haircut. He combs it to the left side. His eyes are deep brown like mine and he has a strong chin. He lives in a little apartment. I saw the street sign. It's on Warren Street. He must have moved there after I died and…"

The more Rita described Jake and where he lived, the more Mya could visualize it. It was just like at her funeral: all she had to do was think of someone to be with them. Before she knew it, she was transported to Jake's apartment. She was afraid to open her eyes in case it broke the trance.

"I see him," she said. "He's sleeping, I think, in a chair in front of the TV. There's a bottle of something…liquor I think, on his lap."

"He started drinking after I died," Rita said. "I've seen him when I used the mirror. It's my fault."

"Don't do that," Mya said with her eyes still closed. "I need to stay focused. What do I do?"

"Call to him," Rita said.

"Jake? Jake Delmar, can you hear me?"

Jake's eyes were sealed shut. His head dipped to the right and he held onto the half-empty bottle of Scotch with his left hand. He snored quietly against the low murmur of the TV.

"Jake, please, I need your help," Mya said. In her mind, she stood in the background. Jake slept in the recliner, his feet propped up in the air, and his hand wrapped around the bottle like a lifeline. She called his name again. He squeezed his eyelids tighter and gripped the bottle harder.

"Please, Jake. You have to hear me. My daughter needs you," Mya said. "This visit isn't for me. It's for her. I swear. I only want to help her."

"Go away," Jake mumbled in his sleep.

"I can't until you hear me. Her name is..." Mya stopped when she saw the image of her daughter on the TV. The reporter spoke about the trial and Mya's murder. "That's her," Mya said. "Jake, open your eyes. That's Rachael, my daughter. Look at her. She's innocent."

In his sleep, he muttered more fiercely, "Go away. I don't want you here."

Mya began to fade. She fought it. Eyes squeezed tighter, she took a deep breath and reached for the chair where Jake slept. Her hands disappeared into the cushion. "Please, don't send me away. Help me. Help Rachael. Don't be afraid. Your great-grandmother would want you to help me. She would. Even if you couldn't help your mother."

Jake's eyes popped open.

Mya was gone; back to the cold farmhouse with Rita.

"Why did you say that to him? You had no right!" Rita shouted.

Mya collapsed onto the floor. She could barely lift her head. Rita's shouts sounded miles away.

"You were with him," Rita hollered. "You weren't supposed to go there, damn it!"

What little strength Mya had left, she used to form the words. "What are you talking about?"

"You left. You disappeared. I heard some of it. You were with Jake. That's not what you were supposed to do."

"I was right here," Mya said while she labored to stand. Her knees wobbled. She felt too weak to lift her head. When she did, she saw terror on Rita's face.

"Your spirit left. I saw you slip away." Rita eyed her with caution. "How did you do that? It's the hardest thing for a spirit to do, let alone a new one like you. Where did you get the energy? Did you take it from my son? Did you?"

"No. I...I don't know what you're talking about. I visualized Jake like you said."

"And then you appeared to him. You had to because you weren't here, not all of you. I heard your voice." Rita covered her face with her hands. "Oh, sweet Lord, why did I let you try this?"

"Why are you so upset? I made contact. Isn't that what we wanted?"

"Through thoughts only, Mya. Thoughts. Don't you see? You became...a ghost. A spirit not in this dimension and not completely in theirs. You opened a doorway before you returned here. Only a strong willed spirit can do that."

Mya smiled. "I guess I'm one strong willed spirit."

"That isn't something to be proud of. It's dangerous. It brings danger to the living. That thing you said to my son...about how he couldn't help me. Why did you say that? You should have never said that."

"Something told me to. I...I think I saw something in the corner. It told me what to say."

Rita covered her mouth. "What was in the corner?"

Chapter 13

Rachael parked her car in the driveway of the home she once shared with her mother. She looked up at the two-story house. She hadn't returned to it since her mother's death six months ago. It might as well have been six years.

All the window blinds were shut tight. A stack of newspapers, piled high on the front porch, were damp and faded to a yellowish tint. The lawn was months overdue for a cut, and the rose bushes her mother loved so much were buried in thick weeds.

She sat in her car lost in thoughts about that horrible morning. Visions of blood, her mother's lifeless body, and the cold, hard steel of a knife's blade danced in front of her eyes. The sudden rap on her driver's side window startled her.

Burke Ivy smiled at her through the glass. His smile was big and bright like nothing was wrong and he was just glad to see her. He always smiled at her like that.

Rachael lowered the window. "Hi Burke."

"Hey, Rach." He continued to smile. "I thought you pulled in and I was right, so I ran right over. It's good to see you, Rach." He bounced up and down on the balls of his feet. With his hands shoved in his pockets, his pants hung lower. Even though he was nearly a foot taller than her five foot three inches, with the waist of his pants barely hugging his hip, he looked like a dwarf with stubby legs and no knees. A Cheshire cat smile, his voice squeaked as if he was thirteen and not the same age as Rachael. "I knew it was you. I don't know how. I just knew even before you pulled in."

Rachael climbed out of the car, trying to be pleasant. She really wished he hadn't intruded. "Nice to see you, Burke." He stood close, hardly leaving any space for her to close the door or move past him. "Burke?" She gestured for him to step back. Awkwardly, he did.

"You look good," he said with a broad grin and lowered his eyes bashfully. "Real pretty. You always look pretty, Rach."

Rachael ignored him. "I just have to get a few things." She went to the trunk of her car.

"Sure is good to see you, Rachael." He continued to smile while he followed her. She knew he would follow. He usually did. Just like he usually stood too close and stared at her exactly the way she felt his eyes on her now. And, just like always, she was too busy to bother with him and he didn't get the hint.

He kept watching her, saying nothing, and it made her nervous. *Some things never change* she thought with a long sigh.

"How are you?" Rachael broke the awkward silence. She finally looked him in the face and saw the black eye. "What happened?"

Burke lowered his head and shrugged a shoulder. "You know me." He chuckled. "Clumsy. I tripped and banged my eye."

"That was one heck of a fall," Rachael said. She suspected he didn't tell her the truth. He was clumsy, but he seemed to have an awful lot of bruises for someone who spent most of his time either on the computer, or playing video games. She'd known him since they were five years old. In all that time, it wasn't uncommon for him to have bruises on his face, his arms, or his legs, and he always had some excuse for it. It was no different than the way he made excuses for his mother. Rachael didn't press him too much. She knew he had a strange connection to Doris Ivy. Was it fear? Whenever he spoke of his mother, he got a weird glint in his eyes and then the glint turned cold before it returned.

Rachael didn't care much for Doris. The way Doris stared at her was creepier than Burke's stare. And the things Doris insinuated in her high-and-mighty tone, were twisted. Ever since Doris caught Rachael and Burke playing an innocent game of doctor with all their clothes on in the basement years ago, she took a disliking to Rachael. She overheard Doris telling Burke she was a slutty girl. At six, Rachael had no idea what that meant, but it didn't sound good.

There were other times too when she overheard Doris say, "I don't know why you bother with that tramp. She doesn't even know you're alive. She's a snob and a selfish girl. She'll use you. She's nothing but trouble."

Doris said it loud enough, knowing her kitchen window was open and Rachael was in the yard. Rachael ignored it and went inside, never saying anything. Whenever she saw Doris, she forced a polite wave or said a quick "hello, Mrs. Ivy." Under her breath, she cursed a few choice four-letter words at the woman.

Rachael asked Burke once if his mother hit him. He got very nervous and stammered, but never answered the question. He was always a little slow and innocent, so she let it go although she often wondered if she should tell her parents.

"Where have you been? I haven't seen you much," Burke said. He watched her take boxes out of her trunk and grabbed one just before it fell out of her hands. "What are you doing with these?"

Rachael frowned at him. "Burke, you know my mother...died, don't you?"

His face offered little expression. He nodded and then glanced at her with a shy smile. "Of course I do, Silly. I live right here." As if it just occurred to him, he said, "I'm sorry about that."

He helped her carry the boxes to the kitchen door and grinned. "So, are you home now to stay? Cause I've been keeping an eye on the place for you. Do you want me to mow your lawn? I was going to, but Mother said I should ask first and it was probably something you would take care of. I told her it would be nice if I helped but...you know Mother. She said I shouldn't bother you and if you wanted it mowed, you'd do it. I was going to take in the newspapers, but Mother said I should stay away because of...well, the police and everything. I don't mind, Rach, I don't mind helping."

Rachael unlocked the door and brought in the boxes with Burke right on her heels. She barely listened as he went on. Her mind was on the feel of the house–cold, empty, lifeless–and on that morning six months earlier, when she screamed at her mother, the awful things she said, and how angry she felt.

Tears welled in her eyes. On the kitchen table was her mother's daily calendar. A sweater hung over the chair and a coffee cup with dark, murky liquid in it–the remains left over too many days ago with no one to wash it.

The police had searched the house. She could tell by the way dishes were disturbed on the counter and drawers not open but slightly ajar. The thought of going upstairs, of what she might find there caused her stomach to tighten.

Suddenly, Burke's presence wasn't so annoying.

"Burke?" she said, her voice shaking, "Would you go upstairs with me?"

Burke's smile dissolved and for a moment, she feared he'd say no. His cheeks turned red. Rachael realized he might thing she meant something different.

"I...I have to get a few things," Rachael said. "And I'm...well, I haven't been back since...you know and I'm a little...scared."

"Sure," Burke said, but his eyes looked as nervous as Rachael felt. He covered it by forcing a smile. "Anything for you, Rach. You know that, right?" He grew serious in a way Rachael seldom saw him do. With a deep tone and an intense gaze, he took hold of her arm and said, "You know I'd do anything for you."

It was awkward. Rachael felt unsure of whether she was more nervous about going upstairs or being with Burke. She shook off the feeling with the knowledge Burke was inexperienced socially. He was someone with few friends if any; a guy picked on all through school; a man-child who lived at home with an overbearing mother. He was a damaged child who desperately wanted to be liked.

"I know, Burke," she said and smiled warmly at him.

He seemed relieved. "Good. I want you to know."

"You've always been a good friend."

He blushed. "I know. I have been, huh? I always said I'm a good friend to Rachael and she knows it because that's important, right? To be a good friend, I mean. So...I was thinking...what I mean is, maybe we could...I mean, you and I could—"

She stopped him fearing what he was about to say. "How about we go upstairs now and I can pack up some of my stuff."

He creased his bushy brows. "Pack? You aren't staying?"

"No. I...I'm staying at my father's."

"But why? I thought your mother left you the house?"

Rachael frowned. "How did you know that?"

Nervously, Burke laughed. "Well, I...I know your mom would want to do that, right?"

"She did." Rachael eyed him. "Right now, I'm not comfortable being here alone."

"You're not alone, Silly. I'm right next door."

"That's nice, Burke, but...the house just doesn't feel like home anymore. I may sign it over to my father and he'll probably sell it."

"No," Burke was quick to say, "he can't. You can't." He grabbed her arm a little too tight.

"Calm down, Burke, you're hurting me."

He let go and lowered his head. "I'm sorry. I just don't…I like having you live here."

"That's nice." She carried two boxes to the stairs.

"I think you should keep the house and maybe someday…soon, you'll stay here again and it won't be so bad 'cause it's all yours."

"It's the money," Rachael said and, standing on the bottom step, turned to face him. "I might need money for my legal fees."

"Oh. I hadn't thought of that." He lifted his eyes to her. "But your father, can't he help?"

"I don't want to talk about it right now, Burke. I just need to get through today."

"I have some money saved, Rach. Maybe I could help. I don't want you to leave."

"That's sweet," Rachael said and hugged him. He winced when she wrapped her arms around him. "What's wrong?"

He looked away from her again. "Nothing. When I fell, I hurt my back," he said. He took the boxes from her. "Come on. Let's go upstairs."

*****

An hour later, Rachael had four boxes filled with clothes, books, and the family photo album. She closed the lid of the trunk and turned to face Burke. "Thanks for your help."

"I could go with you and unpack the boxes," Burke said, his childish smile frozen on his face.

Rachael shook her head. Her mind flashed on the police tape that outlined where her mother's body had laid on the bathroom floor. The whole bathroom was a mess with dried, caked blood on the walls, the shower door, and tracks of it going into the bedroom. When Rachael went in there, she felt sick. Tears sprang to her eyes. The smell of chemicals the police used, turned her stomach. The dark carpet stains reminded her where she first heard the words that her mother was truly dead. She wanted to vomit. After realizing her father never called the company the police had given them to clean the house, she was disgusted.

"It's not so bad," Burke said, reading her mind. "I mean, yeah, upstairs was pretty gross. I didn't know blood could dry like that. Kind of reminds me of the time I found something...I still think they were rats...in my garage. Mother put poison in there. I told her not to, but she did, and then something else...never figured out what...got in there and ate them. Made a mess. Blood all over the floor. Little pieces of fur. These tiny bones...you think it's easy to get that off a cement floor? Mother told me to use a scrub brush. I scrubbed but...hey, you still look white as a ghost. You sure you don't want to sit? I could get you something to eat. Come over to my house."

Rachael shook her head and stared at the ground. "Thanks again." She played with her keys on the way to her car door.

Burke followed. "I could clean it up if you want," he said as naïve as a child suggesting he rake leaves or help bake cookies. With a little too much jubilance, he added, "The bathroom, I mean. I don't mind. And then maybe we could roast hotdogs in the fireplace and..."

She glanced up at him torn between screaming this was neither a damned game nor was it the time to have a sleepover, or giving in to her emotional exhaustion and crying. Either way, she wasn't about to give Burke or his mother an opening.

"Burke," Doris Ivy shouted as she slammed her car door shut. She marched across the yard like a mother bear protecting her cub. "What are you doing here?" She eyed Burke before she glared at Rachael, then smirked. "Oh, it's you. I'm surprised to see you."

"I'm just here to pick up a few things," Rachael said and opened the driver's side door.

"Not staying? I'd offer Burke's help but..." she continued to smirk.

Her grin vanished the moment Rachael said, "He already helped me. Thanks, Burke. I couldn't have done this without you."

"You mean you've been in the house? Both of you?" Doris asked and turned darker eyes on Burke.

"Yes, Mrs. Ivy," Rachael said and wanted to add 'don't worry, your son is still a virgin,' but she bit her tongue. "This wasn't easy, and having Burke here helped." On tiptoe, she leaned in and kissed Burke on the cheek, not knowing why, and wishing afterward she hadn't, especially with that look Doris gave Burke. "Thank you again." She got in the car and backed out of the driveway.

*****

Burke's stomach tightened as Rachael backed up and his mother glared harder at him. "Get in the house," Doris said.

"But, Mother, I helped."

"Get in that house now and go up to your room. Wait for me there. You know what to do." When Burke hesitated, she lowered her voice to a growl. "Go."

"Yes, Mother." He glanced down the driveway once more at the back of Rachael's car as she drove away.

*****

Jake Delmar reached for the wallet in his back pocket at the same time he yanked open the coffee shop's door. He bumped into her, and her coffee cup spilled all over the front of her navy blue coat and then onto the floor.

"Shit. I'm sorry," Jake said, looking down at the mess on her coat and on the tile.

She stood with arms out, still recovering from the surprise. Jake expected her to call him an idiot or worse. She didn't.

"Well this just adds to my already not so perfect day," she said. "Don't worry about it. There's a dark cloud over me and there's nothing anyone can do."

He looked up at her for the first time, and her simple good looks captured him. Her complexion was rosy, probably from embarrassment, her full red lips moist. He smiled at her cute nose, but felt instantly saddened when he looked into her blue-green eyes.

"I'm sorry," he said again and continued to stare.

She moved to the side with him when other customers came through the door and staff at the coffee shop came over with a mop and bucket. She took napkins from the bin and wiped the front of her coat.

"I know this sounds like the oldest line in the book," Jake said, "but…do I know you?"

Even with her head down, he saw a weary smile come across her face.

"You know," she began, "there was a time when I would have been flattered or even laughed, but…" she glanced up at him, "you probably know me from the papers or the news or both."

Jake's forehead creased. "Oh, so you're a famous person."

"You could say that." She went on cleaning her coat. "But, and trust me on this, fame isn't all it's cracked up to be."

"I don't get it," Jake said and then his breath caught when she looked him square in the eyes. "Hold on. I have seen you before." His mind raced and he knew. "Rachael West…"

"Westcott." She nodded before he said another word. "That's right. Now, if you'll excuse me." She tried to slip past him, but Jake took her arm.

The second Jake touched her, his mind flashed like a movie in warp speed and the feelings flooded in all at once. He sensed sadness, with anger and regret underneath.

He heard a terrified scream. Saw blood on the wall and on her face. The shimmer of a knife's blade in the morning light. A panicked plea for help. A voice far away calling out, 'please help my daughter. Help her,' and mixed into all he saw, was a dark shadow. It made him want to turn and run, until the voice cried out again, 'she's innocent.' He would have blocked all of it if not for the look in her eyes that kept him there.

"Please, let me go," Rachael said.

"I just have one question. Are you innocent?"

Chapter 14

"You said there was something in the corner," Rita said. "What? Tell me."

"I don't know." Mya rested her head in her hands at the table, amazed by how exhausted she felt.

Rita vigorously rubbed her hands along her thighs as she sat on the edge of her chair next to Mya. "Come on, think. Tell me what you saw."

"I was concentrating on Jake and he was pushing me away. I could feel it. Like hands pushing me and a wall coming up between us."

"Jake blocked you. He does that to protect himself."

"He's pretty good at it. I started to fade. No matter how much I wanted to stay, my energy was leaving. Then I saw something in the corner. A white sort of mist at first and then it formed a little."

Rita slid further forward in her chair. "What did it look like?"

Mya held her head in her hands. When Rita shook her arm, she looked up. Rita's face was a mixture of concern and fear. "I told you. A white kind of vapor. It was too quick. Why?"

"Why? I told you the danger if something followed."

"I don't think it followed," Mya said. "I think it was just, I don't know, there. But whoever it was, seemed to know your son."

Rita squeezed Mya's arm. "What did the form look like? Even for a second, you must have noticed something."

"I think a woman. Silvery hair up, maybe in a bun. Older type clothes. And there was a smell. Sweet. Maybe honeysuckle? I don't know. I'm so tired."

"That smell...the hair. It sounds like my grandmother. Jake's great-grandmother."

"Maybe it was. Maybe she's with him."

"No. There's no way. Why did you say what you did to him?"

"The voice...your grandmother told me too. Why are you so upset?" Mya said. "Maybe it's good that your grandmother is with him. Maybe she's protecting him."

"It wasn't my grandmother. She wouldn't do that. She wouldn't tell you to say what you did. You told Jake he knew he couldn't help me. She'd never, ever tell anyone, especially a spirit to say that."

"How do you know? You said the smell and the description could be her."

"Because my grandmother taught Jake and she knew the dangers in traveling through portals. What this thing...this voice told you to say was mean. Only a mean spirit would use something negative and cruel against another. We should never have done this. This is just what I was afraid of."

"But it worked. I got through."

"You got through all right. That doesn't mean it was a good thing. Do you want to know why? Because you traveled the dimensions disembodied. New spirits don't do that. They can't. They don't have the energy or the knowledge it takes to protect themselves and the living. The fact that you saw something dark in the shadows proves that point. Something followed, and it followed you to my son."

"I'm sorry, Rita. I don't know how it happened. I guess I just wanted to connect with him so badly."

"And the other problem is what you said to Jake. He has nothing to blame himself for or any reason to feel guilt. It's the last thing I want him to think, especially now if something followed you. You have no idea how dangerous that is. I hope he was able to block it."

"Why does he block it?"

"I told you. He got frightened when he was a child."

"No, I can see it in your face. There's more to it." Mya waited for Rita to lift her eyes. When she didn't, Mya said, "He's strong. You said he used to help people and he knows how to protect himself, so why wouldn't he let just a small piece in if he could help a lost soul, instead of blocking everything? That wall he put up was hard to pass. I know I'm new at this, but there was no way to get through to him. He refused to hear me until I said what I did."

Rita stared down at her hands. "He's angry with me. Why shouldn't he be? I killed myself."

"Anger." Mya nodded. "I felt it. And something else from him too. It's weird, but it gave me some kind of strength. Energy. Not a lot, but some."

"You can't feed off of him," Rita said, her eyes intense. "You can't get an appetite for that, and especially not from my son, or so help me, this whole thing stops now. I mean it."

"What's wrong?"

"I told you."

"No, there's more to it. What aren't you telling me?" Mya said.

"I don't want to talk about it anymore. I'm tired. You're exhausted. We both need to get some rest."

"There isn't time to rest, you know that. Tell me what's going on."

"You have to rest. And I...I need to think about this," Rita said.

"What's there to think about?"

"You can't appear to him again," Rita said. "Not as a disembodied spirit or voice. If you want to reach him again, it has to be in thoughts only, and to do that, you'll need all the strength you have, that is, if you decide to try again."

"If?" Mya frowned. "Of course I'm going to try again. We can't afford to fail. Rita, you know what our fate will be if we don't do this."

"There's so much about this you don't understand," Rita said.

"Well, maybe I would if you'd stop shutting down every time I ask what's going on. You don't want to discuss you and your son, fine. It's private, but what else is there I don't understand?"

"Any of this. About traveling the dimensions. Contacting the living." Rita began to pace, her spirit lifting a few inches off the floor. Apparently unaware that she floated in the air, Rita began to wring her hands together nervously. The more she did, the more it fueled Mya's own fear until Mya couldn't handle it and she took hold of Rita's waist.

"Stop floating back and forth and talk to me," Mya said and brought Rita back to the floor.

Both women looked at each other. "Maybe this was a mistake," Rita said.

"Okay," Mya said. "Now you're really scaring me. We've been over and over this. There's too much at stake here, Rita. You know it. Tell me what in the hell is going on. It's more than appearing to Jake. He didn't even see me. He probably thought he was dreaming."

"The problem isn't whether he saw you—"

A strange scratching at the door startled them both and they both latched onto one another.

Mya put her finger to her lips and whispered, "Quiet. Do you hear that?" She hoped Rita would say, 'no, don't be silly,' but the way Rita clung to her told her that wasn't the case.

The scratching grew louder, and with each scrape, more desperate, and faster. Slowly, they turned their heads toward the door.

Then, as quickly as it began, it stopped.

The silence was almost as bad. They held their breaths, waiting.

Holding tightly to each other, neither woman dared to speak.

Gradually, Rita, her voice shaking, whispered, "Is...is it gone?"

Mya paused for a second and released her grip on Rita's arm. "I think it left."

A light tapping started at the window. Rita and Mya looked wide-eyed at each other.

The tapping increased in both speed and sound until it erupted into a harsh pounding. They almost jumped into each other's arms as the banging became constant and the window glass cracked from the invisible force behind it. The doorknob began to jiggle lightly as the crack, barely an inch at first, spread quickly until it split into a weblike design.

The rattle turned more urgent. The knob shook so violently that Mya feared it would fall off.

A voice on the other side of the door cried Rita's name.

Rita whimpered as she and Mya backed in a corner away from the door.

"It's going to be okay," Mya softly said, her gaze glued to the door.

Rita sank to the floor, crying and covering her face.

Mya reached for her, but a high-pitched, insistent whistle came from the basement. The tune froze her blood.

She covered her ears and squeezed her eyes tightly closed.

"Stop it," she begged.

Rita pressed deeper into the corner and cried quietly. The pounding at the door intensified.

"It's not real," Mya said.

The whistle grew louder. Mya pressed the heels of her hands harder over her ears.

"It's real," Rita cried, still huddled in the corner. "This is the place where we face our fears and they're very real."

"I'm not afraid of you anymore," Mya shouted over the whistling and banging. "You're a monster." She stormed to the basement door and screamed at it. "You chased a little girl in the woods. I don't know how you got in the basement, but I'm not afraid of you anymore. Do you hear me? I'm not a little girl anymore. You're a monster and I'm not afraid!"

The whistling stopped...for a second, then started again as harsh as before.

"Go away!" Mya slapped her open palm on the door. "Go away, damn you!"

A raw, deep voice laughed at her, then it was gone. She felt it leave and sighed in relief.

Fooled only for a brief second, the silence was broken when the pounding at the kitchen door became as insistent as before.

A hollow voice chanted to Rita, "Why didn't you answer? Why did you let me die?"

Rita withered in the corner. Right before Mya's eyes, Rita's hands shriveled and she started to fade.

"No!" Mya shouted and latched on to her friend. "You can't leave me alone. Damn it, Rita, yell at it! Tell it to go away. Tell it you're not afraid."

"I can't." Rita sobbed. "It's my mother."

"Tell her to stop. Tell her you aren't afraid. Please, Rita, I can't do this alone."

"It's going to take over," Rita cried, her complexion as white as a sheet of paper. Her lower body began to fade into a thin mist.

"Don't let it take over," Mya begged. "Don't let it win."

"The beast will take me," Rita said.

Mya clung to her. "Be strong."

130

A harsh wind blew throughout the room. The door to the farmhouse and the cabinets inside shook. The kitchen table lifted, dropped, and lifted again. It hovered in midair for a moment and then slammed down onto the floor.

Mya shouted above the wind, "Be strong, Rita! You can do this. For us! For Jake! Don't be afraid."

Rita's form zapped in and out like an electric current on the fritz. She looked at Mya and said, "I'm not afraid. It isn't fear."

Mya's grasp was slipping; there was barely any solid form to hold. She grabbed Rita by the ankle, but it dissolved in her hand. She reached for the other leg and an arm. She was left with only Rita's thumb and index finger to grip.

"If it's not fear, then what is it?" Mya shouted over the banging and the fury of wind. "Please, Rita, you have to fight. You have to be strong."

"It's the guilt," Rita said in a whisper. "It's more powerful than fear."

"I know you feel guilty over killing yourself," Mya shouted.

"This isn't the same. I wasn't there to help her."

"How could you have known?"

"I should have," Rita said. Her form appeared one second and disappeared the next only to return as fuzzy as bad TV reception. "I didn't answer the phone."

The icy voice shrieked, "Why didn't you help me?"

"Did you know it was your mother calling?" Mya said. "Did you know she was ill?"

"No." Rita sobbed. She appeared one second and dissolved the next, only to reappear.

"If you knew, would you have answered? And if you did, could you have stopped your mom from dying? Rita, you're blaming yourself for something you couldn't control and you're giving that thing, that ghost, who probably isn't even your mother, power over you. Isn't that what guilt does? It wears us down and twists our fears about what we could have done when we couldn't have done anything to begin with. You didn't know. It wasn't deliberate. But that guilt you feel is. It's deliberately hurting you."

Rita's body began to return. She lifted her head and looked at Mya and nodded. Color came back to her body as she solidified more. "You're right. I didn't know it was her. The doctor said it was a massive heart attack. She was gone in a few seconds. Nothing could have stopped it. It wasn't my fault."

She took a deep breath even though she didn't need to breathe, got to her feet, and went to the kitchen door. Rita placed her hand on the wood and said, "I loved my mother with all my heart. I couldn't have stopped what happened even if I had answered the phone. I don't know who or what you are, but I know my mother loved me. She'd never blame me. She'd understand." Rita laughed while tears ran down her cheeks. "She would say, 'Rita Ann, stop blaming yourself. My time was up, so go on and stop wasting tears.'" Rita smiled with her hand over her heart. "That's what she would say. I know you're not my mother. In my heart, I know." She glanced over her shoulder toward Mya. "I'm not afraid. This guilt isn't mine."

The pounding stopped.

Rita rested her head against the door. "I'm sorry I scared you." She turned to face Mya. "You're right. Guilt does awful things. It makes a spirit weak. Demons know it. They use our weaknesses to trick and deceive us. It gives them some kind of power over us. That thing in the basement has power over you."

"I won't let it," Mya said.

"Do you know what it is?"

Mya glanced at the silent basement door. "I know exactly what it is. It's something that scared me as child. But I'm not afraid of it now."

"If you're not afraid of it, then what's keeping it here? Whatever that thing is, it's here, it followed you to Jake, and it's something dark."

"I don't think what I saw at Jake's was dark," Mya said. "If it was, why did it help me reach him?"

"That's what you still don't understand: darkness is a cunning thing." Rita let out a long sigh. "I don't know. Maybe it was my darkness. I killed myself. There's darkness in that. I just keep thinking about the blame it had you use on Jake. He doesn't have any reason to blame himself. If whatever this thing is, a demon or vengeful ghost, is trying to use negative energy to break Jake and stop us, we can't contact him again. Our energy has to be pure and positive. I won't let anything bring evil to my son, not even to help you."

*****

Rachael hurried to her car. Jake Delmar followed. Rachael whipped around and shouted, "Are you a reporter? Because I have nothing to say."

"I'm not a reporter," Jake said.

"Then what? A pervert? A freak?"

Jake scratched his head and smiled. "I haven't been called a freak in a long time."

"That's a surprise," Rachael said and unlocked her car. "Go away and leave me alone before I call a cop. And trust me, freak, lately, I don't like cops."

"I asked if you were innocent for a reason," Jake said.

"Why? Are you some kind of self-appointed judge and jury?"

"I didn't mean to blurt out the question, but it's important."

"Really? You're not a reporter. You're not a vigilantly. So you're just curious. Well, you know what they say, curiosity killed the cat, and hey, if I could kill my own mother, what's a cat to me?"

"Did you? Kill her?"

"Are you nuts? Leave me alone." Rachael opened her car door and got inside. Jake held the door so she couldn't shut it. "I mean it. I'll call the cops. I still have some rights."

"You were angry that morning. You blamed your mother for your father leaving."

Rachael's jaw dropped. "Are you a private investigator? Are you working for the D.A.?

"Your car...this car," Jake said, "had a flat tire and you used your mother's car. You're wondering if the killer thought you were home instead of your mother or if it was random. You did have a knife...but then I can't see."

"Get away from me, freak!" Rachael said and yanked on the door.

Jake refused to let go. "I see things. I can hear...things."

"I bet you can. Well, let go of my door or I swear I'll scream rape, fire, or whatever I have to. Now, let go of the damn door."

"I know it sounds nuts. It usually does. I'm rusty at this. I've blocked it for a long time and I'm surprised I'm doing this now, but I saw...heard...how desperate your mom is to help you. You look like her. Except her hair is a little darker and shorter." He gestured to his shoulder to show the length. "Haven't you ever had faith in something you didn't totally understand? In something that seems kind of crazy? I just...this time...it won't let me block it. Or maybe, seeing you...I don't want to. Whatever it is, I think I can help you."

"You *are* crazy."

"Let's get a cup of coffee. I owe you one anyway. We can talk."

Rachael gazed up at him. His eyes showed sincerity. His voice made her knees a little weak. He grinned at her reassuringly and winked as if he knew what she was thinking. She supposed if he was telling the truth about hearing things, maybe he heard her thoughts. She blushed. "How did you know those things? It wasn't in the paper. Not about my car or...what I thought."

"I told you. I see things."

"Like what? Dancing bunnies? Unicorns? You see dead people?" Rachael laughed.

"No, no, and yes."

"That's it, buddy, let go of my door or I swear I'll scream."

He touched her hand and saw a flash. Shutting his eyes, he said, "You're name is Rachael Marie Westcott. You're in college for business, but you'd rather be a writer. You have a scar on your wrist from the time you jumped off your bed when you were ten. You were pretending to ski down a mountain. Your mother said she would take you skiing. She never did."

Jake glanced into Rachael's wide eyes. "I know how it sounds, believe me. I never wanted this...gift. That's what my mother called it. It never felt like a gift. It's lonely. Just like I'm sensing you feel all alone right now. This damn gift, that does make me a freak, feels like that too. So, come on. Let me help you. What could it hurt, huh?" He smiled and Rachael melted.

"I swear, if you're a reporter playing some sick game with me..."

"I'm not. I'm an out of work contractor who wanted to be a photographer. I get insane headaches because I try to block this thing I can do. Last night, someone...your mother, came to me and begged me to help you. She kept screaming at me that you're innocent. Your mother believes you didn't kill her."

"My mother, huh?"

"Yes. I got a quick glimpse of her. She's the woman I described. That's your mom, right?"

"You saw her? Last night? Or maybe you saw a picture of her in the paper or on the news."

"No," Jake said, "it was her."

"And she believes I'm innocent?"

"Yes. So, are you, Rachael Westcott?" He smiled again.

Rachael looked at him with tears building in her eyes. "No, I'm not."

Chapter 15

Mya sat at the table, focused with her eyes shut, and smiled. "I see Rachael. She's with…Jake. Jake is there. Rita, he found her."

"Where are they?"

"Looks like the street in front of the bank on Westport Avenue. She's in her car and Jake is talking to her." Mya strained to hear. "Damn it. It's muffled."

"Concentrate," Rita said.

"I am, damn it. I can't…wait. I hear Jake's voice. He's saying… 'I try to block the thing I can do'…something. 'Last night…'" Mya strained harder. "Oh for crying out loud. It keeps coming in and out. Wait. Jake said, 'Are you innocent?'" Her eyes popped open. "Oh my God."

"What?" Rita asked. "What happened?"

Mya turned her head away from Rita. "Nothing. Nothing happened."

"You're lying. I can tell. You're whiter than a ghost, and that's saying a lot. Now tell me."

"It can't be. I heard wrong."

"You said you heard Jake ask Rachael if she's innocent. What else did you hear?"

Mya's eyes welled with tears. "She said…Rachael said…it can't be what she meant."

"Tell me, Mya. Remember what I said before this began, about the truth and facing that? You have to tell me what she said."

"She said…she's not innocent."

As Mya cried, Rita hugged her. "What are you going to do now?"

"What can I do?" Mya said with a sniff. "My daughter says she killed me. She's not innocent. Could she have really hated me that much? I don't understand and to make matters worse, it's getting harder to remember that day. All I've been able to see is a form in the mirror, a hand over my mouth, and then a stabbing pain. How could she have done that?"

"You're angry. You can't go back to Jake. I won't risk him."

"But I have to understand. I have to know why."

"You have your answer. The why she did it is for her to face."

"I just don't believe it. Rita, if she did do this, I could forgive her. I could let Jake know and he'd tell her. Maybe I *was* a terrible mother. I worked a lot. She didn't know the truth about her father."

"How can you forgive something like this?" Rita asked. "She took your life."

"Please. Let me just go back one more time. Just to say goodbye."

"You said goodbye at your funeral. The hourglass doesn't have much left in it. You did what you could. It's time to face Tricia." Rita exhaled a shaky breath. "And, time for me to face my destiny."

"Jake should know how much you love him."

"It's too late for that, and besides, Tricia said we can't mention me. Even if you did, he would block it and he should. It would bring darkness to him and he doesn't deserve that."

From far away, Mya heard Jake's voice without even trying.

"What you're talking about is guilt," he said. "That doesn't mean you're guilty of murder."

"Wait, Rita, Jake doesn't think Rachael's guilty," Mya said.

"What are you doing? You can't still be there," Rita said.

138

"I'm not trying. But...I can hear him. It's like a radio station. I'm tuned in."

Rita frowned. "Somehow you got connected. But how?"

"I need to go back. I have to."

"I don't like this. Something's wrong."

"My daughter is innocent. What's wrong is the ugliness of her facing a trial."

Mya closed her eyes and focused. She could smell Rachael's gardenia perfume. She could feel a warm tear travel down Rachael's cheek. Her energy built and she appeared, unseen by anyone else, in the corner of a coffee shop.

Cups clattered. Chairs scraped across the wood floor. Voices talked all at once. Everything around became clearer to Mya. A server hurried from one table to another with a coffee pot in her hand. A man stirred his coffee then tapped the spoon on the edge of his cup. Even the glide of a knife over a piece of toasted bagel sounded loud and clear.

Mya forced all distractions from her mind and concentrated only on Rachael seated in a chair with Jake sitting next to her.

Gently, Jake gazed into Rachael's eyes. "You don't really believe you killed your mother, do you?"

"I did. Why can't you understand that?"

"Because I know...I know...you didn't."

"You don't know me. You don't know a damn thing about how I felt or what I was thinking."

"Then tell me," Jake said.

"My mother died six months ago..."

Six months? How was that possible? Mya shook her head at the thought. It felt like only a few days ago to her and yet, it all slipped into a strange place as if being stripped away from her.

Rachael said, "A month ago, I turned twenty-three..."

That's right. Rachael's birthday. Tears slid down Mya's face. "Happy birthday, my sweet girl. I was going to order those boots you wanted. I never did."

"When I look back," Rachael said, "I get it now. I was a twenty-two-year-old spoiled brat. A spoiled, pain in the ass, bitch. I was angry all the time, especially at my mother. I blamed her for everything. How could I do that? How could I forget all the things she did for me? She worked hard and the harder she worked, the more bullshit I dumped on her. She gave and I took and never even said thank you." Rachael wiped her wet cheeks with the napkin Jake handed her.

"So you were young. Kids do that."

"Yeah, well I guess it took my mother dying to help me grown up. Six months later, I finally get it. A little too late."

"She knew you loved her."

"Everyone says that. How do you know? I mean, besides a gift you keep talking about. But, really, how? The things I said to her, especially that morning, were awful. It was horrible. I killed my mother, Jake. I stabbed her in the heart. I told her I hated her. I might as well have stabbed her with that damned knife. I'm not innocent. Whoever murdered my mother, they just finished what I started. But it's on me, Jake. I killed my mother when I screamed those horrible things at her."

Mya stood beside Rachael and looked down at her. "I wish you could hear me," she said. "You didn't kill me, Rachael. Mothers and daughters argue. We're so much alike. We're both stubborn and loyal. You were loyal to your father and I didn't help the situation. We both made mistakes, but in the end, we love each other and nothing can change that."

Rachael shivered. She glanced up as if looking for a ceiling vent. With her hands wrapped around the warm coffee cup, she said, "I left. I left, and the last thing my mother heard me say was I hated her. I should have gone back inside, but I left."

Jake's eyes darted toward Mya, and for a second, Mya thought he saw her. If he did, he didn't let on.

"Do you think," Jake said, "you could have stopped what happened? You might have been killed too."

"But if I had stayed home that morning or been there somehow," Rachael said. "But no. Instead, the last thing my mother heard from me was I hated her. I'm not innocent. My words cut her and I broke her heart."

Jake lifted his eyes in Mya's direction again. It frightened Mya this time. The look on his face frightened her. He turned pale and his eyes opened wider as if seeing something that terrified him.

"We have to stop now," Jake said and looked away from the corner where Mya drifted.

"What's wrong?" Rachael said.

Mya felt it too. Something else was there, behind her. She turned...

"I...I can't do this," Jake said. "I thought I could but I can't." He tossed some money on the table and pushed his chair back. "I'm sorry, Rachael. You're a nice girl and I believe you're innocent, but I can't help you. I'm sorry." He rushed out the door of the coffee shop to the street.

The connection was broken. Mya's energy pushed back through an unseen doorway, to her grandfather's house, and returned to spirit form in that dimension. She sat, weakened. She trembled, but it wasn't from exhaustion, it was the uncertainty of what she felt that gripped her.

"You did it again," Rita said. Angry, she shook her head. "You swore you wouldn't travel to that dimension, but you left again. Your shell was here, but not your essence."

"I couldn't help it," Mya said. "Something pulled me there. I had to hear. I had to know." She shook harder with a fear she didn't understand.

141

"What happened?" Rita asked. "You're shaking."

"He said he knows she's innocent but he can't help her." Mya didn't want to tell her about the feeling of someone standing with her at the coffee shop. "Why would Jake say he couldn't help her?"

Chapter 16

Jake tossed two aspirins in his mouth and swallowed them with the gulp of Scotch he took straight from the bottle. He grabbed two more aspirins and did it again.

He didn't consume enough pills or Scotch to kill himself. That wasn't his intention. What he wanted to kill was the throbbing headache unlike any of the others he suffered. It was that and what he saw at the coffee house combined with what he heard that he tried to block.

He saw a dark shadow: one he hadn't seen in a long time.

One he sensed now was centuries old, and...he heard the whistle.

It was an ungodly whistle, high-pitched like the one he heard as a child.

Jake switched on the lamp. At the coffee house sitting opposite Rachael, he saw her mother. Her image didn't frighten him. On the contrary, the woman he saw looked kind and he sensed love for Rachael. In fact, there was a radiance about her clouded slightly by concern.

Jake decided not to tell Rachael he saw her mother standing right next to her. Why lay that load on her at the moment she confided in him? She needed to confess her feelings of guilt and voice her sorrow. Besides, he wanted to gain her trust. Telling a person their dead mother was next to them probably wasn't the way to do it. From past experience, Jake knew it was best to go slow and ease the terrified girl into this stuff. After all, most people didn't believe in it, and those who did, often had doubts.

He could tell Rachael's mother listened to what her daughter said. From the sad look on her face and the sense Jake got, she wanted to communicate, but that was extremely difficult for the departed. A moment later, her expression and the air in the room changed. Rachael's mom looked scared. At first, Jake thought it was because she appeared before him. She floated to the corner as if to hide and that's when he saw the shadow. He wasn't sure if Rachael's mom knew it was there or not, but she vanished and the shadow began to whistle.

That's the fear Jake felt.

It was evil.

He had to get away before it embraced him.

Never again. He promised himself. He would never let it get close again.

The lamp bulb flickered twice. He held his breath, preparing for the something he sensed. The soft glow of the light finally stayed on and he exhaled.

He lowered himself into the armchair, the bottle of Scotch held between his legs, and rubbed hard at his temple. Maybe what he thought he saw and heard—the shadow and the whistle—was only his imagination conjured up from a long ago fear.

He was rusty.

Dealing with lost souls and spectral beings wasn't something to play with. What was dead should stay dead, even if they fought it.

As true as it was, there were those who needed help. Rachael's mom did. However, the help she sought wasn't for herself; it was for her daughter. That's what intrigued Jake. The vibrations he got were unselfish and pure...until a blackness overwhelmed them. Why was it there?

He took a swig from the bottle. The burn of the alcohol made him cough. He stopped it by taking another drink, but before he swallowed...the whistle began. Low and distant at first, it got stronger, louder, and surrounded him.

Jake shook his head. "No. Stop it!"

The whistle continued.

"Get out, damn it!" Jake screamed to the walls, the ceilings, and the corners. Once on his feet, he threw the bottle of Scotch across the room.

The cabinets in the kitchen flew open simultaneously. As if to match Jake's anger, they slammed open and shut incredibly fast. Drawers burst open in a rage and dishes on the counter crashed to the floor. Papers in the living room swirled as if a tornado blew in. Books hurtled across the room. More drawers in the living room ripped open and everything in them was tossed to the floor as if the force behind it all was searching for something.

Jake cowered on his knees in front of the armchair, his hands shielding his head from the flying debris. Then, as quickly as it began, it stopped. Jake lowered his arms and saw at his knees the photograph of him and his mother taken five and a half years ago, the one he pushed into a drawer and forgot about.

With his hand trembling, Jake lifted the photo. "Who are you? What do you want?"

A white mist rolled down from the ceiling and Jake hid his face in the cushion of the chair.

"Please," he whimpered, "leave me alone."

"She needs you," Mya's voice called out.

Jake's face buried in the pillow, he shook his head and cried, "Leave me alone."

"Rachael needs you," Mya said. "Help her."

"Help her?" Jake lifted his head. "This is how you ask for my help? Get out of here."

Mya appeared as light sparkles, flicks of white with lavender specks. When Jake glanced at her, she transformed into a fuzzy but more solid wave. She tried to smile at him. That confused him. She didn't appear vicious or harmful dressed in a white gown with soft features that resembled Rachael, but he was certain she caused all the damage. That confused him even more–she didn't demonstrate an innocent gentleness this time as she had in the coffee shop.

Confusion turned to anger. He held up the photograph of him and his mother. "Now I'm beginning to understand. She sent you, didn't she?"

"No one sent me."

"The way you let your presence be felt at the coffee shop, wanting to help Rachael, was all a trick, wasn't it?"

"No," Mya said.

"You're lying. She's been sending your kind to me for years. Why? Why can't you all just leave me alone? Why did you come in here and do this?"

The room was a mess. Tossed books, broken glass, a busted drawer, and the kitchen was just as bad. "I didn't," Mya said. "I would never do this."

"You wanted to scare me."

"No. I'm new at this. I just want to help my daughter."

"How? By scaring the crap out of me? Did you really think you could scare me into helping her? Or, is the real truth that you want to give me a message from my mother? Either way, it won't work." Jake stood and faced Mya with contempt. "I can't help her and I won't help you or anyone from that world, do you hear me? I won't."

"But you know she's innocent. I heard you."

"You heard me say what you want." Jake laughed. "What I said is that I believe she *might* be innocent. I never said she was."

"She is. I swear to you, she is."

"Tough. Go back to Hell and leave me alone. I've had enough."

"I'm not from Hell."

"Right. And I'm supposed to believe that? You're a poltergeist and you're using my mother."

"I'm not any of these things." Mya zapped in and out. Her vibration manifested like a snowy picture on an

146

old television set. Her sparkles disappeared. Her eyes changed into black circles.

"Did I offend you? Tough."

"Your mother didn't...she isn't..." Mya stopped. "Please, calm down. What you're feeling is...it hurts. It's too much energy for me."

"Anger does that."

"Then stop. I can't control it. I told you I'm new at this."

"Didn't get the owner's manual? No afterlife 'how to haunt the living guide'? Well, don't look at me for lessons. If you're using my mom, it won't work. And if my mom sent you, tell her...don't tell her anything. Just leave me alone."

"Your mother...I'm not permitted to discuss her." Mya tried to calm herself with thoughts of soft clouds and Rachael's smile, but the negative energy that rose from Jake was powerful. She worried it would consume her.

"I bet. Get out."

"I didn't do this." She struggled to remain a white flicker of light. Instead of the blackness absorbing her, she washed herself in the love she felt for Rachael. "I came to ask for help. I came because..."

"Because you're a lost soul who can't rest. You had me fooled at first. I thought maybe this time, a genuine 'I give a shit about what happens' mom appeared. I should have known better."

"You're wrong. Please, listen to me."

"And you got me wrong. I'm not your savior. I'm not buying this angel spirit thing you got going. You look harmless, but it's a trick. It always is. Go whistle for your hellhounds someplace else and leave me the hell alone."

"Why are you so angry?" Mya hovered over the couch and then grounded herself behind it.

"Angry? I've blocked your kind for years and now you come floating in here asking me to get involved with

147

this dark crap? No thanks. I tried to help years ago when I was a kid and you took advantage. You showed me things no kid should see."

"I swear that wasn't me."

"Right. Well, if you want to play the mother card, you should know this: my mother wants me to forgive what happened. I can't. I'm surprised Hell even lets you out for this kind of thing. Let her rest in peace, for Christ's sake, if that's even possible." Before Mya could respond, Jake said, "You have to leave if I say so. That's how it works. Go whistle your tune somewhere else. Now go," he screamed at her.

Mya's energy flickered on and off just like the blub in the lamp. "Whistle? You hear it too?" Her voice was too faint to be clear. She appeared in a white light one second, only to fade to electric static and reappear pale, and gray the next. Like a brownout, the connection finally broke, and she vanished.

Jake wiped his tears away and held the photograph in his hand. "I'm sorry, Mom, but I can't forgive what you did. I know, okay? I know what you did was my fault."

*****

"Why did you go back?" Rita asked. "I told you this is too dangerous."

"I had to," Mya said, her form still flickering.

"Look at you. You don't have much energy left. You keep this up and you'll disappear. You have to rest."

"The hourglass is running out and we're losing time."

"You have to stop."

"I can't," Mya said. "Something…something scared him. I think it might be that thing I felt when I was with him at the coffee shop."

"What thing? You never told me that."

"I didn't want to worry you and now…I think it was at his place. He accused me, but I didn't throw the furniture around."

"Throw furniture around? That's it, Mya. This has to stop. I'm begging you. This is my fault. The whole idea to try this. I should have listened to Tricia. You're telling me something evil has come. It has to be my darkness that follows you. I don't want it to, but it must have attached itself to you. Don't you see, Mya? I can't have my darkness harm Jake. I can't. If…if I have to stop you myself, I will."

Mya glanced over at the basement door, still locked with the chair pushed against the knob. "He said…whistle."

"What?" Rita followed Mya's gaze. "What did you say?"

Mya looked at Rita and knew she was as frightened as Rita was. "I don't think your darkness is attached to me. I think it came from…someplace else."

*****

A gentle knock at Jake's door made him jump. He stomped over to it, took a deep breath, and snapped the door opened.

Rachael gasped and she blushed.

"Rachael? What…how did you find me?" Jake asked.

"You gave me your address," Rachael said. "I just wanted to make sure you were okay. You ran out of the coffee shop so fast, I was worried."

Jake stood in the threshold just admiring her. Her eyes were soft and warm when they gazed at him. Her rosy cheeks made her appear so young and vulnerable that, for a moment, he forgot to breathe.

"Could I come in?" Rachael asked.

Jake snorted and stepped back. "Yeah, sure." He ran a hand through his hair and watched her walk inside, all the time admiring the back of her as much as he admired the front. When she turned, he could feel his cheeks flame.

"Not much of a housekeeper, are you?" Rachael giggled as she glanced around.

The room was a disaster. She picked up a book by her foot and handed it to him. When her next step crunched on a broken liquor bottle, she said, "Maybe I should go."

"No," Jake said a little too quickly, causing Rachael to startle. "I mean…it's not usually like this."

"I have bad days too." She looked down at the busted bottle. From where she stood, the condition of the kitchen with knives thrown on the floor, cabinet doors flung open, dishes broken, caused her to back up to the front door. "Look, I don't need any more trouble, okay? So, whatever you're into, or whatever kind of temper you have, I don't need it."

She placed her hand on the doorknob. Jake stopped her from turning it.

"Don't be scared," he said.

"Famous last words often said by a serial killer." Rachael held onto the knob. "The walls are thin in places like this. I'm a very loud screamer."

"You don't need to scream."

Rachael tightened her grip on the knob and her pocketbook. "Let me go," she said.

"I'm not a serial killer or any other kind of killer," Jake said and released her hand. "If you want to go, then go. It's been a long night and I'm tired." He heard the doorknob turn and then added, "I didn't do this. Not all of it anyway. But you probably won't believe me so go ahead and leave."

"Are you in some kind of trouble?"

Jake laughed. "Trouble? That depends. Let's just say I want to help someone because I'd like to, but if I do, who knows what could come through the door?"

"I don't understand."

"Neither do I."

"Why did you leave the coffee shop like you saw a ghost or something?"

"Weren't you listening? I'm psychic. I see dead people. I can hear dead people."

"You were serious?"

"What do you think? You think I use that as a pickup line?"

"You did seem to know...stuff."

Jake flapped his arms. "Yeah, that's me. The guy who knows stuff. Even when he doesn't want to." He went into the kitchen, stepped over pots and pans on the floor, silverware scattered everywhere, and took a broom from the closet...the only door the demon didn't rip open. "If you're here to beg me to help you, I can't."

"I told you," Rachael said, "I came because I was worried about you."

"Yeah, well, seeing dark shadows can get on a guy's nerves." He began to sweep, and Rachael started to pick up the trashcan that was tipped sideways against the wall. "You don't have to do that." Jake took it from her.

"I don't get you. When I was in the hall, you looked happy to see me and now...what's with you? Are you on meds or something?"

"I wish." He kneeled to pick up the trash and put it back into the can. "Look, you're right, okay? You wouldn't understand. There's no way you could understand."

"Are you serious?" She picked up a pan and slammed it on the counter.

"Now you're pissed?"

"Of course I am," Rachael said. "I couldn't possibly understand? Get real, Jake. This hasn't exactly been my year, you know." She slammed a cabinet door shut and then another. "My mother was murdered. I'm accused of killing her. And to top it all off, I feel guilty. I didn't stab her with the knife, but my words sure as hell did. Feeling the way I do is probably why I failed the polygraph test. So don't tell me I couldn't understand whatever the hell you're going through."

"You got a temper." Jake curled his lips into a smile.

"And that makes you happy? You should be running for the door. Pissing off a killer is dangerous." She threw spoons into a drawer and slammed it shut.

Jake took her arm. "The only danger I see is to my pots and cabinets."

Rachael's face relaxed and she smiled shyly. "Sorry."

"It's okay," Jake said and turned a kitchen chair upright. "You and me aren't that different. Except for the fact that you didn't kill your mother."

"You're sure?"

"I'm sure. A killer can always recognize another killer."

"What are you talking about?"

Jake turned and faced her, his eyes as intense as his words. "I killed my mother."

Rachael began to laugh, but when Jake stared at her, she dropped the smile and tensed. "Are you joking?"

"No. Murdering someone is not something to joke about."

"Sure. Right." Rachael slowly backed away. "I think I should go now." She got closer to the door, realized she held a frying pan in her hand, began to hand it to Jake, changed her mind, and put it on the table near the door while she gripped the doorknob. "Nice meeting you. Take care."

"Hold on," Jake said, and took her hand. "It's not what you think."

"No, of course not." Rachael giggled nervously. "How could it be? But I do have to go. I have an appointment. I—I forgot about it. You, um, you take care, okay?"

"My mother shot herself," Jake said before Rachael could turn the knob. He looked down at his shoes. "That's the first time I ever announced it like that. I usually just say my mother died in an accident. But the truth is…she shot herself in the head and I'm the reason."

Rachael released the doorknob. When Jake finally lifted his head, he was amazed at how gentle her expression was. He felt ashamed and she looked at him without judgment.

"The reason I'm telling you this is because…like I said, we have something in common. Our mothers are dead. You're accused of killing yours and I should have been ."" His gaze lingered in her eyes along with the silence. "Aren't you going to say anything? Call me a freak again and run?"

"No," Rachael said. "I'm just going to go over here, sit on the couch, and wait for you to tell me when me you're ready."

"This could take some time."

Rachael sat on the couch and crossed her legs. "Well you better get started. My trial starts in a month." She laughed in a way that caused him to laugh at himself.

"I like you, Rachael Westcott."

She smiled. "Why's that, Jake Delmar?"

He joined her on the couch. "Because you make me question everything I thought. For instance, I get it now that my pickup line for pretty girls was all wrong. I should have led with 'I see dead people'.""

Rachael smacked his arm. "Very funny. You're avoiding. Now talk."

"Talk? I thought I was." He caught her hand before she smacked him again. Turning in his seat so they faced each other, he said, "Okay, I give. Be warned. This gets dark." He glanced at her waiting for him to begin, and sighed. "The thing is, for years, I've been able to block this crap and now, after someone or something manages to get in, this stuff starts again."

"What stuff?"

"Exactly."

"Are you trying to confuse me? What stuff? What something?"

Jake looked her in the eyes. "Something dark. First, it came begging me to help you. She sounded nice and even managed to appear nice, but it's dark. I know it and I won't open the door to that. Not again."

"What door?" When Jake got up and went into the kitchen, he returned with two opened bottles of beer. He took a gulp from one and offered her the other. Rachael accepted the drink and insisted, "What door?"

"There are doors in this world that open to the next. Things can get in. Usually bad things. If it *was* your mother who came to me, then she's one of them. A dark thing."

Rachael, her voice rising, said, "My mother is not dark."

"That's when all this started."

"I don't care. If my mother came to you, she's an angel and not some...some dark thing."

"So you believe in angels? If you do, you also believe in evil."

"I don't know what I believe, except my mom isn't evil. She was murdered and she didn't deserve it. She's never hurt anyone. Me, I hurt her with the horrible things I said. But she...never did anything bad to anyone."

"That's the thing I don't get either. When I saw her the first time and even the second, there was a light around her."

"You saw her twice?"

"Yes. I told you. You look like her."

A tear sprang in Rachael's eye and she lowered her head. "Stop it. If this is bull, it's mean."

"It's not bull. I don't know what I can do to prove it."

"What did she say? How did she look?"

"Like I said, at first like an angel in a white gown and a light was around her. Her voice was soft and she kept saying you were innocent and I had to help you. She said she heard me say I believe you're innocent."

"She heard us?"

Jake nodded. "They can do that if the connection is strong enough and they're motivated. From what I saw and heard? Your mother is very motivated and strong, which is weird."

"Why weird? Haven't you ever heard of a mother's love?"

"Of course I have but...your mom passed away what? Six months ago? It usually takes longer for a spirit to get strong enough to manifest, and then they need lots of energy to do it. But for her to do this..." Jake gestured at the mess, "takes a hell of a lot of energy."

"You think my mother did this?"

"Well, something did. It was dark energy with a damned whistle. Scared the shit out of me."

"Whistle?"

"Yeah." Jake scratched his head. "I know it sounds weird. I haven't heard it since I was a kid. I heard it a few times in the last couple of days, but now it's...I don't know. More evil, I guess. I can feel it. It's not just creepy. It's —"

His jaw dropped when Rachael whistled the macabre tune in a slow mid-level pitch almost identical to what he knew.

"Like that?' she asked, her face ashen.

"How did you..."

"I've heard it."

"Where? When?"

155

"That's one of the reasons I couldn't stay in my house anymore. After my mother died, I heard it and once, just before she died. Jake," she said and held his wrist so tight Jake felt her nails dig in through his shirtsleeve, "what does it mean?"

"I don't know," Jake said. "You say you heard it in your house before your mother died?"

Rachael nodded.

"How soon before?" Jake said.

"A couple of weeks. What does it mean?"

Jake lowered his head. When he looked up at Rachael again, it was with a new determination. "It means that's where we have to go. I'm not going to let this thing scare you or me anymore. If what I sensed when I first saw your mother is true, and her motives are just to help you, then I accused her of some rotten things. This thing didn't come to scare me into helping you. It came to scare me away. Well, not this time. Whatever it wants, this time, I'm going to figure it out and put an end to it."

Chapter 17

Rachael sat uneasily in the passenger seat of Jake's metallic gray Honda. "You haven't finished telling me about your mom," she said.

"Not now. We have to focus on this." He glanced over at her worried expression and added, "I'll tell you. I will. Later. I have to concentrate on this first."

"I'll accept that. For now. But, just remember, I opened up to you and you should open up to me. That's what friends do."

Jake smiled. "Friends? So now we're friends? A few hours ago, you called me a freak. You threatened to scream rape. You told me to get the hell away from you."

"Shut up." She chuckled, and her laugh made him smile more.

"I forgot the serial killer part."

"A few hours ago," Rachael said, "you did act nuts. Now, we're on the way to my house where a ghost might be hanging out trying to drive us both crazy. I'd say that fact makes us friends."

"You've come a long way from disbeliever, Miss Westcott."

"I don't know what I am or how any of this will help my trial. All I do know is you and me hearing the exact same thing has to be more than coincidence. Maybe it'll give me some closure too."

"That's the spirit," he looked at her and grinned, "friend."

As they drove, Rachael directed him. They pulled down the street to her house, and Rachael noticed a car parked along the curb.

"Stop," she told Jake. "Pull over."

"What's wrong?" Jake slowed the car to a stop and looked in the same direction as Rachael. He saw a mint green 2002 Ford Focus across the street. No one was in it.

"I know that car," Rachael said. "But I don't know where I've seen it before."

Jake heard her gasp and turned toward her. Her hand covered her mouth and her eyes were wide open.

"You see that man walking down the street? That's Ted...oh what the hell is his last name? He worked with my mother." Rachael glared at him. "He's a piece of work. A real slimeball. He was like a damned stalker or something, always coming around me and saying things about my mother. He's part of what my mother and I argued about that morning. I accused her of having an affair with him."

They both watched as Ted walked in long strides, too fast for his short legs. He carried a brown bag held tightly to his chest.

"He looks nervous," Jake said.

"He's coming from the direction of my house. Why would he be here?"

Ted got to his car, looked around, and unlocked the passenger side door. He tossed the bag into the front seat, and checked the street once more before he went to the driver's side. Once in the car, he started the engine and pulled out to the road.

"I don't know," Jake said. "Let's find out."

He made a U-turn and followed.

"I don't understand," Rachael said. "I always thought he was creepy. He acted like he wanted to be my friend. He said we should all go out and it would mean a lot to my mother if we got along. When I told Mom, she acted like she had no idea what I was talking about. I accused her of lying."

Jake kept pace with the car ahead and said, "When was the last time you saw him?"

"At my mother's funeral. He came over to me a few times saying how sorry he was and how much he missed her. He had the nerve to ask if I could come over to his place sometime and talk about my mom. I ignored him. There's something weird about him. The things he'd say and his eyes, the way he looked at me. It gave me the chills. Jake? You don't think...I mean, my mom said he meant nothing to her. What if...he wanted more?"

"And she didn't?" Jake said. "Could be a motive."

Ted turned right three blocks down and continued for a few more miles until his right blinker signaled once more and he drove through the gates of Mercy Hill Cemetery.

"Why is he coming here? Where my mom is buried?" Rachael said.

Jake slowed the car and watched as Ted drove up over the hill. "I don't know. But I think we should find out."

"How? We can't just go up to him and say, 'Hi there, Jackass, did you kill my mother?'"

"You forget. I can see things. I'll know. He looked scared on the street. That always leaves them open."

Jake parked about a hundred feet from Ted's car. He and Rachael had a clear view as they both watched Ted walk with hunched shoulders across the green lawn. Five rows in and three tombstones over, he stopped and dropped to his knees.

"Come on," Jake said. "Be quiet."

Ted's back was to them both as they stepped lightly along the gravel to the edge of the lawn.

"Watch him," Jake whispered to Rachael.

He snuck back to Ted's car, quietly opened the passenger side door, and took out the paper bag. After he peeked inside it, he waved for Rachael to come over.

"Do you know what this stuff is?" Jake said.

Rachael pulled out a lavender and buttercream silk scarf and a woman's gold watch.

"These are my mom's things," she said. "They were in her bedroom. Why did he take them?"

"Come on," Jake said. With quick steps, he came up behind Ted.

Ted was still on his knees facing the grave. He trailed his hand over Mya's name etched into the stone, sniffled, and muttered, "This should never have happened to you. I tried to warn you it could. You never listened. Nothing is the same now. Nothing."

"What are you doing here?" Jake said.

Ted nearly jumped out of his skin. He fell forward into the tombstone scraping the palm of his hand on the rough corner before he turned and looked up at Jake and Rachael looming above.

"Why are you here?" Rachael asked.

Ted used the stone to help get to his feet. He brushed dirt off the knees of his pants and said, "I...I was just paying my respects. How are you, Rachael? It's nice to see you."

"Is it?" Rachael smirked. "I wish I could say the same."

"For what it's worth," Ted said, "I know you didn't kill your mother."

"Gee, thanks," Rachael said. "That isn't worth much to me."

"I tried to contact your attorney," Ted said. "I wanted to offer myself as a character witness for you. Your mother would want that."

Jake stepped closer to get a better look at Ted's face. Ted glanced at him and then cleared his throat.

"I don't believe we've met," Ted said and put out his hand.

Jake shook the hand and, in an instant, flashed on a vision of Ted searching through bedroom drawers, holding up a pair of pink underpants, sniffing them before stuffing them into his jacket pocket, and going back to rifle through another dresser draw.

Jake's mouth formed a hard line and his tone hardened. "Got a thing for ladies' underwear?"

Ted frowned. "I beg your pardon?"

"Why did you kill her?" Jake said.

Ted darted his gaze between Jake and Rachael. "I'm sorry. What?"

"You heard me. Why were you going through her dresser drawers? And…" Jake kept a grip on Ted's hand, "you were there that morning. The morning she died. Outside. In your car."

Ted yanked his hand back. "I don't know who the hell you are…but…"

"Tell the truth," Jake said.

Ted ran. He scrambled across the lawn, nearly slipped, and rushed to his car.

Jake ran after him and, just as Ted was about to get in the car, Jake pulled him back and tossed him to the ground.

"Rachael," Jake said, standing over Ted with his fist ready, "call the police. I think we have our killer."

"No!" Ted yelled, sitting on his butt in the middle of the road. "I didn't kill anyone, I swear!"

"Right. Tell it to the cops. You broke into Rachael's house. You have her mother's things in that bag on your seat, and…" Jake pulled out the pink underpants from Ted's pocket, "you have these."

"I…I just wanted something of Mya's," Ted stammered, "to remember her. That's all." He struggled to get to his feet. "I miss her so much."

"You sick son of a bitch!" Rachael pushed Ted up against his car.

Jake took her arm. "Calm down."

Rachael pulled away and pushed Ted again. "I won't calm down. How could you do that to her? How could you kill her?"

"Rachael, you know me," Ted said. "I didn't kill Mya. I loved her. You have to believe me."

"I don't know anything about you," Rachael said, "except for the fact that you're a pervert."

"I'm not." Ted put up his hands in defense. "I love...loved your mother. I have since the day I met her."

"But she didn't love you," Rachael said, "so you killed her, didn't you? Didn't you?"

"No, you have it all wrong. I would never...I could never hurt your mother."

"Then what's all this?" Jake said. "Souvenirs?"

"No," Ted squeaked. "Yes. I mean...I just wanted something that belonged to her."

Rachael snatched the paper bag from the seat and shook the scarf in Ted's face. "Like this?"

"I loved that scarf on your mother," Ted said. "It brought out her eyes. I always told her that. She just laughed and blushed a little. It was sweet."

"And this? Her watch? Planning to pawn it?" Rachael said.

"No," Ted said and grabbed it out of her hand. "How dare you. This was a gift."

"Liar!" Rachael said and shoved Ted. "You never gave that to my mother."

"I...I didn't." Ted lowered his eyes. "I mean, I like to imagine I did. A group of us collected money to get a gift when your mom made partner. I picked out the watch and I liked to pretend, when she wore it, it was just from me."

"Why did you run just now?" Jake said.

"I was embarrassed. I knew it was stupid to break into the house, but I just wanted to be close to Mya again." Tears began to roll down Ted's cheeks. "I'm not proud of it. Taking her…things like that…but they all mean something to me." He took the underpants from Jake and said, "You have to believe me. I never meant to be disrespectful. I know she didn't really love me. I just liked to pretend she did. I pretend I meant something more to her than just a friend. That's why I came around you all the time, Rachael. You look so much like her and I hoped maybe, if you thought I was a nice guy, you'd tell your mom and she'd look at me differently. Maybe, she'd want to go out with me."

"None of this explains why you were there the morning she died," Jake said.

"How do you know that?" Ted asked.

"It doesn't matter. You were outside her house."

Ted looked at Rachael. "I was. I'm ashamed of myself for that. I drove by and saw her car. I heard sirens and police, and then an ambulance. I knew something was wrong. I didn't stick around. I thought if I went in to see if Mya was okay, there would be a bunch of questions and I'd look like a fool."

"Did you see anything? Anyone?' Rachael said.

"No. I wish I could say I did, but I didn't."

"I heard you," Jake said. "Just now. At the grave. You said you were sorry this happened and you tried to warn her."

Ted glanced at Rachael. "I always told your mother I thought it was strange your father kept contesting the divorce. I thought maybe he was doing it so he wouldn't have to pay alimony and, if anything happened her, he'd still legally be her husband."

"You knew about the divorce problems?" Rachael said.

"Your mother needed someone to talk to. At least, at first, when they separated. She spoke less about it to me after a while. I think she listened to me a little and that's why she put the house in your name. Your father agreed, but he didn't like it. He made sure there was a clause that if anything ever happened to you, it'd go back to him. I saw...the documents on your mother's desk and I read them. I'm not proud of myself, but I wanted to look out for her."

"What do you mean you warned her? About what?" Rachael said.

Ted turned his head toward the grave. "I just have to wonder if maybe...someone who stood to gain from all this is the one who murdered her."

"You mean my father, don't you? Well, he didn't. I know he didn't."

"I don't want to upset you."

"Too late," Rachael said. "Blaming someone else is a good way to get suspicion off you."

"I'm not trying to accuse anyone," Ted said.

"No. Just get me to question my own father."

"Is there anyone," Jake said, "you know of who might want to murder Mya?"

"Besides..." Ted glanced at Rachael. He bit his bottom lip. "No. Everyone who knew Mya respected her."

"Anyone at work?" Jake said.

"No. Like I said, everyone respected her. She was a great boss. Even after she made partner, she never changed. It wasn't easy to be the head of the contract division, but she managed it with a lot of grace. Even when she had to fire Melissa, she did it with dignity and fairness."

"Fire Melissa?" Jake said.

"Yes. Melissa was screwing up contracts and paperwork. Misfiling things. She always had some excuse, but really, she was a backstabber. Mya was right to let her go."

"When was this?" Jake said.

Ted shrugged. "The beginning of October."

"A week, two weeks before the murder?" Jake said.

Ted creased his brows. "Two weeks. You don't think...?"

"Doesn't hurt to check," Jake said.

"Give me back my mother's things," Rachael said. "And just so we're clear, no matter what you think, my father would never hurt my mother. Never."

Chapter 18

Silently, Jake and Rachael rode out of the cemetery and onto the street. Jake gripped the steering wheel in his hand, fighting with himself, trying not to say what he was about to.

"Rachael, what that guy, Ted said…"

"Don't," Rachael said. "There's absolutely no way."

"Why did your father contest the divorce? They were separated for how long?"

"A long time. It doesn't matter. My father hoped he and my mom would get back together. That's all there is to it. Ted is a creep."

"Is that what your father told you? How did your mother feel about it?"

"I don't want to talk about it."

"It's important."

"Look, Jake, I'm happy for your help, I am. Just…just don't push me on this. I know my father. He's a good man. There are things…Let's just leave it as stuff I don't want to go into. But this Melissa Porter Ted talked about? I mean, who knows, right? She's angry with my mother and wants revenge. It's a motive, right? I think we should call my attorney and tell him about it. Let the cops handle it."

"Sure. You think the police are going to jump all over this? They have their suspect. And you think this Melissa is going to confess to your attorney?"

"You think she's going to confess to us?"

Jake smirked. "You keep forgetting, don't you? I'm the secret weapon. All I have to do is get close enough."

"And what? Come right out and ask her like you did Ted? You remember how he ran? And he was only

166

embarrassed. What do you think this woman will do if she's the killer? What if she gets spooked? What then?"

"I have an idea," Jake said. "Don't worry."

"Famous last words. I'm pretty sure 'don't worry' comes just before the wrongly-accused is convicted."

"You're not going to be convicted."

"So sure? I didn't know you predicted the future too. And besides, I thought you only believed I might not be guilty."

Jake turned his head to face her. "Well, now I know for sure you're not guilty, okay? We'll figure this out." He studied the traffic ahead of him, not saying that he hoped when they did learn the truth, the killer didn't end up being the one person Rachael was convinced was innocent.

"The address Ted gave us is 189 Senator Street," Rachael said. "That's up one more block. What's your idea?"

"Well first, you have to stay in the car."

"Why? I want to meet her and see for myself if she's lying. I can judge these things too, you know."

"I'm sure you have a gift," Jake said. "But you look too much like your mother, she'll figure it out."

"Figure what out?"

"That we're there to accuse her."

"So how are you going to get close?"

"Doing something I always wanted to do. Go undercover. I'm just someone working for the prosecutor's office looking to speak to people who worked with Mya and might have overheard something about your tainted character. You know, maybe I can get her to open up and hint that Mya was the type that could piss someone off so much they'd want her dead, maybe even her own daughter. I'll work the angle if Mya had a bad temper, maybe her daughter did too. Not much of a stretch. You do have a temper."

"Smart. You're an ass, but smart. For the record, I don't have a bad temper."

"Sure you don't. Tell that to Ted. I think he peed his pants when you pushed him. And when you shoved the scarf in his face, he almost had a heart attack."

"He deserved it. Sicko. I should have slapped him."

"No." He rolled his eyes at her. "You don't have a temper." Jake parked the car and looked across the street to the apartment building. "Not too shabby. Better than my dump. I wonder if she got a new job or if she's sweating unemployment will end soon. If her lifestyle is going to change and not for the better, she can't be in a good mood. That should open her up and I'll be able to read her."

"Jake? When you touch me, do you read me too?"

Jake smiled. "Sometimes. Like the way you really wanted to rip that swell guy, Ted, a new one. Sometimes, I don't even have to touch you to read you. Like now."

"Oh really? And what am I thinking right now?"

"You're thinking I'm damn cute and you'd like to kiss me. Sorry. I have work to do. Being a savior is exhausting and I need all my energy. Now, sit here like a good girl and keep those thoughts coming."

Rachael held up her middle finger. "Besides the fact that you're a jackass, what else am I thinking?"

"Don't fight it." Jake climbed out of the car, turned and blew her a kiss through the open window. "That'll have to hold you for now." He tucked in his shirttails. "Do I look like a legal assistant?"

"No. You look like a bum."

"I'll improvise the outfit. Trust me. I'll have her eating out of my hands and then we can call your lawyer and tell him to check out her alibi, which, of course, will be a lie. If you get bored, think of ways to thank me."

"You're in a good mood. Why?"

Jake leaned his head through the window. "Cynical, aren't you?" His smile grew serious and he said, "Look, I know I came off as all doom and gloom. Very dramatic, but...we haven't seen anything dark so far or heard any damn whistles. I think we might just be able to pull this off without ending up in the psych ward. Ever wonder why psychiatric and psychic come from the same root word?"

"Yes, dummy, because they both have to do with the mind."

"Yeah. Which goes to show that when you fool around with the mind, you go insane."

"Shut up and hurry."

"A temper and bossy." Jake smiled and waved while he strolled across the street.

He knocked at apartment 3-C and, after the door opened, was surprised. "Melissa Porter?"

"Yes."

She looked completely different than he expected. For some reason, he thought she would be a young, snobby type, glamor magazine pretty who counted on her looks to get by. He counted on the fact he'd be able to charm her. Instead, she was middle-aged, no make-up, hair uncombed, hard-edged woman, wearing a sweatshirt and pants with a half-gallon of rocky road in her hands.

"If you're selling, I'm not buying," she said and moved to shut the door.

Jake pressed his hand to the wood and stuck out his foot in case she tried to shove the door closed. "I'm not selling. I work for the D.A's office. The prosecutor for Westcott versus the State case."

Melissa looked him up and down. "You sure aren't dressed to work for the D.A."

Jake flashed his smile. It dissolved when he sensed she couldn't care less. "I'm a little embarrassed by that. See, it's my day off and I realized I forgot to check on a couple of people. My boss would fire my ass...excuse me, I mean, he'd be less than thrilled, if I messed this up."

"Life's tough." She tried again to shut the door.

"Please. It'll only take a minute and...your ice cream is dripping all over the floor."

"Damn it." Melissa huffed and hurried down the hall.

"I'll just step inside," Jake mumbled. He glanced around, but didn't see much. He stood in a narrow hall that led to what he assumed was the rest of the apartment. He tried to tune in to the environment but couldn't pick up on any vibrations.

Melissa rushed back with a handful of wet paper towels. "Great. Just what I need. Things just keep getting better." After she wiped up the gooey puddle, she stood and looked at it. "I hate sticky floors. Now, who are you and what do you want?"

"You worked for Mya Westcott, didn't you? You know the case is coming to trial soon. My office wanted to follow-up with people who knew Ms. Westcott. We want to get a better idea of the type of person she was."

Melissa nodded with no smile and a look that told Jake she was suspicious.

"Hope you don't mind. I showed myself in. I won't stay long. I just need to ask a few things and please, you can tell me anything."

"Sure," Melissa said. She studied his face for a moment before she led him down the hall and into a living room that, to Jake's surprise, was even messier than his apartment.

On the dining room table there was a laundry basket of unfolded clothes. The olive green carpet was layered in piles of newspapers. The end table next to the couch was decorated with three diet Sprite cans, one of which had a cigarette butt poking up from the opening. Today's crossword puzzle, missing one block horizontally and two vertically, lay on the coffee table. Jeopardy played on the TV. She muted the sound and sat on the couch.

"It's a horrible thing that happened to Mya," she said.

Jake cleared his throat and sat in a chair three feet from Melissa. "Yes, it is." He kept trying to get a read on the setting, the woman, anything to connect, but either she was blocked or there was no energy, positive or negative, to read. "You worked for her? What was she like?"

"She was brilliant."

Jake creased his brows. He hadn't expected that reaction. "Brilliant?"

"Yes. I respected her very much. She worked hard to get where she was, and she deserved it."

"Deserved it?" Jake sat on the edge of the chair. Did she mean she deserved to be murdered? Was this a subtle jab? "How long did you work for her?"

"A year before she made full partner and then seven months after that."

"Not very long. I believe I read that she…fired you, is that correct?"

"She had every right," Melissa said. "I screwed up and made mistakes."

Jake's scowl increased. "Most people don't react like that after being let go."

"I take responsibility for what happened. Mya was a decent boss and a decent person."

Jake smiled. "Come on. You can be honest. Was she a tyrant? I heard she had a temper."

Melissa frowned. "I don't understand why you're saying that."

"I'm just trying to figure out if she was the type who could really piss a person off. Make someone, perhaps even her own daughter, want to kill her."

Melissa shifted in her seat. "I wouldn't know about that."

"But you worked with her. I mean, come on, even my own boss drives me nuts sometimes. Sometimes, I could kill him."

"Are you accusing me...?"

"No," Jake said, quick to cover his mistake. "Not at all. We have the killer."

"What happened to innocent until proven guilty?"

"Well the D.A's office doesn't prosecute people we think are innocent. No, what I'm looking for is what drives a person, even a person's own kid, to murder them."

Melissa was silent. He couldn't read her at this rate. He was too rusty. He needed to touch her. He didn't have to be psychic to know it wouldn't be easy. He did pick up on one thing—that there was more to her than being an understanding, well-adjusted woman whose recent termination was just one of those things. She was smart. The game show she watched, the crossword puzzles she obviously had a knack for added to the way she came across as praising Mya, could mean something. Maybe it was a scam. On the other hand, maybe she was too good to be true. "It just occurred to me," he said and extended his hand, "I never introduced myself. I'm Glen Fry."

"Glen Fry? Isn't he a member of the Eagles band?"

An Eagles fan. Jake chuckled. "I believe he was." He offered his hand again.

Melissa finally reached out and shook it.

Jake flashed on her circling job ads in the newspaper. He heard her inner voice say, *Mya Westcott, you're a bitch and you got what you deserved.*

Jake lowered his hand. "Where were you the morning Ms. Westcott was killed?"

"Excuse me?"

"Just for my report. I mean, how did you hear about it?"

"I was here that morning updating my resume." *Thanks to her. I don't know what in the hell I'll do for recommendations. I could get my neighbor to be my reference. I'll say she was my supervisor. Who would know the difference?*

"Ms. Porter?" Jake asked, glad to have established a connection, with her guard down, he could finally read her thoughts. "You were here?"

"That's right. I heard about it later that day on the news. A friend of mine from the office called right after that." *Her Highness dead. Stabbed. I hope one of the wounds was to her heart. The nerve of her telling me I wasn't competent. Well, I'm the one still standing, so who's laughing now?*

"You ever been to Ms. Westcott's house?"

"Are you kidding?" she asked with bitterness in her tone. "Of course not." She realized her mask cracked and relaxed the acidic scowl. With her calm façade recovered, she said, "I mean, we weren't...close friends." She looked at him as if looking through him. "What does that have to do with this? I thought you said you wanted to know if Mya was the type to upset someone enough to kill her? As far as I know, she was a brilliant, hardworking woman. A role model for her peers." *Who thought she was better than anyone else was just because she was a single mother raising a daughter on her own. She had those narcissistic partners eating out of her hands. Bunch of dirty old men! There's no way she was that smart to climb the ladder. Wouldn't surprise me if she went to bed with one or two of them. Tits and good looks, that's what they wanted. I bet she misfiled plenty of things in her day.*

Jake cleared his throat again. "Ms. Porter? Was there anyone at the office, anyone you can think of, that might have wanted Ms. Westcott gone?"

"No," Melissa said and curled her lips into a smile. "I told you. She was loved by all of us." *Especially by Ted. You should talk to him.*

"We already did," Jake said. When he caught the quizzical frown, he stammered, "We've already looked into the office. Lots of people felt like you do. I just wondered if you could think of...anyone that might want to see her dead."

Yes, her daughter. If Mya was my mother, I'd want her dead. Brave girl. Not very smart, though. If I ever killed anyone, they'd never find... "I thought you said the D.A has who they believe did this? I mean, as sad as it is. A tragedy."

Melissa turned her head and Jake swore he saw her grin a little.

"Yes, we do," Jake said. "We just want to cover all the bases. You know how defense lawyers work."

"But I read they caught her there, covered in blood, holding the knife. They did have a strained relationship. You know how gossip flies in a small office. Anyway, that's what I heard. Mya wasn't perfect. I mean, just look at her marriage. That was stressful. I overheard her once arguing with her husband...ex-husband, I guess. Well, they were supposed to be, but he never signed the papers. He kept coming up with excuses and she was furious with him for that." Melissa pursed her lips and chuckled. "I mean, that's what I overheard."

"When was that?"

"I remember it was the day she fire...let me go. I heard her talking on the phone and she was upset. She said something like, 'Doug, for the last time, stop stalling and let's be done with this. Why are you fighting me on it?' I couldn't help overhearing. She was really angry. She said 'You come up with one excuse after another. Changing lawyers has gotten old. Getting medical excuses so you can avoid court dates, running to Las Vegas and telling the judge that was the only place where a specialist with your kind of heart condition could be found. It's all bullshit.'"

Melissa laughed, glanced at Jake, and covered her mouth. "I know it's not funny. Her ex was pathetic. But this next part is kind of funny and that's why I remember it. She said, 'Doug, you don't have a heart condition. How could you? You don't have a heart.'" Melissa laughed again before she changed her expression to a sad one. "Poor Mya, having to deal with that. My heart ached for her and when she told Doug she was signing the papers and proceeding with a no fault divorce whether he agreed or not...well, I knew she meant it. That's when I stepped away from the door. It was none of my business. Poor thing. She deserved better." *A lot better. Like having her hair pulled out and being set on fire.*

Melissa grinned and rubbed her fingers across her mouth to remove the smirk. "The rumor was he was fooling around on her. Why he didn't finalize the divorce, I couldn't say. She never confided in me. But, the rumor was, he wanted alimony from her. Divorce can be so messy." She glanced up with a glint in her eyes that made Jake's stomach tighten. "Oh, and Mya said 'there's nothing you can do to stop it this time, Doug. I've made sure.'"

"When was this?"

"A week before her murder."

"Well," Jake said and stood, "thank you, Ms. Porter. You've been very helpful."

Jake headed for the door with Melissa following and she said, "Will you call me to testify? I don't know what good I can do, but if I can help the poor woman get justice, I'd do what I could."

"We'll be in touch." Jake touched the doorknob at the same time as Melissa and her thoughts rushed over him. *Maybe it was the husband. Or the daughter and husband together. I can't wait for this trial to start. I want front row seats.* Jake pulled his hand away and tried to hide the contempt he felt. "Thank you again. Good luck on the job hunting. And don't worry, maybe no one will figure out just how much you really did hate her."

Melissa's jaw dropped. Jake smiled and hummed on his way to the elevator.

"Well?" Rachael said, anxiously waiting in the car.

"Good news and bad. I could read her disgusting mind. She had motive, but didn't do it. I almost wish she had. I'd love to see her get the death sentence."

"Are you sure? Maybe she was hiding something."

"I'm sure," Jake said. He didn't want to tell her about the accusations made against her father. "To my face, she said all the right things about your mother. Underneath, not so much. I could read her though, and she wouldn't be any help to us."

Rachael deflated. "Now what? We've got no leads."

"We go to your house. Maybe I'll be able to pick up on something." He bit his lip. What they were about to face was something evil, but which kind? If it was supernatural, that scared him, but he was also afraid of the other kind— the kind that could break Rachael's heart.

"Are you sure, Jake? What about the shadow and…the whistle?"

"I know," Jake said and started the car. "But we don't have any choice. Like it or not, it's time to face it." He looked over at her. "We're about to meet the dark."

Chapter 19

Mya stood at the front window of her grandfather's house. She could see the old willow tree where she played as a child. There was nothing beyond that. A thick fog engulfed everything else. It lingered with a still sadness Mya saw and felt.

She focused on the willow tree and the happiness it once brought long ago. Under the huge limbs and cascading foliage of that tree, she felt safe. She'd pretend it was her castle and the leaves that hung down, her guardians. Fairies lived up in the branches of the tree and she was their royal princess.

From behind her, in the dimly-lit kitchen, Rita's heartfelt sigh brought her back to the present. When Mya looked toward Rita, she saw someone frightened. Rita's inner light faded. Her glow, the one that provided enough energy to keep her spirit in a solid form, diminished with each passing moment. The swirling cloud in the hourglass was also dissolving. While time meant little in this dimension, Mya guessed there was maybe a day, two at the most, for the mystery of her death and for her daughter's innocence to be resolved.

"We can't give up. I can go back," Mya said. "I'm stronger now."

"No." Rita shook her head adamantly. "It's too dangerous. Something followed you. It had the energy to get through the door, and once it has enough, it won't stop."

"How do we know it doesn't already? It might still be there."

"I pray it isn't."

"But if I go, maybe I could stop it."

"Are you crazy? You don't understand."

177

"Then explain it to me. If that thing…that darkness knows how to travel, it isn't me it needs. It can go on its own. I'm not even sure I brought it to them. But, maybe I could protect them." She nodded. " Yes, I—I really think I could."

"Really? From this thing…this something you don't know? Well, I know what it is." Rita sat at the table with a faraway look. She kept her head down and her hands in her lap. She appeared slightly frailer and smaller than even a minute ago.

"You only think you do." Mya glanced over her shoulder at the still-locked basement door. Just like Rita, she guessed what was behind the door, but she wasn't sure. All she did know was there had been no noise from it in a while, and that worried her. "It's possible you're wrong." She hoped they both were.

"I'm not wrong. I know what it is," Rita said and lifted her head. "And it's my fault. My guilt brought it here to this dimension where we are now. It's my guilt that gave it life and power."

"Guilt over what? Your mother and how she died? You faced that. You couldn't have stopped it no matter what. Whatever remorse or regret you felt was with yourself. Besides, that thing wasn't even your mother. It was a trick to frighten you."

"Because evil could read my mind and knew how I felt. It used it against me."

"You took away the power it had when you forgave yourself."

"What about my other guilt? The sin against myself? I took my life, Mya. That's a violation against life, against our Creator."

"Anyone with a heart and soul would feel guilty. You have a conscience. I have guilt over things I've done and things I should've done."

"This is different. It was intentional without thought for others. The guilt in me feeds on despair and that gives evil the strength it needs to exist. I shouldn't have come here. This is what Tricia warned us about."

"We made contact," Mya said with hope in her voice. "Don't you see? If it hadn't been for you, I could never have reached Jake."

"And our attempt to reach him was supposed to be pure," Rita said. "You promised me. You promised to keep the purest intentions. No vengeance or spite. No self-motivation that might be used against us in some dark way . That's why Tricia wanted no mention of me.

"And what good did it do? You said Jake refused to help Rachael because of the dark shadow. He knows, and I do too, that darkness…that entity he saw is pure evil and it's coming for him. If we don't stop, it won't stop, and I won't risk Jake. That kind of evil is real. After everything we've seen, you know it. It can hurt the living physically. It possesses, even kills. It'll try to take his soul." Rita shook her head. "I won't watch that happen. This is what Tricia tried to tell us, but I was too vain to listen. I wanted forgiveness no matter the cost. It was self-serving. The darkness saw its chance and took it. I'm so sorry, Mya. My guilt is consuming my soul. I've nothing left. Look at me. I'm barely here and it's what I deserve."

"Stop it!" Mya gripped the edge of the table and shook it. "Stop feeling sorry for yourself! You have to be strong. Don't lose your faith now."

"I do have faith. I have faith in my son. I believe with all my heart that he's right to protect himself. I brought this evil thing to him." Rita turned her back and cried.

Mya didn't know what to say to prove Rita wrong. She didn't even know if Rita *was* wrong. This evil entity was real. Mya could sense it. It had power that came from some place… some other plane, like a foul stench, a blackness that hung in the air like smog, and a hatred that matched nothing she'd ever imagined. It would be hard to fight this monster without knowing the source. Like all things, it had a creator. Something motivated it. What? What did pure evil want? She found it hard to believe some demon spawn of Satan would care about her, but they did collect souls. Maybe there was value in one almost heavenly spirit and one lost soul. Mya assumed the real prizes were two innocent souls like Rachael and Jake.

The mere thought of Rachael opened the door to the living. Tempted to walk through, Mya became translucent, but as she glanced toward Rita who still had her back to her, she hesitated. If she stayed in this dimension, maybe the monster would too.

Mya could hear Rachael's voice in her own thoughts. Somewhere between dimensions now…not there and not exactly here, covered in a dense fog, Mya captured everything. She stood in the middle of it miles from her grandfather's house and the willow tree, away from the woods she'd gone to as a child, and gone from the Lobby or Waiting Area. She was nowhere and somewhere all at once but, wherever it was, wasn't dark. She reached out to touch the fog, expecting something solid like a wall, but her hand went through the fog and she felt cool air. Mya stood on ground that wasn't there either, and yet she wasn't floating.

She quieted her fear and focused. Not wanting to go to Rachael, she still needed to know what was happening. In a strange way, she felt summoned and, as she listened, she confirmed it.

Rachael's voice was soft like a child's. Her thoughts radiated a pure light. She was praying. Mya could hear her. Nevertheless, the one she prayed to wasn't God: Rachael prayed to Mya.

"Mom," Rachael whispered, "I don't know if you can hear me, but I miss you. I'm so sorry for what happened. I don't understand it all, why it happened or how, but Jake is with me and I'm not so alone. Did you send him to me?

"Mom? I'm scared. Not about the trial. Well, yes that, but, there's something else, and I don't know what it is. I'm scared for Jake too. He wants to help, but if he can't, I don't know what it'll do to him.

"Mom, remember when we went to that horse riding camp? You got stuck with a horse that had no tail and it kept hopping on its hind legs to get the flies away." Rachael laughed so sweetly it brought tears to Mya's eyes. "I don't know why I thought of that. We had so much fun that day. I miss riding with you. I miss so many things. Things I took for granted. I guess I always just expected you to be there.

"That day...the day you...died, I was horrible and I'm sorry. I blamed you for so many things. I'm mad at myself for that."

No, you mustn't, Mya wanted to answer, but she couldn't. She opened her mouth and no words came. She focused her thoughts. As she did, she saw the fog begin to part and sensed the door she didn't dare go through open.

She desperately wanted to tell Rachael not to feel guilty; it would do no good and only open her to regret and despair. Darkness looked for any weakness to get inside a person's soul. She was beginning to understand the power of the monster now.

"Mom," Rachael said, "I don't know if you can help us. I want you to be at peace, but there's something here: something in our house. I felt it even before your death. There's some kind of weird anger here. I can't explain it. It's some kind of ugliness in the air, and a presence, I don't know what, causing it. I thought it was my imagination, but I'm not so sure now. Jake talked about seeing it too. He told me about invisible doors that open and let these things in. Is that possible? Maybe my anger towards you let it in our house. I don't know anymore. Maybe this is silly. I want...I need you to know, Mom, I'm not angry with you. Not anymore. I'm sorry. I'm so sorry. Please forgive me."

Mya reached out, tempted to go through the mist to her daughter. "Stop, Rachael, please." She could feel Rachael's sadness. It was heavy, like a sack of bricks, and the negative energy it created was too much to bear. The fog around Mya grew with an electric charge powered Rachael's pain.

"I don't know if you can hear me," Rachael said as she cried, "but I love you, Mom. And I pray for protection for Jake and me against whatever this thing is. It's some kind of dark, black shadow. And when it whistles..."

Mya took a step back and the fog swirled.

Whistles?

She backed away from Rachael's thoughts as quickly as she could.

She had no way of knowing if the darkness was with her, listening in wait, or not. If it was, Mya wanted it away from the door that could bring it closer to Rachael.

Aware that she had returned to the farmhouse, Mya faced the locked basement door. The thing she knew as a dark shadow, which also whistled, existed behind that door. Was that the evil Rachael spoke of? Why was it there? Why did it exist at all?

"Rita," Mya said, keeping her voice as calm as she could, "maybe you're right. Maybe you should go back and talk to Tricia. Tell her we were successful. We reached Jake and did as much as we could."

"But we didn't succeed. We didn't find who murdered you."

"Our deal was to reach Jake and not mention you," Mya said. "We accomplished that. We shouldn't be punished."

"Mya, you wanted to prove your daughter's innocence and we haven't done that."

"First you don't want to do this anymore, and now you do? There's no making you happy, is there?" Mya glanced at the basement door again, hoping whatever it was didn't decide to make itself known until she could convince Rita to leave.

"I know you," Rita said. "You won't be able to rest if you don't know what's happening to Rachael. And, as much as you don't want to think about it, what if she did kill you? How can you move on with that hanging over your head?"

"Boy, you're stubborn." Mya forced a laugh. "Look, if it makes us both feel better, I can forgive her, okay?" Mya said. "God's will be done and all that. No matter how my murder plays out, it's time to move on. You can talk to Tricia. She'll spare you."

"I haven't been forgiven for what I did. I know I won't be. I can't be spared. I accept that. I came close to heaven and that's further than I deserved to be."

"No, Rita, you deserve much more. You risked a lot to help me."

"If you're sure about this, that's good. What matters are the children. They'll be safe." Rita's inner light brightened. "I'm sorry we didn't get all the answers, but this is for the best." She stood in the center of the room, her hands clasped together. "Are you ready?"

"You go. I'll follow," Mya said.

"We should go together."

"I...I just want a moment alone to say goodbye."

"You can't contact Jake or Rachael. It's too risky."

"I want to say goodbye to this place," Mya put her hand on Rita's shoulder to reassure her. "Whatever waits up there, I just want to say goodbye to my memories here."

Rita hugged Mya and said, "Goodbye. I don't know if I'll see you again. Once you're processed, I hope the gates open for you. Be at peace, Mya." She vanished.

"I'm sorry I lied to you, Rita," Mya said to the emptiness. "I had to get you away from here. You think you brought the darkness and it attached to me when I visited Jake, but you didn't bring it. I'm beginning to understand. It's been with me all the time. It must have been with me when I was alive and I brought it with me in death. Whatever it is, it followed me when I went back. It wasn't your guilt that caused this monster. For whatever reason, this thing is attached to me. Now I have to figure out why before it hurts our children."

*****

"Let's not go to the house tonight," Rachael said.

Jake pulled the car over and stopped. "Why not? Rachael, we have to face this thing and figure out what's going on. Your trial starts soon."

"And what do we say to the judge? Your Honor, some dark demon thingy killed my mother?"

"I'm not saying the dark shadow did, but we both agree it's weird you've heard it and so have I. As far as the murder, someone did it. Now, maybe this thing was responsible somehow, and maybe it wasn't. But if I can get in your house, I might get a vision and I'll see what happened that day."

"And maybe this thing will hurt you...or worse."

"Worse? I know what this thing can do. What else can we do if we don't confront it? You wanna hide? You want to be sent to prison for something you didn't do? Or...maybe you're scared of something else."

"Like what?"

"Rachael, when I read Ted's thoughts and Melissa's, they both said the same kind of thing. It was about...your father."

"My father had nothing to do with my mother's murder."

"Just hear me out, okay? He had motive. He had opportunity."

Rachael shook her head. "No. I won't listen to this."

"I'm sorry. But we have to consider all the angles."

"Not that angle. First, why would my father want to hurt my mom? He loved her."

"He didn't agree with the divorce. He found ways to postpone it, which means, if anything happened to her, he would still be her legal husband."

"The only thing my father was entitled to was an old insurance policy my mother forgot about. She never changed him as benefactor. On everything else, she named me. The house, her bank accounts, all of it."

"And if something happens to you?"

"Right, your theory is what? My father plans to kill me too?" Rachael laughed. "Do you hear yourself? That's crazy."

"He wouldn't have to kill you. All you have to do is go to jail for murder. Your mother's estate would go to him, or he could contest it."

Rachael looked at Jake. He didn't have to be a mind reader to see the disbelief on Rachael's face. "That's the most...are you serious?"

"And if you got the death penalty, even better. I bet you have life insurance too; and I'm pretty sure they pay out on things like that."

"You're insane. You don't even know my dad. My father would never..." She opened the car door and then slammed it shut just as quickly. "Take me back to my father's house. I mean it, Jake, I've had enough of this."

"You're willing to bet everything? Look, Rachael: I hope, I really hope, your father had nothing to do with any of this. I hope to God I'm wrong. But I swear, with or without you, I'm going to find out."

"Now you want to play hero? Less than twenty-four hours ago, you told me you couldn't help and ran out of the coffee shop."

"I'm not willing to let you go to prison," Jake said. "Dark entities, evil, whatever, they're out there. Now, whether this thing got into someone and made them do it..."

"Possession?" Rachael laughed at the windshield. "Yeah, right. Something possessed my father." She laughed at him this time. "Listen to you. It's insane!"

"Or," Jake continued, "someone was evil all on their own enough to do it. Whichever it is, you don't deserve to pay the price."

He started the car. "It's late. We'll go to your house tomorrow." He pulled out onto the street.

"Fine. Take me to my dad's place."

"No."

"No?" She stared hard at him. "You're stubborn, you know that? Where in the hell are we going?"

"To my place," Jake said. "You'll be safer there."

Chapter 20

"Who are you?" Mya stood by the basement door and placed the palm of her hand against it. "Tell me your name."

She heard nothing, but felt, deep in her soul, something lurking behind that door. Instinct told her it was something from her childhood, and maybe, something even older than that.

She pressed her ear against the door and concentrated. Silence. From under the door, she smelled an odor both familiar and wicked: the scent of sulfur; a mix of rotten eggs and death so vile it made her shiver. She saw her breath. Cold air whooshed around her head, and soon, she was engulfed by a frigid, white cloud.

A laugh, deep and menacing, erupted from behind the door. She backed away and grabbed a chair, holding it in front of her like a shield. She waited, listened, and tightened her grip on the chair for some sense of protection. No other sounds came. Slowly, Mya lowered the chair and took one tentative step after another toward the door. She lifted her hand to place on the wood but dropped it just as quickly. "Come on, you can do this." She steadied her nerves and placed her hand on the door again.

"Answer me." Mya softly said, fearing it would answer. Near tears, she was ready to beg it to stop, to leave her alone, but too much had happened and she knew it would do no good.

Trembling, she listened. The laugh began again, stopped and then the whistling started again. Once more, it was a forbidding tune of an old song she couldn't quite remember.

"Who are you?" Mya's voice shook. She stood up straighter. Her anger rose. "Stop it!" she shouted. "Tell me who you are, dammit."

The thing behind the door simply whistled louder.

She gasped and took a step back. The thought to run overtook her...but where would she go? What would become of her, and more importantly, what about Rachael? "No," she said more to herself than to whatever it was. "I won't let you defeat me." She smacked the door. "You don't scare me!"

It laughed again.

"You're just my imagination. You aren't real. You don't exist."

A fierce bang on the door let her know it indeed existed. She covered her mouth, but her scream pierced the air anyway. She backed up into the chair and screamed again. Another hard bang on the door. She covered her mouth and muffled the cry this time. It taunted her, she could sense it.

With the chair as a barrier, she swallowed and forced herself to say, "Are you the one who followed me? Have you appeared to Jake and Rachael?"

Two distinct whistled notes indicated yes.

"Why?"

No reply.

"You leave them alone!" Mya slammed the chair to the floor. "Do you hear me? Stay away."

A cackled laugh, followed by two deeper notes, mocked her.

"You didn't follow," Rita said, and Mya jumped.

"What are you doing here?" Mya spun to face Rita, holding her chest. "You scared the crap out of me!"

"You said you would follow. Why are you still here?"

Mya took a deep breath. "I had to figure out something, and I think I did. Your darkness didn't attach to me, Rita. It has nothing to do with you at all. It's me. Me and that…whatever it is behind this door."

Rita's eyes widened. "What are you talking about?"

"That thing. Behind this door. It's come to me like the evil version of your mother came to you."

"Guilt? Is there some guilt you have over something?

"No. I don't think so." Mya pressed her hand to the door. "I don't know the reason."

"Fear? It must be. Or something else you haven't dealt with?" Rita said.

"I thought you were going back to talk to Tricia."

"I was. I went looking for her, but I realized you gave in too easy and that meant you might be up to something."

"I needed to do this alone."

"We agreed to stop this for the children, to keep them safe."

"I didn't want to tell you any of this and make you worry."

"Too late." Rita said, "I'm worried. What else haven't you told me?"

"I sent you away so I could deal with something," Mya said. She glanced toward the basement door and wondered if the thing that tortured her was still there listening to everything. "There's just something…something I believe is after the children."

"What are you talking about? Mya, stop protecting me and tell me what's going on! If my darkness does anything to hurt Jake, I'll never forgive myself."

Mya faced Rita and let the tears well in her eyes. "Not your darkness. Mine. Rita, I heard Rachael's thoughts calling me. She's scared for her and Jake. She said Jake saw something, and she's seen it too. In my house, even before I died. She's felt it and…heard it. A whistle. It must be the same whistle I heard here and when I was a child."

"But how?" Rita looked around the room and shrugged. "I don't understand."

"I don't know. She said Jake has heard it too." When Mya saw Rita turn her back, she said, "You know something."

"I just remember once, when Jake was ten or twelve, he said he heard a demon whistle and saw a dark shadow. It scared him so much he cried. I told him it was just a dream and just like his great-grandmother, he was protected. It didn't help. He was sure it wasn't a dream."

Mya glanced at the basement door and back at Rita. "How could that be? Is it the same or…"

A growl from behind the door started low. Mya went to the door and attempted to unlock it, but Rita stopped her.

"You can't." Rita started to shake. "We don't know what we're dealing with."

"I have to know what this thing is. If it intends to hurt Rachael, I have to stop it."

"How? Before we do anything, we have to know what it is," Rita said. "And whatever it is must be powerful. It could be the one Jake also heard or…a different evil from the same type of demon. You were a child when you first heard it?"

"I told you about that day."

"Try to remember it again with more detail."

"What good will it do?" Mya said.

"Because if you can remember, you can try and face it, just like I did with my mother's death."

"That was different. You were dealing with guilt, regret. I don't have any reason to feel those things."

"What about fear?"

"Fear of what? I'm not afraid. I was. But I dealt with it. My grandfather took care of it. My grandparents saved me. It's all just a bad memory of something that's over now."

"There has to be more. Something you're not facing. Just try to remember. If you don't, then it doesn't matter if we stop this now or not, Jake and Rachael could be in danger."

The thing behind the door laughed and whistled the chilling tune.

Mya smacked the door. "Whatever you are, you're not going to hurt anyone anymore."

She closed her eyes. While she focused on that early fall so many years ago and began to talk about what she saw, the room filled with light and transformed into what she remembered so vividly as a child: a pale yellow color on the walls, pinewood cabinets her grandfather built and stained white, the table in the center of the room held a vase filled with the last daisies of the year her grandmother picked from the field. Mya smelled oatmeal cookies baking, and heard her grandmother humming 'Amazing Grace.'

"Why can't I go into the woods?" Mya saw herself as a ten-year-old child whining behind her grandmother who took a batch of cookies out of the oven.

"I don't want you going into those woods. Not today," her grandmother said.

"But why? I have to make my treasure," Mya said and held out her hand. "See? I have a shiny new nickel. I want to make it into my treasure."

"Child, if you don't stop nagging me, you'll go to your room. Now hush."

Mya's grandfather came in from outside. His dark green work shirt had dirt and straw stuck to it. His faded denim trousers had black patches sewed to the knees.

"Poppy?" Mya whined, "Nana won't let me go to the woods to make more treasure. I go every other day and today is every other. Can I go, please?"

Nana tossed Poppy a stern look. "I already answered her."

"What's wrong now, Em?" Poppy asked and lit his pipe.

"I told you. Mrs. Evans and Mrs. Leroy were all talking yesterday about vagrants being seen on trains and jumping off to rob people. Good Christian people. It happened two towns over twice last month. Mrs. Leroy said Mr. Turner's cousin's son saw one jump off the train near town last week. I don't want Mya near them woods 'till we know it's safe enough."

Poppy blew smoke up in the air and chuckled. "You know as well as I do that Nat Turner's cousin's son is a drinking man who talks before he knows the words are coming out of his mouth. Besides, what fool bum would jump off a train in our woods miles from town?"

"To rob us," Nana said.

"Well hide the silver and put away the crystal, Woman." Poppy looked down at the cherub eyes of Mya begging him. "Child's always gone in those woods."

"Not today," Nana said and placed the fresh baked cookies on a dish.

Mya took hold of her grandfather's hand, her bright eyes large, and still pleading. It was a look he couldn't, and never would, resist.

"What if I go with her?" Poppy asked and Mya clapped.

"You, old man? I thought you had to fix the tractor. I asked you to take me to town, and you said there was no time."

"Well…" Poppy glanced down at Mya, "this will only take a little time." He winked at her and she tried, with both eyes, to wink back.

Nana faced them while she rubbed flour off her nose like an annoying itch. "Fine. You two together wear a soul to bits. If you go with her, old man, then fine. Be back in an hour or I call the law."

"Yes, Dear," Poppy said and smiled. "Come on, Princess of Treasures, let's go."

"Mya, put on your sweater," Nana said. "And tie your sneakers, Child, before they fall off your feet."

Mya put on her red sweater and followed her grandfather outside, skipping behind his long strides. She held the nickel in her hand like a prize and smiled more when the sun reflected the silver back into her eyes.

"Let me stop in the old chicken coop first," Poppy said.

He headed around the barn, down a dirt path about forty feet away, and glanced over his shoulder toward the house.

Mya followed his look, wondering why. There were no chickens in the old coop anymore, and no way to see from the house. Poppy built the new coop and moved the chickens there so they'd be closer to the barn. He wanted to be able to see if any foxes or coyotes tried to get to them after he lost a couple in the early part of summer, which Mya thought odd. She counted the chickens. They were all there. When she mentioned that fact to her grandfather, he scratched his head and said she must be wrong.

Poppy stopped just next to the coop and said, "Wait here." He hitched up his overalls and went inside the small wood structure surrounded by barbwire.

Mya tossed the coin into the air. It landed in the dirt. She swept it up, wiped it clean on her plaid pedal-pushers, and said, "Come on, Poppy, the train comes when the sun's up like now."

She heard a clang and a pop, a hiss, and a metallic bang. Then she heard Poppy curse in a way that made her cover her mouth. Poppy never cursed, not like that.

"Damn thing just popped a hole," Poppy said as he came out of the coop. "Right in the seam."

"What did?" Mya said and tried to peek around him. "What's in there?"

"Nothing. Nothing to worry about. Gotta fix it though. Can't let it run all to hell."

"Poppy, the train. I gotta get there now."

"Just have to wait. I got something in there I can't afford to waste." He grabbed an old bucket next to the coop and hurried back inside.

Mya followed and when she saw the still, she let out a loud gasp. "You told Nana you smashed that. She said it's bad and you said you smashed it!"

Poppy let the liquid run from the tap into one bucket while more ran from the ripped seam of the metal still. The spill caused a muddy puddle on the dirt floor. Caught by his deception, he chuckled and scratched his balding head. "Well, Child, I did kind of smash it and then...I kind of rebuilt it. Now, don't go telling Em. Let's make this our secret, okay? No sense in getting her worked up."

"But, Poppy...Nana says this is bad water."

"For her. For some. But for hard working folk like me? It's good. It cleans out the dust in my veins. You don't want old Poppy to have dust in his veins, do you?"

Mya thought for a moment. "No, Sir."

"Good. Now promise me. No telling."

Mya spit on the ground and stomped it. "I promise."

Poppy imitated and said, "I promise too. Now give me a little time to fix this."

He headed for the barn. Mya looked at the coin in her hand. She shouted after him, "it's okay, Poppy. I won't take long at all. Promise."

She ran to the woods across the field. Once the familiar trees surrounded her, she felt at home. Through the dense forest, across a shallow creek no deeper than her ankles, she climbed over a dead tree limb and ran down the hill to the tracks.

The noon train was coming. She heard it and felt the rails. The tremble of the iron under her small hand always excited her.

She spit on the nickel and polished it to a shine. Satisfied, she placed it on the tracks and stepped back.

The train rumbled past her. She jumped up and down, clapping her hands, and laughing.

Her sneaker was untied. She sat down and carefully, just the way Poppy showed her, made the rabbit-hole loop and used the other shoelace as the rabbit going in the hole. She tightened the knot, stood, and brushed off leaves from her backside.

The coin would be cool enough now. She grinned when she saw it waiting there for her all flattened and still shiny: her treasure to add to the jar.

She started up the hill and stopped. A whistle filled the air. She frowned at the sound. The train was too far away now to be heard and even if it wasn't, the whistle didn't sound like that.

She started again and stopped once more when she heard the high-pitched whistle. The tune was familiar.

The bushes shook. She waited, expecting to see a rabbit. That's when a tall, thin man, with tattered, dirty clothes, pants ripped in the knees, and a scruffy, bearded face jumped out.

Mya froze for a second. He stopped and watched her. He lowered the black hood of his coat, licked his lips, and grinned. Something in Mya screamed at her to run.

She took off, jumped over the fallen limb, tripped, and fell to her knees. He grabbed her. She kicked, and scrambled to her feet. He was right behind her. Branches snagged her hair and pulled out strands. She felt her cheeks get wet. Her feet pounded the floor of the creek slapping water on her and soaking her pants.

She stumbled on a rock, fell face first to the ground, and he was on top of her. He yanked at her pedal-pushers. The zipper ripped. He pulled them down, and covered her mouth.

She kicked and managed to bite his finger. He hollered. She twisted and got to her feet.

Screaming, she ran out of the woods and across the field. She saw her grandfather running toward her with a shotgun in his hand.

The man who chased her deliberately slowed down. He started to whistle again, and, when she looked over her shoulder, she saw him grin with no fear. He walked in long, easy strides as if he had time to catch her.

Mya's grandfather seemed an equal distance from her and the man. With every ounce of strength in her, she lifted her legs, bloody knees and all, and ran with only one wish—to reach her grandfather.

She heard a shot and saw the puff of smoke from her grandfather's gun. The whistling stopped. Unable to catch her breath, Mya fell to the ground, sobbing and wheezing. When her grandfather got to her, she waved her arms hysterically as if still fighting the stranger. Poppy shook her, screaming her name. Mya stopped fighting, then began to tremble with a vacant look on her face.

Nana came outside, scooped up Mya, and hurried to the house. She rushed with Mya cradled in her arms upstairs and looked over her body. Mya's cheeks, stained with dirt and tracks of dried tears, had scratches and blood beginning to cake. Her knees bled. Her small hands were filthy with cuts and mud even under her fingernails. Mya's hair was a fuzzy mess, with sticks poking out and damp leaves tangled in it.

Nana removed the soiled plaid pants with the button torn off and the zipper ripped. They were damp and caked with dirt. Mya's underpants were also wet and smelled of urine. She unbuttoned the red sweater, which was ripped in the shoulder. The back of it was covered in sticks and grass. Mya's sneakers, untied once more, her socks soaked with creek water, also had mud and grass stuck to them. Nana took the clothing and dropped them all to the floor.

She placed Mya in the bathtub, wrapped a towel around her shivering body, and then hugged her. As she filled the tub with warm water, Nana helped sit her down, and then washed her back.

The whole time, Nana said nothing and Mya, with hiccups from crying, stared blankly. She had been bad and something bad happened because of it.

Poppy cleared his throat. He stood in the doorway. Mya glanced up at her grandmother and saw rage in the wrinkled face. She wanted to say not to be mad at Poppy, but the words didn't come.

"Is she all right?" Poppy said. "He ran off. I didn't see him."

"Go downstairs and boil some tea, old man," Nana said in a tone Mya knew meant they were both in trouble.

Nana lifted Mya to her feet, dried her still trembling body, and wrapped a towel around her. She kissed her forehead, hugged her, and said, "Praise God that you made it back. If that monster had hurt you...I'd have hunt him down and, once he paid with his pitiful soul, I would have laid down and died."

Mya opened her mouth to say how sorry she was, but still no words came.

"You just put this right out of your mind, sweet child," Nana said. "Go get on your nightgown."

Mya went to her room. The tears still running down her face made the cuts sting. Her knees hurt to bend them. She thought about her nickel and sobbed into her pillow. It wasn't the coin she cried about. She heard her grandparents arguing downstairs. The anger in Nana's voice was extreme.

"You said you would go with her, old man," Nana shouted and slammed down a pot. "You knew. You knew what I was afraid of, and it happened."

"I'm sorry. Don't you think I'm sorry?" Poppy said.

"You don't think. You don't think about that child or me. You're a selfish old man."

"You stop right now, Em. I ain't proud of what happened. I told her to wait and she run off."

"Of course she did. She's pigheaded like you. I told you to go with her. I told you what Mrs. Leroy said and about Nat Turner's cousin's son and did you listen to me? No. Why? Because that still of yours and that devil water that's more important. If that child been harmed in anyway, I'd have taken a butcher knife to you and that monster. You hear me?"

Mya heard the squeak, bang of the kitchen door, and knew her grandfather left. She had to tell her grandmother it wasn't Poppy's fault. And she had to tell Poppy she hadn't broken her promise not to tell about the still. She didn't know how Nana figured it out, but she spit swore and would never betray her grandfather, she loved him too much.

In her soft, flannel lime green nightgown, Mya tiptoed into the kitchen. Her head hung low, her voice small, she called to Nana.

Nana turned, but anger was still set deep in her eyes. "Go down in the basement, Mya, and bring me up a jar of peaches. I'm going to get the clothes off the line before it rains."

Mya nodded. Barefooted, she stood on the top stairs of the basement, flicked on the light, and stepped carefully down. She forgot to be afraid of the basement. All she thought about was how bad she had been not to listen and now Poppy was in trouble and Nana was madder than she'd ever seen.

Poppy's fishing pole bumped the wall as Mya took a step. His fishing hat hung on a hook, but she didn't even bother to touch it like she always did. She held the railing, and when her feet hit the damp ground, she shivered. She swore she could see her breath. It was dark. The light bulb suspended flickered, crackled, and went out. Normally, she would have turned and run, but she didn't want to upset Nana any more than she already had, so she set her mind on getting the jar of peaches.

She heard a whistle and froze. Her breath caught. Her heart stopped. A hiss, rattle, and the furnace turned on. It glowed as if it had red eyes behind the grate.

She stood on tiptoes to reach the jar of peaches. Another whistle scared her to the bone. A whoosh of wind slammed the door to the basement shut. She turned and he stepped out from the shadows, the grin spread across his face. She dropped the jar and glass shattered.

Mya ran for the stairs. He grabbed her. She tried to scream. He covered her mouth. His hand smelled of something sour. His breath had a foul odor of rotten eggs.

He laughed deep in his throat. Mya's eyes were wide open, but his hand now covered both her mouth and her nose, making it hard to breathe.

She struggled and twisted, squirmed and kicked, but he just laughed.

She felt a scaly, rough hand under her nightgown. It scratched her skin. He pulled on her underpants. She heard the cotton material rip. He pressed down on her, heavy, she gasped for breath, fighting against his hand covering her mouth and the weight of his body crushing her.

She slapped his back, pounded her fists, wiggled like a worm on Poppy's hook, while he forced her legs apart, and worked himself in between.

Her hand went to the floor and felt a sharp shard of glass along with something sticky and slippery. She fisted the piece of glass and pushed it into his back.

He lifted his head and cursed at her as if the glass was just an annoyance. With a sloppy, wet smirk and the same deep, vicious laugh, he leaned into her again.

Mya held the glass tight and stabbed it in his neck. His eyes popped wide. He pushed himself up enough that

Mya could wiggle and twist out from under him. She screamed, running up the stairs, and pushed past her grandfather who had just opened the door. She didn't stop screaming until she heard the gunshot. She ran to the barn and hid up in the hayloft.

Mya closed her eyes. Tears trailed down. When she opened them again, she was back with Rita, in her grandparents' home aged with dust, cobwebs, and the memory she tried for years to forget.

"I never went down in the basement again," Mya told Rita. "And I never went near the woods after that either."

"What happened to the man?" Rita said.

Mya wiped her tears away. "I don't know."

"Did your grandfather..."

"I can't remember."

The whistle started behind the door. That distinct, grisly tune which haunted Mya from the first day until now. It grew louder and more insistent.

She pounded on the door. "Go back to Hell! Leave me alone."

"If that's what followed you," Rita said, "then it knows how to travel to the living."

"I think it's been with me all these years."

"And now..." Rita said, "it's here to get what it wants."

"I won't let it haunt me anymore." Mya banged on the door. "Do you hear me, you bastard? No more."

"It wants to hurt you and...our children."

"How could Jake hear the same whistle when he was a child?" Mya asked, her gaze pinned on Rita. "*Why* did he hear it too?"

Chapter 21

"Are you trying to get me drunk, Mr. Delmar?" Rachael asked. She curled her legs under her on the couch and rested her head on a pillow.

"If I am, is it working?" Jake poured more wine into her glass and then his.

"Why did you bring me here?"

"I told you. To keep you safe."

"Safe from what?" When Jake didn't answer, Rachael said, "You don't really think my father is guilty, do you? You don't even know my father."

"True, I don't. But Rachael, you're too close to this thing to see all the possibilities."

"Like what?"

"Like the fact your mother was murdered in your own house. Who did it? The police arrested you. You're innocent. So that leaves a murderer running around. Now we have to think motive. Why kill her? Ted, whatever his name is, was in love with her. Motive? She didn't feel the same for him, so he decides to kill her so no one else can have her. An old cliché but it happens, except in this case. I read him and he didn't do it."

"He took my mother's underwear. He's a whacko."

"Yes, but not the one who killed your mother. Obsessed, insane, okay, but not the murderer. Now, let's consider Melissa. A disgruntled employee. The type that smiles to your face and stabs you in the back, but still not the killer. I read her and, while she's smart, her thoughts let me see she didn't do it even though she's not exactly broken up over it."

"Jake, don't take this the wrong way, but I have to say it: you said you're rusty with this stuff and even if I believe in any of it…no offense…you're ruling out some real suspects based on what? Intuition?"

"I thought you believed me." Jake put down his glass and looked her straight in the eye. "Or is this your way of getting off the subject of your father?"

"I know my father. You don't. If you want to make him a suspect, then I might as well leave."

Jake took her hand and played with her fingers for a moment. "Don't leave. I really want to help."

"Then help. But not by making a case against my father. He's all I have left, Jake. I couldn't handle…" Rachael's eyes filled with tears. "I just couldn't."

Jake wrapped his arms around her and held her to his chest. The smell of her hair reminded him of fresh flowers. A few strands tickled his nose. He smiled. A vibration, a good one, warmed his insides in a way he forgot possible. Softly, he said, "I get it. I do. The only way I know how to help you is doing what I do. The truth is, I hate this damn gift if that's what it is. Problem is, I've learned to trust it. That's why I never wanted it. Seeing the things I have, knowing there's real evil out there, is no way to grow up."

With Rachael's head pressed to his chest, he felt her relax in his arms. He smiled again.

"Wicked Witch of the West," he said.

Rachael moved out of his arms and lifted her head. With a bewildered look, she said, "What did you say?"

"You were thinking about the time when you were six and you sat on your father's lap while you watched *The Wizard of Oz*. The witch came on. The part where Dorothy is flying in the house and looks out the window. She sees the old woman on a bike, the music is scary, and she turns into the witch. You buried your head into your father's chest and he held you so tight."

"He did," Rachael said with amazement. "That part scared me, but I felt safe with him. I peeked out and he said—"

"'Don't be scared. It's a pretend story. It's okay if you don't want to look. Shut your eyes and I'll tell you when she's gone.' And then he whispered, 'they get rid of that mean witch in the end.'"

Rachael nodded. "He did say that. All of it just like that." She curled her lips upward. "I do believe in you, Jake. I'm sorry I doubted."

Jake shrugged. "Happens to the best of us. I'm sorry I keep bringing up your dad. You love him and I shouldn't try to get you to doubt him."

"So we're back to zero suspects." Rachael sipped her wine, lowered her legs, and combed her hand through her hair. She smiled when she saw Jake smile at her. "What?"

"You're beautiful."

"You've had too much wine."

"No, I haven't. Only enough to have the courage to say it. You're beautiful."

Rachael giggled. "Stop it. If you fall in love with me, you'll be stuck visiting prison every other Sunday."

"That's not funny."

Rachael sat up. "Well, what do you want me to say? My trial starts in three days. We have no leads. I can't prove a damn thing. My mother and I argued...a lot. Neighbors heard us. The cops showed up and found me over the body, knife in my hand, and blood on me. Damn it, why did I pick up the knife? I've see cop shows. Never pick up the weapon."

"You were in shock. No one, especially someone innocent, would be thinking about evidence at a time like that. As for the arguing with your mother part, what kid hasn't argued with their parent?"

"Not like we argued. I said awful things. I'm ashamed of myself. Jake, if you were anyone else, I wouldn't say this, but sometimes I think..." her eyes grew intense, "I think something made me say those things. I heard my voice, but I swear it wasn't me." She searched his face. "Is that possible?"

"Can be. If there was enough negative energy in the house, it gains power. It can take over and make people do things they might not."

Rachael scoffed. "That's crazy. It is. Think about it. It's like some old seventies saying. 'The devil made me do it.'"

"There's more to that then most people know. I've seen it."

"The devil?"

"No. Jesus, I hope not. I'm talking about demons. Something demonic. Scared the shit out of me. When I was a kid, there was a boy who went missing. He was only about seven or eight. I didn't know him. The whole town looked for him for over a week. I was the one that told the police where he was."

"You found him?"

Jake lowered his head. "Not in time. He was dead."

Rachael was silent and then reached for his hand. "I'm sorry."

"It was bad. This monster...this demon came to me and showed me firsthand what he did to kill that kid. I could see it happening. I heard the kid crying. The fear. I felt what he felt. The spirit wanted me to know. He wanted me to feel. What kind of vengeful spirit does that?" Jake turned away and stared at the floor. "It possessed me," he said.

Rachael burst out laughing. "You're kidding." She stopped laughing when he looked at her. "You're not kidding."

"Pretty weird, huh? Now you know why I don't talk about it."

"I didn't mean to laugh," Rachael said. "I'm new to all this. Before I met you, this kind of stuff was only in the movies. Remember? Wicked Witch of the West? Hiding my head? That's me. I never even went to see *The Exorcist*." Her eyes grew wide. "Is that the kind of thing you're talking about?"

"No pea soup," Jake said. "I don't think my head spun." He saw the terror in her face. "I'm kidding. Sort of. It was inside me though. It started when I could see through his eyes. His hands tying the ropes on that poor kid. The knife he held. The blood. The excitement of hunting down someone innocent, the thrill of taking them, and the power that came from torturing them until they were dead. It wanted me do things…awful things. I thought I was going nuts. My mom tried to help me. Kids at school found out I told the police where the body was, and they made fun of me. Some were scared of me. Their parents didn't want them around me. Hell, even the police were suspicious at first. You think you had trouble believing? Try explaining how you know where the body of a dead kid is and you're not the one that did it to him. Then there's the voices I kept hearing. The black shadow I saw. Visions of things that make nightmares. After all that happened, I fought to stop it. I blocked all the visions with everything I had.

"It still tried. The damn thing was powerful. For a long time, I'd hear this whistle and I knew it was trying to get to me. The only thing I could do was try to figure out what it was. That's the only real way to get rid of it."

"Did you find out?" Rachael asked.

Still staring at the floor, Jake shook his head. "It was old. That's all I knew for sure. Something around for decades, maybe more. It could take different shapes. It tried to take over. My great-grandmother had the gift same as me. She taught me some things to do if a willful spirit tried that kind of thing. She died just before this happened to me, but I swear, I think she was there helping me to get rid of it."

"I can't even begin to imagine something like that."

Jake huffed. "It's not the best feeling, I can tell you. It started like a rage in me. I'd feel sick. My chest hurt. I'd black out. I woke up in different places. One time, I woke up in the kitchen with a pair of scissors in my hand. I had scratches all over my back and arms. I started to lie. I told my mom it was from climbing a tree or playing in the woods. Sometimes weeks would go by and everything was fine and then…it would start again."

"Why didn't you tell your mom?"

Jake shrugged and took both their empty glasses. "You want more wine?"

"Don't do that," Rachael said. "You promised you'd tell me about your mom."

"Not now."

Rachael put out her hand for him. "Yes, now."

Jake sighed. He put down the glasses, took her hand, and sat next to her on the couch. "My mom." He sighed again. "I loved my mom."

"You said she tried to help you. Why did you lie to her?"

"My mom, her name is…was Rita. She was a good woman. Gentle. Fragile, I guess. A good cook. We were close. She didn't have the gift. Her mother didn't either. Actually, I don't think my grandmother believed in any of it. She was a tough woman. I remember her telling my mom not to encourage it and that her mother was crazy and did she want her son to be crazy too? My dad sure as shit didn't believe in it. He'd get so pissed whenever my great-grandmother came over and talked to me about it. My dad didn't get just a little upset. No, not him. He'd yell and scream and then he'd leave. I'd hear him shouting at my mother all the time. I knew it was my fault."

"Your fault? Because your father wasn't open-minded? You can't blame yourself for that."

Jake grinned. "That's what my mom said. I could see how it wore her down. She wasn't strong enough to stand up to him. She'd cry in her room. My dad would slam things. And all my mom would say is I had a gift. I never thought of it as a gift. I would have given it away in a second. People wish they knew what others think. They wish they could see things, and here I was able to do that and wished to hell I couldn't. Nuts, huh?"

"No," Rachael said and rubbed her hand down Jake's back. "I mean, yeah when I first met you, I thought you were insane, but I've seen what you can do, the things you know. It must be hard and awfully damn scary. Why did you stop blocking yourself now?"

He turned to look at her. "Why do you think? You need me." He brushed a strand of hair from her eye and leaned in to kiss her.

Rachael backed away. "Don't, Jake."

"Why? You don't like me?"

Rachael grinned. "I like you. I just don't want either of us to get hurt. I know you want to help and, if anyone can, I believe it's you, but…what if you can't? I don't want you to blame yourself."

Jake turned away. He sat on the edge of the couch and looked down at his feet. "You mean like with my mother?"

"What?"

He let out a long breath. "My mother. It's my fault she's dead."

"You said your mom shot herself. I don't understand why or why you blame yourself."

Jake shrugged a shoulder. "Because it's my fault. My mother was ill. Not terminal or anything like that. It was depression. I always knew something was wrong when I was a kid, but she coped. Then my father took off. Just like that, one day, he said, 'so long,' and he left. I never saw him again. I figured, 'so what?' He thought his son was a freak and his wife was nuts."

"I'm sorry, Jake."

"Me too. I mean, at first. At first, I tried to blame everyone else. My mom for not making him understand. Me. If I didn't have this stupid gift then the old guy wouldn't have just picked up and left. But then I realized he was just a piece of scum. People get divorced all the time. He didn't have to abandon us…me. It was all just some lame excuse because he didn't want to be married anymore and he sure as hell didn't want to be around me. At least when your dad left…"

"My father didn't abandon us," Rachael said. "I really do think he wanted to get back together with my mother."

"And you blamed her because she didn't."

"That and…there was more. I'd hear her argue with him about money. I thought that's all she cared about. She worked all the time, was hardly home, and I thought my father was frustrated with a wife who was never there. I got angry and took it out on my mother. My father said he wanted to be more involved with my life but mom wouldn't let him."

"Do you really believe that?"

Rachael handed him her glass. "I think I will have some more wine."

Jake stepped to the kitchen and called back over his shoulder. "Now who's avoiding?"

He came back, handed her a full glass of red wine and grinned at how comfortable she made the old, lumpy couch look.

Jake sat next to her. "You said you felt like something made you say the things you did to your mother. Did you believe the things your father told you?"

Rachael sipped her wine and set the glass on the table. "Now that my head is clear and I know what I've lost, I can honestly say I don't know. It doesn't seem like my mom to do that. When I was little, we had a lot of fun together. We'd play dress-up, play with makeup, do lots of things together. She's the reason I love horses so much. She put me on a horse when I was three and it was love at first saddle."

Jake's lips spread into a smile. He wanted to kiss her so badly. "You love her."

"Are you reading me again?" Rachael laughed.

"No. I can see it when you talk about her."

"She worked hard. Was very smart. She worked her way up in her company. Even as busy as she was, she always came to my games, my plays, to watch me in horse shows. She taught me to be determined and set my mind on what I wanted and then go for it. I've never known a stronger woman."

"Yours was strong and mine was...not. Don't get me wrong. My mother was amazing in her own way. She'd do anything for anyone if they needed her to. I think that was the problem. I think after my dad left, she didn't feel needed. He didn't need her for a wife and didn't want her for a wife. 'Course, there was also my grandmother. Like I said, not the nicest person. I think she piled a lot of guilt on my mom. Add me to the mix. I grew up." He sighed. "You know. Not her little boy anymore."

"Of all the nerve." She laughed. "Come on, Jake. You can't blame yourself for that."

"I don't. I blame myself for not knowing, not seeing. All because I was scared as a kid about my gift."

"Some demon tried to possess you. That would scare anyone."

"But I blocked myself, and because of that, I didn't see what would happen. Rachael, I never admitted this to anyone, but if I'm supposed to be so damn psychic, why didn't I know my mother was going to kill herself?"

Rachael's brows rose. "You're really tough on yourself."

Jake nodded. "I guess I am. Doesn't change the fact she killed herself. My mother used my father's gun. Of all the ways to do it, why that? Why didn't I know it would happen? I was making all these plans to go away and travel for a while before college, knowing she was depressed, alone, and I did nothing. I blocked my visions so I wouldn't see anything and if I hadn't, maybe I could have stopped her."

"I'm sorry, Jake, but listen to me, okay? If a person wants to end their life...they usually find a way no matter what. How could you know anyway? You don't read the future."

"But I was having visions. I don't know if it was my great-grandmother sending them. All I know is I had dreams and I pushed them away. I was more scared of the whistling demon trying to trick me than in protecting my own mother."

"How could you protect her? Stay with her night and day? Give up your life?"

"My life?" He scoffed. "I never ended up doing anything. I took a few classes here at the local college, that's about all. That and running from job to job."

"You gave up what you wanted? You think that would make you mom feel better?"

"She shot herself, Rachael. I doubt she felt very good to begin with."

"And what about her spirit? You think she can rest with all this guilt?"

"It isn't her guilt. It's mine. I didn't stop her. I didn't help her. How can I ask her to forgive me for that?"

"Wait a minute. She killed herself, and yes, that's sad, but you want her to forgive you? I don't think giving up your dreams or blaming yourself is healthy. It doesn't help anyone, least of all your mother, but Jake, she…well, she did it to herself. Don't you think she should ask you to forgive her? I'm not sure if I believe in all that restless spirit stuff, but it seems to me if I took my life, I'd want to know the people I loved forgave me."

"Since my mother died," Jake said, "the voices and the visions started to come again. I blocked it as much as I could."

"Why?"

"Why?" Jake exhaled a long, uneasy breath. "Because it was too late and I didn't want to face it…or her. Because part of me was angry with her for leaving me and part of me…a huge part….felt responsible. If I had let Great-Grandma in, if I had been opened to the visions, it might not have happened."

"And now you're not blocking."

"I opened up when your mother came to beg me to help you. She's damn persistent."

"Sounds like my mom. I still don't understand how she knew about you."

"I have a feeling it came from…my mother."

"You think your mom tried to contact you?"

"Not her exactly," Jake said. "I think she sent others. I sensed it and I wouldn't let them in or maybe they just weren't strong enough. For some reason, I felt more of a connection to your mom."

"Jake, if there is life after death and our moms are together, how did they end up in the same place?"

"You mean because my mom took her own life and yours was murdered? I worried about that. I believe…or at least believed a person ended up in hell when they committed that kind of act. Another reason I blocked. I didn't want to know for sure."

"I'm not very religious," Rachael said, "not like my mom's family and sure as hell not like her grandparents.

According to my mom, they could recite the whole bible. I used to pray. I used to pray my parents would get back together. After a while, when they didn't, I stopped praying."

"You don't believe in anything?" Jake said.

"I believe there's *something,* I just don't know what. I guess I take after my father. I'm more of a realist. It's just…all of it just makes me curious. I had believed when you're gone, you're just gone. But after, all this? I'm questioning everything. "

"There's a lot we don't know."

"Here's another question," Rachael said, "If my mother knows who killed her, why doesn't she just tell you?"

"Either she can't or she doesn't know except for the one thing she does know." Jake grinned at her and brushed the side of her hair back. "She knows you didn't do it."

"Well, thank God for that. I'd hate the idea if she was…wherever she is and blamed me."

"She'd probably forgive you anyway." Jake nudged her and then took her hand. "She knows you. You could never hurt anyone."

"I hurt her plenty in the things I said."

"I bet she forgives you for that too."

"Just like your mother would."

"I guess. Forgiving myself, though, isn't so easy."

"You said your mom used a gun to…you know, kill herself?"

Jake drifted his glance to her. "She shot herself in the head."

"Who found her?"

Jake nodded. "Me. I can't make sense of. The gun she used. My father took everything else with him so why leave the gun? My mother hated guns. She was scared of them and never wanted it in the house. So why did she use it? She could have taken pills. There were other ways. And why didn't I make sure the gun was gone? I knew she was depressed."

"There you go again. You're asking questions about things you couldn't control, not now or then. Why this and why that. She was ill, sad, and she decided to commit an act out of desperation. I bet if she could talk to you right now, she'd say how dumb it was and how sorry she is. Whatever her reasons, she probably didn't think at the moment what it would do to you."

Jake put his arm around her. "Here you are, facing a crime you didn't commit, and you're worried about me and my mom. I'm glad I met you, Rachael Westcott. And we're going to figure this out."

"If we can't..."

"We can. We will." He leaned in to kiss her, and this time, Rachael didn't back away.

Chapter 22

Outside by the driveway, Doug Westcott was fully aware Doris spied on him from her bedroom window. He easily pretended not to notice. Most people, when they lied, became self-conscious, but Doug knew better, he had lots of practice. Lying was a talent, a skill that, like any other skill, required training to perfect. Too bad so many considered it morally wrong, otherwise, he would have loved to boast about it.

He shook hands with the real estate agent and begrudgingly agreed with her recommendation. "I'm sure you're right. It's a bad time to put the house on the market with all the publicity."

"If it wasn't for that, Mr. Westcott," the agent said, "I'm sure this house would sell fast. It shows very well. But the stigma…you understand."

Doug nodded again. His true thoughts revealed something more cynical. What the agent really meant was that a murder in the house would turn off too many people with delicate stomachs.

He patted her on the back and said, "Timing is everything." The agent narrowed her eyes. He felt her back tighten.

Any good liar would recognize the signals since reading the opponent was a vital part of the skill. Quick to appear remorseful, he dropped his hand and added, "My daughter needs the money, you understand. If not for her pushing me to sell, I'd never even consider it this soon." He glanced over his shoulder just enough to make sure the agent could still see his regret. "My wife…" he pretended to choke, "loved that house."

The agent sympathized. Her voice softened and she nodded. "I do understand. It's an unfortunate situation. Let's give it a month or two after the trial and the media frenzy dies down. People forget. And I'm sure once they see this place, they'll fall in love with it and overlook anything...distasteful."

Doug waved from the driveway while the agent backed her car onto the street. Doris still watched. He felt her eyes cutting into him. He fisted his hand on the opposite side of her view and cursed under his breath. He wanted the house sold now, not months from now. He was sure he could get Rachael to sign it over; it was just a matter of timing. He just had to strike while she was vulnerable.

He glanced at his watch. The meeting with the bank was in three hours. He was finding it harder to stall them, and now he couldn't even buy time by telling them the house was on the market.

Tired of being hounded and threatened, he was desperate to repay gambling debts, bank loans, and take a three-day trip to Rio he promised his newest long-legged conquest; desperate enough to go see Mya's aunt two weeks ago. He never liked her, and she sure as hell didn't care for him.

With an unshaved face and a little makeup strategically placed, he made his complexion appear gaunt. He even added dark circles under his eyes. Pinching his arm until tears sprang; he trudged up the steps to Aunt Rose's house and rang the doorbell. He figured the old lady would be watching from her window. He confirmed the fact when she opened the door just as he rang the bell.

She eyed him with contempt. He was ready for it.

"Hello, Aunt Rose." He made his voice quiver for added drama.

"You." She grasped the top of her housecoat as if he might try to rape her.

"I'm sorry to bother you," Doug said and looked at his feet. "I miss...you. It's good to look at you. You have Mya's eyes." He lifted his eyes to check whether he had an effect. He could tell by her sour expression and how she crossed her arms over her chest he didn't. He'd anticipated that too.

"What do you want?" Rose said.

"You know about..." he made his voice sound choked, "Rachael's situation?"

"I spoke to her. That lawyer you got better be good."

"He is," Doug said. "That's why I'm here."

She waited. He cleared his throat.

"The lawyer is very good," Doug said. "And good lawyers are expensive."

"Rachael said it wasn't a problem."

Doug scoffed and ran a hand through his unkempt hair. "Well, I didn't want to worry her."

"Is that so?"

"I was hoping...I hate to ask, and of course I'll pay it back, but I was wondering about a loan. For Rachael."

"For Rachael?" Rose smirked at him. "I'll give her a call."

"No," Doug said a little too quickly. He chuckled nervously. "Don't do that. I don't want her to worry. I told you that."

"Do you really take me for some kind of fool, Doug Westcott? I know your type. Mya was my niece. We talked. I know about your gambling and chasing women. You have money. Plenty of it. At least, you would if you didn't gamble it away."

"You misunderstand," Doug said.

Rose took the broom next to the door and swept it at his feet. "Get off my porch. I warned Mya years ago not to marry you. Go on. And so help me, Doug, if I find out you murdered Mya and you're coward enough to let Rachael take the blame, I'll come after you myself. Now, get." She held the broom, ready to swat him.

He glared at her while he mentally called her all kinds of names. Some people were immune to his charm; he learned that a long time ago. Even so, he hated to fail.

"You don't need to call Rachael about this," he said.

"We don't want her to worry," Rose mocked.

Doug turned on his heels and left. He felt her eyes cut into him just the way Doris Ivy's did now.

With a heavy sigh, the idea of going to Plan B didn't sit well, but then again, over-extension at the bank was a tough pill to swallow. He looked up at Doris, his best smile in place, and waved. She slid the curtain back with the look of superiority he despised.

Doris answered the door before Doug came up the last step. "Well, look at you," she said. "In a new suit and everything. Hard to believe you broke down and bought one."

Doug straightened his tie. "You were the one who always said I should dress better."

"What can I do for you, Mr. Westcott?"

In his best, innocent tone, he said, "I know you're angry I canceled the other night. Business pressures." He smiled wearily. "I've missed you, Doris."

"I bet." She sipped her martini and when she finished, she ran her tongue around her lips. To him, she resembled a viper.

"Of course I have. This hasn't been easy for me." He stepped inside, making sure to brush her arm for added appeal, and smiled. "Are we alone?"

"As alone as we can be for now," Doris said and shut the door. "I saw you with that real estate agent."

"Yes," he sighed as if exhausted, "Rachael is begging me to sell the house. She wants nothing to do with it."

"Really? That's a surprise. I would think the brat would want it to sell herself."

"She'll sign it over to me. It's only natural. It is my house."

"I doubt Mya would agree."

Doug shrugged his shoulder. "Doesn't matter. We placed Rachael on the deed in name only. I agreed to it and now...I don't."

"That simple?"

"I have a very close understanding with my daughter. She knew how her mother broke me down. Rachael understood that Mya, out of spite, would just as soon see the house go into bankruptcy than let me have it. Rachael agreed to have her name on the deed and, in the event anything happened to her mother, she and I would share the profit. She's very smart."

"And low and behold, something did happen to her mother and now you want her to sign it over to you."

"It was an unexpected tragedy," Doug said. He rubbed his forehead. "I wish you would show just a little bit of compassion for me. She was my wife." He lowered his eyes when Doris grinned at him. She cocked her head and raised her brows with doubt similar to the real estate agent's. Except Doris was more blatant and looked amused. He was beginning to feel like he'd lost his touch. "Selling the house makes sense. Rachael's facing murder charges, for Christ's sake, Doris. No point in having the house in litigation for however long this all takes. She's not exactly in the position to pay taxes, upkeep, and all that, now is she?"

"I understand. You might as well clear the plate. At least, when she's found guilty, the house issue will all be resolved."

Doug hesitated before he spoke. "I pray she isn't found guilty." He pushed his hands into his pants pockets. He looked down again finding it harder and harder to make eye contact.

L. Thomas Cook

He felt Doris's stare. "Why do you seem so unbelievable?" She strolled over to the bar and poured the remains of her drink from the shaker into her martini glass. "You know what I think? I think you're so wrapped up in yourself, you don't even realize how serious all this is. You're like a child who thinks as long as he gets what he wants, everything will miraculously be fine for the rest." She plopped two olives in her glass, swirled them with her finger, and when she looked over at Doug, she put her finger in her mouth. "Pray is it? You? Really? You seem to miss a very important point, Doug. If your prayer is answered, and that would be a laugh because I doubt very much God takes time to listen to men like you, then there's still the matter of who killed Mya."

"Well, it wasn't my daughter," Doug loosened his necktie when he sat on the couch.

"You know what's interesting about the morning of the murder?" Doris asked as she grinned and sat next to him. "I happened to look out my window and I saw…you." She crossed her legs and rocked one back and forth. "I'm just saying."

"Stop whatever you're saying." He quickly stood and unbuttoned the top of his shirt. "You've mentioned it before. I told you. It wasn't me either."

"Then why did I see you hurry down the driveway to your car parked down the street?"

"I…I needed to get into the house and find something I left there. I thought it best to wait for Mya to leave rather than get into anything with her."

"You left in a hurry."

"I was behind the garage waiting, and when Mya's car left, I was going to go in, but when I saw Rachael's car, I left. I thought she had classes and realized I must have been wrong."

"And yet you drove off when the police showed up. Why would you do that? Weren't you worried or at least concerned something happened to your sweet baby girl?"

"I thought it would be awkward to explain why I was there. I never dreamed it was something so...tragic. Doris, you know Mya refused to sign the divorce papers with excuse after excuse. She just delayed everything. She threatened to get a restraining order against me if I came around again."

"Really?" Her reply was slow and deliberate. Her eyes burned through him. "Do I look like a fool to you? You led me on for years saying Mya wouldn't sign; Mya contested; Mya wanted mediation; and all the time it was you. Close your mouth and don't look at me like that. Don't look at me like some misunderstood child, for Christ's sake. You played the game at everyone else's expense. What was it, Doug? You wanted the house and knew Mya would probably get it? Was it a matter of child support? Disclosing how much you were really worth...or how broke you really are? Or was it the insurance policies?" Doris smiled smugly. "All of it, I'm sure. You could never allow yourself to be left in the cold, so the best way to keep your only ally, your baby girl, on your side, was to play the martyr. That way, you and Rachael could gang up on Mya and, if something should happen to her in the meantime, so much the better. You'd come out like the poor, heartbroken widower, smelling of all the money you got."

He puffed out his cheeks and stuck out his chin. "That's a horrible thing to say!"

"Is it? You overspend, Doug. You always have. You like women, booze, horses, and you have a nasty affliction towards work. The bank won't lend you any more money, you have no credit, and now, with your daughter facing murder charges, you're trying to steal the house right from under her. Let's see..." Doris paused and sucked on an olive, "did I miss anything? Oh, yes. Aunt Rose." Doris laughed. "Your mouth is hanging open again."

"How did—?"

"I know plenty." She placed another olive in her mouth.

Doug's jaw opened and closed. He massaged the back of his neck wondering how and where his skill had failed him. He decided outrage was the route to take and tossed in the sympathy card for luck. His voice high-pitched, he said, "How can you say all that to me after what we've been through? Wasn't I here for you after your husband disappeared? When they questioned you, didn't I stay by you? All the time I worried more about your reputation than mine and this is how you act?"

"Oh just shut up." Doris shook her head at him before she gulped her martini and chomped on the swizzle stick.

"Shut...what in the hell is wrong with you today?" He felt himself sweat and ran his fingers across his forehead. She was making him work for it today and he couldn't afford to quit...not yet.

"Today. Yesterday. Last week. I'm tired of it, Doug. Right now, you're more floored I figured it all out. Well, it doesn't take a genius. A little eavesdropping, my son hanging around your daughter needing someone to confide in, and some discreet calls to the bank manager, who happens to be a personal friend, and before long, all the pieces fall into place. Of course, a good private investigator doesn't hurt either."

"You...followed me?"

"Not me, a detective...and he was worth every penny." She looked up at the ceiling like she was reading a list, and began counting on her fingers. "Let's see. There was that waitress last month. Oh yes, and your competitor's secretary a week ago. Let's not forget that slut in accounting where you're barely holding onto your job."

She shook her head at him again. "Of course, I shouldn't forget about those expensive dinners at places where you never took me. Oh and what about hotel rooms and room service? Usually paid for by the whore you bedded that night, am I right?" She laughed. "Then, for good measure, let's toss in the bets you made and lost badly at the track."

She walked away from him, but before Doug could say a word, she whipped around and pointed a her finger at him. "You borrowed ten thousand from me and took a female member of the Lion's Club to Vegas." She placed her hands on hips and snickered. "Under the pretense of seeing a heart specialist...have I got that right, Doug? "At least that's what you told me and the courts. Now that takes nerve, Doug, real balls."

Doug's eyes grew large. Nowhere in his autobiography on lies and deception did he have a page for this. Defeated, he tossed up his hands. "Okay, you got me. What can I say, Doris, I'm just a son of a bitch."

"Please don't bother trying that 'oh, Mother, I'm just a bad boy but I'm so damn cute' routine with me."

"So what now? You toss me out?"

"Not exactly." Doris swayed her hips over to the bar and mixed another martini.

Doug fumed behind her while images of choking the life out her danced through his head.

"Careful, Doug, I know what you're thinking." She chuckled.

"What are you? Some damn witch?"

"You never know." She laughed. "Perhaps I'm just a smart woman with too much experience. You're just lucky you're so damn good in bed, Darling. No, I won't toss you out, but I will tell you how things are going to go: you're going to sell your condo and put the money in my bank account."

"You're insane. That condo is worth a hell of a lot more than ten grand."

"The rest is interest plus damages. Emotional damage. Then, you'll tell your darling daughter about us, move in here, and help plan our wedding."

"No. I'd rather have you toss me out."

"And risk telling your daughter the truth?"

"Rachael is loyal to me. She'll never believe it. Hell, she believed me over her own damn mother."

"Oh, did I forget to mention you'll also testify your daughter and her mother had a volatile relationship and while it breaks your heart to say it, you had to tell the truth?"

"There's no way in hell...No way, Doris."

"Then I guess I have to tell the police I saw you outside the house that morning and you ran away just before the police arrived. I didn't say anything at the time because I'm in love with you, but my conscience wouldn't allow a young, innocent girl, to be convicted of murder and face the death penalty without telling everything I know. Like how you wanted to get Mya's money and if Rachael should go to prison, then Mya's estate would go to you; her legal husband, and, may I add, just in time too, before Mya could shut down your con. But she never did make it to that final court date, did she?"

"Your word against mine."

"Really? Mya's friends and family all knew how she wanted the divorce to be finalized. People she worked with knew. Sounds like a motive to me." Doris smiled and then pouted when she looked over at him. "That face. I've never seen you so...humbled. And nothing to say? Doug, just so you know, you're good at the games you play, but there's always someone out there who's better. You recall the old hair color commercial? Don't hate me for being beautiful? I always added the line, 'just hate yourself because you're not.' Clever, isn't it?" She hoisted her glass to him and sipped. "Your move."

"I will not testify against my daughter."

"Too late for a conscience now, Darling. You will. You must."

"But why? What did Rachael ever do to you?"

"I just want to see justice play out as it should. Someone has to answer for murder."

"But she's innocent."

"None of us are innocent, haven't you learned that yet? I plan to marry you, Doug. I have always planned that. You've kept me waiting long enough. I'm not about to have the man I wed go to prison for murder."

"I didn't do it."

"So you say. A lifelong liar. You're good, Doug, but under pressure, you'd break. Now do what I say. And I'll make certain that nasty bank manager stops bothering you. Just in time, too. I hear through the grapevine you're about to be terminated for missing funds. Let me guess: you didn't borrow against the corporate accounts with that whore you took to Vegas, did you? Or was it the other one you took to Puerto Rico? I guess it doesn't matter. Either way, you're screwed."

She sashayed over to him and cupped his deflated face in her hands. "You're so adorable when you're beaten. I like it. So will you. You might say giving my men a whipping is something I'm extremely good at." She laughed and he felt like vomiting.

With sunken shoulders, Doug labored to the door. "I'll call you later."

"Where do you think you're going?" Doris said. "When my puppy has his tail between his legs, I have him lie down. Go upstairs and wait for me. Tonight is a night you'll never forget."

"I have an appointment."

"Tough. Keep her waiting like you kept me. Go upstairs now, Doug. This is my game and we've only started."

"You haven't won."

"Wait. I could call Rachael and tell her everything…and I mean everything. Think she'll sign over the house then?" She pursed her lips. "Don't look so grim, Darling. I could tell and toss you out. Is it true when you have gambling debts they send a big, apelike man…Gaetti, or something like that; after you?"

Doug clenched his jaw. "Mind if I pour myself a drink?"

"Take the damn bottle with you." Doris slapped the whiskey bottle in his hand. "I'll be up in a few. Oh, and close the bedroom door. Burke will be here soon."

Doug trudged up the stairs wondering how the talent he had spent years mastering could betray him so viciously now.

Chapter 23

Positive that Doug was upstairs safely consuming the whiskey Doris had put a sedative in, she grinned at the ease with which she could predict others' actions. Doug's lust for alcohol was as much a part of him as his thirst for women, but liquor was the primal vice he'd turn to when pushed too hard by a woman.

Doris had dealt with his type so often it was hardly a challenge anymore. Her husband, Louis, would be the first to agree with that...if anyone could find him.

Doris married Louis Ivy when she was thirty-five; five years after her first husband, Mitch Jordan, died. He'd killed himself in their garage one night when stars twinkled and a patch of clouds partly hid the full moon for a moment. It was a warm June night perfect for so many things...even death.

Mitch simply went to sleep in his car with the motor running and the garage door shut.

Doris, the grieving widow with a small child to care for, sobbed when the police found him and couldn't explain why a man in the prime of his life with a devoted wife, a nice home, and comfortable lifestyle would do such a thing. It must have been, she explained to the police, because she found out Mitch was having an affair. She told him she forgave him, but the poor man must have been so distraught he took his own life.

Her life went on with no financial concerns thanks to insurance policies and investments Mitch had made. Doris's only child, Burke, was five at the time of his father's death, so she lavished her attention on him.

But, the boy needed a father and Louis came around at the right time. He adopted Burke, and Burke adored him. Then one day, Louis disappeared. Eight years later, Doris

L. Thomas Cook

rarely thought of Louis except for those times when she went into the basement.

She pulled a key from her pocket and unlocked the basement door. Her high heels clicked on the wood steps and along the concrete floor as she walked through the basement. Beyond the washer and dryer; past some old chairs she meant to give to Goodwill; and past stacks of bundled newspaper, she paused at the upright freezer. She slid the freezer away to reveal a wooden door sealed with a combination lock. She turned the dials, inputting the code, opened the lock, and pushed the door.

A cool breeze greeted her. It was dark inside the small four-by-eight room. With flashlight in hand, she guided the beam of light around the tiny space until she found her target.

Naked and with his hands and feet tied, he shivered on the cold floor. He squinted in the light, trying to adjust his eyes but he knew who came for him...there was only one who ever did.

"Have you repented for your sins, Burke?" Doris kept the bright light aimed at his face.

"Yes, Mother," Burke said in a dry, raspy voice.

"Why do you make me punish you?"

"I'm sorry, Mother."

"You have to stop lusting." She stepped inside the windowless cell and squatted near her son. Ten hours with no light, no sound, and nothing to eat or drink, he lay curled in the same position she left him. Running a hand through his mussed, blond hair, he looked too much like his biological father, which made Doris's stomach tighten in a knot. "So much like your father," she said, brushing Burke's hair. "When will you learn that young, beautiful women are selfish, greedy sluts? I have to come first, Burke. A mother's love for her son cannot be replaced."

Burke sniffed. "Yes, Mother. I only wanted to help her."

227

"She doesn't need your help. Rachael Westcott is a tramp. She never liked you and she never will. She'll use you. Is that what you want, Burke? To be used like a servant and then tossed aside?"

"No, Mother. I'm sorry."

"I wish I could believe that." She began to untie his hands and, as she stood, said, "Look at you. Your face is dirty. Your hair needs a cut. You've scraped your knees on the floor. How many times have I told you the floor is rough? You never listen."

Burke sat up slowly. He whimpered when he bent to untie his feet and even more when Doris pulled him to his knees and pressed his head to her chest. She hummed a soft tune that made him cringe.

"You're tightening your muscles, Burke. Don't you like Mommy's song?"

"Yes, Mother. It's very pretty."

"Good boy." She kissed his forehead and then his lips. "I don't like punishing you. You give me no choice. You have to stay away from that evil girl and obey me. You promise to obey me and think of only me?"

"Yes, Mother."

"Say it, Sweet Boy. Make the promise."

"I promise to obey and think of you."

She yanked his hair until he hissed. "Only me. Say it."

"Only you, I promise."

Doris smiled. "Good. Now I want you to go upstairs very quietly. I have a guest and I don't want any noise, do you understand? Take a bath and go to your room. We'll say your prayers together before bed."

"I'm hungry," Burke said. With his mother's help, he got to his shaky legs. At full height, he would stand six inches taller than her five feet six, but he had to bend so he didn't hit his head on the low ceiling. "Mother, may I have something to eat?" His body was underdeveloped and

228

nearly hairless with peach fuzz on his chin. He had a flat chest and ribs that showed through under pale, pink skin. His thin legs showed bone where they shouldn't and didn't appear strong enough to hold him.

Doris wrapped a blanket around his trembling body. "I'll bring you something after your bath. Now go on and remember to be quiet."

He nodded and slowly thudded up the stairs. Doris knelt on the floor and prayed, "Help me guide him away from temptation. May he never know the true evil of flesh without the ultimate love only a mother may offer. Give me strength to conquer those who would betray that bond so he may serve as You have designed."

She ran her hand over the porous floor where Burke had laid so often over the years. She was proud of herself for making this room with no help from anyone except some from Burke. He asked questions. She ignored him. Together, they placed the cinder blocks, cemented them in place, and. hung the thick, wood door. But the floor was her secret. She poured the cement floor without anyone knowing. It didn't start out to be a cell but rather, a secret place for secret things. The fact it had multiple purposes pleased her.

"And," she said, still trailing her hand over the floor, "give me strength to conquer those who would betray me." Doris's lips curled upward. "Like you, Louis. So much like the rest who lusted for young female tramps. I was enough. I'm all you needed, but you were weak. I come first. You should have known it, but I had to show you your mistake."

She showed others. If only she had this room then. She made do and, along the way, honed her skills. From a young age, she made sure no one betrayed her.

Her desire to be first began even before she wanted to be prom queen. She should have been, but the fools picked her best friend instead. Her boyfriend made the same mistake when he also picked her best friend. He cheated on Doris that night in the backseat of his car with Karla.

Karla never should have tempted him, and Bruce should never have picked someone over Doris. While she couldn't punish the whole school for choosing Karla over her, she could put her skills to work on the main sinners.

Karla's house burnt down that week with her and her family inside. Doris got the opportunity to practice her talent for drama.

"I was supposed to spend the night with her," she sobbed when she spoke to the police. "I had a horrible headache, otherwise I would have been at her house and burned too. I just wish I had Karla come and stay at my house that night. Then she'd still be alive."

They all felt sorry for her, the poor girl who lost her best friend. Doris was the center of attention for weeks.

Bruce drowned a few weeks later.

"He took me swimming to help me forget Karla," she told everyone, "and now he's gone too. I feel so bad for his parents. They don't even have a body to bury." She cried real tears she got from biting the inside of her cheek. "And I have no place to put flowers."

She planned it all at just the right time when the attention she got after Karla's death began to fade. For the next two months, she had all the sympathy.

Even before then, Doris's gift began. At the age of seven, she was jealous of her father's attention to her younger sister. How she was inspired to place her wet, chewed bubble gum on the sleeping five-year old girl's pillow, she couldn't remember. In the morning, her sister's long, curly hair that everyone adored, was a tangled mess. Their mother had to shave the hair to the scalp.

Not long after, Doris didn't care about her father's attention so much. She lost interest in him and her mother. Her focus became other children in the neighborhood and those she could manipulate or blackmail into being her slaves.

Then He came—the dark shadow with a his menacing whistle intended to scare her. She laughed when she thought of it. Even with all his darkness, he was surprised he didn't frighten her.

He wanted to kill her, but she made him a deal. A special deal that brought other malevolent beings to her, along with rewards she never imaged. She became the pupil, the star student, teacher's pet.

Nothing stopped her. Later, when she was in college, both she and her roommate ran for freshman president. Her roommate died in a car accident. Another rival also had a car accident and, fifteen years later, was still in a coma.

Doris stood and brushed cement dust from her hands. Yes, she thought, Doug Westcott was no match for her. He would serve her well and learn his share of lessons. She came first, always did, and always would. All the men in her life who ever betrayed her soon learned how wrong they were. And Burke would learn too that the only woman he needed in his life, was her.

She began the lessons early with him but like so many, he was stubborn. Doris's patience endured, although she'd never allow anyone, not even Burke, to take advantage of her. She controlled him in every way. It had to be so. As he grew older, he was twenty-two after all; she had to pull the reins tighter. When he craved sex, she would say who and when. He would need her approval and her permission. He had a destiny to fill. She always told him that. Why he allowed himself to lust after Rachael Westcott was beyond her.

"I guess when a tramp gets her claws into someone; it's hard to pry them loose." Doris sighed. *Burke, you must learn Mother knows. I've seen the signs in that girl since the first day we moved here. She was no five-year-old*

*innocent. She had the look and smell even then of
something vile. My son is too pure for the likes of her.*

She closed the wood door, latched the padlock, and
slid the freezer back in place. "Rest well, Louis, you dirty
son of a bitch."

Further, toward the back of the basement, Doris
went where the shadows made it darker. She lifted the
black sheet off the table and knelt before her homemade
altar.

An inverted cross, burnt candles, and a pentagram
waited for her to worship. She lit the candles, speaking in
tongue as old as time, and closed her eyes.

"I call upon the Father of Dark. I am first. You are
first. I serve you. You serve me. Hear my call. Make me
strong. And, with your help, make my enemies weak."

The candles sizzled. Doris bowed her head. She
hummed along with the insidious ancient tune that whistled
close to her ear.

Chapter 24

After securely locking the basement door, Doris leisurely climbed the stairs to the second floor. She opened the door to her bedroom and, just as she expected, Doug was snoring, the half-empty bottle of whiskey by his side.

How easy it had all been. Timing and patience were all the virtues required. He would sleep, probably not even remember dreaming, and when he woke, stripped and tied to her bed, the lessons would begin.

She'd have to work fast though. Rachael's trial began in two days.

Doug would drink until he begged her for no more. They would have sex until he had nothing left to give. He would bend to her will. His fate was sealed with the darkness as witness. She would be his first and only until she grew bored, and only then, she would release him or kill him; whichever she decided.

She turned her attention to Burke. He was her pride and joy. Humming, she strolled to his room, didn't bother to knock, and found him kneeling alongside his bed with the whip in his hand.

His eyes closed, he repeated the chant she taught him as he flung the leather strap over his shoulders to slap against his back, creating welts. Red blood beaded and oozed down his spine. Naked, his pale, thin body appeared frail, but she knew it was well-acquainted with the whip.

Self-sacrifice and self-mutilation, were all part of the ritual he practiced under her teaching since he was six years old. Self-flagellation was the nightly practice. A time to renew vows, a time to meditate and repent, a special time to be close to their god—their master.

"Obey my mother first and only," Burke chanted and then slapped the strap across his back.

"Not like that," Doris said.

She came to him and snatched the whip from his grip.

"You said you were old enough to do this yourself." Doris shook the whip in his face. "You hold it in the palm of your hand, like this, and go from the opposite side. Left to right, right to left, cross over and relish the sting." She stood behind him and hit him repeatedly with the whip so all his self-inflected welts bled more.

"Please, Mother," Burke said and winced. "I can do it."

"Not if you don't do it correctly. You must be punished. Time in isolation is not enough. You are weak. You must be strong." She slapped the whip back in his hand. "Now, show me."

"Obey my mother first and only." He crossed his right hand over his left shoulder and brought the whip down, then bit his lip and hissed. Doris saw that as a sign of weakness.

"Again. Harder," she demanded.

"Obey my mother first and only." He slapped as hard as he could.

"Better," Doris said. "I love you, Burke." She took an already blood-stained towel from the floor and dabbed at Burke's wounds.

"I love you, Mother."

"And..."

"Only you know what is good for me."

"Very good." She sat on the bed and put out her hands. "Come to Mommy."

Burke stood, wrapped an infant's blue fuzzy blanket around his shoulders, and sat with half his body on the bed and his upper torso cradled in her lap.

"I have your milk so you can sleep," Doris said and lowered the left side of her blouse.

A sagging breast exposed, Burke nuzzled close and sucked in her nipple.

234

Doris smiled at the tug she felt all the way between her legs.

"Be careful of your teeth," she said and traced her finger along his cheekbone. "Do you like Mommy's milk?" Burke nodded and suckled more. "You're my baby. Only mine. No one understands us. Louis didn't, did he? No. He thought you too big to drink from me. He didn't understand growing boys need nourishment only a mother can give. That's why so many men lust after tramps. Those poor babies denied their mother's breast too soon with want unanswered. Not my boy. Not my sweet baby."

She cuddled him closer and hummed as he fed. She ran a finger down his side and he giggled with her nipple still between his lips. She smiled at him and then lifted her head with eyes shut while her flesh tingled.

"You need me," she hushed. "My milk. My love. One day, I'll permit you the flesh of a woman when I feel you're ready. But for now, you are still growing and I'm all you need."

He sucked faster and she caressed him between his legs.

"I know the weakness of the flesh. That's why you must do penance. I know what a young boy needs." The harder he sucked, the firmer she stroked until his erection filled her hand.

"That's why I offer you release, my sweet boy. Release and be pure in mind and body."

He came and she licked her sticky hand clean.

"I feed you." Doris kissed his flushed cheek. "And you feed me. Had enough?"

Burke nodded and kissed her breast before he sat up in her lap. "Thank you, Mother."

She covered her wet breast and handed him a glass. "I'm sorry my milk is so dry."

"No, it isn't. I can taste it. Warm and sweet," he said. Strands of hair framed his face and a few wisps hung over his eyes.

He looked so innocent to Doris. She brushed the strands away. "You're very kind. Drink this and go to bed."

"Yes, Mother." He crawled under the covers and Doris tucked in the sides.

"Don't ever disappoint me, Burke," she whispered close to his face.

"I won't. I promise." Burke drank down the milk without tasting the sedative she put in it.

"Sleep well, my sweet boy." She blew him a kiss, turned out the light, and shut the door, locking it.

It was only nine at night, but with the amount of sedative she gave him, he would sleep until noon the next day.

*****

In an oversized New York Jets football jersey Rachael found strewn over a chair, she padded out of Jake's bedroom. Jake slept on the sofa in the living room, a little bit of drool trailed from the corner of his mouth.

Rachael smiled. He was handsome and apparently, a gentlemen. An empty bottle of wine on the coffee table was proof. She touched her lips in remembrance of the kiss they shared last night. She liked it and him. He could have taken advantage of her because she was tipsy, but he didn't. She had mixed feelings about that. No, she decided, he was goofy in a sweet way and smart to take it slow. Besides, liking him or not, she was in no position to start something complicated.

While Jake slept, she snooped. Books on photography lined some shelves. A badly-formed clay bowl that looked like something a third grader would make sat on another shelf.

She glanced at the titles of some travel books: Italy, Spain, and Costa Rico. There was also a book on how to play the guitar and one that was a collection of poetry.

On a side table, she found the only photograph there was-a picture of Jake with an older woman. He had the same soulful eyes as her.

She walked to the kitchen. In the refrigerator, she saw a bottle of ketchup, a half-eaten, stale jelly donut on a paper towel, a small plastic container with contents she couldn't recognize, and a carton of expired milk.

While she continued to explore, she muttered, "I swear this is the worst use of an appliance I've ever seen. There should be a law against this." Her heart jumped after she heard the cough behind her.

"I'm afraid I don't have much," Jake said, scratching his scalp under sleep tossed hair.

"Much? Try nothing. You've seriously lost points with me."

"I have instant coffee," he said, opening the upper cabinet.

"Instant coffee? You've just committed the ultimate sin against any devout coffee lover. Shame on you. Repent." She put two fingers up to form a cross.

Jake shielded his eyes. "Forgive me." He laughed, looked at her, and took her hand in his. "My jersey looks good on you."

Rachael felt her cheeks heat. "It's the only clean thing I could find."

"How about I take you to breakfast?"

"Now we're on the same page."

"Good," he said while he opened and closed a couple of drawers. "Where's the damn aspirin?"

"Drink too much last night?"

He rubbed the top of his head. "You think? It's weird because I've been known to go through a bottle of Scotch like water, but that wine hit me."

"Probably because we never ate."

He smacked himself in the forehead. "Shit. Did I not feed you?"

"No, you never did." She rubbed the spot he hit. "But don't beat yourself up over it. As I recall, we were trying to solve a murder. That kind of thing usually makes a person forget to eat. By the way," she picked up the photograph, "is this your mother?"

Jake took the photo and smiled sadly at it. "Yes. Rita Delmar. My mom."

"She looks like a nice lady."

"Was. Was a nice lady and very troubled." He stared at the picture and said, "Thanks for what you said last night."

Rachael covered her mouth. "Oh, God. What did I say? Something dumb? Mean?"

Jake frowned. "No. Why would you think you said something mean?"

"Because when I drink...sometimes I say mean things."

"Good to know, but I wouldn't thank you for it."

Rachael giggled. "That's true. So what brilliant thing did I say?"

"Oh, now you're brilliant?" He laughed when she shrugged. "What I mean is what you said about my mother and why she might have done what she did. I've been confused by that for a while and I guess, you know, mad at myself about it and I took out my anger on her."

"How?"

"Just...trying not to think of her. That picture? I tossed that in a drawer. Others, I threw out. I was angry and didn't want to let anyone in."

"You mean souls?"

"I think...no, I know there have been souls who tried to contact me and I'm pretty sure my mom was behind it. That photograph only came out thanks to our friend, the Dark Shadow Thing."

"DST. I like it." Rachael pulled her hair into a ponytail and then let it go. The soft strands willowed across her shoulders.

"I think you were right, too, when you said with or without me using my gift to predict my mom killing herself, she would have found a way."

"'Suicide is the permanent solution to a temporary problem.' I read that some place. I'm not excusing it, but I get how someone desperate enough or in enough pain, might do it. It's internal. But, if she knew how it would've affected you, I bet she would have handled her pain differently. I bet if she had it to do over...well, who knows?"

"And if I had it to do over with my fears and blocking my gift...well, who knows?"

"There's still something I don't get," Rachael said. "The whistle. You said you heard it when you were a kid. I've heard it too. How is that possible?"

Jake sat at the table. "I think it has to do with opening a door. I think when I was a kid, I felt bad that I couldn't find that boy before he died. I started to think 'what's the point of having some damn gift to know things if I can't save someone?' I was angry. You, you might have opened a door when you were so angry with your mom. Dark stuff feeds off negativity and waits for that moment when we're vulnerable. They gather energy and, when they have enough, they have the power to do things."

"What kind of things?"

"Mess with our minds. Make us do and say things we wouldn't. They can possess us. Hell, there are cases where demons have killed."

"Oh my God." She wrapped her arms around herself and shivered. "I always hated horror movies when I thought they were made up. Now, you're telling me there's some truth to them?"

"No one really knows. In this case, I think the reason I saw the dark shadow again after your mom came, was because something followed her. It somehow knew my guilt over my mom, how I blamed myself and turned that blame against her, and it used it."

"But the whistle? Is it the same one?"

"I'm not sure. Maybe. It's possible different demons come from a shared negative source. This is pretty old stuff dating back thousands of years. If you listen to the stories, and know the history, not all those people who wrote about it can be wrong. I want to show you something." He hurried out of the room.

Rachael heard him opening draws and tossing around papers. When she came into the living room, she saw him searching.

"Where is that damn thing?" Jake snapped his fingers. "I remember." He went to a bookcase and, after sliding books out of the way, he brought one out and showed it. "I hid it. A few times. The last time, I was kind of drunk. I thought just having it here might be bad."

He opened the thick, leather-bound book to a creased page. The drawing alone scared Rachael.

The pencil sketch showed a large, black figure. The misshapen head was bigger than the body with small horns on top. It had no face only blood-red eyes. Clawed hands reached out, ready to strike.

"What is this?" Rachael said. There appeared to be no title for the book, only a symbol etched into the front cover. She turned some pages to find more drawings of things just as horrifying.

"An old book I found a few years ago in the attic of a house I was working on," Jake said. "Once I saw what it was, I took it. This isn't the kind of book that should be hanging around."

"I still don't know what it is."

"It's filled with stories, myths, legends on demons. There's a section on how to call some of them too," Jake said. He went back to the creased page and pointed. "When I saw this, something told me I had to take the book and hide it. The owner didn't even know she had it. You should have seen her face. She was terrified. She told me to get rid of it." He put his finger under the picture of the faceless, clawed demon. "Read this."

Shedim—Hebrew word for demons. Demons can take many forms. They are false gods who often require a sacrifice, such as a child or animal. Sinful people sacrifice their daughters to the Shedim through murder or for sexual satisfaction of the demon.

"Are you serious?" Rachael said.

"Keep reading."

Whistling may call a demon. Even saying Shedim out-loud may invoke it.

"Whistling," Jake said. "And this part. 'Certain chords resonate well with darker spirits, like the forbidden chords of a medieval tune.' I could never figure out what that darkness whistled. It sounded familiar, but I think it was meant to fool anyone who heard it." He turned the page. "Read this."

El Tuchi–legend from Peru about an evil spirit that haunts the rainforest. They say he's the ghost of a troubled man who got lost and died in the woods. His evil spirit roams the forest, whistling... Rachael glanced wide-eyed at Jake. He nodded.

Its high-pitched whistle gets louder until it's unbearable. Legend says you must never acknowledge it. If you do, it will get louder and draw nearer. Whatever you do, never answer the El Tuchi's whistle. He will kill you in the most hideous way.

"Oh my God, Jake. It's a legend, but...is it true?"

Jake began to read: *According to legend, a young Catholic nun, Sister Bernadette, heard it once. She claimed it sounded like fingernails scraping against a blackboard, but different, like a strange creature. The nuns with her refused to acknowledge it. Sister Bernadette insisted. She answered the whistle and it stopped. She continued to whistle. The nuns blessed themselves. That night, the nuns heard a piercing scream coming from Sister Bernadette's room. They rushed in and recoiled in horror. There was blood from the floor to the ceiling. Sister Bernadette was gone.*

Days later, they found her body in the forest hanging from a tree. Her throat torn out. Her arms and legs were twisted in weird angles. A look of utter horror was frozen on her face.

"Stop, Jake," Rachael said and placed her hand over the page.

"You need to know. We both do," Jake said and read: *A young girl was said to have seen a dark shadow in the forest near her house. She heard a strange whistle and imitated it.*

Her father found her at the window whistling an odd tune. She told him she was whistling to the dark figure. Her father was terrified. He knew the legend of El Tuchi. He hid his daughter upstairs and bolted the door.

A crash against the door almost broke it down. Her father pushed the girl into the closet, locked the door, and broke off the key. The bedroom door burst open and her father screamed in terror. The window shattered. The girl covered her ears and her father's screams faded in the distance.

The villagers found her. To this day, the body of the father goes undiscovered. The girl lives in fear that one day, El Tuchi will return for her.

Excited, Jake looked at Rachael. "This has to prove something. The book has hundreds of stories from around the world. Not everyone can make this shit up."

"Okay," Rachael said. "I admit the description is similar. There's just one problem: if it's real, we still don't know how to stop it."

"I never said this would be easy."

"Jake, what if…what if our mothers are stuck in a place with a monster like that?"

He patted her shoulder, closed the book, and placed it back in the hiding spot. "I started out this morning wanting to thank you. You gave me some things to think about with my mom."

"Well I'm glad I could help." She let out a heavy sigh. "Now, answer my question."

"We'll figure it…somehow. I'm going to take a shower, then we'll have breakfast, and after, we'll check out your house."

"I think I just lost my appetite."

"Don't be scared."

"I think it's perfectly reasonable for me to be scared," Rachael said. "I…I did a lot of thinking last night about my father. Jake, it couldn't have been him. Not just because I believe he loved my mom, but…he wouldn't let me go to jail for something…you know."

"Something he might have done?"

"Jake, please. You don't know my father."

"Then I think I should meet him. After we go to your house, call him and we'll find a place to talk."

"Jake, I just want you to know that no matter how all of this goes, I'm glad we met. It hasn't been easy going through this alone and not having anyone to confide in."

"It's going to be fine. You'll see."

"If it's not…"

"Think positive. That's what we have to do. We can't give the darkness anymore power."

"Right. No more power for DST."
Jake smiled and kissed her.
"I like positive," Rachael said and kissed him again.

Chapter 25

Rachael turned into the driveway of her mother's house and parked the car. "That's my father's car." She pointed next door. "What's he doing at Mrs. Ivy's house?"

Cutting across the lawn, Rachael peeked inside the tan Lincoln sedan. All the doors were locked, her father's briefcase was on the front seat.

"I don't understand." Rachael glanced at Jake. "He barely knows Mrs. Ivy."

She went up the front steps of Doris's house and rang the bell. Doris opened it, and her smug expression turned colder.

"Rachael Westcott. Aren't you supposed to be in jail?" Doris said.

"My father's car is in your driveway. Why?"

"A little car trouble. He's waiting for the tow truck," Doris eyed Jake. "A new victim?"

"Why do you hate me so much, Mrs. Ivy? What did I ever do to you?"

"You mean besides the smut you tried on my son?"

"Smut?" Rachael lifted her brows. "You mean when we were five? Are you serious? We were kids, Mrs. Ivy, and we didn't do anything."

Doris rolled her eyes. "I'm sure."

"The only smut is your imagination. Is my father here?"

"No."

"You said he was waiting for the tow truck."

"Did I? Well, he's tied up right now." Doris rocked back on her heels with a smirk on her face and started to shut the door.

Rachael stopped it with her hand and used her foot as a wedge. "Is my father here or not?"

"He's not. He gave me the keys and asked me to take care of it. Now, if you don't mind," she pushed against the door, "I have an appointment."

Rachael didn't budge an inch. "Why is my father's car in your driveway to begin with?"

"Oh, for heaven's sake. He stopped by to ask me to keep an eye on the house." Doris glanced at her watch. "Now, if you don't mind, I'd like to run my errand before the tow truck gets here. Oh, and by the way, your father will be talking to you about us in a couple of days."

"Us?"

"Me and him. He'll explain, and when he does, try not to be thoughtless. He's been through enough lately."

"What are you talking about?"

"I've said enough. Just try to be mature about it and not resort to being a brat." She began to close the door again, but when Rachael stood there glaring, she said, "Go on now. Take your…friend and leave. And young man," she called to Jake, "I'd be careful getting involved with the type of woman she is. She's wanted for murder, you know." She slammed the door.

"Bitch," Rachael hissed. "What in the hell is she talking about? Her and my father? What's that mean? My father always said she was a nosey, lonely, miserable woman, and I shouldn't pay her any attention. Now he wants to talk to me about…it's crazy."

"There's something about her," Jake said and glanced back at the front door. "I got a weird feeling. Something's not right about her."

"You can say that again."

"Let's do what we came to do. We can deal with that later," Jake said. "Come on. Take me in the house."

*****

Doris watched out her bedroom window as Jake and Rachael went into the house.

246

L. Thomas Cook

Doug, tied to the bed, his mouth covered with duct tape, grunted and squirmed.

"Oh shut up," Doris snapped at him. "What does she want in the house? And who's that young man?" She ripped the tape off Doug's mouth and stared down at him. "Well? Answer me."

"Why are you doing this?" Doug asked, trying to catch his breath.

"You know why. To punish you. Who is that boy with Rachael?"

"I don't know. Untie me, Doris, damn it! You can't get away with this."

Doris sneered. "You don't know what I can get away with. You belong to me now. I come first. You'll do what I say and you'll thank me." She prepared a hypodermic needle and held it up in the afternoon light. "You'll like this. Pretty soon, you won't be able to live without it or the person who gives it to you…me."

"No!" Doug shouted and twisted. "Stop it, Doris. Let's discuss this calmly. You know I love you."

"Love?" Doris laughed bitterly. "Oh, you'll love me, all right. I'll be your whole world. For now, you need a little push and this'll do the trick."

Doug wiggled and shouted, but the ropes were too tight. Doris slapped his face and pushed the syringe into his arm.

Within moments, he began to relax. Doris patted his cheek. "Be a good boy, Doug, and I'll give you a surprise later." She stood back to admire how the drug worked so quickly. "Say yes, Doris, my love."

Doug slurred the words behind half-lidded eyes and a silly grin Doris knew was part of the drug's charm.

She adjusted the ropes and secured the knots. At Burke's door, she listened and, satisfied that he was still asleep, she strolled downstairs.

247

In the garage, she used the remote to open the overhead door, and backed her Volvo around Doug's car. She glanced over at Rachael's house and then drove down the street.

At the corner, she pulled over. With black tinted sunglasses on, she took a small wooden box carved with some ancient symbols out of her bag, and opened it. Inside was sacred dirt, taken from an unholy place, a ruin from a distant land that knew mayhem, death, and evil rituals, a place that thrived on slaughtered innocence, and sacrifices made in offering to a dark god.

In tongue, she spoke the words, *Serve me as I serve you. Appear and be seen. Show your might and power now.*

She took a pinch of dirt, rolled it between her fingers, and let it rain back into the box.

With a smile, she placed the box back in her purse, fixed her hair in the rearview mirror, and rubbed her red lips together before she drove away.

*****

Burke froze curled in a ball, holding his breath and keeping his eyes sealed shut. He heard his mother come to his door and expected her to come in and check him. Surprised she didn't, instead, he heard the click of her heels across the floor and go down the stairs.

He sprang out of bed and watched from his window as she drove out of the garage. He gave no thought to the tan Lincoln in the driveway, but when he saw Rachael's car parked next door, he got excited.

Rachael Westcott was beautiful, an angel in Burke's eyes. He didn't understand why his mother didn't like her. She was nice, smelled good all the time, and she didn't make fun of Burke like the other kids at school had from kindergarten through graduation.

Rachael always made room for him on the bus. She told the other kids to stop when they called him *freak* and *mommy's boy*. She even shared her sandwiches and cookies with him when his mother packed nothing but rye bread and a thermos of milk for him.

She gave him a Valentine's Day card once. It was in the third grade. He cherished the card that simply read: *Jump up and down let's hear you say it's Valentine's Day, Rachael.*

He kept the card, worn from reading and re-reading it, hidden away in a special place under his dresser where his mother never thought to check. The fact he kept this secret from his mother made him smile. It was his only thrill aside from his thoughts of Rachael.

He imagined her all the time. During the day when he sat in his room, at night when he supposedly said his prayers, even when he fed from his mother…he wondered what Rachael would taste like and how sweet her milk might be. He had to be careful, though. If his mother even suspected what his dreams were, she'd whip him until he couldn't sit and then lock him in his bad place for weeks.

He wanted her to understand. Mother told him that one day, when the time was right, he could know the flesh of a woman so long as Mother came first. He wanted Rachael to be that woman and he'd gladly obey his mother if only she would allow it.

A few times, he thought about asking his mother to have Rachael, but it would crush him if she said no. He decided to be patient. His mother would prepare him for that special moment and until then; he had his fantasies to keep him; especially when he was locked in his bad place. Mother tied his hands so he couldn't touch himself, but Burke was clever. She never got the ropes so tight he couldn't wiggle his thin wrists out. On his knees, he would think of Rachael, how he wanted to touch her, cuddle to her breast, and have her touch him.

He covered his mouth to muffle his grunts and groans. His other hand stroked and rubbed, playing him, until he came harder than even when his mother released his seed.

He lapped up the sticky mess from the floor so she wouldn't see. He never understood, though, how she didn't smell it in the small cell or on his breath, but he was glad. His mother would never tolerate masturbation. She'd consider it a vain act of self-indulgence and a sin against her.

Careful there were no signs of his misdeed, he'd wiggle back into the ropes, tighten the knots with his teeth, and curl into the position his mother demanded. With thoughts of Rachael still swimming in his head, he'd sleep.

Today, his mother would be gone for at least two hours. She went to get her hair and nails done. Two hours alone without her eyes on him, Burke hurried to dress. It was naughty and he knew it. If caught, he'd faced punishment, but it would be worth it if he could see Rachael.

*****

Rachael unlocked the back door and Jake stepped inside. The kitchen was quiet. The whole house seemed still. He didn't sense anything at first except for Rachael's anxiousness.

"It's okay," he tried to assure her.

She wrapped her arms around herself. "Something isn't right. I can feel it."

"Who's the psychic here? You or me?" He teased her with a smile and took her hand. The instant he did, he flashed to a scene that happened in the kitchen.

In his vision, Rachael stood by the table and shouted at her mother. Jake could feel her outrage. It overwhelmed him with a darkness he tried hard not to let in. Rachael's anger appeared directed at her mother, but Jake sensed there was more to it.

He saw Rachael snatch a set of car keys and storm out the door. The car started, and tires screeched out of the driveway.

"The back door was left unlocked," he said to her. "I don't think your mother realized it."

"You can see her?"

"Not exactly. I saw you. You were really pissed."

"Now that's embarrassing. How bad did I look?"

"I'm not going to lie. Your face was burnt red and you looked like... let's just say, really, really mad."

"I looked like I wanted to kill her, is that what you were going to say?" Rachael stood by the table as she had that morning. Tears formed in her eyes. "I'm so ashamed."

Jake flashed again, and this time, he saw Rachael come back in through the door. She searched through some books and paper on the table.

"I see you again," Jake said. "You came back. You're in a hurry looking for something."

"My English paper. I forgot it."

"But you unlocked the door first. When you came in."

"Yes. It was locked."

"Something happened between the time you first left and when you came back."

"Are you sure it wasn't locked?"

"Yes." Jake put his hand on the doorknob. "It wasn't locked the first time you left."

"My mother must have locked it."

Jake went over to the counter where his vision had shown Mya standing. He placed his hands on the top and flashed to an image. "No. She was crying. She stood here for a minute, refilled her coffee, used the phone, and went through there." He pointed down the hall.

He headed in that direction, got to the bottom step of the staircase, and stopped; overcome by some type of force forbidding him from going further. He felt paralyzed.

"What's wrong?" Rachael said.

Jake's face turned pale. His lips barely moved and he whispered, "Something's here, Rachael. Something…very dark."

Chapter 26

"Mya, you have to remember," Rita said.

"I can't. It's like looking at a blank screen."

"That thing is still here. Can you feel it?" Rita stood by the basement door, heard the deep growl, and stepped back. "There has to be more to the story."

"I'm not afraid of you!" Mya shouted and banged on the door.

The thing behind the door laughed more viciously.

"I'm not," Mya shouted and pounded the door. "You have to be that monster that came for me when I was a child. I'm not a child now. Leave me alone. Leave my daughter alone."

For the first time, the monster spoke. In a tone deep and hollow, it rasped, "You are a child filled with fear, but not innocent. You fear what you refuse to face."

Rita's eyes were huge. "Oh my God. What is that thing?"

"Your God," the monster cackled, "has nothing to do with this."

It began to whistle the tune Mya's grandmother hummed long ago...Amazing Grace. The whistle was dry, steady, and mocked Mya's memory.

"Stop it." Mya covered her ears. The whistle filled the room.

The monster said, "Pitiful and weak. Sorrow and tears. Why not end this? Give in to your fears. It was your fault. You know it was. Deny all you want. You brought this on."

"Shut up," Mya screamed.

"What's he talking about?" Rita said. "Mya, you told me to face my fears, now you have to do the same."

"I think…" the monster's gravel voice said, "that I should see what Rachael, our precious, sweet, Rachael is doing. Is she crying for mommy?" It laughed and then, in Rachael's voice said, "Oh, Mommy. I'm so sorry. I hated you and…" the voice changed to its own, "I still do." The laughter was deafening. It sounded as if a thousand lost souls screeched together. The air filled with a foul stench of decay. "Sinful soul, sacrifice a daughter, sacrifice just one. Give in to it. No rest until you do." It laughed and began to whistle a piercing tune.

Sorrow consumed Mya with a weight she could hardly bear. Weakened by it, she fell to her knees. Her inner light began to fade, but she still tried to fight.

Straining, she said, "You stay away from my daughter, you beast!"

It laughed. "Beast. Just one of many. I answer to the name I'm called. Monster from those who were foolish and don't understand. The rational ones seem to prefer that name as if there is some human quality in me. Dark One. Dark Shadow. So many names. My true name is one they fear to utter. Tell me, Rita, does Jake still fear the shadow he saw? Let's find out."

"No!" Rita shouted and charged the door. She was about to unlock it when Mya stopped her.

"We can't. We don't know what it is," she said.

"You're fading," Rita said. "I can't fight this thing alone. I won't let it harm Jake."

"Harm Jake," the monster imitated Rita and then its real voice sounded, "He is beyond harm. His mommy killed herself. He knows darkness. Pain, regret, and guilt. All those delicious human vices. You can understand that, Mya, can't you? Guilt eats at you and has since you were a child. Poor, poor, Mya. What Poppy did. Sin for some. Shame for others. Shame, you're to blame." The laughter from a thousand demonic souls thundered through the room. The windows rattled. Doors shook on their hinges. "Oh, my sweet Rachael, let's play."

"Mya, you have to stop it," Rita begged.

"How?" Mya couldn't stand. Her light was nearly gone.

"He said guilt. What is he talking about?"

Mya struggled to take a breath. She flickered in front of Rita, there and then gone, and then back again. She mumbled, "Poppy," and worked to stand.

"Yes, yes, Poppy," the monster said as if bored. It began the whistle more high-pitched than before. "You know the tune. Everybody sing." It laughed and the door shook enough to crack the wood.

"Mya, that thing is strong enough to bust through that door," Rita said. "You're still strong. You're strong enough to keep it there."

"Yes," the monster chuckled, "but for how long? Rita? If I were you, I'd..." His voice shrieked and the whole room erupted with falling drawers, and shattered glass. "Run."

Rita held on to what she could of Mya. "You have to remember."

In the distance, Mya heard Rachael's voice. It was pure and sincere, not like when the monster pretended. It called to her, faint, but there, *Mom, I'm scared. Mom, help us...*

*****

"Jake?" Rachael tried to pull him back from the stairs. He felt her tug but remained frozen like a statue; held there by something she couldn't see.

Jake's eyes were large balls, fixed on something he couldn't comprehend. He had no control over them to close them from this thing.

He was aware of Rachael. She seemed miles away. He stared at the dark form of something that crept up the stairs. He sensed movement filled with longing that motived it. And something else. Something powerful guided it. Helpless to move or speak, Jake could only watch. The form, tall, thin, hooded in black, carried a knife, and took each step carefully. Sunlight hit the blade of the knife, making it shine. Slowly, the form climbed each step.

Jake heard someone humming and the sound of running water. He recognized the tune...Amazing Grace, and then a whistle came from the form still creeping up the stairs.

Jake opened his mouth, but only a gagging sound came out. He began to wheeze and gasp for breath.

Rachael cried, terrified, and yanked on him. He felt her slap his face, felt the sting, and felt her pulling on his arms, but a power he never experienced before kept him paralyzed.

Jake's spirit, ripped from his body, propelled to a place that appeared blurred at first. He heard the muffled sound of running water, saw a vaporous cloud around him, and then everything came into focus. He floated, unable to call out. He didn't want to see what was there. Something forced him.

The naked silhouette of a woman behind beveled glass. Steam rising. Humming that seemed filled with sorrow. A low, lonely whistle in a macabre tune approached. As it grew louder and more unbearable, it came closer. Whoever was behind the glass began to whistle idly as well.

Someone tall stepped into the bathroom. Jake couldn't see the entire face. Only a chin protruded from the cloak. He or she carried a knife clinched tight in a black gloved hand. The shower water turned off. The beveled glass door opened.

A woman with wet hair and beads of water on her flesh began to step onto the tile floor.

The form came from behind. It covered her mouth and lifted the blade.

Jake tried to look away, but it was useless. The blade came down. The woman raised her hand and tried to fight but the blade came again and blood shot onto the walls, the floor, the ceiling. Red oozed from her body in streams and puddled at her feet.

She dropped with gurgle, a wheeze as air passed from her lungs, and then, the form backed away, turned, and looked toward the doorway. It lowered the knife, lifted its hand to the hood, and was about to speak...

Rachael screamed Jake's name and begged him to hear her. "Oh, my God, Mom, help me. Mom, I'm scared. Help me..."

*****

"The monster is with them," Mya cried.

"It can't be," Rita said. "It's still here, behind the door. I can hear it laughing."

"Here. There," the monster taunted them, "could I be...everywhere?"

"You have to stop it," Rita said. "You're the only one who can send it back to Hell where it belongs."

"That...that day," Mya said, her voice weak, "I ran up from the basement. I ran to the barn. I heard a gunshot. I didn't stop running. I hid in the hayloft. Poppy came in. I saw him through the floorboards. It was my fault. If I hadn't gone in the woods...that monster wouldn't have followed."

"Poor, poor Mya wanted her treasure," the monster laughed. "Poor, poor tramp lost in the woods just wanted to taste a sweet young thing. Is he here? Does he haunt? Give up. Give in."

Mya held onto the back of a chair and gripped it for strength. "Nana came in and I heard her. She said, 'We can't let that child go through anymore. If we call the police, they'll want to talk to her.' Nana sobbed pulling on Poppy's shirt. I could see red spots on it..."

"Blood," the monster said and laughed. "Blood for sins and sacrifice."

"Nana begged him," Mya said. "She said, 'she's been through enough. If we have to tell what...what that monster did to her...' and Poppy shook her. He said, 'what he tried to do, woman. We don't know he did.' Nana cried harder and said, 'you saw him with his...pants down. He came close or...did. She's a child, old man, an innocent child.'"

The monster rasped, "Innocent? Disobeyed her Nana. Wicked. She brought this upon herself."

"Go on, Mya," Rita said. "Don't listen to that thing, keep going."

The monster chuckled. "I live inside you, Mya. I have since that day. I stayed with you, watching, waiting. Patience is a virtue. I grow strong with your shame. Your blame feeds me. Guilt gives me life hereafter."

Rita pleaded, "Mya, try. Say what happened."

"Nana kept begging my grandfather. 'The town will talk. They'll whisper. They'll never treat us...her, the same. She'll be marked. She's ten years old. Oh, Heavenly Father, how do we explain it to her? How do we help her?'

"Poppy took a shovel and told Nana, 'go to her. Take her in the house but don't let her look. I know what has to be done.' Nana came up to the loft. She found me hiding behind bales of hay. She held me. I remember crying so hard my chest hurt. She picked me up and, when we went back into the house, I begged her not to. I wiggled and tried to get out of her arms, but she held me tight. She covered my eyes and hummed her tune that I used to love but now, I couldn't stand hearing it. I buried my head in her neck as hard as I could. She washed me in the tub and the whole time, I never said anything. I wanted to say I was sorry. I wanted to ask her to forgive me, but I couldn't talk and I couldn't even cry anymore.

"She put me to bed and..."

"The lie was born," the monster taunted. "Shame. Blame. Guilt. Gone the innocence."

"The next morning," Mya said, "I looked outside and...there was fresh dirt mounded under the willow tree." She pointed out the window. "My willow tree and I knew...I knew all the fairies were gone and I wasn't their princess anymore." She sobbed into her hands.

"But that's the best part, isn't it, Mya?" the monster said. "Oh child of the night with lies to hide, keep from the light." It started to whistle 'Amazing Grace' in sour, bitter, notes.

"After that," Mya said, "I never went into the woods again. I never went into the basement. I never played under the willow tree. I never told my mother, my sister. Nana said to keep silent. She said it was a bad dream that was dead and buried. Poppy started to drink all the time. Nana cried a lot. We never talked about it, ever. When I was twelve, Poppy died. Nana passed two months later, and..."

"And?" the monster urged. "Say it. Say it now."

"It was all my fault."

The monster laughed and whistled a happier tune. "I stayed with you...in you. You tried to forget me. But guilt eats at a person. Shame whittles the soul. And blame burns the weak. Lonely for something, you find Doug, but not love. Anger. Regret. Hate that grows. Kept me going. I longed to be free. Rachael, sweet and pure. Her hatred tasted good and gave me life. I became strong and finally broke free." The monster pounded the door. "Now let me out and you can go on your way. The sinful must sacrifice the daughter for me. A quick stop for Rachael just to seal the deal for her destiny, and we'll let you get some rest."

Mya lifted her head. "No."

"Sorry, couldn't quite hear that through this door," the monster said.

"I said 'no'." Mya stood taller. "I will not let you touch my daughter."

"You misunderstand," the monster said. "I've already touched her. I fueled her hate. I gave her the best months of my existence."

"Well, no more. I understand you now. Demon. Monster. Beast. The spawn of evil. I get where your power comes from. You're right. I blocked it all. I pushed it down in me, and I refused to face it. I blamed myself, but no more. I won't be your victim anymore. You...you came after a child. A child who didn't know better. I was safe, loved, and innocent."

It hammered the door. "Not innocent...you disobeyed."

"I was a child. I had no reason to see evil or think about it. I didn't disobey. I was curious like a child and, like a child, I believed I would be protected."

"You let Poppy kill for you. Nana lied for you," the monster shouted.

"He protected me and so did she in the only way they thought possible. Poppy would never have killed if you hadn't come for me."

"And he drank himself to death with his own guilt," the monster hissed.

"He has to forgive himself just like I have to forgive myself," Mya said, her inner light growing brighter. "He paid the price with a conscience. He suffered for what he did over something that was a true monster. He confessed his sin to God, the God he believes in, one with mercy. He doesn't need to answer to you, the darkest of all things, never to you. I remember one other thing: the day Poppy died, I held his hand. He said love protects and forgiveness comes. Now, get out. Get out and go back to Hell!"

The basement door shook until it splintered, cracked, and burst opened.

Mya faced the monster, his form black, his blood-red eyes. He towered over her with a grisly snarl cut across his face.

"I'm not the only one," he growled at her. "I come from many. Send me away. It won't end for others who let me in." It swirled into a black tornado, but its voice still sounded, "Those who summon my brothers. Those who are closer than you think. It wasn't me there the morning of your murder. My father will not be cast away." In a puff of smoke, it vanished.

Mya shook and took a deep breath. "It's gone." She looked at Rita who shivered in the corner. "I can feel it." Mya smiled. "For the first time in as long as I can remember, I feel lighter. It's really gone."

In the threshold of the basement, a faint light emerged. It grew brighter until two people appeared.

Mya gasped. "Poppy? Nana?"

They smiled at her. "Sweet child," Nana said.

"We're here," Poppy said. "We've always been here but we couldn't break through. The demon kept us trapped here with our guilt and shame. The harm we caused you in not facing it haunted us. It gave evil power, but now, with faith and your strength, we're finally free."

"You're stronger than you know, sweet child," Nana said. "We're so sorry we left you to face it all these years alone."

"We were wrong," Poppy said. "Wrong in what we did, and when we never told you that you did nothing wrong."

"You were always fearless," Nana said, "and strong enough to face it. You'll need that strength now...don't be afraid."

With tears streaming down her face, Mya wanted to go to them and throw her arms around them. She didn't. The light surrounding them was intense. It was all she could do to look at them, even shielding her eyes.

261

"Don't be afraid," Nana said again. "They will use it."

"Find them," Poppy said. "Love protects, my Princess of Treasures."

They disappeared.

Mya wiped her tears away. "I love you both," she called out to them. "Rita? Did you see?"

Rita nodded. "I did. But what did they mean?"

Chapter 27

The force that held Jake released him, and he dropped to his knees. Gasping for air, he struggled for breath, choked, and fell over on the floor.

Rachael tried to lift him, but she couldn't.

"Jake? Jake, are you all right?" she shook him. He was pale and cool to her touch. He looked at her for a second and then closed his eyes. "Jake, please get up. Get up." Again, she tried to move him, but he was too heavy. "I'll get help," she said. "Hang on."

Rachael searched her pockets for her cell phone. When she realized it was in her car, she rushed into the kitchen, hoping the phone there still worked.

"Hi, Rachael," Burke said with a shy, awkward smile.

Rachael screamed until she recognized his face. "Burke, oh, my God. Thank God."

"What's wrong?" Burke asked in an impish voice. "You okay, Rach?"

"Help us. You have to help us."

Burke's smile faded. "Us? Who?"

Rachael grabbed his shirtsleeve and pulled him towards the living room. "We have to get out of here. Something...something's here."

Burke's smile was completely gone when he saw Jake passed out on the floor. Pointing at the body, he said, "Who's that?"

"Never mind," Rachael said, lifting Jake's head up into her lap.

"Don't do that," Burke said, his tone flat.

"Help me," Rachael said and struggled to move Jake. When Burke didn't react, she frowned up at him. "What's wrong with you? Help me. I have to get him out of here. It's still here. Don't you hear it? Can't you feel it?"

Rachael heard the low, steady whistle. She covered her ears.

"I like that song," Burke said.

She glanced up at him. He couldn't be this dumb. His empty, dewy eyes and the silly grin he always had pasted on his face, told her maybe he was.

Rachael grabbed onto Jake's shoulders and tried to slide him along the floor. Finally, the load got easier, and she realized Burke helped.

Together, they hoisted Jake to his feet and, while his arms dangled over their shoulders, dragged him outside. The door slammed behind them. She hadn't closed it. Neither had Burke.

"Let's get him to my house," Burke said.

Terrified, Rachael strained with her share of Jake's weight. She glanced over her shoulder toward her house. She swore she heard the structure groan as if it was ready to fall in.

Anxious to get away, she hurried Jake into Burke's house. "Shut the door," she shouted to Burke. "Lock it."

Jake moaned and slowly lifted his head. Dazed and weak, he stumbled along while Rachael got him to a chair.

"Are you all right?" Rachael asked, kneeling next to him.

Jake rubbed the back of his neck and nodded. "I think so. What the hell happened?"

"It came at you," Rachael said.

With his sappy grin, Burke stood next to them. "What did, Rach? What came?"

Rachael creased her brows at him, wondering what world he lived in. "I don't know, Burke. Something...dark." She got to her feet. "You...you heard it, didn't you? The whistle."

Burke shrugged and pointed at Jake again. "Who's he?"

"That's Jake...my friend," Rachael said.

Burke's eyes turned dark and the grin melted. "Friend? I don't know him."

"You don't know all my friends, Burke."

"I don't like him," Burke said.

Jake still rubbed his neck. "Nice to meet you, too."

"Get him some water," Rachael said.

Burke pouted. "I don't want to."

"Burke, please. Can't you see he's hurt?"

Burke sucked in his lips. "Okay, but only because you asked," he said and turned toward the kitchen.

"Toss in some aspirins if you got 'em," Jake shouted after him.

Rachael knelt next to Jake and lifted his chin so she could see his eyes. "Are you sure you're okay? You scared me."

"I scared you?" Jake cuffed. "How do you think I feel? I saw it, Rachael. The murder."

Rachael held her breath. "My...father..."

"I don't know. It was someone tall. Is your father thin?"

"No. He's not that tall. Five-nine, I think."

"No, this was someone tall and thin. I think I saw a small scar on his chin."

"That isn't my father," Rachael let out her breath.

"Well whoever it was whistled a tune and...I don't think he was alone."

"Two people? A break-in?"

"No, I...I had the feeling this person knew the house. He or she moved slow and acted as if they had time. They used a knife from your kitchen. Damn it, they were about to take down the hood and say something and then...it was over."

"Was there anything else? Anything?"

"No." Jake massaged his forehead. "I wish...I saw this tall, thin figure in a black hooded sweatshirt. Black gloves. A scar on the tip of his chin. And…there was a hole in the sleeve of his sweatshirt. A hole in the left elbow."

"Here's your water," Burke said, his sudden presence startling Rachael.

"Thank you," Rachael said and took the glass. Curiously, she looked at Burke and saw him blush when her hand touched his.

"Why is he here?" Burke said.

"He's trying to help me," Rachael said.

"I can help you, Rach. All you had to do was ask."

"It's a different kind of help, Burke. Jake's trying to help me find out who killed my mother."

Burke looked down at Jake with no expression.

"Jake is a psychic," Rachael said. When Burke continued to stare, she explained, "He sees…things and can hear things."

"What kind of things?"

"Spirits. Voices."

"Ghosts?" Burke chuckled like a child. "That's stupid. Nobody can do that."

"He has a special…gift," Rachael said.

"My mother has a special gift, but I don't think she sees ghosts. She just," Burke shrugged his shoulder, "knows stuff."

"We better go," Rachael said.

Burke was quick to object. "No. I…I mean…you should stay here."

"Burke, you've been sweet, but I don't want you to get into trouble with your mother. She doesn't exactly like me."

Burke grinned at her. "You care about me, Rach, don't you? You always did."

"We better go. Just let me go to the bathroom," Rachael said.

Jake forced a smile when he noticed Burke glaring at him. "So, you know Rachael."

"Better than you, I bet. She's mine."

"Really? That's nice." Jake stood, wobbled, and gained his balance. "Well it was sure nice to meet you." He took a step and then everything went black.

Chapter 28

Burke placed the bronze figure of an elephant back on the side table, ignoring the spot of blood on it. He dragged Jake's unconscious body to the basement and, after he located the hidden key, lugged Jake down the stairs, making his head thud on each step as they went. At the bottom, he pulled Jake to the furthest corner and dropped him there.

Upstairs, he locked the door, straightened his red and white plaid shirt, and waited for Rachael.

"Where's Jake?" Rachael asked. "Did he go out to my car?"

"I took him upstairs, to my room. He was tired."

"Burke, we can't stay. We really have to go. I'll get him."

"No," Burke blocked the way. "He tried to stand but…he passed out again."

"I'll get him to a hospital," Rachael said, attempting to side-step around Burke.

"No. He said he didn't want that."

"You told me he passed out."

"He did and then…then he came to and I said, 'let's go to the hospital', and he said, 'no, tell Rachael I just want to rest here.'"

"Burke, you've been very nice but…"

"It's the truth, Rach, honest. Besides," he lowered his eyes and played with his fingers. "I kind of wanted to talk to you and I couldn't before. Not with him here."

"Burke, if Jake is hurt, I have…"

Burke quickly lifted his head and eyed her. "No!" His abruptness scared Rachael. She took a step back and Burke lowered his voice. "You have to listen before my mother gets here."

"That's just it," Rachael said, trying to keep her voice from shaking. "Your mother will be angry, Burke, very angry if she finds me here."

"She won't be back for a while, Rach, and I won't let her hurt you. I'd never let anyone hurt you." He giggled and shyly bowed his head. "You're the one."

"The one what?"

"The one I want." He looked up at her with that sappy grin and those dewy eyes again. "You're the one." He said it like it should mean something to her. "Mother said I could..." he giggled again, "have...you know."

Rachael backed away one inch at a time. "Have...what, Burke?"

Burke took her hand. It was all Rachael could do not to scream or run. He glanced at her with wisps of blond hair hanging in his eyes like a sheepdog, but something told Rachael he wasn't a sweet innocent dog.

"I dream about you, Rach, all the time." His eyes trailed to her chest. "I bet you taste sweet and creamy. I lie to mother and tell her she's sweet but her milk dried up a long time ago."

Rachael's eyes nearly fell out of her head. "You...what did you say?"

"Mother's milk is gone, but you...I bet you taste good. When I suck on Mother, I dream about you and pretend that I get full...but I don't. I'm hungry, Rach. I'm really hungry."

Working for calm, Rachael suppressed the shriek in her throat. She stepped back an inch while he clasped her hand. "Okay. Well, I really have to go now, Burke. My trial starts tomorrow you know, and I have to meet my lawyer. So...let's talk more later, okay?"

"Mother said I can know the flesh of a woman. I know where to put my penis." He smiled with flushed cheeks. "Mother finally told me what it's really called. She used to say it was my pee-pee place, but then I got scared because it swelled, and Mother released it for me. She said it was my seed growing. But then...she showed me where to put it, and last month, told me what it's really called. She said I could put it between a woman's lips here..." he touched Rachael's mouth, "or here." He reached between her legs.

Rachael pulled her hand free and backed away. "Stop it, Burke. You're sick. Your mother is sick."

"Don't say that," Burke demanded. "She's not. She wants to be sure I'm ready. I am. You're the one. You just have to know that Mother comes first. She has to always, always, always come first."

He took a step toward her. She took another step back.

"Mother's lips are kind of dry. Her..." he giggled, "Virginia. I know that's not what it's really called, but I like it. When I put my penis in her, it was dry. Is it supposed to be dry? I bet you're not."

"That's it." Rachael turned and ran toward the door.

Burke was right behind her. He grabbed her. She pulled away. Turning, she twisted her ankle and fell into the door.

Burke hovered above her. "Don't do that, Rach." He peered out of the window on the side of the door. "Mother will be here soon."

Rachael rubbed her forehead. Slowly, she used the door knob to help her to her feet. "Burke, let me go. Please. Just let me go."

He crushed her to the door and held her there. Rachael screamed. Burke covered her mouth. His voice a harsh whisper, he said, "I wanted to tell Mother that you're the one, but I was scared she'd say no. So I waited until I knew how to do it. Mother says I'm very good, but it took practice to go slower. She said I was too fast and made a mess." He lifted Rachael's chin and glared into her eyes. With his breath hot on her cheeks, he said, "She's worried I

L. Thomas Cook

have lust and that's bad. That's why I have to obey Mother. I have to eat, and when Mother's mad, I don't get anything. That makes Mother madder because she can't have anything to eat. I taste good," He smiled and nodded.

"Burke, let me go or so help me…"

"Rachael, don't be mad. I know you like me."

"Burke, just because I was nice to you doesn't mean…please, let me go, you're hurting me."

"We can go away together. You and me. I'll make Mother understand. If I can't, we can live here. Don't be scared, Rach. You can feed me and I'll feed you and Mother. We'll have fun. We can play games. All kinds of games."

"Nobody is feeding anybody," Rachael said and brought her knee right in Burke's groin.

He folded. She scrambled to her feet, raced to the door, and fumbled to unlock it. "Jake!" she screamed while she tried to work the lock. "Jake!"

"He can't hear you," Burke said and grabbed her again.

When she looked at him, his eyes were black and his mouth curled into a snarl.

"Mother said you were a whore. I bet you let Jake taste you, didn't you?" He shook her. "You're mine, Rach. You can't let him know your flesh." He shook her like a rag doll.

"Burke, please." Rachael held on to him as he rocked her back and forth. "Please. You need help. Your mother is a sick, twisted woman."

"Don't you say that. Don't you dare! You're mine and you have to stay with me."

"But I have my trial."

Burke stopped shaking her. "What happens if you don't go?"

"They come looking for me. The police will look for me."

Burke quietly held her. "I...I'll have to hide you."

"Where, Burke? Do you know how?"

"Mother...she would help. And then she'll see and I'll tell her that she always comes first and I'll obey her, but she has to let me have you. I can keep you like Mother is keeping your father."

Rachael's jaw dropped. "What did you say?"

Burke laughed. "She doesn't think I know, but I do. I saw him."

"Where? Where is he?"

"Upstairs. Tied in her bed. He must have been bad. But Mother didn't use the whip yet. She lets me whip myself now, you know," he proudly said.

"Oh dear God." Rachael twisted under his grip, but Burke picked her up and carried her across the room. When he set her down, she begged, "Let me get you help, Burke. You can be free from your mother, just let me go, and I'll bring help."

He traced his finger along her cheek. "You're soft and pretty. I'm hungry." He reached for her blouse and Rachael slapped him.

Burke touched his face as tears welled in his eyes. His shock was like that of a surprised two-year-old. "Why you'd you that, Rach?"

"Because you're insane," she said and stood tall. In an authoritative voice, she demanded, "You let me go, Burke Ivy, or so help me...I'll never, ever be your friend again." She held her breath hoping he would buy into it. For a second, he looked like he would, but when his expression changed to one of hurt and determination, she realized she failed.

"That's not nice, Rach. I helped you. Mother is very mad at me for that. She told me never to help you again, and I disobeyed. Now she's going to be home soon."

"Then let me go, Burke. I won't tell."

"No, and no matter what you say, you're still the one I want. I could hide you, but Mother would find you under my bed or in the closet. Don't worry. I'll put on my best smile for Mother and explain everything." He picked up the bronze elephant. Rachael put up her hands to block it. As the heavy object came down, she felt a horrendous pain on the side of her head, saw stars, and then grayish black.

She felt herself dragged and placed on a cool, hard floor before she heard a door shut. After a scraping sound and a heavy thud against the door, she passed out.

Chapter 29

Winded after the struggle with Rachael and pushing an oversized chair to barricade the closet door, Burke dropped into the chair. "Mother is going to be so mad at me," he said, wringing his hands together.

He stomped up the stairs and retrieved the whip from his bedroom. He knew what he had to do to appease his mother, so why fight it? If he was careful enough to do everything she wanted, maybe she would allow him this one thing.

He heard the car come down the driveway and puffed out his cheeks. He tried not to shake when he heard the back door open.

"Burke?" Doris called out.

Burke swallowed, gripped the whip in his hand, and lingered for a moment at the top of the stairs. Mother's temper was vicious, but he had no idea what to expect in this situation.

"Burke!" Doris shouted. "What in the hell? Why is my good chair in front of the closet?"

Burke steadied shaky legs by grasping onto the railing. When he heard his mother begin to slide the chair, he rushed down the stairs.

"Mother, don't," he said and stopped her in time.

"Don't what? Why is my chair here?" She eyed him curiously and noticed the whip. "Burke? What have you done?"

Coy, Burke grinned. He combed his bangs away from his eyes, and, in a tiny voice, said, "I had to, Mother. I didn't know what else to do."

She glared at him. "Tell me what you did, right now, young man."

"Well...see...Rachael was…"

"Rachael? What did you do, Burke? Tell me right now." She shook him and his hair fell back over his eyes.

"She's in..." he pointed to the closet, "there." The look on his mother's face changed from confused surprise to outright anger. He held up the whip to her. "I was bad."

She snatched the whip out of his hand. He removed his shirt and turned his back to her. She slapped the whip against his flesh, and with each violent whack; her anger seemed to increase instead of settling.

"How...many...times..." she gritted, and with each word, took out her wrath, "have...I...told you...to stay away...from that girl?"

Burke hissed with each lash, but he took it. He didn't try to run, there was no point in that, and he didn't object. He flinched, tried not to because Mother would see that as weak, but as the whip shredded his skin and the blood trickled down, he couldn't help the tears in his eyes.

When Doris exhausted herself, she threw the whip at him. Burke took this as his opportunity to explain. "I'm sorry, Mother. But she's the one. I wanted to tell you before that...I want her as the one."

"The one what?"

"You said I could know the flesh of a woman. I want to know her. But...but Mother, you will always be first. You will always be the one I obey. I promise."

"You promise, do you?" She snarled at him. "You'll always obey me?" Doris slapped his face. "Then why didn't you obey me this time?"

Burke whimpered like a sick pup.

"Lust," she muttered under breath. "I sacrifice all I have for what?" She turned away from him, shaking her head. "You stupid, stupid boy. You've ruined everything. Everything!"

"No, Mother, I didn't. Honest. Now that we have her here...we can..."

"Can what? She's on trial for murder. You do realize that. The murder of her mother? Does that sound familiar?"

"Yes, but..."

"'But' nothing. I need to think." Doris stomped to the wet bar and poured a glass of bourbon. After she gulped it, she poured another.

"Mother, I'm hungry," Burke said and came up to her. He started to unbutton her blouse and she slapped his hand away.

"You're hungry?" she said. "Well that's just too damn bad. Do you honestly think I'd feed you after this?"

Burke lowered his head. "I'm bad. I know." He lifted his eyes, brighter this time and said, "But now I can show you. I can practice everything you taught me with Rachael and you won't have to get so tired anymore."

"Shut up. You didn't do this as any favor to me or out of any concern. It was pure lust, Burke. Pure lust just like all men. You disappoint me. I warned you never to disappoint me." She looked at his childish face and then combed back the strands of hair from his eyes. "But I love you." she said softly. "Damn it, I love you."

She let out a long sigh. "Now, tell me everything that happened. How did she get here?"

"I saw her go in the house."

Doris's eyes filled with panic. "You...you didn't go in that house, did you?"

"When I went in, Rachael begged me to help her. I had to, Mother. She couldn't lift him by herself."

"Lift...who?"

"The guy she was with. I don't like him."

"Oh, my...she was with a man?"

"Yes. A man," Burke said, sour-faced. "She shouldn't have been there with him."

"What did you do with him, Burke?"

"He's in the basement."

"The...our basement?"

"Yes. I locked him down there."

She began to strike him all over. Burke recoiled, but her fists kept coming. "Are you a complete imbecile? You brought that tramp and her toy over here?"

"Don't call him her toy, Mother. I want her to play with me."

She stopped hitting him. "You want her to play with you? Is that what I taught you? No, it isn't. And I warned you about lust. Filthy, dirty, sinful lust. I should just let you face all this alone. That's what I should do."

"No, Mother, please don't. I'll do anything you want. Just let me have her. I'll keep her quiet and you can teach her how to behave. You can have your toy and I'll have her."

"My toy?"

"Mr. Westcott. I saw him upstairs."

"Oh hell. I almost forgot. You see how upset you've made me?"

"And Mother, you and me can still play. I won't get mad when you want Mr. Westcott. It's okay because I can have Rachael, but only when you say, Mother. Honest. Just when you say I can." He grinned proud of his defense. Mother had to believe him and approve now, but, just in case, he handed her the whip again, got on his knees, and said, "If I don't obey, you can punish me. You can put me in my bad place. You can even keep Rachael away until you're not mad at me anymore. I'll behave. I promise, please, Mother, please?"

"Get up. For God's sake, you sound like you did when you were ten and wanted a goldfish. I got you the damned goldfish, remember? You killed it when you wanted it to sleep in bed with you."

"I forgot it needed water."

"And now you want to keep a grown woman?"

"You can show me how. You said when I was ready, I could have one."

"I meant one time. I didn't mean to keep one as a pet. I spoiled you, that's the problem. A mother's love can do that sometimes." She went to the window and looked outside. "Did anyone see you come here with them?"

"No."

"Good. I want you to open the garage over at her house. We'll hide her car there for now. We'll hide Doug's car...No. Wait." Her lips curled into a wicked grin. "I have a better idea."

"Can I keep her, Mother? Can I?"

Doris patted his cheek. "For now."

Burke's eyes glowed, but then he pouted. "How long? The last time you let me keep a pet and said, 'for now,' it was gone in a week."

"Long enough. Now, do what I say. Take her out of the closet and bring her to the basement."

"What about him? His name is Jake. I don't like him."

"We'll take care of him. He won't be a problem."

Burke beamed. "Really?"

"I promise he won't be an obstacle. Burke, when you were in Mya's house, did you see anything?"

"No. But I guess Rachael did. She was scared and that guy, Jake, he passed out."

"Good. But you saw nothing?"

"I heard the Whistle Man."

"That means he's still there. In that house." Doris rubbed her hands together. "That's very good."

"Mother? Rachael said that guy can talk to ghosts and hear voices." Burke laughed. "Isn't that silly?"

"He can?"

Burke shrugged. "I don't know. It's dumb, isn't it? She said he has a gift. I bet it's not like yours. I bet he made it all up. I bet he lied."

Doris thought for a moment. "Well, I guess we'll have to find out." She turned and smiled at her son. "Maybe this'll all work out."

"You're not mad at me anymore?"

"Not as much."

"Can I have something to eat?"

"You are such a naughty boy. I should say no, but...later, after we take care of this. Now, bring her downstairs."

Burke pushed the chair back and opened the closet door. Rachael lay passed out on the floor. He lifted her easily over his shoulder and trudged to the basement door.

Doris used duct tape to bind Rachael's hands together and then pressed a piece over her mouth. "Follow me." She carried a butcher's knife with her and stepped lightly on the stairs.

"Mother, the knife isn't for Rachael, is it?"

"No," Doris said and grinned up at him. "Of course not. But if that fellow, Jake, is awake, well, Mother might have to stop him from hurting you."

"You take such good care of me," Burke said with Rachael's head drooping over his back and while her taped together arms dangled to the side. She looked like a rag doll with her hair hanging down. When Mother wasn't looking, Burke sniffed her and smiled. Rachael always smelled good. He put his hand between her legs. She felt warm in that place he longed for. He chuckled to himself and quickly lowered his hand when he thought Mother might notice.

The basement was quiet. Doris pulled a chain and a ceiling light came on in the center of the room. The bulb, suspended from the rafter, cast a soft, dim glow.

"Where is he?" Doris asked.

"I put him way back there," Burke said.

With the knife held tightly in her hand, Doris stepped toward the rear of the basement. She saw a lump lying on its side. She knelt next to Jake, felt a pulse, and noticed some dry blood caked just above his ear. With the duct tape, she wrapped his wrists together, and made sure they were secure.

"Bring Rachael over here," Doris said.

Rachael began to moan. She lifted her head for a second and dropped it down again.

"She's waking up, Mother," Burke said.

"Calm down," Doris said. "You won't touch her until I say so."

"I know," Burke smiled. "Thank you, Mother. I'll be extra, extra, special good."

"Lust," Doris said with a sigh. "Men are all alike. I should have made you into a girl. I could have, you know. I could have cut off your pee-pee place and dressed you like a little girl. But no. I was sentimental. I wanted a boy to learn about a mother's love. True love and he'd never, never want anything else." She looked at him. "I come first, Burke. Don't ever forget that."

She slid the freezer to the side, removed the padlock, and pushed open the door. "Put her in there."

"My bad place?"

"Yes. Do you have a better idea?"

"I thought she could stay in my room."

"Really? I don't trust you." She gripped his groin and felt the erection. "You already need release just from carrying her down the stairs. Honestly, Burke, you're trying my patience."

He held her hand there. It helped the ache and throb. "I'm sorry, Mother. It gets like that when I'm hungry."

"You're a growing boy. I knew this day would come. Now put her down and lock the door. I have to get things ready."

Burke rested Rachael gently on the floor. The cement was abrasive and damp. He worried the surface would be too rough for her tender flesh.

He arranged her so she lay on her back. Gently, he fussed with her hair and placed her arms across her lap.

He admired her features and her body. When he was sure Mother wasn't behind him, he parted her blouse with trembling hands like a child opening a precious gift. He licked his lips. All his years spent suckling on his mother had reinforced one thing–when he saw a breast, saliva filled his mouth.

While he viewed the thin, pink bra she wore, he giggled and then covered his mouth so Mother wouldn't hear. He liked the silky feel of the garment. And then, checking for Mother once more, he lifted the bra and stared at her breast. The flesh was smooth, taut, not sagging like Mother's. The nipple was dark pink and the ring around it had a mole that he wanted so badly to lick.

He sucked back the drool and palmed the breast. It was firm and warm. He ached between his legs–another reaction after years of training. Lowering his head carefully, he felt tempted by the need that overpowered him. Licking his lips, he wanted just a taste, but before he could take the nipple between his lips, Mother shouted for him to come to her.

"Bad boy," he said quietly. "Don't make Mother mad. I can have her. Mother said. I just have to be extra special, special good." He lowered her bra, fixed her blouse, and smiled. "You're the one, Rachael."

"Burke? Damn it," Doris shouted again.

"I'm coming," Burke said. He latched the padlock and hurried.

Chapter 30

"What did that thing mean, there are others?" Rita said. "And your grandparents said you'll need your strength. Why?"

"There must be more than one demon," Mya said. "It doesn't matter. Look around, Rita. Isn't it so much brighter now? I feel brighter. I conquered it. My grandparents are free. I'm free. It can't hurt Rachael or Jake anymore. If the demons feed on fear, and we have none, then we've won."

"Then why don't I feel better? If there's more demons, what does that mean? That monster said it like we aren't safe yet…maybe we never will be."

"Don't be so negative. You know they love that. Besides, demons lie, don't they?"

"They can't lie about how we feel. They only use it."

"So feel happy. Jake is helping Rachael. When I was dealing with that thing, I heard Rachael calling me. She was scared. I don't feel any fear now. It must have vanished altogether." Mya's grin began to slip away with a new feeling.

"What is it?"

"It's weird. I can't sense Rachael at all. I've felt her this whole time, and now, I can't feel her."

"That's not good."

"Maybe it is," Mya said. "Maybe she's okay."

"And what about your murder?"

"My what?"

"Don't forget it. Now isn't the time to forget," Rita said.

"What if I am? I think I am." She wrung her hands together. "Rita, maybe I'm slipping away again and Rachael is fading. I can't let that happen." She began to pace. Touching her arms and her face, her eyes pleaded with Rita. "I can't slip away. Not yet."

"Try to reach her. If that demon is gone, then it should be safe."

"Try to reach who?"

"Rachael," Rita said. "Your daughter wanted for your murder."

"Murder? I was...oh God, Rita, my memory is...where the hell am I?"

Rita maneuvered Mya to a chair and helped her sit. "Focus on me, okay? We're here, in this dimension, to contact my son, Jake, so he can help find who murdered you. Rachael, your daughter, was arrested for it. Look around. This is your grandparent's house."

Dazed, Mya glanced at the room. "I'm so tired. Why am I so tired?"

"Because you just took on a demon and he put up one hell of a fight. You're strong, Mya. You are. You were able to appear to Jake and make contact. New spirits can't do that. It takes years. So now you have to grab hold of that strength and fight not to forget." Rita stood straight. "Maybe that's what your grandmother meant."

"My grand...Nana? Was Nana here? I'm sorry, Rita." Mya rested her head on her folded arms. "I'm just so tired."

*****

Doug Westcott twisted the knots that tied him to the bed. He lifted his head and scanned the room. A pair of Doris's shoes lay tossed in the corner by her makeup-covered dresser. A jewelry box in the center had a watch and a pair of earrings next to it. On the nightstand, there was a photograph of Doris and Burke. She grinned along with him, but his smile was overly toothy, and his eyes were half closed.

Doug shuddered at the picture. If he had known how manipulative and deceitful she really was, he'd have never bothered with Doris. He made a mental note, *stay away from needy, insane women.*

When he tugged on the ropes again, he was reminded that this was no joke. If he ever did write that book on how to play others, he'd have to figure out how to deal with this new chapter.

Doris Ivy truly caught him off guard. When he met her over eight years ago, she had an air of mystery about her, along with a flair for the kinky that teetered on domination, which, of course, turned him on. She looked damn good holding a whip and wearing leather. Many of the younger women he preferred wouldn't be able to pull that off half as good. Naturally, the biggest attraction came because she had money. A widow twice, well, at least once, and a husband who disappeared that she had legally declared dead, she was financially sound. That sealed the appeal–no jealous husband to worry about. She wasn't a bad looking woman. A little worn around the edges, but in soft light and with enough whiskey, Doug could deal. Besides, the younger women, especially lately, had become obsessive. Once they caught the scent he was separated, he turned into London Broil at a half off sale.

Women flocked to him. He enjoyed it. If they got too demanding, he'd explain that his divorce wasn't final, he was married to a real bitch who wanted to take him to the cleaners, and he just didn't have the conscience to keep them waiting for something that could very easily go through the courts for years.

No, he'd explain, *the best he could offer was a night here, a weekend there, and some tokens of his affection.* He'd give a gold bracelet he could borrow back later saying his wife had locked his accounts, a jeweled necklace he'd hock weeks after to tide him over because his wife had maxed out his credit cards. They'd be sympatric. Some even offered him money while he dealt with this ordeal.

They'd insist dinner was on them. They'd lavish gifts on him: a Gucci shirt, a Vanderbilt silk tie, one even gave him a Swiss Army wristwatch. He had them eating out of his hands. The separation from Mya came with benefits and open doors. He could play without getting dirty. He could sample without buying. It worked.

Until now. Tied to a bed, Doug was certain Doris drugged him. How she knew half the stuff she did, confused him. No private eye could possibly be that good at discovering all his lies...and yet, Doris knew them. She also knew motive, which was a complete surprise. Hell, sometimes he didn't even know his true motive. Like the times he lied to Rachael. He felt bad about that.

She was the only one who truly seemed to love him. She believed him, trusted him, all without asking for anything in return. She just seemed to accept him. Of course, she didn't know the real him. Even so, whenever she looked at him with those big eyes, it made him want to be a better person.

How would he explain all of this? What was Doris's game? She went on and on about him telling Rachael of their affair, how he would sell his condominium and give Doris the money, and that he must learn that she came first. Not likely. On top of that, she expected him to testify against his daughter. Never. How she thought she could force that one...then he remembered.

Doris would go to the police and tell them he was there the morning of Mya's death. He was there and he ran. The motive? Money. Any detective worth half his salary would discover Doug Westcott was in financial trouble. No bank would give him a loan or extend the ones he had, he had borrowed against the life insurance policy he kept on Mya...the one where he forged her signature, and borrowed against the one Mya forgot named him as beneficiary. How could he explain all that? Then there was Aunt Rose who would be all too happy to testify he'd come to her using

Rachael as bait. The real estate agent would testify Doug tried to put the house on the market and steal it from Rachael. Rachael would be devastated. The jury would view him as scum. Doris would grin like the cat who ate the canary, and the D.A. would throw the book at him.

He couldn't let that happen.

A desperation swept over him to get out of Doris's bedroom. There had to be some way.

He looked around: the phone on the nightstand. If he could just wiggle enough that way, maybe…

*****

At her handcrafted altar, Doris removed the black cloth, lowered a black, lacy veil over her face, and kneeled. Two lit black candles flickered. She took the knife, cut across the palm of her hand, and let three drops of blood fall into a tarnished silver bowl.

"Bring me that jar on the shelf," she told Burke.

"What are you going to do, Mother?"

"Just do as I say."

Burke brought her the jar filled with a red goo. "Mother, is the Whistle Man going to come?"

"Please, Burke. Mother has to concentrate. Go upstairs and make sure Doug isn't getting into trouble."

"What if he is?"

"Then stop him."

Burke walked to the basement steps, stopped, and turned. "How?"

Doris let out a sigh. "Hit him over the head. Must I tell you everything? I swear I'll have to add brain enriched vitamins to your milk." She heard him stomp up the stairs and called, "Burke? Don't hit him too hard. I want him alive."

"Yes, Mother," Burke said and closed the basement door.

"It's partly my fault," Doris said to the altar. "I did try to smother him once in his crib. Maybe I left the pillow on his face too long. Or perhaps the time I tried to drown him in the tub." She lit another candle. It sizzled and smoked. With the silver bowl in one hand, she uncapped the jar, and dipped the knife blade in the thick goo.

She used the blade to stir the bowl and then took an old chicken bone and the feather of a crow. She dipped those into the bowl as well.

In ancient tongue, she spoke. Waving her hand over the bowl, the contents began to bubble.

"Dark Knight. Savior of Lost Souls. Lord of the Night, come to me. Bring forth your powers. Test those who deny you in righteous flight. Show your commands and tally their fears. Use them as you will. For those with sight, show them their sins. For those who hear the dead, let them know your wrath. Teach them, mighty darkness. Use their blame, their dread, their weakness to serve you as you will. Take a soul tonight by the name of Jake. Make him pay for his sinful ways. I offer as always my body and my son as sacrifice to give you power. Use our bodies for your pleasure."

She gave thanks, blew out the candles, and removed her veil. With a knowing grin, she turned. A black form whirled behind her.

"Master." She bowed. "He's there," she pointed, "and ready for you." She bowed again. "I leave him in your darkness." Upstairs, she locked the door.

*****

Doug inched and edged to the side of the bed. He pulled the ropes as hard as he could and, even though it cut into his wrist, he could feel the rope give a little. He paused and glanced toward the door. His shoulder ached with each attempt to fight the rope, but he made progress. Little by little, the nylon stretched, the knot loosened, and he crept closer to the phone.

Once more he stopped, held his breath and watched the door. He had hope but worried about time. How long had it been since Doris was here? His stomach growled. He needed to use the bathroom. Even with the closed blinds in the bedroom, he sensed it was night. The same day? He wasn't sure. All he knew was he had to get out of here, away from Doris, and then figure out what he would do. There was no way he would take the fall in Mya's murder. As much as he loved Rachael, he wouldn't do it, even for her and if that bitch, Doris, thought she could...

Burke burst through the door. Before Doug could slip back on the bed, before he could say one word, Burke bashed his head with what looked like a small baton.

*****

Back downstairs, Burke said, "Mr. Westcott is sleeping now, Mother." He tossed the baton with a smidgen of blood on the couch.

"Good," Doris said, finishing a martini and pouring another. "Now, let's go up and I can give you your bath."

"Oh, Mother, I'm not a baby. I can bathe myself."

"I want to do it tonight," Doris said and tugged his hair. "Maybe I'll cut your hair too. It's gotten too long."

"But what about that guy?"

"It's being taken care of."

"What about Rachael? I should see if she needs anything."

"Who comes first, Burke?"

"You do, Mother."

"And when it's time to check on Rachael, I'll give you permission. For now, it's best not to go in the basement. Do you understand?"

"Yes, Mother," Burke said.

Doris, in stockinged feet, walked up the stairs. Behind her, Burke glanced toward the kitchen, wishing he could slip downstairs just to check Rachael was still there. The mere thought of her excited him like his birthday always did. Mother would surprise him with a trip to town for ice cream.

Besides school when he was younger, Burke never went any place. He was lucky Mother even allowed school. She wanted to teach him at home, but Louis, his stepfather, convinced Doris to let Burke go.

She checked on him all the time, though, finding excuses to take him home early, keep him out of school for days, and insisted on daily reports from both his teacher and him.

Sometimes, he would come home from school crying. The other kids were mean to him. Everyone except Rachael. Once, a boy pushed him down in a mud puddle and ripped his shirt. Burke was hysterical and the principal called his mother. She said she would never send him back, but Burke begged, and for days, refused to eat even when she tried to force him. It was the first time he ever disobeyed like that. Punished severely for it, it was worth it if he could return and see Rachael every day.

Doris relented and allowed him back to school. Weeks later, he overheard the boy who pushed him fell out of tree and landed on a spiked fence. He died in the hospital.

That's when Burke began to understand his mother's special power. He knew she could conjure things like shadow people. She could make things, like his toy cars, move without even touching them, and she knew things, which is why he took special pride when he could fool her, like the time he went to the library and looked up how to make babies. If Mother knew the school had a book like that, she'd burn the place down. Nevertheless, Burke didn't know until then how she could punish others. He didn't fear her power. He wished he could do the things she did.

"Your bath is ready," Doris said. "I checked on Doug. He was busy trying to loosen the ropes. I tightened them. I gave him something to help stay calm. Now I can take care of my little boy." She took Burke's pants off, slipped off his underwear, and held his hand while he stepped into the tub. "Too hot?" she asked when he winced as he lowered himself in.

"No. My back hurts."

"From your punishment. I did whip you hard, poor baby, but you were naughty."

"I'm sorry," he said while she sponged his back.

"I know you are, Burke, but sometimes I think you're testing me. Do you appreciate everything I do for you? Like right now. I'm tired. But here I am, giving you a bath. And why? Because a mother's work is never done. Because a mother's love means she has to be everything for her baby. I keep a roof over your head, don't I? I feed you. I bathe you. Give you clothes to wear. And what thanks do I get? All I ask is that I'm the only one. The first for you in every way. I ask that you obey me. And do you?"

Burke played with a small sailboat. His mother's voice melted into the background. He thought about Rachael and how good she smelled. He pictured her bare breast and the raised nipple. He wanted her to feed him so badly, he could almost taste it.

With his long legs bent so his knobby knees stuck up in the water, he made motor noises while he pushed the boat along. Doris washed his back, still talking about something he ignored as he envisioned Rachael washing him.

"Do you hear me, young man?" Doris asked and yanked his hair.

"Yes, Mother," Burke said.

"You went over to that house after I told you to stay away," Doris said.

"I know. I was bad."

"You went over there because you lust. Your father had lust and so did Louis. I won't allow it, do you hear me?"

Burke nodded but his thoughts went back on Rachael. She felt warm when he touched her, soft, but not mushy...

He felt his head forced under the water. It surprised him. His mother's strength was overpowering. She pushed him down and held him there. His legs flew up. His feet banged the wall. He reached for the side of the tub to lift himself, but she was too powerful.

He could see her face hovering above him. The water made her look wet and rippled. He couldn't hold his breath any longer and tried to grab her, but she glared at him as her lips formed a horrible grin. His lungs began to give. He gasped. Water stung his nose and filled his lungs.

She released him and he popped up. Choking, gasping, he bounced up like a jack-in-the-box trying to both cough out the water and get air at the same time.

"You were thinking of her," Doris said. "Her. You weren't listening to me or thinking of me first. It was her."

"I...I'm sorry," Burke said, still struggling for a breath.

"I should put an end to her right now."

"No!" Burke grabbed her arm. "Mother, please. I...I shouldn't have but...when you take me for ice cream, I get excited too. She's...like a present."

"I'm the only present you need. Me," Doris screamed. "I saw your penis get hard. I knew what you were thinking. You forget who I am. What I can do."

"Mother, I won't forget. Not ever. You're the best mommy in the world. I can do better. Please. Let me do better."

"Get out of the tub."

Burke stood and took the towel she offered. Dried, he followed her to his bedroom. Doris took off her clothes and lay naked on his bed.

"Get on top of me like I showed you," she said.

Burke obeyed.

"You can have her once. Only once. And I will watch. You will think of me and do it like I taught you. You need practice. Enter me slowly and move in the way I've told you. If you do it right and I'm pleased, then tomorrow you can know her flesh."

"Yes. Mother. Thank you."

"Wait. You better feed first. You must be starving."

"I am." He took her nipple in his mouth and sucked until she moaned, digging her nails into his shoulders.

"A growing boy needs to be fed," she purred. "You love Mommy's milk, don't you? Hers won't taste as good, will it? Even though I know I'm getting old, I have to be sure you will always be taken care of."

She held his head to her breast. His drool ran down her chest. Burke forced his thoughts to be only on her. He couldn't afford for them to betray him.

"You are hungry," Doris said. "That girl is only a slut, but I will allow you to have her. Your flesh is weak. I'll find ways to make it strong. I will pick the next tokens for you, and when the time comes and I can't...you'll have to trust Mother knows what's best for you. Will you do that for me?"

He nodded while he suckled. Pretending he could taste her milk, filling up on air, he groaned, acting satisfied.

He lifted his head to see her flushed cheeks. He kissed her breast as part of the ritual she liked and, in his way, to give thanks.

"Let me feel," she said and slipped her hand under his body.

He lifted his torso and slid up the bed so she could check his erection.

"You're ready. But don't hurry it. I'll guide your hips."

He did as she said, the way she showed him. He knew by her reaction that he was a good boy doing it the way she liked...the extra special way.

She moaned. Her body tensed and relaxed. He opened his eyes. Her face contorted. She looked at him with black eyes and grinned wickedly.

The image used to scare him. Not anymore. It was the beast who took her so it could take him.

"Our master demands it," Doris had said. "Our sacrifice of body and soul allow him to provide. We must serve."

The first time she told him that, he cried in fear. She slapped him and told him weakness would anger the darkness. *No crying when whipped. No crying when the beast scratched his back until it bled. His purpose was to submit, to be a tool, and to be only a vessel the beast commanded for acts of pleasure.*

The beast growled deep in its throat. Claws dug into his flesh. He moved swiftly as directed. The beast took all of him into utter darkness. Even when Burke whimpered with exhaustion, it showed no mercy and devoured more of him.

Chapter 31

Jake opened his eyes. Unsure where he was, he rubbed his head and felt a bump. It hurt worse than any hangover he ever suffered.

A small, familiar room came into focus. He found himself standing in the living room of the house where he grew up. For a second, it felt like some whacky dream. He was there but it wasn't possible, not unless someone transported him a hundred miles from where he now lived. Maybe this was like the ghost of Christmas past from A Christmas Carol, a movie he thought was cool. He especially liked the moaning, chain burdened ghost and the dark cloaked figure that haunted Ebenezer, those characters never frightened him, that is, until he turned around.

A black cloaked form towered over him. It had to be eight feet tall with a hollowed out face and burning red eyes.

He patted his cheek. "Okay, Jake, time to wake up."

When the figure still loomed before him, he smacked his face harder. He didn't like the whole movie idea so much anymore, especially if he was starring in his own horror version.

Jake closed his eyes. "Wake up now." He pinched his arm. "Ouch."

After he opened his eyes, he found he remained in his childhood home, but at least the ominous, cloaked figure was gone.

"What in the hell is going on?" The house smelled like home–a mixture of his father's cigarette smoke and his mother's lemon Pledge. A soft light radiated from a lamp in the corner. His baseball and bat leaned against the wall with his catcher's mitt and grass-streaked sneakers. A stain on the edge of the couch cushion where he'd spilled grape juice one Saturday morning was still there. Books, knickknacks, a vase with dried flowers, all the things that reminded him of home, filled the room.

He wandered to the kitchen. Dishes in the sink, a coffee cup stained by tea, even the misshapen clay bowl he made in the fourth grade was there on the counter. That child-crafted art was the only memorabilia he took with him when he left this house. It reminded him of the crush he had on Ms. Polanski, his art teacher, and the thrill he felt the day she covered his hands with hers to help him form the clay. To this day, whenever he saw the scene from Ghost with Patrick Swayze and Demi Moore at the pottery wheel, he smiled as he remembered a schoolboy's fantasy.

Jake scratched his head. The vivid dream seemed real, but there was no way it could be. The last thing Jake remembered was being with Rachael.

Rachael!

He rushed through the house. She wasn't there.

"Think." He listed his last memories. He awoke on the couch in his apartment. Why? Rachael had spent the night. He didn't want to move too fast for her, so he took the couch. Rachael, bent over, searched his refrigerator. He liked the view when he came into the kitchen.

They spoke. Breakfast. They went to Rachael's house. Jake saw images of a murder. A weird kid...that's right. Bert? No, Burke. Tall, lanky, a couple of pimples on his chin, Jake found it hard to believe Rachael went to school with him. That would make them the same age, but this guy looked like he was twelve or thirteen.

Jake recalled the strange eyes, the death stare, and the odd giggle. The next thing he remembered-something slamming into his head.

"So how did I end up here?"

In the kitchen, he thumbed through some mail on the counter and then saw a calendar still opened to the exact month his mother committed suicide.

Jake rushed down the hall and froze just outside the bedroom. He was the one who discovered his mother's body. He wasn't supposed to be there that day. He had kissed her goodbye the night before and planned to drive eight hundred miles away to college to drop off some things before his trip to Mexico. He forgot a book he loved and came back to the house.

Jake stood at the closed door just as it was that afternoon. He thought he'd burst in and surprise her, expecting to find her reading in her favorite chair by the window or sewing. That isn't what he found.

"Open the door, Jakey," the black cloaked figure rasped behind him.

In some weird way, Jake expected him. He didn't react to the sinister form with fright or shock. Instead, guided against his will, he reached for the doorknob with dread.

*****

Rita spoke with Mya at the kitchen table in her grandfather's home. The back door rattled. They looked at one another and then, as if a bomb went off, the door exploded, spewing pieces of wood everywhere.

Rita covered her head and, when she looked out the door, she couldn't believe her eyes. She looked right at her son Jake and oddly, he stared back. It was like looking through a window except she was in one dimension and he, in another.

"Jake!" Rita screamed and ran to him, but it was like running into a glass wall. She fell back, tried again, and once more, wasn't able to pass through.

Jake stood on the other side as shocked as she was. They both put their hands on the invisible barrier and gazed at each other.

Tears streamed down Rita's and Jake's cheeks. She called his name. He couldn't hear her. He tried to talk, but she couldn't hear him either.

L. Thomas Cook

Stunned, Mya started to come toward Rita when a power overtook her. Thrown backward, she was pinned to the wall.

In that instant, the setting changed for Rita. No longer in the old farm kitchen, she found herself in her bedroom at the home she once shared with Ed and Jake. She was in the small, one-story home on Barley Street, that she and Ed purchased a year after they were married, and where she raised Jake, the place that, over the years, felt less like home and more like an empty shell.

It was here one day that Ed unexpectedly decided to leave. He packed his things, said he was leaving, and told Rita she was worthless.

Rita sat on the edge of her bed as if she'd never left. Next to her, a distorted black form of a person also sat. It didn't upset her. That form had been with her for years. She came to know it. The darkness was part of her. It lived in her, filled the room, and consumed her life. It had for as long as she could recall.

The times in her life when she thought it was gone didn't last. It always came back. It was a black, bottomless pit she'd worked hard to crawl out of only to slip back in at some other point.

"You know me," the blackness grumbled next to her. "We're old friends. Ed is gone, isn't he? And now, Jakey is leaving too. Poor Rita. All alone. No one wants you. No one needs you."

It whispered in her ear all the fears she had, and all the self-loathing that bathed her soul. It fed off her until there was barely anything left.

"Do everyone a favor," it hissed. "Put an end to this misery. Stop wasting space. Go on," it nudged her, "do it."

She lifted the gun off the nightstand and held it. The heavy, cool metal filled her palm.

297

"I whispered in Ed's ear," it chuckled, "I told him to leave it just for you." The darkness laughed again. "It's the only thing he did leave you, so use it. Go on."

"Jake," Rita whispered.

"Jake doesn't need you. You're a burden to him. You always were. An embarrassment. Sad, pathetic, silly Rita. Useless. Worthless. You have nothing to offer anyone. Your mother is embarrassed by you. Ed sure as hell was. What have you ever done for anyone worth remembering?"

She held the gun firm in her hand. From the first day Ed brought it home, she feared it. He told her she was silly and paranoid.

"Did he care how you felt?" the darkness asked. "No. And now he's left the very gun you were so afraid of here just for you. Use it and let me take you away from all the self-hatred and pain. Come with me, Rita."

Water-filled eyes, she glanced up and, at that moment, saw a mirror image of her room except she wasn't sitting on her bed holding a gun, it was Jake.

The dark form sat next to him. It whispered in his ear, "Do it, Jake. Use the pain. It was your fault. You were so scared of facing me you never bothered to help your own mother."

Jake held the gun in his hand, looking at it, tears falling down his cheeks. He nodded. "You're right. I knew my mother was ill."

"Ill?" the darkness snickered. "Okay, call it that if you want. Doesn't matter. She was weak and you were too. All because you got scared. Some psychic you turned out to be. You couldn't even sense your mother's pain."

"No," Rita said. "That isn't true. What I did wasn't his fault."

"That gift of his," the darkness said close to Rita, "he hated it and you. He didn't see it as a gift. It was a curse. He couldn't wait to get away from this house and, most of all, you."

The black form lifted Rita's hand with the gun to her temple.

Opposite of her, the darkness raised Jake's hand with the gun to his temple.

"Don't, Jake!" Rita shouted. "You didn't do anything wrong. You're not to blame."

"I should have helped you, Mom," Jake said, the gun at his temple. "I blocked out everything and I should have known. It's my fault."

"That's right," the darkness croaked. "It was. But did he face it? No. He blamed you for his own failure. He took out his anger on his own mother. Shameful. I don't know about you, Jake, but I think you should give up your miserable life and never look back. I mean, really, you can't hold on to a job, your drink to forget, and you're ashamed of what your mother did. Now that's the kind of thing I fed from. I've actually enjoyed it all. Nevertheless, it's time to turn out the lights, Jakey boy."

"Jake, don't," Rita cried with the gun aimed at her temple. "I never meant to hurt you."

The black form laughed. "Really? Should have thought of that sooner. You did him a favor. No more burden. He could go on with his life and never have to deal with you."

"That's not true," Jake said. "Mom, I let you down. I understand now. I did blame you because I was mad at myself. I took it out on you by denying you, by burying it, and trying to forget. I'm sorry. I understand the pain you felt and why you thought this was better. I'm not excusing it, but I understand. This is a horrible place to be stuck. It feeds on you. It sucks life out of you. I get it now. It wore you down."

"This is getting boring." It swatted the form of a hand at nothing in the air. "Just do it and get it over with."

It sighed a foul breath. "Fine. I'll take you, and afterwards, you and Mommy can be together. Hash this out for all eternity if you want. At least you'll be together and you can play the blame game all you want. Sometimes her self-pity will win and sometimes, she'll let your self-righteous, 'But Mommy,'" the darkness mimicked in Jake's voice, 'I could have stopped you.'" It chuckled. "That's the attitude that might win. Now, doesn't that sound fair?"

"Jake, you aren't to blame. I made a choice. A horrible, terrible choice that I'm responsible for. Please, Jake, don't listen to that demon. Don't let him fool you."

"Demon?" the darkness laughed and said, "If I'm a demon, then what in the hell is sitting next to you?"

"My own demon," Rita said. "I listened to him for too long and I won't do it again." She lowered the gun. "I won't make that mistake again. Now, get away from my son."

The black form next to Rita stood. "What's done is done. You will do it again."

"Come on, Jake," the darkness rasped, "you know this is the best way to punish yourself."

"I would never do it again," Rita shouted. "I forgive myself for all the weakness I showed back then. For letting you in at all. And I swear, I would never make that mistake again."

"Mistake?" the darkness said. "That's one hell of a mistake."

"It was my mistake," Rita said. "I let loneliness and despair in. I let it consume me. I let it swallow me. What I should have hung onto..." she looked at Jake with a tender grin, "was love."

Jake lowered the gun. "No more blame for either of us. I love you, Mom. I always will."

"Live a good life, Jake. And, when you find love, hang onto it."

The darkness next to Rita grew larger. She faced it. In a high-pitched screech, it broke apart. Like a reptile, it slithered up the wall and dissolved. The remains turned to black smoke and sank into the floor.

Rita was back with Mya in the farmhouse.

"What in the hell happened?" Mya said.

"You have to get to the children." Rita grabbed onto Mya. "That monster was right. There's more than one. You have to get to them and make sure they're okay."

Chapter 32

Jake woke on the basement floor, his hands and feet wrapped with duct tape. It wasn't a dream he had and he knew it. He saw his mother, and together, they banished their demons. No time to celebrate, he had to figure how to get out of there and find Rachael.

Jake wormed his way along the floor. He got to a wooden table and spotted a nail sticking out from the leg. Using the nail, he sliced through the duct tape, and with free hands, pulled off the tape from his ankles.

He didn't know who was near, so, in a low voice, he called her name. "Rachael? Rachael can you hear me?"

He heard a knock and, when he got closer to a small door, called for Rachael again.

"Here, Jake!" Rachael said and banged harder. "I'm locked in here."

He found a hammer on a bench and used it to pound off the padlock. When he pushed the door open, Rachael flew into his arms.

"Are you all right?" he and she asked at the same time.

Rachael noticed the blood along Jake's temple. "That bastard! He did this."

"Who? Where in the hell are we?"

"Burke. This is his house. His and that sick mother of his. I always knew Doris Ivy was nuts, but now...Jake, they have my father."

"What? Why?"

"I don't know, but Burke said he was upstairs." She looked closer at Jake and said, "You...look different. Something about you is different."

"It's a long story." He stood by Doris's makeshift altar and said, "Right now, we have to get the hell out of here."

"What is all of this?" Rachael picked up the jar with red goo and made a disgusted face. After she looked at the dried bones, the inverted cross, and examined the steel knife with dried blood; she got a chill up her back. Her whole body shivered. "What in the hell is this stuff?"

"It's not good," Jake said. "It's used to summon demons."

The basement began to vibrate.

The floor shifted.

Jake held onto Rachael and said, "We have to go. Now!"

*****

Upstairs, Doris and Burke felt the house rock.

"Mother, what's that?" Burke asked.

Doris got off the bed. "Quick. Get dressed and bring Doug to the basement."

"What's wrong?"

Doris glanced upward. The ceiling cracked. The walls trembled. "Something. Something is very wrong. Hurry up." She wrapped a robe around herself while Burke pulled on a pair of pants and tossed a sweatshirt over his head.

Doris rushed downstairs. Burke went into his mother's bedroom to grab Doug.

Downstairs, Doris took a knife from the drawer. "Dark Master, I'm coming." She tore open the basement door and faced Rachael and Jake.

"Get back," Doris said and held up the knife. "You have no idea what I can do."

"I think I have some idea," Jake said and backed down the stairs, holding Rachael's hand.

"That's right," Doris said with a snarl, "you're psychic. Well, can you tell what's going to happen next?"

Jake snickered bitterly. "I don't usually read the future."

Doris took one step down for each one Jake and Rachael took. Holding onto the knife, she kept a smug, superior look on her face. "Don't read the future? Then what good is your…gift? Oh, that's right. You hate your gift so much you blocked it and couldn't help your own mother."

Jake chuckled keeping Rachael close behind him. "Really? That's the best you got? Look, we've already covered that, okay? It's all resolved, so drop it."

"That easy?" Doris asked as they got to the basement floor.

"Easy?" Jake scoffed. "No. But it's done. I guess that's why your pet demon decided to have a temper tantrum, huh? Did he run crying back to hell?"

"He failed," Doris said. "The Beast doesn't like failure."

"Tough. I guess he'll have to get over it. They have counseling in hell?"

"You think you're funny?" Doris peeked around him and grinned at a trembling Rachael. "How about you? How is Mya? Did you resolve your guilt over her death?"

"Leave her alone," Jake said and backed up further with Rachael.

"How much of her death was your fault, Rachael?" Doris said. "Your anger, your hate for her, all the blame you laid at her feet, how did that work for you?"

"You're sick, Mrs. Ivy," Rachael said, her voice quivering.

Doris laughed. "Me? I'm not the one who killed her own mother."

"I didn't," Rachael shouted.

"Tell it to the jury." Doris stepped closer as Jake and Rachael backed up more. "That is, if you make it out of here."

"Mother?" Burke called. He dragged a groggy, semi-conscience Doug down the stairs and dropped him.

"Dad," Rachael shrieked and started to go to him, but Jake held her back.

In a lump, Doug Westcott groaned on the floor. He opened his glassy eyes and looked up at the others. "What have you done, Doris? Why?"

Doris stood over him with the knife at his throat. "Me? This is what you did. You and your lies, deceit, lust. Go on, tell your precious spoiled brat what you did. Don't you think she deserves the truth before she dies?"

"Mother, no," Burke said. "You said I could have her."

"Shut up," Doris said. "You can. And then she dies."

"Darn it." Burke pouted and stomped his foot. "I wanted to keep her."

"Well we can't have everything we want. She's a no good slut and a tramp who tempted you," Doris continued holding the knife to Doug's throat.

"Me?" Rachael scoffed. "What about you and incest? You and your son, it's sick what you've done to him. You're both sick."

"You shut your filthy mouth!" Doris's face turned beet red with a vein that throbbed along her neck. She flew at Rachael. When Jake blocked her by pushing Rachael behind him, she snarled like a wolf ready to devour a meal.

Jake stood tall and unyielding. Doris paused. Her snarl was replaced by a wicked mocking. "You don't know how vile she is. Just like all men, all you see is sweet, young flesh, but I've taught my son the right way."

"By taking him to bed?" Rachael asked from behind Jake. "By making him your puppet? It's disgusting."

"It's what our Master commanded, you silly, ignorant girl. A sacrifice worth the cost for all our god provides."

"You sacrificed you own son?" Rachael asked, her brows furrowed with deep creases. She shook her head. "How sick are you?"

Doris sighed. "You don't understand. Well of course how could you?" She waved a dismissive hand. "What is important in doing all this," Doris said, "is that I showed him a mother's love and taught him. He knows I'm first after our master. The master and I are the only things that should matter. I taught him the weakness of the flesh, how to find release without lust, and showed him the truth in how far I would go to provide for him," Doris said. "Like all men, he needs the flesh of a woman, and when that day comes, he'll be prepared. Lust is sinful. Our master does not permit such things. Lust clouds the mind. Our master is to be worshipped just as I am. Burke's penance will keep him pure."

Jake scoffed. "What penance is there for lust?"

"To create a child and sacrifice it–flesh of his flesh– as I sacrificed him. In body, blood, and soul. His firstborn will be the offering in blood. Slayed in innocence. After that destiny is complete, he'll always have me. A tramp like Rachael won't destroy that."

"I learned really good, didn't I, Mother?" Burke said. "I didn't even cry when the Master hurt me. I want Rachael, Mother. I want her to be the one I do penance with for my sins. It won't hurt…not too much, Rach. And don't cry. The Master gets really angry when he hears crying. I'll help you. You'll see. The Master will use my body to take yours, right Mother? You can get nice and fat with our baby and feed him. You can feed me too, isn't that right, Mother? After the baby is served to the Master, there will be plenty of milk. Rach won't dry out for a long, long time. Only, Mother, can I have her first, please, before the Master uses me to take her, please?"

"I'm gonna be sick." Pale, Rachael pressed tighter into Jake.

"Burke, stop whining. I told you, you could," Doris said. "I keep my promises. She'll be made a sacrifice after the Master rewards you. All we do comes with a price." Doris turned her attention back to Doug. "Just like you must pay the price. Tell her. Tell the truth for once. Tell her what you did and why."

"Dad?" Rachael called to him. "What's she talking about?"

"Tell her," Doris shouted and kicked Doug in the side.

"I made mistakes, okay? Just...just let her go," Doug said.

"We've come too far for that," Doris said. "It's time to confess." She leaned over him with the knife to his face. "About everything."

Jake kept backing up with Rachael. He got to the altar, and bumped into it. The silver bowl tipped, and he noticed the 9 mm Smith & Wesson he hadn't seen before. He picked it up, but Doris's senses were keen. She placed the knife at Doug's throat once more. "Drop it, Jake, or his death will be your fault."

Jake dropped the gun. "Okay, you win. You have powers, so how about this? You make us all forget any of this ever happened, and then you and Junior can go back to whatever twisted crap that gets you off. We'll handle the rest. You know, let ourselves out. Lock the door."

"Why do you insist what my son and I share is so disgusting?" Doris said.

"Um, because it is," Jake said. Doris squinted her eyes at him. He put up his palms. "You asked."

"I'll look forward to seeing you dragged to Hell," Doris said. "But before that, Doug has a story to tell. Now talk." She kicked him again in the ribs.

"Okay! All right." Doug put up his hands. He could barely look at Rachael when he said, "I lied to you about…well, pretty much everything. Your mother and I separated because I was having an affair."

"With her?" Rachael asked, pointing a finger at Doris. She placed her hand over her stomach. "Now I am going to be sick."

"No. Yes. But..." Doug rubbed the back of his neck, "there were others at first."

Burke had moved to stand behind Rachael. He sniffed her hair. She nudged him away, holding tighter to Jake.

"Down boy," Jake said. "Doris, you want to call off your toy? I don't think he's thinking about you or your damn Master right now."

"So smug," Doris said. "My son is on his way to becoming a man. I've taught him that flesh is weak and desire is used to appease our Master." She smiled at Burke. "Sweetheart, give Mommy the gun."

Burke picked it up. "Heavy." He tried to twirl it with his finger. Doris put up her hand. "Stop playing and give it to me," she ordered. Burke pouted and handed his mother the weapon before he moved into the corner.

"Now don't sulk," Doris said. She shook her head. "Burke can be very sensitive."

"When can I have Rachael?" Burke whined.

"Well, your son doesn't seem to be satisfied with homeschooling anymore," Jake said.

"Rachael's the one," Burke said with a sappy grin.

"He keeps saying that," Jake said. "Why not shop around?"

"Don't," Rachael said, sticking as close to Jake and away from Burke as she could.

"He's made his choice," Doris said. "He doesn't have to chase after it. He'll never be a fool like some men. He knows I come first and he'll always obey me. Not like his father. Not like Louis. Not unless he wants to end up buried under the floor in that room."

Burke frowned. "My father is buried in my bad place?"

"No, stupid boy," Doris said. "Your father is buried in Cedar Cemetery. I put him there after I found out about his lustful ways. He made the mistake of not making me first. I don't share well. I never have. I drugged him, put him in his car, and let the fumes from the engine do the rest. Tragic. To be a widow so young like I was. Under the floor. That's where I buried Louis. He lusted too. Let that be a lesson to you, Burke. Never disappoint me." She glared at Doug. "You've disappointed me. You played me for a fool. I'm no fool. Now, go on with the story."

"I don't know what you want me to say," Doug said.

"I want you to stop the lies and tell the truth for once. Tell Rachael how you lied about the divorce. About the money and the house. Did you know, Rachael, that your father had a real estate agent at the house to put it on the market? That he told the agent you wanted to sell the house? That he only agreed to have your name on the deed because he knew he could talk you into letting him get a loan on it? Or give it to him if something happened to your mother? In fact, you father had the means, the opportunity, and the motive to kill your mother, let you take the blame, and go on his way…without me, isn't that right, Doug?"

"No…yes…but, Rachael, Honey, don't believe her. Yes, I had the means…"

"He was here that morning," Doris said.

"But I left," Doug said. "I just wanted to talk to Mya about a loan. I'm in debt. I've used all the money I had. I screwed up, Honey. It wasn't your mother who bled me dry. I did that to myself. I begged, borrowed, stole whenever I could. I mortgaged the house. It was your mother who saved it and she did that for you. I owe money…"

"He stole from the company he works for," Doris said. "He used his relationships with the accountants, all desperate, stupid, and believing fools, to get the money and cover for him. He owes gambling debts. Overdue loans. Even his car is about to be repossessed. He was about to be caught for all of it. Some anonymous tip to his boss...I wonder who made that call?"

"You bitch!" Doug snarled and lowered his hands. "How in the hell did you even know?"

"You really don't know who I am, do you?" Doris pressed the knife closer to Doug's neck. A tiny dot of blood oozed. "Or the things I can do?"

Rachael gasped and covered her mouth. "No, please don't. Don't hurt him."

"Mother is special," Burke said, his head bobbing up and down. "But I'm sad. I liked Louis."

"Dark magic," Jake said. "She's special all right. Satan's slut."

Doris charged over to Jake and slapped his face. "Don't be rude again or so help me...I will place your bones to the fire with the rest of you still attached."

"Isn't that the plan?" Jake asked. "To call your demons and send us all to Hell?"

"You're clever."

Doug took a step toward Doris. She turned to him with the knife ready and raised over her head, the gun aimed in the direction of Jake and Rachael. "Don't try it, darling." She waved the knife. "Who shall be first the first sacrifice?" She went back to Doug and put the blade of the knife to his cheek. "Blood of a liar." She pointed the knife toward Rachael. "Blood of lust." Then she aimed the knife at Jake, "and the blood of a lost soul. I have all I need. But, not Rachael learning the truth about her father. That is still missing."

"There is nothing else," Doug said. "Yes, I had motive. I could get the house and bank accounts since I am still legally Mya's husband. But that's not why I put off the divorce. I didn't plan for her to die. And I didn't kill her. I didn't. The whole truth is…" he let out sigh, "I used the marriage as a way to fool around without having to commit to anyone. Is that what you want, Doris? I lied to you for years. I never intended to marry you. I wanted money and freedom without paying child support or taking responsibility for my credit card debt. I left that mess with Mya."

"You…you let me blame her for everything?" Rachael said and cried. "You said you wanted your family back and Mom was too selfish. How could I have listened to you and believed you?"

"I guess not all demons come straight from Hell," Jake said. "He took advantage, Rachael. He used your love for him."

"Now you see how destructive lust is," Doris said. "Lust for sex, lust for money does nothing except feed greed and the weaknesses of the flesh."

She held the gun tightly and went to her altar. With the silver knife in her hand, she wiped off the blood, and gave the gun to Burke.

"And don't play with it," she warned Burke. "Just aim it right at Doug." She smiled and took a deep breath. "Let me tell you a story."

"Oh goody," Burke said with a bright smile. "I like mother's stories." His smile slipped away when Doris tapped her foot. He pointed the gun at Doug and pressed his lips shut.

Doris shook her head. "Now if I may without interruption, " she eyed Burke. "When Mya and Doug moved here, all I heard from Louis was how genuine Mya was, how beautiful. Mya this and Mya that. The whole neighborhood went on and on about her and her beautiful house, her devoted husband, her precious daughter. I got sick of Louis talking about her and I knew he lusted for her.

Well, I put an end to that just like I put an end to the facade. The surface of anything is easily destroyed when the foundation is flawed. All I had to do was dangle the right prize in front of Doug. I would be first again. I would be the one everyone paid attention to."

She leaned over Doug. With the knife firmly in her hand, she pushed the blade into his gut. Doug withered in pain. Rachael ran to him.

"You monster!" Rachael screamed.

Doris pulled out the knife. The tip of it dripped blood. "The essence of a liar." She held up the weapon to admire it. "Even you, Rachael, temptress of my son, fornicator of my innocent little boy, are with sin and blind to it. I fed him, I provided for him, and I taught him the curse of lust so he could control it through release meant only for the Master and me."

Rachael stayed by her father's side and shouted, "You're sick and hateful! You just want to control everyone."

"Burke obeys me," Doris said. "He knows the true evil is in smug little sluts like you. Temptation born of evil."

"You killed Rachael's mother, didn't you?" Jake said. He rushed to her to grab the knife.

Doris wrestled with him. Jake froze. The second he touched her, he flashed. A sharp knife. It came up and then struck the body. The blade stabbed over and over with a vengeance. Blood puddled on the floor.

Jake looked at Doris. "It was you."

Doris put up her hand. That single movement tossed Jake back. He flew across the floor, landed against the wall and slipped to the ground.

Doris snarled at him with teeth clenched and eyes blacker than coal. "You're next. The ultimate death." She set her gaze on Rachael and said, "Once I appease my son with you, his need will be filled and he'll have release from

L. Thomas Cook

temptation. But first, I need the offering of that temptation." She stepped toward Rachael, chanting a summons for the darkest of all dark.

Jake scrambled to his feet and headed for Rachael, but Burke held the gun on him.

"Mother says no." Burke aimed the weapon. Jake slapped away Burke's hand that held the gun and punched Burke in the jaw.

Doris threw up her hand and once more, Jake soared into the wall. Again, she came at Rachael.

"Stay away from me, you sicko!" Rachael screamed.

Doris kept coming, closer, chanting words in a deep, graveled voice, calling the evil to bring forth its power, to open the gates and bring hopelessness, to feed on fear, and guilt.

Each step, she wielded the blade, her face bitter, her eyes black holes. The sweeping motions of the knife longer and longer until she reached Rachael. She cut a one-inch gash along Rachael's lower arm, and all the time, her words grew more intense and demanding.

"You're the sacrifice," Doris growled at Rachael.

Suddenly, bright light burst through the basement and Mya Westcott's spirit charged, blinding everyone for a second.

Silvery and glowing, her features showed. She screamed as she flew, "Stay away from my daughter!"

Stunned at the spirit, Doris's surprise changed to contempt. Snarling, she recited the words to bring the darkness.

A black cloud swirled, growing larger, until it encompassed nearly the whole room. It took form in the shape of a cloaked man with fierce, red eyes.

Rachael fell to the floor. Mya shielded her. "Stay away from her!" Mya commanded.

The darkness swept Mya up and cast her back. Pinned to the concrete wall, Mya couldn't move.

Doris tossed her head back and laughed with the power she held.

The darkness came at Mya with its arms extended, claws reaching, fanged mouth ready to swallow her.

A brilliant light appeared.

It beamed in a way Mya had only seen in the Lobby outside the gates of Heaven.

The light filled the room. In the center, Tricia radiated, her form evolved into a magnificent spectrum.

She stood in front of Mya. Her eyes pools of aqua and the robe she wore was a golden shimmer. In Latin, she chanted, "Exorcizote, omnis spiritus immunde, in nomine Dei Patris…"

The darkness growled. It waved its arm. Its cloak whirled before it charged the light.

Tricia extended her arms, pushing the darkness back against the far wall. Light bulbs sizzled, and one after another exploded. The electric charge in the room was so intense it smelled like fire.

The darkness grew larger and once more raced at Tricia. Its claws grabbed at her. Flung to the wall, a demonic power held her, compelled her, and prevented any movement as she tried to release herself.

"Mya," Tricia called, "you can do this. You have the power you need with you."

Mya, still held by an unseen force, struggled to lift herself from the wall. Each attempt drove her back. She pushed against the force and began chanting the same words Tricia used, "Exorcizote, omnis spiritus…" The words came easier as she fought to move. Somehow, she knew the words and had no fear. The power flowed from within. She felt the strange sensation, as if this was her destiny: to rid those she loved of evil.

Tricia joined in. Together, they recited the words and then a chorus of voices sounded from the ceiling and then the walls. The words resonated all around. Clusters of light appeared around them like soldiers on a battlefield. More joined them and they grew stronger. The invisible force that held Mya disappeared. She floated, unburdened, upward and loomed over the darkness.

"Forgive us our trespasses…" she said, "and lead us not into temptation but deliver us from evil."

The demon whirled in a mad frenzy like a black tornado. The tail of it stretched out behind it. It traveled toward the altar.

With the weight finally lifted, Jake jumped to his feet. He rushed to the unholy altar and flipped it over.

The darkness spun and turned on Doris. She screamed and clawed at her throat like she was trying to pry away unseen hands. Doris fell to the floor and the darkness wrapped its cloak around her consuming her and leaving nothing but a dry, lifeless husk. The darkness sank into the cement floor feet from the place Doris buried Louis years ago.

"Mother?" Burke's small voice cried and then louder, he shouted, "Mother!" He turned the gun to Rachael. "It's your fault! You were supposed to be the one. Mother comes first. You killed her!" His finger shook on the trigger.

Jake rushed him. They struggled over the gun. A shot rang out. Rachael screamed. Burke stepped back, holding his chest. Blood spurt. His eyes were wide with shock and his mouth was open in surprise. The blood oozed between his fingers. He looked at them and then at Rachael. He dropped to his knees, tipped, and fell on the floor next to his mother's body.

Rachael turned him to his back and leaned over him. "Hold on Burke. Just hold on."

Burke gurgled. He hissed and then sucked in air. "Rachael…"

"We'll get help," Rachael said.

"I…I killed your mother," Burke strained to say. "I wanted you…to be the one. I went to your house. I took a knife from your drawer. I only wanted to scare you. I went upstairs and heard the shower. It was your mom. I was going to leave but…the Whistle Man told me to do it. Mother put him there a long time ago. He was strong. He said I should help you. I wanted to help you." A tear drifted from the corner of his eye. He sucked in more air and shook. "You were angry with your mom. I…I thought if I got rid of her….you'd be happy. Then you'd want to come with me."

Jake stood over Burke and noticed for the first time, under the only remaining lightbulb that swung from the ceiling, a scar on Burke's chin and a hole in the elbow of his black sweatshirt. "I'll call for help," he said.

Burke winced. "I stabbed her. Mother…Mother was there. She said I did it wrong. She took the knife and….kept stabbing her. There was blood…so…so much of it. Mother took me out of there. She cleaned me. Said I would be punished. She said I ruined everything….but I didn't care. Not if I helped you. I just wanted…to help."

"Hang on, Burke," Rachael said as tears fell from her eyes.

"Rach," Burke labored to say, "you were the one. You'll always be the one."

Chapter 33

Three days later, Jake helped Rachael pack up the last of her things from the house. He did a cleansing, but he couldn't promise the demon was totally gone.

"So long as no negative energy goes in the house, it should be okay," he said.

"That's good," Rachael said. "I'd hate to sell a house with a devil attached." She glanced at Jake, who grinned. "What? It's not funny. I never thought I'd hear myself say anything like that either, but, sadly, it's true."

"So, how does it feel to have all the charges dropped?" Jake asked as he loaded boxes into the car.

"Thank God Burke held on long enough to confess to the police," Rachael said. "It's so sad that no one came to his funeral."

"How's your father?"

"He gets out of the hospital today," Rachael said. "I suppose, in time, I'll forgive him, but it will never be the same between us."

Jake hugged her. "I'm proud of you. You've been very strong through all of this."

"I think I get that from my mother. Funny how the police believed everything except that part of her spirit coming. Why is it that people don't want to believe in the good things?"

"Human nature."

"Well, it wasn't a hallucination."

Jake put up his hands. "Hey, I'm a witness. She really loved you. What she did was amazing." He closed the trunk. "So now what?"

"I was just about to ask you," Rachael said.

"Well…" Jake took her hands between his and smiled. "I see you finishing school, getting a great job, traveling with a guy who likes to take pictures, and...having a house with three...no, four bedrooms."

Rachael laughed. "Really? And what about you?"

"Me? I see me traveling and taking pictures with a beautiful, super amazing woman, and then building her a house with four bedrooms. One for the mommy and daddy and one for each kid."

Rachael laughed harder. "I thought you didn't read the future?"

"It's my newest gift."

*****

In the Lobby, Mya glowed in her creamy white gown. She hugged Tricia and said, "Thank you. You came to help and I can't say how much that means."

"It was your destiny, Mya. There are things we're not permitted to reveal so nothing is altered. What happened was always meant to be as long as..."

"As what?"

"As long as you found it in you. Your love and devotion for Rachael, and your willingness to sacrifice to save others, it all brought you where you were meant to be."

"So, you knew." Mya smiled. "And all the bull you gave me was for what?"

"To set up the challenge you were meant to face. You see, we have it all very well organized up here. We don't usually make mistakes."

"What about Rita?"

"Rita received her redemption and her forgiveness. The greatest kind of all. Not just from the one she hurt...but from the one she hurt the most...herself. Her willingness to accept responsibility and to pledge she would never make that mistake again if given the choice, saved her soul. You'll see. In your vision of Heaven."

"My vision?" Mya said.

L. Thomas Cook

"Yes. We all have our own vision of the afterlife. We make it what we want. Some, like you, have the vision of family and friends. But, you mustn't shirk your primary duty," Tricia said. "You have been selected by the Highest of High to be a Guardian. Your training starts now."

"A Guardian? Me?"

"You've shown strength and loyalty. And, in a few years, by human time, I believe you will have your first assignment...a sweet child named Mya Rita Westcott Delmar."

*****

"Jake," Rachael said as she got in the car, "that thing that took Doris, how did that happen if she summoned it?"

"Demons need to collect souls. She failed."

"How did she learn to do all that stuff?"

"Who knows?" Jake said. "It was probably in her for a long time. It fed off her hatred and her lust to be the center of attention. Once a person has enough darkness in them, they open a door. The darkness gets stronger and takes over. When that door is open, you never know what can come through."

He started the car. Rachael latched her seatbelt. She glanced up at her house and then over at the Ivys' house. "Looks quiet," she said. "No one, not in a million years, could ever guess what happened there. I hope it's at peace now." She shivered for a second when a chill ran over her.

"You okay?" Jake asked.

"I'm fine. Let's go."

*****

As they drove down the silent street, Doris Ivy's house was still.

A flock of sparrows nested in a tree. One moment, they were peaceful and calm, and the next, they scattered in a frenzy to the sky.

Then, the front door of the Ivy house creaked open.